"At least they're not real dragons," Rig said, relaxing a little. His eyes darted back and forth between the two creatures blocking the exit of the cavern.

The beasts flicked their barbed tails, flexed the claws on their hind feet, and took a step closer. Two sets of large, pear-shaped eyes bored down into the trapped adventurers. The motion of the creatures' leathery wings sent the sand on the cave floor rushing away.

"Wyverns," Palin noted.

"The *brown* dragons my lizard friend mentioned," Feril said.

"I've never seen anything like them," said Blister, a hint of awe creeping into her voice.

"They're not nearly as big as the thing that killed Shaon," said Rig. "I can take them."

"Take what?" one of the wyverns growled. "Something steal? Mad be master."

"Mad be Storm Over Krynn when comes!" exclaimed the other.

The Storm Over Krynn, Palin mouthed. "This is Khellen-dros's lair! We've got to get out of here!"

FIFTH AGE®

Fifth Age®

The Day of
the Tempest

Jean Rabe

DRAGONLANCE® FIFTH AGE®

The Day of the Tempest
©1997 TSR, Inc.
All Rights Reserved.

Distributed to the book trade in the United States by Random House, Inc. and in Canada by Random House of Canada Ltd.

Distributed to the hobby, toy, and comic trade in the United States and Canada by regional distributors.

Distributed worldwide by Wizards of the Coast, Inc. and regional distributors.

Cover art by Jeff Easley. Interior art by Jacen Burrows.

First Printing: August 1997
Printed in the United States of America.
Library of Congress Catalog Card Number: 96-60805

9 8 7 6 5 4 3 2 1

8381XXX1501

ISBN: 0-7869-0668-5

U.S., CANADA,
ASIA, PACIFIC, & LATIN AMERICA
Wizards of the Coast, Inc.
P.O. Box 707
Renton, WA 98057-0707
+1-206-624-0933

EUROPEAN HEADQUARTERS
Wizards of the Coast, Belgium
P.B. 34
2300 Turnhout
Belgium
+32-14-44-30-44

Visit our website at http://www.tsrinc.com

For Harold Johnson,
Tasslehoff Burrfoot,
and the Winter of '87

and for the FIFTH AGE® design team—Steven Brown,
Sue Weinlein Cook, William W. Connors, Steve Miller,
Ed Stark and Skip Williams—Krynn's true champions.

DAY OF THE TEMPEST

Southern Ergoth

Last Gaard Mountains

Caergoth

Castle Eastwatch

The Tomb of Huma

Zhea Harbor

Edgerton

Morgash Lake

Straits of Algoni

Daltigoth

Silvamori

Pontigoth

Qualimori

Ankatavaka

Qualinesti

Thunder Bay

Porliost

Qualinesti Forest

Ahlanlas River

Enstar

Wayreth Forest

Symbol	Legend	Symbol	Legend
● City		〰 Glacier	ℵ
☆ Capitol		〜 River	
····· Trail		‒‒‒ Border	
⛰ Mountains			
🌲 Forest			

0   150   300

Miles

Prologue

A Red Shade of Greed

Malystryx the Red lay on a plateau on the highest mountaintop amidst an arid wasteland. From this lofty position—in what once had been called the Goodlund Plains—she could survey a large portion of her domain. Smoke curled upward from her cavernous nostrils, clouding her huge, dark eyes. Twin horns curved gently away from the sides of her skull and tapered to sharp points. Her scales were as large as a knight's shield, and they glowed like hot coals in the late afternoon sun.

Those rare individuals who accepted invitations here, to her favorite lair—like the Knights of Takhisis standing before her—braved much. Streams of lava from the volcanoes that ringed her plateau ran perilously close to the steep paths that led to her lair. Unnatural creatures prowled the bleak slopes, and the visitors had to endure the intense heat once they climbed to the top—or perish.

The ninety men were here at the command of their governor-general. They were selected for their bravery, cunning, and loyalty. Malys thought little of humans, but she considered these far better specimens than the ones she had slaughtered in the many villages she had trampled since taking over this part of Ansalon.

"You are mine," Malys hissed to the knights. Her words were drawn out, sounding like an ominous wind. Flames licked out around her massive jowls and crackled loudly.

"Command us as you will," the senior knight said as he stepped forward and bowed his head. He was a young man who had distinguished himself in numerous battles under the governor-general's watchful eye. He acted confident and poised in the presence of the great dragon, though he was actually in awe of her and terrified.

He wore the black armor of the knights, with the death lily displayed prominently on his breastplate. A curl of red edged up from one petal—a rising flame that signified that his compgroup had sworn fealty to Malys. The young knight stood at attention, his shoulders painfully square and his arms at his sides, straight as arrows. His eyes met the smoldering orbs of the dragon without blinking. Malys opened her mouth a bit, just enough for her furnacelike breath to escape and wash over him. The knight did not flinch, though beads of sweat rolled down his face.

"You are called . . ." Malys began.

"Subcommander Rurak Gistere," he answered.

"Rurak," the dragon repeated, "Gistere." The words sounded eerie when uttered in her sonorous, inhuman voice. She tilted her head slightly and looked him up and down. She'd already studied him carefully as he led the procession of knights up the path to her plateau, but she wanted to make him uncomfortable, wanted to see if he would squirm beneath her intense scrutiny.

Malys growled softly as her eyes met the knight's. He did not falter, and she noticed with satisfaction that his lips did not tremble, his hands did not shake. The knight was trained very well and was indeed brave. Or he was terribly foolish. In either event, Malys decided he would do.

"Rurak Gistere," she said again, this time holding onto each syllable and letting the deep tones echo off the volcanoes.

"Yes, great Malystryx?"

"Take off your armor."

The other knights' eyes widened, but not those of Rurak Gistere. The dragon was amused. To her, the other knights' faces asked dozens of silent questions. Was Rurak to be eaten? Tortured? Who was to be next? Still, she was mildly pleased that they held their positions and watched attentively, though fearfully.

Rurak maintained his stoic composure. He took off his gauntlets and laid them at his feet. Next came his helmet and his flowing black cloak, which he carefully folded and set upon the gauntlets. Then he removed the epaulets, brassards, and elbow pieces that covered his arms. Undoing the breastplate took more work, but he eventually stood it up next to the other pieces. Then he took off the scale chest piece. The tunic beneath it was dark with sweat, and he tugged it off to reveal a gleaming, muscular chest.

"That will do," Malys said.

Rurak snapped to attention and again met the dragon's gaze.

She raised a claw and crooked a talon at him, as if he were a dog she was beckoning. "Closer, Rurak Gistere," she hissed. He stepped around the pile of armor and moved nearer to the dragon's snout. "No. Much closer."

The knight stood a mere foot from the dragon's claw now, and for the first time in her presence, he showed a sign of weakness. His bottom lip trembled ever so slightly, but she decided she would forgive him this fault. Malys had to concede that he was the most suitable subject of the lot.

The dragon rose to sit back on her haunches. Her shadow fell across him, cooling him somewhat, and it occurred to him that this was an unfortunate way to gain some respite from the heat. Malys flicked her tail up in front of her snout and appeared to study it for a moment. Then she tugged free one of the tiniest scales she saw near its tip and held the specimen gingerly before her smoldering eyes.

"Kneel," Malys hissed. The young knight was quick to comply. Then the Red uttered words so exotic and strange that none on the plateau could discern them. There was a melodic resonance to them, and as her inhuman voice droned on and then quickened, the heat on the plateau intensified. Flames darted out of her nostrils and teased the edges of the small scale.

Rurak felt lightheaded and feverish, felt warmer than he ever remembered being in his life. His head pounded, and he gritted his teeth to keep from crying out as waves of heat rolled up and down his limbs. He imagined that his blood was boiling and his skin was starting to melt. The young knight stared at the flames licking around the scale and flickering about the dragon's nostrils. He saw shapes—orange and red winged creatures, miniature versions of Malys flying all around her. The vision was at once mesmerizing and terrifying, and he continued to stare as the tiny dragons of flame darted toward him.

The dragon moved the scale closer to the knight, then suddenly thrust it against his chest. His skin sizzled and popped, and—despite all his training and resolve—the young knight screamed. The tiny dragons of fire swarmed into the scale as it seared his flesh and melded with his body, becoming one with the muscles of his chest. The scale now resembled a small breastplate. It glowed white along the edges from the heat of the dragon's flame.

Rurak pitched forward and clawed at the ground. The pain was excruciating and it consumed him. His throat was dry and he gasped for breath, but was unable to suck enough air into his parched lungs. Tears rolled from his eyes. He thrashed about in front of Malystryx and prayed to his departed goddess Takhisis for death to claim him. But death didn't come. Eventually the pounding in his head lessened, it became easier to breathe, and he was able to push himself to his knees. He was still warm, uncomfortably so, but no longer felt as if he were rolling in a bonfire. He struggled to his feet, and after a few moments stood shakily at attention.

I have honored you, Rurak Gistere, as I have honored only a few other humans on this world. Rurak's eyes widened slightly. The dragon's lips were not moving, but he could hear her—inside his head. *A part of me is with you, knight, enhancing you, making you better than human. Rarely will you require sleep now. You will discover that you are stronger, more alert, your senses keener and your mind sharper. We are joined, Rurak Gistere, and through our link I can see what you see, hear what you hear. You are truly mine.*

"Yours to command," Rurak said aloud.

"You will lead these knights beyond my lands, to the place men call Solamnia." This time the words were audible, for the benefit of the knights waiting behind Rurak. "I will know what is transpiring there, and I will gain that knowledge through you. You and your men will travel from village to village and mingle with those in authority. You will discover where Ansalon's refugees are flocking to, learn who is inciting the populace to oppose the dragon overlords and the Knights of Takhisis, and you will ferret out those who might become my allies."

"As you wish," he replied.

"Seek people who are healthy and clever, with darkness in their spirits. I might be able to put them to good use. Humans only. I will direct you where to deliver them."

"I understand, Malystryx." Rurak risked a glance down at the scale. It was blood-red and shiny, but no longer glowing. He felt around the edges, his fingers slipping between the small gap between skin and scale. "Am I to always wear this?" he braved asking.

"You can never take it off—not without dying in the process."

Rurak Gistere nodded to the dragon and set about donning his armor again. He took a last look into her huge eyes, saw his reflection in them, then pivoted and directed his men down the mountain.

Malys eased her head over the edge of the plateau and watched the Knights of Takhisis wend their way back down the path. She couldn't see Rurak, but she knew he was in the lead. She knew everything he did because now she could see through his eyes. She could see that no one was walking in front of him. She could see the rocks he stepped around, the streams of lava he effortlessly jumped across.

Malys purred with satisfaction, closed her eyes, and pictured something cold.

* * * * *

There was nothing but sparkling white land in all directions—from the once scrub-covered plains and grasslands of the coasts to the eastern slope of the imposing range that cut through the length of Southern Ergoth. Icy winds swept across the terrain, stirring the snow into drifts, constantly-shifting patterns, and ever-thickening banks. Other than the far western part of the country, Southern Ergoth had become a veritable iceberg.

Its foul-tempered master—the dragon overlord Gellidus,

called Frost by men—sat at the edge of a small frozen lake. Except for his eyes, pools of pale blue-green, the dragon was as white as everything else in his domain. Occasionally his scales gleamed here and there with silvery-azure streaks—a reflection of the sky that sometimes appeared through gaps in the cloud cover.

The majestic dragon was completely still, his eyes unblinking, his wings tightly tucked into his sides, and his tail curled around his haunches. His crown, a scaly fringe that swept gracefully back from his massive frosty jowls, sparkled as did the five tapering horns like inverted icicles that grew upward from the fringe.

Gellidus stared at the lake and filled his lungs with the blessed frigid air. He released it all in a single blast, blowing away the snow from the top of the frozen water.

The newly revealed ice shimmered and sparkled, and seemed to flow for an instant, as if it were melting. Then it brightened, turning a pale pink, as it did when it reflected the dawning sun on days when the clouds weren't so thick. But it was the middle of the day, and the ice was several inches thick—in no danger of melting. The pink blossomed into a radiant orange glow, then became a warm vermillion, the shade of dying embers. Finally it turned an intense blood red, and the visage of Malystryx came into focus.

Gellidus stared at the magical image of the massive dragon with rapt attention, then lowered his head. The Red stared back at him across the hundreds of miles.

Your answer? Malystryx prompted.

Gellidus heard the words inside of his head; it was part of the magic the monstrous dragon used in her communication spell. At roughly five hundred feet long, she was twice his size, and she could squash him without a considerable amount of effort. Her fire could easily melt the ice of his domain. When the steam dissipated, his corpse would be found, twisted and burnt, on the plains.

"I will ally myself with you, Malys," Gellidus said. His voice was sonorous and haunting like the frigid wind that whistled through his land's valleys. But it was not so commanding as the Red's. "I will work with you. I will not oppose you."

Malys curled back her lips in the approximation of a smile, and a rumble resonated inside the white's head. The Red sounded pleased. Flames danced amongst teeth that were as white as Gellidus's hide and rose up around her head like a wreath.

The white dragon continued. "And I would deign to be your consort, Malys."

The Red nodded. *Accepted, Gellidus. Together we will make Ansalon tremble. My plans are already in motion, and soon I will tell you what magnificent role you will play in all of this.*

"I am honored," the white dragon answered. "We will meet?"

Soon, she silkily replied. *On the Plains of Dust in the realm called Duntollik.*

"Neutral territory," he said. "You are most wise." Then he felt her mind slip away from his, and watched the red glow on the frozen lake's surface turn to orange then to a rosy pink. Within moments, the ice was milky white again, and the soothing chill wind was blowing snow across its slick surface.

Gellidus raged at kowtowing to any dragon. He was an overlord, and he ruled Southern Ergoth unchallenged. The continent of the Kagonesti elves was a temperate land when he first came upon it. There were vast stretches of ice-covered lands he could have more easily claimed, but only a smattering of ice barbarians lived in those lands, and Gellidus felt a need to rule over a larger population. Since securing Southern Ergoth nearly two decades ago, he had worked to change the climate and much of the terrain to suit his icy, austere tastes. He was quick to take control of Daltigoth, the once-great capital. And he was quick to turn it over to the ogres—after plundering the city's riches. Foghaven Vale fell too, and with it the legendary resting place of Huma, hero of the Third Dragon War.

The ogres of the land were Gellidus's to command. They offered the dragon their loyalty and service in exchange for their worthless lives and some small amount of power. Groups of thanoi—grotesque walrus-men—also served him. Gellidus had captured the thanoi from the southern Plains of Dust and brought them here to use as guards and messengers.

Most of the Kagonesti, the wild elves who once ranged across the island continent, had fled more than a decade ago. But some remained on the western part of the dragon's realm, beyond the Last Gaard Mountains. Though the climate was harsh and the wind bitter, they were relatively free of the dragon's influence there. It wasn't that Gellidus was too lazy to conquer that part of the continent, though the overlord admittedly led a largely sedentary life. The White simply decided to leave a safe haven for people. It would give him something to watch, to study, and a place to terrorize later when he grew too bored.

Gellidus rose on his stubby legs and uncurled his tail. It stretched dozens of feet behind him, ending in a flattened fin-like ridge. He worked the kinks out of his thick neck, then stared at the frozen lake for a moment before thrusting his front claws through the ice and into the freezing water below. The rest of his body quickly followed, embraced by the welcome glacial coldness.

* * * * *

The White was not Malys's first consort. That distinction belonged to Khellendros, the Storm Over Krynn, who was occupying her thoughts now.

"Khellendros uses knights," Malys hissed to herself. "Though not so aptly and cleverly as I." The Red's thoughts often drifted to the Blue who claimed the Northern Wastes and the city of Palanthas. She considered him the most astute and powerful of those beneath her.

"What is he up to?" she mused aloud. She extended a talon toward the dirt floor of the plateau and began sketching an odd-looking symbol. Dust rose around the edges of the diagram, and the air shimmered with cool, blue energy.

Khellendros, I would speak with you—here.

Chapter 1

Deaths and Beginnings

The increasing pressure of the cool blue water snapped Dhamon awake. He was floating just above the lake's silty bottom, his long hair fluttering like the fronds around him, his chest burning for air. He ached terribly from his fight with the dragon, but somehow he managed to summon a last bit of strength, kicking hard and struggling toward the surface. As he rose, he felt his limbs grow heavy and numb. Dhamon felt himself slip toward the comforting embrace of darkness. Then his head broke the surface and he gasped, coughing up a lungful of water and greedily gulping in air.

His hair was plastered over his eyes, but through a gap in the strands he spotted Palin, Feril, and Rig walking up a hill, away from the edge of the lake.

"Feril!" He raised his arm and thrashed about to get the elf's attention. But he wasn't loud enough. She was too far away to hear him, and getting farther with each passing heartbeat.

"Feril!" he called again; then something brushed against him and closed around his leg. His cries were silenced as he felt himself being pulled under. Water rushed down his throat and the darkness reached up and swallowed him.

* * * * *

Just before dawn, *Flint's Anvil* eased away from the Palanthas docks. The green-hulled carrack glided as swiftly and silently as a wraith through the maze of fishing boats already dotting the deep bay. Palin Majere moved toward the bow, listening to the soft splash of the fishing nets hitting the water and the nearly imperceptible creaking of the *Anvil's* deck beneath his sandaled feet.

The son of famed Heroes of the Lance Caramon and Tika Majere as well as one of the few survivors of the Battle of the Rift, Palin was called the most powerful sorcerer on Krynn. Yet for all his magical skills and arcane knowledge, he felt powerless against the dragons threatening his world. He cursed himself for having been unable to save Shaon of Istar and Dhamon Grimwulf when the blue had attacked yesterday.

Palin leaned against the rail and stared at a spot on the horizon where the rose-tinted sky met the waves. His gray-streaked auburn hair whipped about in the wind, and he halfheartedly brushed it away from his eyes and yawned. Sleep had escaped him last night. He had lain awake listening to the sounds of the workers repairing the *Anvil's* mainmast, which the dragon had snapped in half during its assault. When the work was completed, he had listened to the water lapping against the hull and had thought about his dead friends.

"We're far enough out!" called Rig Mer-Krel, the sea barbarian who captained the *Anvil*. He motioned to Groller, the half-ogre standing by the rear mast. Then he raised his arm, pointed to sails, clenched his fist, and brought his hand in quickly toward his chest.

The deaf half-ogre nodded in understanding of Rig's hand signals and started lowering the sails, stepping around Fury—the red wolf sleeping near the base of the mast. The rest of the *Anvil*'s complement stood amidships. The group formed a ring around a human-shaped bundle carefully wrapped in an old sail. Jasper Fireforge, nephew of the legendary Flint Fireforge, knelt next to the bundle and ran his stubby dwarven fingers over the silk cord wrapped around it. He mumbled a few words to the absent gods of the sea, stroked his short brown beard, and choked back a sob.

Behind him stood Feril. The Kagonesti closed her eyes, and tears slid down over the oak leaf tattoo on her cheek. "Shaon," she whispered. "I will miss you, my friend."

"I'll miss you, too," softly echoed Blister, a middle-aged kender. She grimaced as she fidgeted with the white gloves on her small hands. "You're the only person I ever told about . . . about my—"

"Shaon loved the sea," Rig began, his resonant voice cutting off the kender's reflections. "I often joked that salt water, not blood, ran in her veins. She was more at home on the rolling deck of a ship than on solid ground. She was my first mate, my friend, and my . . ." The mariner's big frame shuddered as he stooped to cradle the bundle. His muscles strained, for the body was weighted with ballast to help it sink. "Today we return her to that which she cherished."

He walked toward the railing and paused, picturing Shaon's walnut-brown face beneath the canvas. He would miss the feel of her skin against his and he would never forget

---

her infectious smile. He dropped the first mate's body over the side of the ship and watched it quickly sink out of view. "I will never forget you," he said, so softly that no one else could hear.

Feril stepped to the rail beside him. The breeze fanned her curly auburn hair around her shoulders and teased the tips of her pointed ears. "Dhamon Grimwulf died, too, though we could not recover his body. He abandoned his life as a Knight of Takhisis to take on a noble cause, and he sacrificed himself to slay the blue dragon who killed Shaon." The Kagonesti held a leather thong in her slender hand. She had found it among the scant possessions Dhamon had brought aboard the *Anvil*. She paused to tie the short strip of leather around an arrowhead. "Dhamon brought us together. Let us honor his memory—and Shaon's—by staying together and reclaiming our home from the dragons." The arrowhead and thong slipped from her fingers and plunged into the sea much as Dhamon and the blue dragon named Gale had plunged to their deaths into the nearby lake.

For a long while the only sound was the faint creaking of the ship's masts. Finally Rig backed away from the rail and nodded to Groller. The half-ogre raised the sails, and the dark-skinned mariner made his way to the wheel.

* * * * *

Noon, several days later, found Rig, Palin, Blister and Feril drenched with sweat, standing in the desert of the Northern Wastes. Before them sat a foot-long curly-tailed lizard. It flicked its forked tongue and peered with special intent at the Kagonesti, who was communicating with it. The others looked on, but understood none of the unusual conversation.

"Only for a short time can I share this desert, little one," Feril said aloud in clicks and hisses.

"Run with me across the sand. Enjoy with me my very, very

beautiful home. Plenty of desert for everyone."

"It is a most beautiful desert," Feril admitted. "But I need to know—"

"Catch with me insects. Crunchy beetles. Sweet butterflies. Juicy hoppers. Very, very juicy hoppers. Plenty for everyone."

"I'm not interested in insects," Feril explained.

The lizard looked disappointed and turned away.

"Please don't leave," she hissed, kneeling close to the lizard.

"What are they talking about?" The kender asked, eyeing them with typical wide-eyed curiosity. "Rig, do you know what they're talking about? All I hear are hissing noises. Sounds like a couple of tea kettles."

"Shh!" the mariner scolded.

"I wish I knew how to use magic like that," Blister said huffily. "I'd be able to talk to anything . . . everything." The kender crossed her arms and glared down at the ground, at least what she could see of it over her thin orange tunic that billowed about her short legs in the hot, dry wind. The tunic was another sore point. That morning, when Blister had come up from below deck wearing the large orange garment along with green gloves and a green belt, Rig had said she looked like a ripe pumpkin. The comment was enough to make her doff her matching orange boots in favor of brown sandals and to leave her green hat behind. "Palin, couldn't you cast a spell or something so we can all understand what the lizard is—"

"He's telling me about his big desert," Feril said, briefly glancing at Blister. She reached out and scratched the top of the lizard's head and resumed hissing and clicking.

"It *is* an awfully big desert," Blister admitted as she glanced at the sea of sand spreading away from them in all directions. She had to strain her eyes to see the *Anvil*'s masts edging into the northern horizon. So thin and far away, the kender thought they looked like sewing needles sticking out of the white fabric of the landscape. "I know it's a very big desert because I saw a map of it. Dhamon bought the map in Palan-thas several weeks ago—before we went into the desert way south of here. Shaon was with us." She paused when she saw Rig's lips tighten at the mention of Shaon. "Of course," the kender quickly continued, "Dhamon didn't have the map for very long. Spawn attacked us and frightened away our horses, and the map was on Dhamon's horse, which is who knows where now. Do you think the horse is alive? Do you think we'll need another map? Or maybe the lizard could sort of, you know, draw a map in the sand with its tail. Or maybe we—"

"Shh!" Palin and Rig admonished practically in unison.

The kender thrust out her bottom lip, ground her heel into the sand, and stared at the curly-tailed lizard, which was star-ing attentively at Feril.

"You're very smart," the Kagonesti hissed.

"*Very, very* smart," the lizard added. It sat back on its small haunches and looked up at her smooth, tanned face and sparkling eyes. "Smartest one in this wonderful desert."

"I'll bet you know a lot of what goes on here."

"Know everything," the lizard replied, puffing out its small chest.

"What do you know about a blue dragon?"

"Blue?" Its curly tail straightened for an instant, and it blinked at her quizzically. "Brown like mud?"

"Blue like the sky," she corrected.

Its mind whirled in deliberation. "The very, very big lizard?"

Feril nodded.

"Wings? Like a bird?"

"Yes, the dragon can fly."

"Stay with me away from the very, very big lizard," the curly-tailed one lectured. "It will eat you very, very quickly."

Blister tugged on Rig's pant leg. "I wonder if Feril's telling the lizard this was really all your idea. We all preferred to go to Southern Ergoth after the White. You've got Dhamon's lance, and you might be able to kill it."

"It's *my* lance."

"Now," Blister agreed. "But originally it belonged to Sturm Brightblade, and he used it in the War of the Lance a long time ago. And then it belonged to people who took it apart and kept the pieces as souvenirs. And then Dhamon and Palin put it all back together, and then the lance belonged to Dhamon until he died. Maybe you should have brought it along in case we run into a dragon. Maybe you shouldn't have left it on the ship with Groller and Jasper. Maybe we should be heading to Southern Ergoth instead."

"We *will* go to Southern Ergoth," Rig said emphatically.

"Good, but I still think you should have brought the lance."

Rig sighed and lowered his voice to a whisper. "Listen, Blister. I don't know how to use the lance. Satisfied?"

"I thought you could use any weapon. Feril says you're a walking arsenal."

"Swords, daggers, garrotes—those I know how to use. A bola in a pinch, and a couple of others. But a lance is something different entirely. You need both hands for it, and it's heavy. I want to practice a little bit with it first, become familiar with it. Using a weapon I'm unfamiliar with could do me more harm than good."

"So, you're basically saying that you don't want Palin to see that you can't use the lance. That's why you're whispering so he won't hear."

Rig groaned. "Blister . . ."

"Anyway, why should you drag around a big lance in the desert? It'll only make you sweatier and hotter and grumpier. You know, you could give it to someone who does know how to use it. Maybe Groller could use it or even—"

"It's my lance," the mariner repeated. "I'll have plenty of time—weeks, months—to practice on our way to Southern Ergoth."

"We should just go to Southern Ergoth right now."

"I said we would, but only after we find the blue dragon's lair. That dragon killed Shaon, killed Dhamon as it was dying. Dragons have lots of treasure—so they say. And I aim to get as much of it as I can carry."

"Well, I've never been on a treasure hunt before," Blister said cheerfully. "It all seems so exciting—even though it's so hot. I'm surprised Palin's going along with it, though. He *really* wanted to go to Southern Ergoth."

Rig sighed. "Palin agreed because I'm the captain of the ship, and he needs me to get to Southern Ergoth."

"I agreed because I think we can learn more about dragons by studying a dead dragon's lair," corrected Palin. "We might gain clues that will help us defeat a living one."

"That's provided we can even find the lair," Blister said. "The couple of birds Feril talked to this morning didn't seem too helpful. And now this lizard . . . well, who knows what it's saying?"

"Shh!" Feril interjected. "I can barely hear my little friend here."

"The very, very big lizard eats everything," the curly-tailed lizard continued. "Eats camels and—"

"It won't eat anything again," Feril hissed. "It's dead. A friend of mine killed it."

The lizard closed its eyes and its dark red tongue flicked in what Feril sensed was a sign of relief. "Very, very glad it is dead."

"We want to see where it lived."

"Lizard hole is dark and very, very stinky. Smells like death."

"You were there?"

"Once. Went inside chasing beetles, then went outside. Stinky. Did not want beetles that bad."

"Will you take us there?"

"No." It wrinkled its scaly nose, uncurled its tail, and

turned toward the southeast. "The very, very big lizard lived that way. Near rocks that touch the sky. Far walk from here, three days, four, two. But not so far for you. Only one for you, maybe." It looked at her long legs. "Very glad it is dead. Come run with me across the sand. Search with me for juicy hoppers."

Feril shook her head. "I haven't time today." She rose and brushed the sand off her knees and watched the lizard scamper away.

"Did it know anything about the dragon's lair?" Rig asked. The mariner wiped the sweat from his face and took a long draw from one of his waterskins.

"This way," Feril answered, pointing in the direction the lizard had indicated. "Follow me."

* * * * *

Shortly before sunset the foursome stopped to rest. They could find no cover and simply sat down on the sand, near a small dune. Palin's legs ached from all the walking, and his feet burned from the grains of sand that were constantly getting between the soles of his feet and the leather of the sandals. The thin garments he wore, once pale green, now were dark with sweat and clung to his skin. He closed his eyes and tried to think of something cool.

"You're sure the lair is around here?" Rig slumped a few feet away from Palin and kept his eyes on the Kagonesti.

"In this direction, yes," Feril replied.

"How much farther?" The mariner tugged off his shirt. His dark skin gleamed, and he futilely tried to blot himself dry with the sweat-soaked shirt. Then he put it back on. "We've been at this all day. Maybe talking to animals wasn't the best way to find the dragon's lair."

"And you have a better suggestion? This whole trip was your idea, Rig Mer-Krel," she reminded him. "If you hadn't been so set on finding the dead dragon's lair and getting rich, we'd be. . . ." She let the words trail off. Home, she thought, we'd be well on our way to Southern Ergoth—my home until the white dragon moved in.

Feril turned her back to the two men and concentrated on the warm wind playing across her skin. She was enduring the heat much better than her grumbling companions. A wild elf, she was inured to many of the vagaries of nature, and she savored rather than despised dramatic climates. She stared at the steadily dropping sun. A brilliant ball, it was painting the desert a pale orange-red. It was captivating, and she wished for a moment that Dhamon was alive and here to share it with her.

"At least we won't be sweating when we get to Southern Ergoth," Blister offered. She gingerly raised her gloved hands to her head and fussed with her braids. She sucked in her bottom lip when her fingers started to ache, and decided to leave her hair as it was. "Wonder how cold it'll be there? Probably not as cold as it is hot here. I'm drowning in sweat."

The mariner smiled—his first smile since Shaon's death. He emptied his second waterskin into his mouth, leaned back against the dune, and closed his eyes. He wondered what Shaon would think about him traipsing across the sand and looking for a hole in the ground where a dragon—the dragon who killed her—once lived.

The sound of flapping wings interrupted Rig's thoughts. He glanced at a rise in the sand several yards away. A vulture had come to roost and was watching them; a few more birds circled high overhead.

Feril feverishly worked a lump of clay into a miniature sculpture of the bird. She concentrated on the smells and sounds of the desert around her and then felt her mind floating on the warm wind toward the vulture. She intensified her concentration until the connection was made across the distance and she had entered the vulture's thoughts.

Dying soon? it cawed loudly, the shrill tones filling her head. *My belly rumbles and you would fill it nicely.*

She shook her head. *I plan on living a long time.*

Humans without camels do not live long in this heat, it cawed. *Soon you will stumble and not get up. Soon you will smell sweetly of death and we will feast.*

You like the smell of death. It was a statement, but Feril saw the bird bob its head in assent.

So sweet, it cawed.

Perhaps you know a place nearby where the smell of death hangs heavy?

* * * * *

Just as the stars winked into view, the quartet spotted an enormous rocky rise. It stretched across the sand like the spine of some half-buried beast, and it reached at least forty feet high in places.

"Rocks that touch the sky," Feril whispered, remembering the curly-tailed lizard's words. "The dragon laired here."

Palin brushed by her and walked toward a cave entrance. It was incredibly wide and low to the ground. It looked like a great, dark shadow cast by the ridge above it and was practically hidden by the night sky. Even in daylight it might be difficult to spot because of the shadows.

The mariner raised an eyebrow. "I don't see any dragon tracks."

"The wind," Feril said, pointing at the sand that blew at their feet. "It covered them, just as it's covering ours."

"If there were any tracks to cover," Rig said. "Who knows if the vulture was telling you the truth? It probably wasn't any smarter than the lizard." He looked at the sorcerer. "It's dark out here. It's going to be darker in there."

"We could wait until morning," Feril suggested.

Palin was exhausted, but more than he wanted rest, he

wanted to get this over with, return to the *Anvil*, and leave the hateful heat behind. The sorcerer closed his eyes and concentrated, sensing the energy around him, feeling for the faint magical pulse of the land.

In his youth it was strong and powerful—godly-given and so easy to grasp, able to birth the greatest of spells. But it was like a whisper on the wind now, only detectable by a skilled sorcerer. To craft great spells required much strength of will and perseverance. Palin's mind grasped the natural energy and channeled it toward his open palm, shaping it, coaxing it, and crafting a variation of a fire enchantment.

"Wow!" Blister exclaimed.

The sorcerer opened his eyes. In his hand was a glowing orb of light, brilliant but no hotter than the desert air. It alternately pulsed white, orange, and scarlet, like the flickering flames of a campfire. The rudimentary spell worked better than any lantern. "Let's see what the dragon left behind," Palin said. He led the way into the cave.

The still air inside was filled with the cloying scent of death. It was so strong that Palin's eyes began to water. Near the entrance, broken bones and tufts of fur were scattered here and there. Palin knelt to examine them. "Camels," he said. "Only something big could eat this many camels."

He stood and moved deeper into the cave, where the air was stale, but not as foul smelling. Following the stone floor that sloped steeply downward, he entered a massive underground cave that was a few hundred feet across. The light from the globe in the sorcerer's hands barely lit the walls and the ceiling, and it did nothing to chase away the shadows that clung to niches and other rock formations.

"I've never been in a cave so big!" Blister chirped. "Where to start, oh where to start. Palin, look at this!"

The kender stood near a rocky outcropping, pointing at a spot in the floor where a bit of sand had been brushed away. Palin could see deep gouges in the stone. They seemed to form a pattern. He brushed away more of the sand so he could see all of the design. Blister helped for a moment, then rushed away suddenly to investigate something else. Part of the etching looked familiar, like the written component of some transformation incantation Palin had seen before.

"Interesting that a dragon would rely on this type of magic," he mused aloud. "Dragons have an innate arcane power." He studied the pattern intently. The curved line represented change or rebirth. The wavy line that cut through it had gold dust sprinkled along its length and symbolized strength and energy, and the wax-filled circle that cut through the half moon meant—

"Palin!" Feril called to him from a dozen yards away. She and Blister were kneeling and staring at something in the sand. There was a crack in the cave roof directly above them, and the sorcerer saw traces of sand, like falling snowflakes, filtering down from it. "You'd better take a look at this." There was an urgency in the Kagonesti's voice, enough to pull Palin away from the diagram.

Rig, who had been preoccupied with taking in the size of the place, was quick to join them. "It's part of a big footprint," he observed, leaning in over the Kagonesti's shoulder. "It means your animal buddies were right. This really was that blue dragon's lair. And that means I'm going to head deeper and look for the treasure. I told you this trip wasn't going to take long."

The Kagonesti scowled and pointed toward a depression. "That would be a mark from a talon, and from its position, I'd say it was the small talon of its right front paw."

"Uh-oh," the kender whispered.

"So the dragon had a very big talon," Rig said. "So what? We knew that. We saw it up close when it killed Shaon. C'mon, Blister, I'll need some help filling these." He tugged a couple of leather bags free from his belt and held one out to

the kender. Blister didn't budge, she was engrossed in scruti-
nizing the footprint.

"This mark is too big," Feril said. "The dragon that killed
Shaon and Dhamon wasn't nearly big enough to make this
print. Believe it or not, I think we're in the wrong lair."

"Uh-oh," Blister repeated even more softly.

"And the track is fresh, I'd guess about a day old," the elf
continued.

"Not the lair of the *dead* blue dragon?" Rig asked, his voice
suddenly quiet. He swallowed hard and glanced at Palin.
"The lance is on the ship. I didn't think I'd need it for a dead
dragon's lair. We'd better get out of here before it's too late."

"Late too much," came a deep, rasping voice from the lair's
entrance.

Panic seized the quartet. As one, they turned to face the
speaker. The creature was the color of baked mud, mottled in
places. Dragonlike in form, it had scales and skin covering
most of its body, with patches on its belly that looked like
clumps of gravel. The beast's leathery wings resembled those
of a bat's, and its snout was long and pointed, filled with a
double row of sharp teeth that clacked together menacingly.
Large pear-shaped eyes the color of the night sky bored into
the foursome.

The creature flicked its barbed tail, flexed the claws on its
hind feet and took a step closer. It had no front legs, only the
wings that were barbed on the tips and looked as formidable
as talons. Its wingspan must have measured almost fifty feet,
and its neck was long and supple like a giant constrictor. The
motion of its wings sent the sand on the floor rushing away.

"A wyvern," Palin noted.

"The *brown* dragon the lizard mentioned," Feril said.

"I've never seen anything like it," Blister said, a hint of awe
creeping into her voice.

"At least it's not a real dragon," Rig said, relaxing only a
little. "And it certainly couldn't have made that print." He

drew his cutlass. The blade gleamed in the light from Palin's glowing orb. "And it's not nearly as big as the thing that killed Shaon. I can take it."

"Take what?" the wyvern growled. "Something steal? Mad be master."

"I didn't think wyverns could talk," Palin whispered to Feril.

"They can't," she answered.

"What find?" Another voice, as harsh as chalk being drawn across slate, reverberated in the cavern. "Something find?"

The quartet watched as a second wyvern emerged. It was slightly smaller than the other, and looked nearly identical. Its barbed tail swished back and forth, and it craned its neck around the edge of its fellow wyvern's outstretched wing so it could get a better look.

"People," the smaller wyvern announced. "Found people. Supposed to be here?"

"Don't know," the other answered. "Weren't here when left. Now here. Hot when left. Now cool. People came between hot and cool. Stupid people."

Rig's hand clenched tighter around the hilt of his cutlass. His dark eyes darted back and forth between the two wyverns.

"Searching for a dragon's treasure was a wonderful idea," Feril whispered to the mariner. She cocked her head in Palin's direction. "Studying a dragon's lair would teach us a few things, you said. If you had both listened to me, we'd be on our way to Southern Ergoth."

"It could be worse," the kender offered. "There could be more of them—or the dragon that made that print."

"I feel much better," the mariner muttered.

"Stop talk. Surrender," the large one insisted. Its eyes focused on Rig. "Drop shiny sticker. Now."

"No!" Rig bellowed. His feet churned over the sand-covered floor as he closed the distance to the larger beast. He raised his blade high above his head and brought it down in a sweeping motion, slicing through the hide of the wyvern's belly. The slash wasn't very deep, and the creature howled more in surprise than pain.

"Not they surrender," the smaller observed, seemingly nonplussed by Rig's attack. "Do what now?" it asked its companion. "Do something?"

"Catch people," the large wyvern replied as it dodged Rig's second blow. "Give to master."

"Give to Storm Over Krynn when comes!" the other exclaimed. "Idea good."

The Storm Over Krynn, Palin mouthed. "This is Khellendros's lair! We've got to get out of here!"

"Khellendros? The dragon overlord?" Blister shouted. She thrust her gloved hand into the bag at her side, and her fingers fumbled over an assortment of oddities she kept there. At last she was rewarded, and tugged free a sling. The kender filled it with the next object she grasped—a walnut—and she twirled the sling above her head, then swung it forward. The nut spun free toward the smaller wyvern, striking it on the nose.

"People sting!" it squawked.

Palin blotted out the sounds around him and concentrated on the globe in his hand. He watched the colors intensify and felt the warmth grow on his palm. When it became so hot it practically burned him, the sorcerer let the globe fall to the cave floor and continued to focus on it.

At the same time, Feril dropped to her stomach and splayed her hands in front of her, brushing furiously away at the sand until her fingers touched the cool stone beneath. She felt the smoothness, hard and ancient and powerful. She closed her eyes and let her senses drift away from her, seeping into the stone, merging with it. The Kagonesti felt strong and heavy, sluggish and immoveable and primeval. She felt the sand atop the stone, the feet of her companions, the heat of Palin's magical fire, and the clawed talons of the wyverns.

Be like water, she urged the rock. *Flow with me.* Feril felt the rock responding to her mental commands, and it became soft like clay. She struggled to dig her fingers into the stone. "Softer," she entreated the rock. "Flow like water. Hurry." She was quickly rewarded; her hands sank into the liquid stone, cool and thick like mud. Her fingers worked furiously, sketching a stream with wavy lines. "Away from me now. Run like a river."

"Fire hurt! Don't like hurt," the smaller wyvern complained.

Palin had built his orb of flame into a veritable bonfire, and now a gout of fire streaked toward the smaller wyvern. The creature's chest and one of its wings were badly singed. It flapped madly to put the fire out and cool itself. The sorcerer concentrated on the flame again and coaxed another searing lick forth to strike the creature. Its keening yowl echoed in the cavern.

"Not people surrender!" the smaller wyvern screeched. "People hurt us. Burn us! Still catch?"

"Catch not!" the larger wyvern cried. Distracted by the fire and its companion, the creature did not see Rig dart in close. The mariner took another swing, his blade cutting deep this time, leaving a growing line of black blood on the wyvern's belly. The creature growled and its head shot forward, its clacking jaws narrowly missing the agile mariner as he retreated.

"Kill people!" the smaller wyvern howled as it lashed forward with its tail. The barbed tip struck the mariner's thigh and Rig gasped and fell to his knees, his sword clattering on the stone.

The mariner fought back a scream as a jolt of pain raced from the barb and into his chest. Trails of fire and ice chased themselves up and down his frame, and he doubled over and shook uncontrollably.

"Fair not! Dark one mine!" the larger wyvern wailed as it edged by its companion and closed on Rig.

"Mine, too!" the smaller claimed, its tail swinging forward again, this time finding its mark in Rig's shoulder. "Share! One with fire next!" It dodged a tendril of Palin's flame, and whipped its barb at the mariner's chest.

Rig couldn't contain his scream this time. He writhed on the stone as alternating waves of heat and cold consumed him.

"Mine to eat." The larger wyvern's lips curled up in the approximation of a smile. Its snakelike neck dropped forward and its head angled toward the squirming mariner. It opened its jaws and then snapped upright as a shower of marbles pelted its snout.

"Leave Rig alone!" the kender shouted, reaching into her pouch to find more things to hurl. She filled her sling again and quickly sent a shower of buttons and shiny rocks at the wyverns. Then she rushed to Rig's side and started tugging him out of the way.

"Hate sting!" the larger creature bellowed, its deep voice bouncing off the cavern walls. "Sting! Sting! Get tiny one!"

"Can't!" the smaller growled. "Cave grab me! Move can't!"

The stone, like molten lava, flowed away from Feril, around Palin and Rig and Blister, and oozed across the wyverns' taloned feet.

"Hard," she urged it. "Be strong again." Her sides heaved from the exertion, but she felt the rock responding, returning to its solid state. She pushed herself to her knees, shook her head to clear her senses, and watched as a bolt of Palin's flame struck the largest wyvern. It engulfed the creature's head, and in the close confines its screams were practically deafening. The smell of the wyvern's burning flesh was overwhelming.

Palin, realizing the wyverns were no longer a threat, released his concentration on the orb and the flames died down.

The kender looked up at the larger wyvern's face, and grimaced when she saw bits of bone showing through on its lower jaw. It continued to howl in agony and swing its tail toward them, but the kender and mariner were several inches beyond the reach of either wyvern now.

Palin edged forward and helped the mariner to his feet. The sorcerer glanced at Rig's wounds, gently prodding the swollen area around them. "Some kind of poison, I think," he said. "We should have brought Jasper with us. He'd know what to do."

"What about them?" The kender stared up at the trapped wyverns.

"They're abominations of nature," Feril said. "They'll die here. Let's get going before the dragon comes."

"No argument," Rig said. He gritted his teeth as another wave of heat coursed through his limbs. It was followed by an intense chill that sent him into a fit of trembling. "I feel terrible." He slumped, unconscious, against Palin.

"You'll have to help me carry him," Palin told the Kagonesti. "Once outside we can—" The sorcerer's words were cut off as a spear of lightning struck him squarely in the back and propelled him and the mariner several feet forward. A miniature thunderclap resounded as they landed on the sand-covered floor.

"Spawn!" Blister shouted, as she reached for her sling again.

Feril spun around in time to see the creature step from a shadow-draped tunnel deeper in the cavern. It had a manlike shape, and there was something haunting about its eyes. It was covered in tiny blue sapphire scales that shimmered in the light from Palin's still-burning fire. A ridge of triangular-shaped scales ran from the top of its head down its back and to the tip of its short tail. Gently curving wings swept outward from between its shoulder blades. The creature flapped its wings slightly and rose a few feet above the cave floor.

Feril had encountered creatures like this weeks ago when she was with Dhamon. They weren't easy to defeat.

"Get bad people!" the larger wyvern coaxed the spawn.

"Kill people!" the smaller urged.

The spawn grinned, revealing a pearl-white row of pointed teeth across which miniature lightning bolts flickered. Traces of lightning skittered along the claws on its hands and feet. It sped toward the Kagonesti.

At that moment Blister released her sling, showering the spawn with colorful bits of tile and metal. The creature was unhurt, but surprised, and it dropped to a crouch on the cave floor.

The Kagonesti used the precious seconds the kender had bought to dash toward Rig's fallen cutlass. Her fingers closed about the pommel just as she heard a second crackle of lightning. Blister screamed, and was thrown against the cavern wall by a bolt from the creature's claws.

"Thing of evil!" the elf cried as she rushed toward the spawn. The weapon in her hand felt heavy, but she wielded it as she'd seen the mariner do, rushing forward and raising it above her head. She swept in close, then brought the sword down as hard as she could. The blade cut through the scales of the spawn's shoulder blade. The creature's arms flailed and lashed at her as she tugged the blade free.

This time she aimed for the creature's neck, her blade flashing down and practically severing the thing's head. It struggled for a moment, its eyes wide and unblinking, then it exploded in a ball of crackling lightning. Feril closed her eyes, but too late. Blinded and tingling uncomfortably all over, she stepped back, and felt about with her free hand, trying to find the wall of the cave.

"Blister, are you all right?" the Kagonesti called.

"No," came the kender's reply. "I hurt all over."

"Can you walk?"

"Yes, but Palin and Rig can't. I think they're alive, but they're not moving."

"Keep talking," Feril urged her. "I'll follow the sound of

your voice. You'll have to help me drag them out of here." She was beginning to see bits of color—the gray of the stone, the white sand, the red of Palin's still-burning fire—but the colors were running together. "This isn't going to be easy, Blister."

The kender groaned. "Easy? Try impossible. They're both awfully big."

She tried to concentrate as she moved toward the kender, tried to bring everything into sharper focus. Then abruptly she froze, tilting her head. There was a sound of flapping wings, faint, but it was there, coming from behind her— deeper in the cave. She turned in time to see a smeared bolt of lightning arc toward her from a hazy patch of dark blue— another spawn. Four more blue splotches were behind it.

"Blister, run!" she cried as she dropped to her knees. A bolt of lightning shot over her head. Another spawn opened its maw, and again lightning crackled toward her. She pitched to the side, avoiding the bolt, and fell into the path of another spawn. The lightning struck her shoulder, and she was driven hard against the cave floor.

"Feril?" The kender took one last look at her fallen friends and the approaching spawn, and ran faster than she had ever run in her life.

Chapter 2

Mirielle Abrena

The Knight of Takhisis ran down the dusty path, his sheathed long sword slapping against his leg and threatening to tangle itself in his long black surcoat. He ran awkwardly, weaving around burning huts and the bodies of ogres who had foolishly dared to challenge his talon. They should have surrendered, he thought as he leaped over a decapitated corpse and through a cloud of insects drawn by the spreading pool of blood. The knights had offered them that opportunity. Why hadn't they listened to reason? Other ogre clans were allied with the knights—they knew that to submit to the Order was the only prudent course.

The knight paused a moment to catch his breath and to

stare at the tiny body of an ogre girl. Twisted and broken, fixed eyes bulging, she looked like a discarded toy. She was one of the many children who had been killed during the attack. Couldn't be helped, he knew. The knights typically avoided fighting those who couldn't defend themselves. It wasn't honorable, but sometimes children got in the way.

He dashed toward a clearing at the far end of the village, where part of his unit was gathered. When he spied his commander, he slowed his pace to a walk, squaring his shoulders, taking long, measured steps—as if he were marching—just as he'd been taught since he joined the knighthood nearly three years ago. He brushed the dirt off his surcoat, and straightened his helmet. Coming to a halt in front of his commander, he sucked in his stomach, and snapped to attention. "Sir!" he said as he saluted. "The governor-general is coming, sir!"

"Here, Arvel?"

"Yes, sir! Knight-Officer Deron spotted the governor-general's entourage heading through the gap, sir! He told me to inform you immediately, sir."

"Very good, Arvel. Fall in!"

Arvel was quick to join the front-rank line. It would afford him the best chance to see the governor-general. Arvel was the smallest in the unit, gangly and all of thirteen years old, and he was also the youngest—though not by many months. The Knighthood of Takhisis inducted squires at an early age. It was practically unheard of to accept new recruits over the age of fifteen.

His heart beat in anticipation as his commander quickly, but painstakingly, inspected each man. The governor-general—here—in an ogre village on the border of Neraka and Blöde! He stood at attention, excitedly waiting and trying to stand perfectly straight. His black mail weighed as much as he did, and he prayed to the departed Dark Queen to give him the resolve not to slouch. A trickle of nervous sweat ran down his brow, and he successfully fought the temptation to wipe it away.

"Dress right!" the commander snapped.

The young squire swung his head until his chin was even with his shoulder. He saw her then, riding slowly down the path toward them—Governor-General Mirielle Abrena.

She was astride a massive black stallion that was as black as night and as black as the armor and tabard she wore. Her hair was blonde, though there were streaks of silver here and there on the curls that hung below her helmet and grazed her neck. She had sharp facial features and taut, unblemished, ruddy skin. Her dark blue eyes were narrow and perched above a small nose that looked slightly hawkish. Not an attractive woman, the young squire decided, though not at the same time unattractive. Powerful would best describe her, he thought, one whose bearing and manner drew and held stares.

She was the only officer who had been able to reforge the scattered Knights of Takhisis into a proud Order again. She subjugated the draconians, hobgoblins, and ogres of Neraka, becoming governor-general of the land and head of the entire knighthood. And she was *here*—only a few yards away! Arvel drew in a deep breath and continued to stare. She must be at least fifty, he guessed, though she looked at least a decade younger. She was muscular, rigid, and showed no sign of fatigue under armor much heavier than his own.

Behind her rode more than a dozen men, all on black horses. Most were Knights of the Lily like himself, the warriors of the Order. But Arvel spotted two men with embroidered crowns of thorns on their surcoats—proclaiming them to be members of the Order of the Thorns. Sorcerers.

Mirielle Abrena effortlessly dismounted a few paces away, and nodded a greeting to the commander.

"Governor-General Abrena!" he stated, saluting her and waving his hand to indicate his unit. "We are most honored by your unexpected visit."

"You took the village quickly," she said, as she eyed the rows of men.

"With only a few injuries to report, Governor-General. None of our knights were killed."

She paced in front of the first rank. "The ogres, commander. Did you take any prisoners?"

She stopped only a few yards away from Arvel, and the squire's heart pounded wildly. To be so close to her! This would be a day to remember for the rest of his life.

"Only three, Governor-General. They fought like mad dogs, all of them. And they wouldn't quit even when they knew they were beaten."

"Foolish," she said. "But admirable. Bring the three here."

She stood directly in front of Arvel now, her cold eyes boring into his. "Was this your first battle?" she asked.

"No, Governor-General," Arvel quickly replied. His throat was instantly dry, and his words cracked like dead twigs as they came out. "My third battle, Governor-General."

She pivoted on the balls of her feet and strode to a point several feet in front of the knights. The two sorcerers flanked her, standing silently as the prisoners were brought to her. The three ogres were young, little more than children. Their hands were bound behind their backs, and lengths of rope around their ankles hobbled them. They glared defiantly at her, and the largest muttered curses in the ogre tongue as they were forced to their knees.

"You are undone," she stated evenly. "We have your lands. Your fellows lie dead. You are all who remain of your clan." Her voice was flat and emotionless. "This ground is pivotal to our planned expansion. From here, it will be easier to launch an assault into Sanction. It is crucial that we have access to the New Sea, and Sanction's coast will allow us to expand our base of power."

"Much ground between here and Sanction," the largest growled. "You'll not get your port."

"No?" Her hand shot out, grabbing the young ogre's throat. "Your village was merely the first step, and it fell easily."

"Many other villages," he rasped. "Much larger than this. You'll be . . . undone."

"Tell me, how many ogres are in these neighboring clans?"

His reply was to spit at her. Her retort was to snap his neck. The ogre dropped to the ground, and Mirielle swung toward the other two. "How many ogres in the neighboring villages?" she repeated.

The closest glowered and shook his head. "Tell you nothing."

"Loyal to your fellows," she said in the same even tone. "I respect that." Mirielle flicked her wrist and one of the sorcerers behind her stepped forward. His hand glowed red for an instant, and the insolent young ogre screamed. His skin bubbled and popped, as if he were being doused with boiling oil. His chest bulged outward, and the sorcerer raised his fist, squeezing and chanting. The young ogre pitched forward into the dirt, where he squirmed for a moment more before dying.

She turned to the sole survivor, the youngest of the three. "Perhaps your tongue will be more accommodating?"

The young ogre talked haltingly at first, stumbling over the words of the common tongue and filling in the governor-general on the position—to the best of his knowledge—of the nearest villages and the number of ogres there. Then the words came easier to him as he betrayed the clans' defenses, the names of those chiefs he could recall, the times when ogre fighters were usually away to hunt.

"Much better," she said. The ogre looked at her hopefully, but she avoided his gaze, instead glancing at Arvel. She crooked her finger to motion him forward.

The young squire of Takhisis swelled with pride, took a deep breath and marched toward her. "Yes, Governor-General?"

"This one is of no more use to us," she stated, gesturing at the ogre. "Kill him."

Arvel glanced at the ogre, likely only several years older than the dead child he'd spotted earlier. There was hatred in the ogre's eyes, and fear. The young squire of Takhisis drew his blade, pushed the ogre to his stomach, and in one strong blow cut through the back of the ogre's neck. Arvel inwardly beamed. He'd been given a direct order by the governor-general. He, of all the gathered knights, had been asked to perform this task. He wiped the blade on the ogre's tunic, sheathed it, and snapped to attention.

"See that the bodies are burned," Mirielle said, continuing to address Arvel. "All of them. The huts, too—though not before they are searched. Turn all valuables over to these men, who will see to it that any choice treasures are taken to Neraka." She indicated the sorcerers, then strode toward her horse. "Commander, a word with you."

Arvel watched his commander hurry to keep up with the governor-general, and heard some mention of dragons. Then he fell to the task of dealing with the corpses. What tales he would have to tell of this day!

* * * * *

"Commander, station your compgroup nearby, within sight of this village. Keep watches in the event any ogre clans come to investigate. Slay them. I'll send more wings here within the week to bolster your ranks. When you've gathered enough men, take the next several villages. Use runners to report on your progress. When we are at squadron strength here, I will return and we'll march toward Sanction."

"Governor-General?"

Her steely eyes locked onto his. "Yes?"

"We are near the territory of Malystryx, the dragon over-lord. Does the dragon know we're taking this land for our-selves?"

A hint of a smile crept across Mirielle's face. "Malystryx is well aware of my plans. She has no objections, and we have nothing to fear from her at this juncture. After all, commander, we work with her and for her, not at cross-purposes."

He swallowed hard and risked another question. "Governor-General, you've assigned wings to the Blue, the Storm Over Krynn. Our units run Palanthas, Elkholm, Hinterlund, virtually all of the Northern Wastes for him. And the dragon financially rewards us. We gain nothing from the Red, yet you repeatedly send her knights. I see no reason why—"

"The Red is the most powerful of the overlords, commander," Mirielle said tersely as she settled into the saddle. She gently tugged on the reins, and the stallion wheeled about. "Malystryx gives us our lives. I'd say that's worth some measure of allegiance."

Chapter 3

Blister's Pluck

The kender stared into the entrance of the cave and nervously wrung her aching hands. Palin, Feril, Rig—all down there at the mercy of the spawn! She had been spared, but not left unscathed. Her back stung horribly where she had been struck by one of their bolts.

"Wonder if my tunic is ruined?" she said to herself. "Wonder if I'm bleeding? Wonder if they're all right?"

She cocked her head and listened, but heard only the prattling of the trapped wyverns, their grating voices echoing off of the cavern walls. There was no whoosh of wings or a crackle of lightning. And no sounds from her friends.

"I could go get help," she said. "Sure, I could go back to the ship, get Jasper and Groller, Fury, Dhamon's . . . er, Rig's lance and then we could all come back here and rescue them. If they're not dead by then. If they're not dead already."

She glanced up at the dark sky, then down at the sand that stretched away from her in all directions—it looked gray in the scant light from the stars. "Probably couldn't find the *Anvil* anyway. Can't tell which way's north." The kender sucked in her bottom lip and took a tentative step toward the cave. "Can't see in there without Palin's magic light. Can't see in the dark." She took another step and carefully touched the rock of the cave's entrance. She couldn't feel the stone through the heavy fabric.

"Somebody's gotta help them. And I'm the only somebody here." Blister gingerly pulled her gloves from her hands, revealing crippled, scarred fingers. She took another step forward and let the darkness envelop her. Then she raised her hand to the cave wall, and painfully started to feel her way down.

Shaon had been the only one Blister ever told about the mishap that caused the disfigurement of her hands. Years ago, curiosity had demanded that Blister open a merchant's chest and its magical trap left her with pain in her hands and scars that she tried to hide beneath an ever-growing assortment of gloves. Maybe the fact that Blister had confided in Shaon and told her the tale was one of the things that had cursed the first mate. Blister didn't want to lose any more friends.

The kender cringed as her fingers ran over a sharp outcropping. Her fingertips were so incredibly sensitive. They felt the air flowing in from the cave, the recirculating air flowing back out. And they felt the air stop when she approached an object that blocked its flow, like a rocky spire or the carcass of a camel.

As the gibbering of the wyverns grew louder, Blister took in a lungful of air, and determinedly plunged deeper into the dragon's lair.

* * * * *

I should have gone with them, Jasper Fireforge thought. Not that I have any love for the desert, but if I was with them, I wouldn't be worrying. He leaned against the *Anvil's* rail, stroked his short beard, and looked up at the stars. Feril, she can take care of herself. So can Rig. And Palin's the most powerful sorcerer on Krynn. But taking the kender along. Well, that was certainly a double helping of foolishness. I should've objected, taken her place. After all, I promised Goldmoon I'd help Palin and his friends.

The dwarf heard the deck creak behind him, and he looked over his shoulder. "Evening, Groller," he said. Jasper immediately pursed his lips and shook his head. "Sorry," the dwarf mouthed, waggling the fingers of his right hand in a greeting.

The burly half-ogre grinned. "Jaz-pear not tard?"

The dwarf held up his hands, then whirled them in front of his face. "Worried, my friend. Can't sleep."

Groller nodded in understanding. "Rig strong, need dis trip. He be okay, need dis." The half-ogre's voice was thick and nasal, the words slurred together.

"Needs the dead dragon's treasure you mean. Wants it anyway." Jasper cupped his left palm then placed the back of his right hand in it. He raised his right hand several inches, turned it over and wriggled his fingers. It was a hand sign Groller had taught him. It meant money. Jasper pantomimed scooping up steel pieces and running them through his stubby dwarven fingers.

The half-ogre shook his head. "No. Rig need dis 'cauz Rig loft Shaon. He hurd bad inside."

"He loved her a lot from what I gathered," the dwarf said to himself. He nodded in agreement with Groller.

"Hurd him bad inside dat Shaon's dead," Groller continued. "I tink Rig wants dreasure 'cauz dragons luf dreasure. Dragon took Shaon. Rig take dragon's dreasure."

"Sort of like a payback, even though the dragon's dead?" Jasper sighed. "Well, I suppose that's one way to look at it. I hope Rig finds what he's looking for. But no amount of treasure will bring Shaon or Dhamon back. And no amount of treasure's going to ease his loss. I know. I felt pretty empty for a long while after my Uncle Flint died."

Groller raised his eyebrows and cocked his head.

"Sorry. I just don't know enough of these gestures," the dwarf grumbled. He made the sign for wealth again, then he pointed his index fingers at each other and circled them in front of his chest. It was the gesture for pain. Next, he shook his head furiously.

"I dno," Groller said. There was a sadness in the half-ogre's eyes that Jasper hadn't noticed before. "Dreasure heals nothing. Dreasure can't make you ferget."

"Hey, where's your wolf?" the dwarf said, deciding to change the subject. He curved the fingers of his right hand, centered them over his chest, then flung them up violently— the sign for Fury, the name of Groller's red-furred lupine.

Groller pointed at the deck and rested his head on his hand. "Sleep below," he said. "Jaz-pear should too. Jaz-pear need rest. Morrow help me mend zails."

"I'm not handy with a needle," the dwarf said. He balled his fist, raised it level with the side of his head, and shook it. He had accepted the task. "Yes," he said. Then he pantomimed sewing. "I'll help you in the morning. But I'm going to stay up a while longer."

He returned his gaze to the shore of the Northern Wastes. "I think I'll stand here and worry a little more. I should've gone with them. A double helping of foolishness, taking a kender along."

Chapter 4

A Grim Fate

"Stuck still," the large wyvern grumbled. It struggled against the rock floor that firmly held its taloned feet.

"Forever us stuck?" the other asked.

Feril awoke to the pair's annoying banter. She was surrounded by a solid inky blackness. Her head pounded and her shoulder stung terribly where she'd been struck by the spawn's lightning, but at least she was alive. She expected the spawn to kill her and perhaps reunite her with Dhamon wherever spirits drifted. But, for some reason, the spawn had left her alive.

The Kagonesti's hands were behind her back, tied with a hard, bumpy cord that cut into her wrists so tightly that her fingers were numb. Her ankles were similarly bound, and she was propped uncomfortably against the cave wall.

She concentrated on the odors in the still air and immediately picked up the stench of the wyverns—she was within several yards of them. The Kagonesti's keen sense of smell noticed other scents, too: sweat, blood, the faintly musky odor of the mariner, the smell of leather—most likely her companions' sandals and belts. There was an unusual fetor that she couldn't quite place, but it hung heavy in the air. Spawn, she decided. She listened now, trying to block out the absurd jabbering of the trapped wyverns. There—breathing, regular, human. Rig and Palin still lived. And there was a soft shuffling sound. It was coming closer.

Feril focused on the shuffling, glanced in its direction and forced her eyes to search for heat. Her exceptional elven vision pierced the blanket of darkness ever so slightly, and she saw large spots of pale gray—the wyverns, and a small blob that seemed to be groping its way along the side of the cave toward her. Her vision had not yet completely recovered from the blinding explosion of the spawn earlier.

"Feril?" the blob whispered.

"Blister?"

"Hear something," the large wyvern announced.

"Prisoners wake?"

Feril heard a groan—Rig's voice.

"Dark one wake. See?" the wyvern observed. "Dark one wiggle."

The Kagonesti scowled. The wyverns could somehow see through the darkness, which meant they might also be able to see the kender sneaking toward her.

"Feril?"

"Shh," the elf softly returned.

"Elf wake," the smaller wyvern growled. "Elf hate. Made floor swallow feet. Elf bad."

Feril felt Blister behind her, the kender softly whimpering

as she forced her fingers to untie the cords that bound Feril's wrist. The Kagonesti shifted her position so that she was interposed between Blister and the wyverns, hoping they might not be able to notice the diminutive kender busy behind her back.

"First I was gonna go back to the ship," Blister whispered, "get Jasper and Groller to come help. Then I figured I might not be able to find the ship, since I don't have a map. I used to have lots of maps, but they were mostly for other places. Anyway, I couldn't ask anybody for directions. I can't talk to animals, and I didn't want to be out in the desert by myself."

"Elf talk much," the smaller wyvern observed.

"Talk to self," the other decided.

"Elf quiet!" the small wyvern barked.

"You want quiet?" Rig bellowed. "Then come over here and try to make us be quiet! Why, I'll just talk—" The mariner's sentence was cut off by a flash of lightning and a muted rumble of thunder.

A ball of lightning continued to crackle, like dozens of angry fireflies held in the palm of the approaching spawn's hand. Its glow provided enough light for Feril to see what was nearby.

The wyverns were several yards away. But only a few feet from her she spotted Rig and Palin—trussed up, back to back, their necks bound together by a gold chain. Necklaces with dozens of thumb-sized jewels had been used to tie their feet and hands together, and Rig's sash had been wrapped around the waists of both men and tied with a huge knot. The mariner's shirt was gone, as were all of his daggers. The spawn were smart enough not to leave him any weapons. A sheen of sweat covered Rig's muscular frame. He was still suffering from the ill effects of the poisonous wyverns.

The kender continued to work furiously. Feril felt her fingers tingle, the circulation starting to return. She was almost free.

Rig strained against his bonds, the chain digging into his throat as he glanced toward the Kagonesti. The sorcerer gasped with pain as Rig's movements made the gold cut into his flesh, too. The spawn stepped closer to the men, the lightning glowing brighter in its hand.

"Struggling shall only hurt you," it hissed.

"Old one live," the larger wyvern said. "See! Spawn said none dead. You said old one dead. Spawn not like you. Spawn smart."

"Spawn not stuck," the smaller wyvern muttered.

The scaly blue sentry circled Palin and Rig once, then stood before the wyverns, its back to the prisoners. "I shall go find our master, the Storm Over Krynn," it said. "The Storm shall be pleased by what we have caught."

"You go?" the larger wyvern asked. "Who guard?"

"My brothers shall stand watch over the prisoners."

"All spawn watching?"

"No." The spawn shook its head. "Only two—these." The creature gestured with its lightning-sparking hand, and two more spawn stepped from a shadowy alcove and glided toward Rig and Palin. "They are more than enough to handle the prisoners. The rest of my brothers shall stay below."

"Free us," the smaller wyvern implored as it looked down at its feet and then into the spawn's golden-yellow eyes. "Please."

The spawn hissed and took flight. In a matter of seconds, it flew up the slope toward the desert, taking its illumination with it.

"Feril, are you all right?" Rig asked.

"Hold your tongue, human," the shorter of the spawn sneered. The creature had a barrel-like chest and thick, powerful-looking legs. Its scales glimmered faintly in the dim light. It stared malevolently at the sorcerer, raising its upper lip in a sneer. Traces of lightning darted across its teeth, faintly illuminating part of the cave. "The Storm Over Krynn shall return soon. He shall make you like us, and you shall be added to the army below. You shall know the pleasure and power of being spawn."

Feril bristled. So that was why they were being kept alive— they were to be transformed into spawn! She felt one last tug around her wrists, and then her bonds slipped away. Feril wriggled her fingers, then slowly brought her hands around in front of her and inched them toward her ankles. Blister remained crouched behind her.

"How many spawn are below?" Palin asked.

"That is not your concern," the taller spawn replied icily.

"You'll have to excuse me if we're a little curious," Rig said tersely.

"Your only concern shall be serving the master."

Feril finished loosening the pearl strands around her ankles and could see that the mariner was quietly working on one of the necklaces that held his and Palin's wrists together.

"We proud to serve master," the larger wyvern cut into the conversation. "Only two of us. Wyvern special."

"Many spawn," the smaller wyvern said. "Many humans at stronghold waiting be spawn. Be big army. Only two of special us."

"What stronghold?" Rig pressed.

"Stronghold in desert near—" A glare from both spawn cut the smaller wyvern off. "Stronghold secret."

The mariner wouldn't let the subject drop. "Why does the dragon need such a big army?" Rig had only one necklace left to go, and his strong fingers made short work of it. He reached for the band of his pants and quietly worked at a seam until it came loose. A moment later, he tugged free a three-inch long blade that had been concealed there. He started cutting at the sash around the waists of he and the sorcerer.

"Stop asking so many questions!" the taller spawn snarled. Lightning shot from its claws to the cave ceiling, bursting in a ball and bathing the chamber in a bright white light.

"The elf is free!" the shorter spawn shouted, pointing at Feril. "And there is a little one with her."

"A little one you can't catch!" Blister taunted as she stepped out from behind the Kagonesti. She whipped her sling wildly about her head and released it, sending a shower of pearls toward the two spawn.

The creatures turned toward the kender. Lightning surged out, twin bolts that cut through the still air and narrowly missed Blister as she fell to the floor. Rig snapped the chain that bound together the necks of himself and Palin and with one strong tug broke the necklace that gripped their ankles. Pushing himself away from the sorcerer, he plowed into the pair of spawn and threw off the aim of their second lightning barrage.

Rig ducked as a bolt of lighting, meant for him, passed narrowly above his head. He barely sidestepped another as he hurled his small blade at the tallest spawn. The tiny knife sank all the way into the creature's neck, causing it to howl madly. Its claws tore at the scales around its wound, trying to find purchase on the blade. Black blood oozed down its muscular chest. The spawn dropped to its knees, gasped for air, then exploded in a ball of light.

"What happened?" Blister called. She had been watching Feril and only saw the flash out of the corner of her eye. "Oh, there's one less!"

"Palin, get over here!" Rig bellowed.

Although the sorcerer hadn't been looking at the creature, he was practically blinded by the explosion. He shut his eyes firmly and took a few hesitant steps toward the mariner.

"See cannot!" shouted the smaller wyvern, who had been engrossed in the struggle. "Bright light! Eyes sting! See cannot!"

"Spawn popped!" its companion growled. "Prisoners bad!"

"Palin!" Rig hollered. The mariner grabbed Palin by the

shoulder, pulling the disoriented sorcerer to him.

"Slayers!" the remaining spawn cried. It flapped its wings to rise several feet above the stone floor and spit at Rig and Palin. "I can't kill you," it hissed. "The master would be angry. But I can hurt you. I will hurt you so badly that you shall wish you were dead."

"My pockets!" Rig shouted to Palin. "Reach in! Hurry!"

The sorcerer blinked, shaking his head to clear his vision. The lightning flashes made it difficult to see very well and he struggled to focus amid all the light sparking from the creature's claws and teeth. Giving up on trusting his eyes, he shut them and felt about for the mariner's waist. His hands dipped into the folds of Rig's pockets and closed on the pommels of twin daggers in hidden sheaths.

Rig stepped away from the sorcerer, tugged off his red leather headband, and started swinging it above his head. "Can't kill us, huh?" he blustered. "Too bad. That's just what I intend to do to you!"

He leapt at the hovering creature, just as a bolt of lightning arced from the spawn's mouth. It cut through the air where the mariner had been standing a moment before and nearly struck Palin. Rig whipped the leather thong around the spawn's ankle and yanked hard. It closed tight like a lasso, and the mariner's weight pulled the creature down.

Rig wrestled the spawn to its stomach and drove his knee into its back. His fingers fumbled with the thong to pull it free. "And this time I'll know enough to keep my eyes closed when you breathe your last." He quickly wrapped the thong around the creature's thick neck. But as he pulled back to tighten the strap, the spawn beat its wings furiously, slicing Rig's arms and chest.

"Hold still, damn you!" Rig gritted his teeth and hung on as the spawn thrust up with its arms and legs, pushing off the stone floor. Despite his best efforts, he found himself dislodged, and the spawn whirled on him. Lightning sparked about its claws as it hurled a bolt into the mariner's stomach, sending him flying against the far wall. The spawn grinned malevolently, then turned toward Palin.

Meanwhile, Blister was busy scooping up pearls and loading her sling, while the Kagonesti touched the cave wall behind her and began to chant. "Move," the elf whispered to the stone. "Dance with me. Sing." The stone began to respond, quaking almost imperceptibly at first beneath her fingertips. Then it began to rumble softly. "Sing," she coaxed. "Louder."

"Hey, over here, blue and ugly!" the kender called, trying to attract the spawn's attention. The creature was stalking Palin now, staying just beyond the reach of the sorcerer's adroitly flashing daggers. "Why don't you pick on me for a change! Afraid of small folk?" She whipped her sling at the spawn, pelting its thick hide with pearls.

"Fool kender!" the creature spat as it turned to study Blister. "Kender cannot be made into spawn. My master shall not mind if I kill you."

"I'd mind, you poor excuse for a draconian!" Blister shouted over the growing rumbling noise in the cavern. The spawn darted toward her, its claws outstretched and sparking lightning. At the last second Blister rolled under its claws, wrapped her stubby arms around one of its legs, and tripped the thing so that it fell on top of her. The kender gasped—she hadn't thought spawn could be so heavy. The miniature bolts of lightning that flickered about its form shot into her like hundreds of jabbing needles. She pushed up with all of her remaining strength. The ache in her fingers was intense.

"No!" she shouted as the world seemed to explode in a blast of blue-white light. Her small frame shuddered as lightning raced through it. Then the pressure of the spawn atop her vanished and she was plunged into an inky world that smelled like burnt cloth and singed flesh.

"So death is blackness," Blister said disappointedly after a moment of silence. "I tingle all over and my fingers still hurt. I thought death would be a little more rewarding. Is anyone else here? Am I the only dead one? Dhamon? Raph? Mom?"

"Blister . . ." The voice was soft, but recognizable—Palin's.

"Not you, too! Did the spawn kill everybody?"

"The spawn's dead, not you," Palin said. "I killed it with Rig's daggers."

"Spawn popped!" the smaller wyvern announced.

"Bad prisoner!" the other lectured. "Master not want spawn to pop. Master be mad—punish you!"

"So it exploded and now I'm blind like Feril was." The kender groped about until she found Palin's leg. She pulled herself up and grabbed onto his tunic. "I can't see anything. Hope it doesn't last long. I like to see what's going on."

"So do I," the sorcerer said. "It's dark as pitch in here. Rig? Feril?"

The rumbling of the cavern grew louder and sand was filtering down through cracks in the ceiling.

"Over here!" Rig called. "Say, Palin, can you. . . ." The mariner's words trailed off as a softly glowing orb of light appeared in the sorcerer's palm. "That's just what I was going to suggest."

The orb alternately pulsed white, orange, and scarlet. The light revealed Palin's tunic to be in smoking tatters, and his heaving chest covered with ugly red welts. Blood dripped from his neck where the gold chain had cut him.

"You look terrible," Rig said.

"Thanks." Palin glanced at the mariner. Rig's pants hung in shreds, and he was covered with at least an equal number of claw marks. A patch of hair on his head had been burned away by lightning.

"Is Feril all right?" the kender asked.

The sorcerer turned and spotted the Kagonesti. Relatively unscathed, she was pressed against the cave wall, her fingers playing across the stone. "Dance faster," she urged the rock.

"Jump with me." The rumbling intensified and cracks spread outward from her fingers, racing away from her and toward the dark part of the cave where the lair extended underground.

"Cave shake. What do?" the smaller asked.

"Spawn below," the other replied. "Warn spawn."

"Spawn! Spawn!" the smaller wyvern shouted, its grating voice echoing off the cave and barely rising above the rumbling sounds. "Warn master!" it added. "Storm! Storm!"

"Let's get out of here!" Palin called. "We barely bested two spawn. We wouldn't stand a chance against Khellendros. Feril, hurry!"

The Kagonesti edged away from the wall and took a last glance over her shoulders as the cracks continued to widen and spread in a growing spiderweb pattern.

"Palin, can you leave that globe here with me for a moment?" Rig asked. He was looking longingly at the jewels scattered on the cavern floor.

The sorcerer shook his head. "It will only last a few minutes if I'm not concentrating on it."

"I'll only need a few minutes."

"You're crazy, Rig!" the Kagonesti shouted. "You're thinking about the treasure, and this cave will be coming down on our heads any moment!"

She spun on her heels, grabbed the still-blinded kender by the sleeve and tugged her toward the lair's entrance.

Palin dropped his globe on the floor and hurried to catch up. "Suit yourself!" the sorcerer shouted to Rig. "But you'd better be quick about it!"

"I'll hurry!" The mariner started scooping up handfuls of pearls and the broken necklaces that once had bound he and Palin. With his comrades gone, the mariner stuffed the jewels in his pockets and padded toward the wyverns. "The stronghold you mentioned," he shouted over the rumbling cavern, "where is it?" He retrieved the weapons that had been taken from him, careful to stay out of the reach of the wyverns' tails.

"Secret!" the smallest said, nervously eyeing the ceiling. It blinked furiously as grains of sand drizzled its face. The cave rumbled louder. "Tell not!"

"If this whole cave collapses, you'll die!" the mariner proclaimed. He sheathed his cutlass and grimaced as he noticed Palin's light globe start to dim. "Wouldn't want to take such a nice secret to your grave, would you?"

"Secret is secret," the larger wyvern hissed. "Storm's stronghold secret!"

The mariner steadied himself as the cave floor trembled. From somewhere behind him, he heard the sound of falling rocks. "I suppose you're right!" he shouted. "Besides, the stronghold is guarded."

"Black and blue men. Lots!" the larger wyvern warned.

"Yeah, sounds like a place to avoid. Well, I'll be going now—back out into the desert. If you don't want me to wander into this stronghold by accident, where would you suggest I not go?"

The smaller wyvern furrowed its brow and spit out a gob of sand. "Not go where sun comes up!"

"East!" Rig said, his voice growing hoarse from shouting to be heard over the increasing thunderlike noise of the trembling cave.

Its brother nodded its head. "Not go near big hole where sun comes up!"

"How far shouldn't I go in that direction?"

The larger one shrugged.

"Not go past tall cactus line," the smaller wyvern said smugly. "Not go past tall black rocks!"

The mariner grinned. He had seen a ridge of black rocks early this afternoon on their way here. He sucked in his breath as the ground shook harder. From somewhere deeper in the lair he could just barely hear the shouts of spawn. He inched his way toward the cave opening. "Cactus line?"

"Cactus with arms. Cactus big as men. Cactus near big hole. Near stronghold at Relgoth. Not go that way!"

"Thanks for the advice!" the mariner called as he bolted from the collapsing chamber.

* * * * *

The air was cool outside; it felt almost chilly as it washed over Palin's face. The temperature was in stark contrast to the heat they'd experienced several hours earlier. Judging by the position of the stars, the sorcerer guessed it was an hour or two after midnight.

Blister's vision had continued to improve as Feril tugged her away from the cave. Palin had paused only long enough to pick up the kender's dropped gloves and hand them to her. He had repeatedly glanced back over his shoulder, expecting to see the mariner.

It was several minutes, however, before Rig finally emerged from the lair. Palin turned and watched as the dark figure of the mariner rushed across the sand toward them. As he came closer, it was clear that what remnants were left of his pockets were bulging.

"Feril!" The mariner picked her up, swung her in a circle, and kissed her. Then he released her and thrust his fingers into his pockets, drawing out pearls and emeralds and gold chains and holding them in front of her face. "Not what I hoped for, but it will do!"

The startled Kagonesti felt a flush of embarrassment rise to her cheeks. She took a step back.

"These will pay for supplies for the *Anvil* for several years," he said, a wide grin decorating his face.

"Wow!" A re-gloved Blister exclaimed. The kender's sight had begun to return and her eyes locked onto the bright gems. "So we got some treasure after all."

"Do you want your daggers back?" Palin asked.

The mariner shook his head, putting the jewelry back in his pockets. He had noted Blister's interest and made a mental note to check his stash from time to time. "Keep 'em. I've got plenty. I got back what the spawn had taken from me."

The Kagonesti shook her head. "You're a walking arsenal, Rig Mer-Krel. Your headband's a garrote, and you have more daggers than fingers. What else?"

The mariner smiled. "The rest is a secret. And speaking of secrets, I managed to persuade the wyverns to tell me where the dragon's stronghold is. There are people there that are doomed to be turned into spawn. I hope Groller will hold the *Anvil* for us, 'cause we're going to take a little side trip—see if we can do a little rescuing."

"Four of us against a stronghold of spawn?" Feril wondered aloud.

"We can at least take a look at it," the mariner said.

"Not before we get some rest," Palin stated.

Two hours later they found a rocky ridge and huddled together in a comfortable niche. Dawn would soon be upon them, and none of them seemed able to take another step. Feril fussed over the cuts and burns on Rig's chest and arms. He enjoyed her ministrations, but he was too tired to stay awake. He leaned his head back against the rocks and snored while she finished applying a salve she had concocted.

Then she turned her attention to Palin. "You mentioned the name Khellendros back in the cave." She made Palin sit still while she rubbed the salve into his cuts. "He's the dragon overlord controlling this area."

Blister, who had been studying the stars, became instantly interested and shuffled over. The kender settled back against a rock and cocked her head toward Palin.

"Most call him Skie," the sorcerer said. "My divinations revealed he laired far to the south of here. Otherwise I wouldn't have agreed to traipse anywhere near this area."

"Maybe he does lair to the south," Blister interjected. "Maybe he has several lairs. I would think an overlord could live pretty much wherever he wanted. So he's called Khellendros *and* Skie?"

"Skie was the name Kitiara uth Matar called Khellendros, and it's a name that's far easier to pronounce. They were partners in service to the Dark Queen. They made quite a pair, so all the stories claim. Both were ruthless and incredibly cunning—and fiercely loyal to each other. Kitiara is said to have died decades ago, and Skie disappeared shortly after. No one knows where he went. But when he came back, he was massive, and he became one of the first dragon overlords."

Feril shivered. "I thought the dragon that killed Dhamon and Shaon was big."

"Skie dwarfs that dragon," Palin said. "My sorcerer associates and I have been studying the overlords, and Skie is in some respects the most intriguing of the lot. He appears to meddle the least of all in the affairs of the people in his realm—not directly anyway."

Feril shook her head and yawned. "I'd say that might make him the cleverest of the overlords. Why should he bother to directly involve himself?" She yawned again. "He has an army of spawn to do the work for him. He can lay back and count his treasure—or do whatever dragons like to do."

"And he has the Knights of Takhisis in Palanthas working for him," Blister added. "The knights run the city and the land around it. How does the dragon spend his time? Counting treasure would get boring after a while."

Palin rubbed his neck. "He must be up to something if he has his underlings running everything. After we find this stronghold Rig's interested in, I'll contact my associates, see if we can figure out just what the Blue is up to. Perhaps we could—"

Blister had fallen asleep. The sorcerer glanced at the Kagonesti. She had curled up into a ball, her head resting on her arm.

"Perhaps we could discuss it later," he said quietly. He closed his eyes and let sleep claim him, too.

Chapter 5

Spawning Ground

Khellendros glided several hundred feet above the desert floor. It was cool this night, too cool for his liking. He could make it warmer just by concentrating and casting an enchantment that would comfortably raise the temperature of the air around his massive body. But he knew the sun would bring the cherished heat with it in a few hours, and that would do. He had the patience to wait until then, and he pledged to devote at least part of the coming day to basking on the white sand and plotting.

He angled his sleek body toward his northernmost lair, soaring past a small ridge in which two men, an elf, and a kender slept. He didn't notice them, so intent was he on reaching the underground cave. Nor did they notice him, for he seemed to fade into the dark sky. Khellendros's belly was the lightest part of him, thick plates of iridescent azure ran from just under his jaw to the base of his tail. The rest of his body was covered with sapphire blue scales that were almost black in some places on his massive back. His dark wings were leathery and covered in small scales, and his claws were long and as white as the single, pale moon that hung low in the sky. Only Malys was larger than he; the Blue stretched nearly four hundred feet from nose to tail tip. Despite his immense size, Khellendros was incredibly graceful on the ground—fast and dexterous. But in the sky, his element, he was even more agile and could turn and bank in smooth, quick motions.

As he neared his home, he tilted his head and unleashed a bolt of lightning that shot up and buried itself into a cloud far overhead. The dragon closed his eyes for an instant, called to the cloud and merged his senses with its milky-gray tendrils. A moment later the cloud answered by caressing his body with soft rain. He released another bolt and another.

The flashing light revealed his magnificent visage. A spiny midnight-blue crest framed his huge head. His eyes, elegantly slanted orbs, were the color of lightning and had a hint of malevolence about them. Horns curved up and away from his jowls, twin spiky growths the shade of cream at the base and turning to steel blue at the tips. Khellendros was a most impressive dragon.

The rain came harder now, so he could better feel it against his thick hide. He rolled onto his back and let it run across his stomach plates. He rolled again and dove toward the sand, aiming for a large rocky ridge that sheltered an enormous cave. As he flew through the cave opening and down the tunnel, his claws never touched the ground. He tucked them in close to his body and the dark maw of the cavern swallowed him up.

"No!" the dragon bellowed, pulling up to a stop and hovering in the air. Khellendros narrowed his eyes to golden slits, and peered through the darkness to observe that part of his beloved underground lair had collapsed. There was barely enough room in the one chamber left standing for his massive form and the two wyverns who trembled nervously.

"Master home," the wyvern stated. "Master free us?"

The dragon's wings, flapped only a little in the now-cramped confines. But it was enough to stir up the sand on the floor, which stung the wyverns' eyes.

"Free please?" the smaller implored as it blinked furiously and jiggled its head to shake off the sand.

Khellendros growled, a rumble that reverberated in his belly and sounded like an earthquake. Lightning flickered around his jagged teeth, and his eyes grew wide. "Explain yourselves! Explain this!"

The wyverns looked at each other, and then the larger one gulped, trembled violently, and swiveled its neck so it could look straight into the enormous eyes of the Storm Over Krynn. "Spawn caught men," the creature began. "And elf. Made prisoners."

The smaller wyvern nodded furiously. "Spawns popped."

"After . . ." the larger wyvern searched its dim brain for a word, "magic. Elf made magic." It looked down at its trapped claws and once more struggled to free itself.

"Elf," the other wyvern agreed. "Elf made floor magic. Made walls fall."

"Bad elf," the larger one said. Then the creature described the prisoners in as much detail as its limited vocabulary allowed—the dark skinned mariner with a seemingly unending collection of daggers, the tan elf with paintings on her skin, the childlike kender who pelted the spawn with pearls, and the older man with brown-gray hair. The dragon paid particular attention to the description of the eldest in the group.

"Free now?" the smaller wyvern asked. "Free please?"

Khellendros growled louder. His huge nostrils quivered, taking in the foreign scents in his lair, and his eyes locked onto the bits of drying blood on the stone floor and along the walls. "Where are these prisoners now?"

"Escaped," the wyverns chorused.

The dragon swung his head around to bring it close to the wyverns. His growl died to a soft rumble, and he sat back on his haunches, his tail trailing behind him and flicking angrily. "And . . ."

The smaller wyvern swallowed. "Prisoners popped spawn. Guards. Only two popped."

"And ones below when cave fell," the other added, then glanced hopefully at the dragon. "Free please now?"

"When Fissure arrives." Khellendros stretched out in the cave as much as possible and closed his eyes. The wyverns' banter faded to plaintive whispers, then stopped. They were afraid to wake the dragon and incur his wrath.

But the dragon was not sleeping. Rather, he was thinking about his lost spawn, his lost hours of work, and of Palin Majere, whom he fully intended to find and slay. The sorcerer was the whelp of Caramon and Tika Majere, Kitiara's nemeses. Therefore the sorcerer was the dragon's enemy. And now, because of the sorcerer and his friends, Khellendros would have to rebuild his spawn army and reshape this lair. The dragon growled softly and let his thoughts drift to the storm outside, his mind playing with it. He ignored the nervous breathing of his ugly brown servants. The wind howled and thunder boomed—sounds he considered preferable to music. Lightning flashed down to kiss the sand. The storm continued to grow more intense, and then he thought of Kitiara.

* * * * *

Shortly before dawn a diminutive figure glided into Khellendros's cave. Not much more than a foot tall, his smooth skin was the color of the rocky walls, His eyes were black, pupilless circles that seemed too large for his pinched face and his ears were flush with the sides of his bald head. He wore no clothes and had long-fingered hands.

The little man shuffled forward, past the wyverns, who looked at him expectantly but kept their mouths shut. He silently approached the Storm Over Krynn, stopping a few feet away from the tip of the dragon's great blue snout. The large yellow eyes opened.

"Fissure," the dragon rumbled. "Palin Majere was here."

The little man looked beyond the dragon and noted the collapsed walls. "Did he discover your plans?"

Khellendros shook his head, the motion sending sand flying in all directions. Fissure's skin shimmered for an instant, and the sand passed through him. "No, faerie, he does not know. I never discussed my plans when the wyverns were present."

"Ah, to return to The Gray. . . ." the diminutive man sighed wistfully. He was a dark huldrefolk, one of the lost race of faeries who, prior to the gods departing from Krynn, could access the many dimensions that overlapped the world. The Gray was his home, a realm of swirling clouds and floating spirits, a place with no land—only mists. He had not been able to return there since the world's magic was suppressed. As was the case with the Blue, he had an innate magical aura about him. But it wasn't powerful enough to transport him beyond Krynn, even with the aid of one of the many portals scattered across the land.

Fissure had met Khellendros at one of those portals. The dragon was trying to use it to return to Kitiara's spirit in The Gray. Perfecting spawn was part of his plan to snatch her spirit and place it in a spawn shell. "To go home," Fissure mused aloud.

"To find Kitiara's spirit," Khellendros said. The dragon had sworn an oath to protect Kitiara uth Matar, the only human he knew who seemed to have the soul of a dragon and a mind as calculating and clever as his own. Decades ago, on a day when she was away from him, she died. Khellendros had felt her spirit drift beyond Krynn, and so far he had searched in vain for it. Vowing to find her spirit, to be reunited with his partner, he had scoured dimension after dimension.

Decades passed on Krynn, while time raced by beyond the portals. When Khellendros at last found her, in The Gray, he returned to Krynn to locate a body suitable to house her lost spirit. He returned as a massive dragon, one century old by Ansalon standards. With his greater size, came greater power. But he had lost the power to return to The Gray.

"How many artifacts shall it require, faerie?" Khellendros hissed.

Fissure stroked his chin. "The ancient magic is powerful. I would say six such pieces should contain enough energy to open a portal and to allow us access to The Gray."

"I have two," the dragon stated. "We must attain four more." Then Khellendros pointed a talon toward the wyverns. The creatures looked toward the dragon and the huldrefolk, then down at their feet. "Free them, then get them out of here. They are useless."

"I promised you other sentries, Portal Master. Smarter ones."

"See to it that you keep your promise, faerie."

The huldrefolk stood and approached the wyverns. Their heads and tails weaved back and forth, reminding him of a pair of excited puppies.

"Free please?" the smaller one pleaded. "Hungry. Thirsty."

Fissure stooped and touched the cave floor. A pale blue glow spread out from his fingertips and raced forward to surround the wyverns' clawed feet. Stone was Fissure's element. He mentally ordered it away from the creatures, and as the rock turned to putty and then parted, the wyverns flapped their wings maddeningly, carrying them above the floor. They were careful not to touch any part of the cave for fear they would be ensnared again, and they watched as Fissure resculpted the stone to look as though it had never been disturbed.

"Free," the larger said with a hint of glee to its deep voice.

"You are truly free," the huldrefolk said. He rose and pointed to the tunnel that led to the desert above. "You are free to return home."

"To forest?" the larger asked. "To cool forest? Shady forest?"

"Hot here," the smaller said. "Go cooler place? Dragon say so?"

Khellendros rumbled loudly. "Go!" he hissed. He watched the wyverns fly from his lair, colliding with each other as they competed to be the first to leave the cavern. "And you should be going as well, faerie. You have duties—help me to gain the ancient magic."

Like a mole, Fissure burrowed quickly through the stone, leaving a ridge behind him to mark his passage. Up and out of the tunnel he hurried. A moment later the stone ridge behind him shimmered and again went flat.

The Blue drummed a talon against the floor. He had places to go, too—away from this lair. Malys had contacted him earlier, requesting his presence. She wanted to know more about creating spawn, for she was gathering human specimens to begin the process herself. Khellendros was furious that she'd discovered his spawn so early in his game. But there was no turning back time and making her oblivious to his scaly children now. So he had agreed to show her how to do it. He had said the process was to be his gift to her.

I shall teach you, Malys, he thought. And then you shall show all of the other overlords—as is your plan—but I shall also show Gale, a lesser blue dragon you have not included in your schemes. There will be more blue spawn than any other color created by the other dragons.

Khellendros wrinkled his scaly brow. It had been some time since he had heard from the younger dragon, his lieutenant. Gale had attacked Majere's ship—as Khellendros had ordered—many days ago.

The dragon glided from his lair and out into the morning sun. He stretched out on the sand, and let its intense, blessed heat seep into his scales. Khellendros would bask here for a few hours, then he would visit Malys. Later, he would get around to contacting Gale. He didn't feel like bothering with the lesser dragon just now. The Blue deserved some time in the sun. Yes, later he would take the younger dragon to his desert stronghold, show him firsthand how spawn were created, let him enjoy the screams of the captive humans and realize just how much power dragons held in Ansalon.

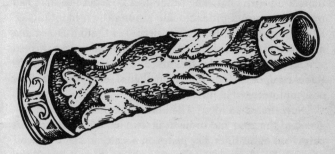

Chapter 6

Sand to Flesh

Fissure sat crosslegged on the desert sand, his gaze drifting to the lone barrel cactus he spotted. Stark green against all the trackless ivory, it looked like a blemish on the face of the Northern Wastes. He reached a slender gray finger up to scratch his bald head. "A giant walking cactus as a guard for the Storm's lair?" he mused aloud. "It could hurl needles and . . . no, that would be no better than the wyverns. What to bring the Blue?"

An hour passed and still the huldrefolk contemplated the matter. The sun was climbing above the horizon. Soon the temperature in Khellendros's desert would be intense and unrelenting.

The heat didn't bother Fissure. A faerie, and a master of the element of earth, he took the weather in stride, willing his body to allow the waves of warmth to pass through it like the wind blew through an open window. But he detested the light that came with heat. The huldrefolk coveted the shadows where they could hide and slip among the inhabitants of Krynn unnoticed. But being here—at this hour—was a necessity if he was to keep the Blue happy and cooperative.

A scorpion skittered across his path, pausing for an instant. It looked up at the odd little man, then skittered away, apparently uninterested in him.

"Now there's an idea." The huldrefolk thrust his thin fingers into the sand and brought up two handfuls. He held his palms out to his sides, like plates on a scale, and let a little bit of sand slip through the fingers of his right hand until the small piles seemed identical in weight.

"Life springs from the earth," he said matter-of-factly. "Let life spring from this sand." His large black eyes grew wide in concentration, and wrinkles formed across his otherwise featureless gray brow. He pictured the scorpion in his mind, and his senses focused on the sand. He felt the pleasing coarseness of the grains of sand agitating in his palms. He directed the magical energy that flowed through his veins to agitate the grains faster, then to meld them together into two liquid blobs. For each of the two shapes, he envisioned eight legs, lobsterlike claws, and a flat, narrow body the color of obsidian. Then he imagined for each a tail that curved up and over the body and ended in a needlelike stinger.

The vibrations stopped and Fissure glanced at his hands. A scorpion sat in each palm—each lifelike, though unmoving, and each roughly eight inches long. Smiling at his constructs, he gingerly placed them on the sand in front of him, a few yards apart, then scooted a safe distance away.

"You'll do. I think you'll do nicely," he said to himself. He pushed his palms against the desert floor and rocked back and forth. "Now, let's make you suitable for the Storm." His fingers glowed blue and the light raced to the tiny statues and engulfed them, surrounding them like halos. "That's it," he encouraged, "more now." The glow brightened and spread outward in a sphere shape, and the scorpions began to move slightly within their prisons of blue light. Their tails twitched, their lobsterlike pincers opened and closed, and their heads turned so they could better see their creator. Then the twin glowing spheres folded in on themselves, and the scorpions absorbed the arcane energy and began to grow.

Fissure watched with satisfaction as they doubled in size, then doubled again and kept growing. "A little larger," he commanded, and the scorpions seemed to comply. Their mandibles rose above his diminutive form, and they kept growing until he could see the underside of their glossy, segmented abdomens. "There. That should do it." He stood and scrutinized his creations. Each was four feet tall from the ground to its chitinous back, and each was a little more than twice that long. Their tails curved upward and writhed like snakes, and the huldrefolk smugly noted a trace of venom on each point.

"Almost perfect," he judged. "Now, unfortunately, for the finishing touch." He shuffled forward, stepping between the two. He tugged on his right hand until it came loose from his wrist, and then worked the hand like clay, forming a ball that he thrust into one of the creature's mouths. Fissure repeated the process with his left hand and the other scorpion, then looked down at his marred stumps. Already the hands were growing back. He could shape his body like a sculptor shaped clay, although now there would be a little less clay to work with next time.

"Can you understand me?" The huldrefolk stroked the underside of one of the scorpions.

The construct clacked its mandibles and its black eyes fixed on the huldrefolk. "I underssstand," it hissed.

"You are of my flesh," Fissure stated. "You share my memories, and I will share yours. You will know my thoughts when I desire it, and I will know yours."

"Your flesh," it repeated.

"Your flesh," the other echoed. "Your thoughtsss."

"You will do exactly as I say. And you will unerringly serve the Storm Over Krynn—for as long as I command it."

"We ssserve the Ssstorm," they hissed in unison.

The huldrefolk had used a similar process to create the wyvern sentries. They weren't very bright, but still he shared their memories. He knew exactly what happened when Palin and his associates came upon Khellendros's lair, knew that the secret of the Storm's desert stronghold had been unwittingly revealed. Fissure had elected not to pass that information onto the Blue.

He had given the wyverns little more than a thumb's worth of himself. His greater sacrifice had been to the scorpions; constructs that had a far greater intelligence and, he suspected, a greater malevolence. Creating them cost Fissure a little of his own magic, and some of his spirit. But such a sacrifice would be worth it if he could again access The Gray and once more feel the mists wrap around him.

"Search my memory, your memories," he ordered the scorpions. "Picture the lair of Khellendros."

"The Ssstorm," one of the scorpions hissed.

"Home," the other added. "We know thisss place."

"Go there," the huldrefolk said. "Go there and follow the Storm's bidding."

Chapter 7

Against the Stronghold

"Palin . . ." The voice, soft and harmonious, gently roused the sorcerer from a sound slumber. His legs and chest ached; his neck was still sore. However, his wounds were healing, and he had to admit that he felt much better than he had last night—even though he'd only managed to get a few hours of rest.

"Palin?" The same voice again, though not audible. At first he thought he'd dreamt a woman calling to him, his wife Usha. He remembered dreaming of her last night. But he was wide awake now, and the voice persisted. He blinked and stared at the face of the rock several feet away. The air swirled in front of it, and the grains of white sand the magical wind picked up twinkled like miniature stars in the early morning light.

Feril slept only inches away, curled up like a dog, Blister next to her. The mariner was deep in sleep, too, oblivious to the voice in Palin's head or to the magical breeze. Though they'd found a crevice in which to pass what was left of the night, and though it protected them from the brunt of the storm that sprang up from seemingly out of nowhere, it didn't entirely shelter them—or keep them dry. But being damp was better than being swelteringly hot, Palin thought. The heat would come soon enough.

"Palin . . ."

"Goldmoon," he whispered. The sands fell away to reveal the translucent image of a woman. Long blonde hair wreathed her slender shoulders, and the hem of her pale cloak swirled like a cloud at her feet. Her startling blue eyes bore into his. He was glad to see her, even if what he saw was only an image borne by her spell. It had been weeks since they'd last communicated.

"I was worried about you," the healer began. She was one of the original Heroes of the Lance, responsible for bringing clerical magic back to Krynn roughly six decades ago, and she remained a close friend to Palin's family. Though human and more than eighty years old, she wore her age remarkably well, and remained exceptionally vital. Goldmoon had managed to hang onto her faith through the years—despite the departure of the gods, and despite the death of her beloved husband, Riverwind. She'd taken many pupils to her side along the way. Among them was Jasper Fireforge, the dwarf who waited on *Flint's Anvil*. Palin greatly admired her and often sought her counsel on matters of the heart.

"I was thinking about the dragons last night," she said. "A vision came to me. I saw the Blue—Skie—and you were in his clutches."

Palin quickly related how he, Rig, Blister, and Feril had escaped from Khellendros's cave several hours ago, then spoke of spawn and how he believed they were being created. "We are heading toward one of Skie's strongholds now," he added. "We must try to free his prisoners, prevent more people from being transformed into spawn. Then we will try to topple an overlord, the White—"

"And Dhamon?"

Palin lowered his head. "I'm sorry. A lesser blue dragon. One that . . ."

Goldmoon's image faltered at the news, and Palin watched as she bowed her head and offered a silent prayer. "I thought he was the one," she said softly. "I believed Dhamon Grimwulf to be a leader of men. I contacted him at the Tomb of the Last Heroes, brought him into all of this, to you. He was to use the lance. . . ."

"Rig has the lance now," Palin said. "I have faith in him."

Goldmoon looked at the sleeping mariner. "He is brave," she admitted. "But he is also reckless and overconfident. Be careful, my friend. See that he doesn't lead you into a fight you cannot hope to win. We will speak later."

Goldmoon turned away from Palin and away from the topmost window in the Citadel of Light, severing her mystical connection with the sorcerer in the desert.

Hundreds of miles from the Northern Wastes, on the island of Schallsea, she now paced across the marble floor. "I was so certain he was the one," the healer said. "My visions, my divinations, they all pointed to Dhamon Grimwulf. I know so little of this Rig Mer-Krel. What's that you say?" She tilted her head to the side, as if listening to someone, though she was alone in the room. "Trust Palin? Of course I trust Palin, you know that. I have always trusted the Majeres. Yes, I agree, Palin is a good judge of character. And if he has faith in this sea barbarian, I should too. It's just that there is so much at stake—the fate of Krynn." Her shoulders slumped and she walked to a narrow, high-backed chair, easing her slight frame into it.

"It was all so much easier when you were here with me,"

she said. "Together we were . . ." Goldmoon closed her eyes and a lone tear edged over her cheek. "When we were together, I was complete."

* * * * *

"Morning already?" Feril yawned, stretched, and stood. She looked refreshed, her eyes clear and bright. "That was quite a storm last night. It woke me several times." She smiled at Palin and ran her fingers through her curly hair in an effort to comb it. She nudged Rig with her foot. "Let's get moving. Palin looks like he's impatient."

"He's been talking to himself," Blister said as she climbed to her feet and gazed up at the bright morning sky. "About the Blue."

The mariner grumbled and pushed himself up. The cuts on his chest still looked fresh. He grimaced when he moved, then allowed Feril to smear what was left of her healing poultice across his cuts. "The stronghold," he said, as his eyes met the Kagonesti's. She was quick to turn away. "It shouldn't be far from here—if the wyverns can be believed." He drained the last of his waterskins, then refilled them by dipping into the crevices where the night's rain had collected. "Let's see if we can make it before noon. I don't want to be traveling in the middle of the day again."

Palin silently agreed, falling in step with Blister behind the mariner and the elf. He fished about in his pocket for something to eat, retrieved a strip of dried beef, tore off a piece, and then offered the rest to the kender. Rig and Feril also ate as they walked.

By midmorning they'd passed by the cluster of cacti and the ridge of black rocks, and the Kagonesti's keen vision spotted part of a black, volcano-like structure between sand dunes located to the north. Even from a distance it looked ominous and unnatural.

"A tower of Khellendros's stronghold," Feril said with certainty. "Relgoth can't be far."

As they drew closer, more of the black sand castle could be viewed, along with the small city of which it was a part. The structure looked as if it had erupted from the earth itself, and its sprawling bulk was stretched across the ruins of almost half of the town.

Palin, Blister, Rig, and Feril settled themselves behind a dune near Relgoth that was tall enough to provide a view over the city wall. Peering over the top, they could see many buildings—most of them in ruins—and a small stone castle in the center of the town. A few people moved about the streets, but it was clear that Relgoth was not all it had once been.

The stronghold dominated the view, its black sand sparkling in the sunlight and smothering the buildings beneath it. The castle had three towers that rose to a height of thirty feet or more, with windows in the shape of dragon scales scattered along their lengths. The tops of the towers were linked by a formidable wall, across which several Knights of Takhisis were patrolling. The stronghold also appeared to be encircled by a deep moat.

"Wow!" Blister said. "I've never seen anything like it."

"Khellendros," Palin whispered. "The dragon must have used his magic to build this place. He must have found a way to harden the sand like stone. Impressive." He stared at the expansive courtyard of the castle, and at a diagram etched into the center of it. The sorcerer was too far away to make out the curious markings. "If only my eyes were better," he said.

"I can make it out." Feril followed his gaze with a frown. "It's like the symbol in the dragon's cave."

"So the dragon turns people into spawn here?" Blister asked.

"Convenient," Palin said. "That way the dragon doesn't have to transport unwilling prisoners, only obedient spawn."

In the northeast quarter of the courtyard, a military formation of a couple dozen Knights of Takhisis stood just beyond a drawbridge. They were taking orders from a black-cloaked man who paced back and forth in front of them. Nearby, a wide path led to the city gates and out into the desert. The path was guarded by knights and appeared to be the only way in or out of Relgoth.

"What are those beasts?" the Kagonesti poked her finger over the top of the dune, indicating four gray, hairless behemoths that were being led into the courtyard. "They're spectacular."

"Elephants," Rig whispered. "Definitely not native to around here. Haven't seen many in my travels, but I know you can find them around Kharolis, and in parts of Kern and Nordmaar. It took a lot of work to bring them here."

"We're a long way from those countries," she said. "I've never seen any animals like them. They're magnificent. Let's move closer."

"Wait a minute," Palin warned as he put a firm hand on her shoulder. "That stronghold's a little too much for us to tackle—even if we did go back to the ship and enlist the others to help. Look at all of those knights, and the brutes."

"Brutes?" Rig followed Palin's line of sight and perceived a quartet of tall, blue-skinned men walking behind the elephants. They were exceedingly muscular and wore little clothing—blue loincloths and primitive jewelry. The men were barefoot. "Knights and brutes. Black and blue men, like the wyverns said."

"That's blue paint," the sorcerer added. "They're warriors, also not from around here. Barbarians, some would call them, but they're not stupid. From everything I've heard, they're pretty formidable fighters. And the blue paint is supposed to protect or heal them in some way."

"I wonder where they're keeping the prisoners?" Feril mused. She was still watching the elephants. "Let's see if we can find out."

The Kagonesti closed her eyes and laid her head against the sand. Warm and coarse, it was pleasing to her, and she let her senses drift into the dune, focusing on one grain and then another. As she slipped further away from Palin, Rig, and Blister, she felt herself become part of the desert, so vast, yet comprised of so many tiny grains of sand. She reached out to the next grain and the next, rapidly moving from one to another until her senses stretched past the dunes, under the city wall, and beneath the assembled Knights of Takhisis.

"What do you hear?" she whispered to the sand, her voice sounding soft and breathy.

"We will leave at sunset, when it is cooler to travel," the Kagonesti heard the knight-commander say to his men. The words were as loud as if the man was standing in front of her. "We will head to Palanthas, take whatever prisoners are in the city's jails and return them here. Their minds are already tainted by evil, and it will not be difficult for the dragon to transform them into spawn. The Storm Over Krynn will be pleased, and we will be suitably rewarded. Your time is your own until sunset. Dismissed."

The knights gathered in small groups in the shade of the walls of the courtyard as Feril's thoughts wandered to the sand beneath the feet of the brutes tending the gray behemoths.

"Share the words with me," she continued. Two of the blue-painted warriors were conversing, their talk centering on the amazing amount of food and water the great animals consumed. But when their conversation drifted to the subject of the prisoners, the elf increased her concentration.

"Prisoners, more the knights want," the larger of the two fellows said. He was more than seven feet tall, with incredibly broad shoulders and a shaved head. His voice was clear and low-pitched, and his accent was unusual. "Prisoners, well more than a hundred now. Tower is almost full."

"Dragon, he wants an army," the other said. "Army, grisly way to gain one. Soldiers, willing ones perform better. Not starving ones."

"Dragon, he be done, they be willing enough," the first said. "Safe they be for a few days more. Me, don't want to watch it again."

"Me, never seen the men change."

"Terrible."

"Dragon, you question what he does?"

The taller one shook his head. "Me, no. Pay, it be good. Dragon, he be better to work for than to be hunted by. Me, just don't want to watch it."

"Fates, worse ones I would imagine. Other overlords, heard they capture people, keep them like cattle and eat them."

"Death, not worse than being turned into a spawn."

Feril shuddered and tugged her senses back to her body. She was quick to relay what she had overheard. The quartet watched the stronghold for the several hours, the sun baking them.

There were about sixty Knights of Takhisis, with half to two-thirds of them scheduled to leave soon—the sun was already edging toward the horizon. Palin suspected more knights would eventually take their place. The troops were probably being rotated. Fortunately, they hadn't noticed any Knights of the Thorn or Knights of the Skull, which meant the fortress was probably devoid of spellcasters.

"I agree we have to try something," Palin finally said. "Even though we're drastically outnumbered." The knights had gathered, and their commander was barking final orders, readying them to march. "But we can't just walk right in there. Even after most of the knights leave, there'll still be too many for us to handle in a fight. We'll be throwing our lives away."

"Maybe we *can* walk right in." The kender was looking over her shoulder, away from Relgoth and toward the south. "Or ride." At the edge of her vision was a small caravan, and it looked like it was headed in their direction.

* * * * *

The caravan consisted of ten large wagons pulled by horses and loaded with barrels of water and other supplies. Each wagon had a driver, and the caravan was accompanied by about two dozen barbarians dressed in flowing hooded robes.

It took one of Rig's thumb-sized rubies to bribe the last driver, who was lagging slightly behind. The mariner and the driver settled on a plan. Palin and Feril were to be the driver's cousins, and Blister their child. Rig was to be a friend of the family. And for a few pearls, the driver provided hooded robes for each of them to wear—even, after some cutting and fashioning, a child-size garment for Blister.

The driver called the stronghold the "Bastion of Darkness." He explained that supplies came to the castle nearly twice a week—food, clothes, paint for the brutes, whips and tethers to replace the ones that were used on prisoners, and, of primary importance, water from an oasis to the south. The prisoners, knights, and elephants consumed a lot of water.

Shortly after sunset, the caravan reached the city gates. Palin felt like he had a fever, his skin burned so, and he imagined the others felt the same. But with the onset of evening, it was cooling a little. A soft breeze washed over the dunes and stirred the air around the town. The Knights of Takhisis wing was just leaving, wending its way down the path and toward Palanthas. The men all wore black mail with death lilies on the breastplates. Foolish military protocol wouldn't allow them to wear lighter clothing.

"Put the barrels in the courtyard!" A knight waved to a tall, hulking barbarian, the caravan master. The wagons rolled through part of the town and into the castle's courtyard. A moment later, barrels were being carefully rolled down planks positioned at the ends of the wagons. They were rolled across the sand, over the drawbridge, and toward the center tower, which had an attached shelter to shade the barrels and help keep the water from becoming intolerably hot. Each wagon carried roughly a dozen large barrels, and it would take several trips to unload them all. On the return trips the men rolled empty barrels that were to be taken back to the oasis and refilled.

Blister darted around the wagon and tried to take everything in, while Feril, Palin, and Rig helped the nomads with the barrels. "The dragon should've built his sand castle closer to the well," the kender softly said. "Would've made things easier on the nomads."

On his second pass over the drawbridge, Palin glanced down into the deep ditch. Scorpions the size of his hand skittered at the bottom, thousands of them. The walls of the ditch were steeply slanted to provide shade. He whispered to Rig and Feril to watch their step. The ditch was more lethal than any moat filled with crocodiles.

The mariner hovered around the barrels in the courtyard, helping to stack the full ones against the wall, while Palin and Feril made another trip to the wagons. He rested his hand against the black sand structure, marvelling at its solidity. Looking closely, he could see the individual grains of sand that made up the wall. They magically clung together without any mortar or moisture of any sort. These were not compressed bricks of black sand. The wall, the entire castle, was made of millions of sand particles that were held together magically.

Meanwhile, Blister grew more anxious. "How are we going to sneak into the Bastion?" she whispered to Palin as he hefted another barrel. Her voice was muffled beneath the too-large hood of her robe. It hung far over her head. "I overheard the caravan master say we'd be leaving as soon as we're done. I thought they'd spend the night here."

"It's getting dark, and no doubt they prefer to travel at night," Palin observed, setting the barrel down on the ground.

"Or they can't stomach staying around here," Feril muttered.

"We'll find somewhere to hide. There." The sorcerer pointed toward a crude stable with four large stalls for the elephants. "That should do." The brutes were putting the elephants away for the night, and Feril brightened at the prospect of being near the exotic animals.

"You two," the caravan master barked as he pointed at Palin and the Kagonesti. "Leave your child be and stop loafing! Move more barrels!"

The pair was quick to comply. Palin relayed their plan to the mariner, and when there were only a dozen barrels left to be moved, the quartet slipped away, sticking to the growing shadows, and stealing into an elephant's stall. The straw that covered the floor was musty and insect-laden, and the animal's considerable dung was pungent and made their eyes water. The elephant took sharing its home in stride, and busied itself eating fresh grasses that one of the brutes had left for it.

"It stinks in here." Blister wrinkled her nose and tried to find a clean spot of hay to sit on. The kender instantly quit complaining when the elephant turned its head and seemed to study her. "Never seen anything like you before," she said. "Wonder if you'd fit on the *Anvil*? I'd feed you and—"

"No," Rig said, then turned his attention to Palin and Feril. "The central tower inside the walls is for the knights. The smaller towers at the corners are filled with weapons and food. Knights are constantly stationed here."

"How'd you learn all this?" the Kagonesti asked.

"I listen well," the mariner continued, his dark eyes flashing mischievously at her. "And I asked a few questions when a couple of knights strolled by for a drink of water."

Palin drew his lips into a thin line and shook his head. "I hope you didn't ask too many questions. We don't need anyone on alert." Then he heard the wagons moving, the cracks of whips against the camels, and he fervently hoped the knights hadn't counted the number of barbarians entering the stronghold and discovered the three missing adults and one "child."

"The medium-sized tower near us has only a couple of draconians in it." Rig seemed pleased with himself for collecting that piece of news. "The administrator of the stronghold, a Sivak draconian called Lord Sivaan, has his office there. Humans are held in the area of the castle near it."

Palin crept to the front of the stall and looked up at the black sand tower. "The draconians are needed for the transformation spell. A portion of their spirit is used to create spawn. We'll have to kill them to keep Khellendros from using them again."

"Fine, you do that. I want to go after the prisoners," Rig said.

"That's the plan," Palin replied. "We'll wait until close to midnight. Most of the knights and brutes should be sleeping then."

"I want to go after the prisoners now—before somebody decides to bring the elephants some water and discovers about half of their new barrels are broken and empty."

"What?" Palin asked, almost too loudly. He dropped his voice to a whisper again and edged farther back into the darkness of the stall. "What did you do?"

Rig grinned. "When I was helping stack the barrels, I used a dagger to make a few strategic holes. "The sand'll absorb a lot of the water, but I suspect there'll be a spreading wet spot that gets noticed sooner or later. I thought drastically cutting their water supply was a great idea. Strike them where it'll hurt the most."

Palin inhaled sharply. That would certainly hurt the

knights—and alert them that something was terribly wrong. They'd be scouring the place for saboteurs soon. "All right, let's move," he said. He turned to address the mariner. "You'll have to be careful—and quiet—going after the prisoners. It won't be easy."

"Sure it will." The kender stopped staring at the elephant long enough to reach into the folds of her robe and pull out a bulging leather bag. It had a cork stopper and made a sloshing sound as she passed it to Rig. "Paint," she said. "Got it off one of the wagons. Figured the . . . brutes, I think you called them, wouldn't miss this little bit. And if it does have magical protection properties, more's the better."

Several minutes later Rig walked toward the area of the castle that housed the prisoners. He had left most of his clothes in the stall with the elephant—along with all but three of his weapons. His cutlass remained strapped to his side, and he carried a dagger in his right hand. Feril had fashioned a loincloth for him out of part of her robe, and a second dagger was carefully thrust into the waistband. Blister had painted the loincloth to match the mariner's skin and short hair. He wasn't as tall as most of the brutes, but he was nearly as muscular, and the growing shadows helped his disguise.

The blue mariner confidently strode past a trio of patrolling knights, who gave him only a casual glance. Then he quietly slipped into the shadows of an archway. A moment after the knights walked by, Palin glided from the stall, clinging to the shadows and heading toward the medium-sized tower. He had two of the mariner's daggers with him, and retained the hooded cloak. If he was caught, he'd claim he was left behind when the caravan pulled away and was just looking for a place to sleep.

Feril and Blister watched the sorcerer disappear into the doorway. Then the Kagonesti crept forward and stood next to the elephant. She ran her fingers over the animal's coarse, wrinkled skin, reached up and scratched behind its massive ear. She was awed by the seemingly gentle creature. Next, she fashioned her lump of clay into an approximation of the elephant, and within minutes she and the elephant were involved in a meaningful conversation filled with "wuffles" and snorts, which Blister complained about not under-standing.

*　*　*　*　*

There were two brutes with pointed ears in a small chamber just inside one of the outside archways of the castle. They were sharpening their swords on pieces of stone and initially paid the mariner no heed. A shadowy corridor stretched beyond them, and Rig started to walk toward it. But the brutes sniffed the air, eyed the mariner a little more closely, and then decided that he wasn't one of them.

The largest, nearly seven feet tall, was the first on his feet, barking words at Rig in an unknown language. The mariner answered by throwing one of his daggers. It lodged in the brute's throat. The large man backed up against the wall, slid-ing down into a seated position. He pulled the dagger from his throat, and pressed his hands over the wound. His breath-ing was labored, but he did not die.

The wounded brute's companion rushed forward, swing-ing his blade and yelling.

Rig darted below the brute's swing and at the same time, thrust upward with his cutlass, intending to skewer the fellow. But the blue man was agile and deftly stepped aside. "Intruder," he sneered at Rig through clenched teeth. The brute was no longer speaking the mysterious tongue.

The brute lunged again, and the mariner barely missed being run through, pressing himself up against the sand wall just in time. As the brute stepped past him, Rig pushed off and drove his elbow into the man's side. But the force of the blow didn't faze the warrior, whose blue-painted skin seemed to function like armor. The mariner ducked to avoid another slash.

To buy himself several feet of maneuvering room, Rig started down the corridor, then turned to face his charging opponent. His left hand dropped to his loincloth and the dagger there. In one motion, he grabbed the weapon and flung it. The mariner's aim was good, and the blade sank into the brute's stomach up to the pommel.

He didn't topple. The healing properties of the paint sustained him and the muscular blue man looked down at the dagger, gripped the pommel, and tugged it free. Bright red blood poured from the mortal wound, but the brute was determined to keep on his feet until he could take the intruder down with him.

With a guttural growl, the brute darted forward, raising his sword high above his head. Rig crouched and raised his cutlass, ready to meet the blow. Then suddenly the brute was flying through the air, his sword clattering at Rig's feet. The brute had slipped on his own blood. The mariner jumped to the side to avoid the falling warrior, and drove his cutlass between the man's shoulder blades. The brute didn't get up.

Rig took a few deep breaths and glanced around. The other brute sat against the wall, his eyes open and unblinking. The effect of the paint had not been enough to overcome the mortal wound.

The clamor had been brief, and likely muted by the thick sand walls. No one had come to investigate—yet. He retrieved his two daggers, wiped them on the fallen brute's loincloth, and tugged his cutlass free. Then he hurried down the corridor in search of the prisoners.

* * * * *

Palin made his way up a curving staircase. With Rig's daggers he had dispatched the pair of unprepared guards at the bottom of the stairs. The sorcerer had briefly considered using a spell that would put them to sleep, but realized he needed to save his energy for future spells.

He thought the way was clear until he suddenly encountered another knight at the top of the stairs.

"You're not supposed to be here, nomad," the knight sneered. He stared into the recesses of Palin's hood. "You'd best leave and catch your caravan."

"It left a while ago," Palin said.

The knight reached over to remove Palin's hood and the sorcerer ducked below the man's grip.

"Intruder!" barked the knight, bringing his blade above his head and driving it down.

Palin lunged away, but not fast enough. The sword cut into his arm and he couldn't help but cry out.

"I haven't time for this!" Palin hissed between clenched teeth.

The man charged him. The sorcerer cast a summoning spell on himself and disappeared. The knight rushed through the empty space where Palin had once been and clattered down the stairs, ending up in a motionless heap near the bottom.

Palin took several deep breaths and glanced down at his arm. The left sleeve of his light brown robe was dark with blood. Ripping off the other sleeve, the sorcerer quickly wrapped it around his wound, then moved toward a door—the only one on this level. There was a small window set into it, through which he could see two Sivaks.

They were the largest of the draconians created by Takhisis, made from stolen silver dragon eggs and bred to follow the Dark Queen's evil directions. One of the Sivaks had an almost emaciated silvery-scaly body. His beady black eyes were downcast and his lizardlike snout pointed at the floor. His head hung in shame as the other Sivak, a larger, more robust creature seated behind a hulking wooden desk, berated him. Palin guessed that the larger Sivak was Lord Sivaan, the administrator of this entire gruesome facility. The skinny one was undoubtedly a minion of the officer.

Palin took a deep breath, and threw open the door. Lord Sivaan stood up from behind his desk, knocking his chair to the ground. Palin raised his unwounded arm and sent a jagged stream of flame into the Sivak's broad chest and out the other side. He turned to find the emaciated Sivak slinking toward the door. Palin paused for a second, pitying the creature, and the Sivak turned to hurl a dagger at the sorcerer. Palin released another burst. The hot light passed through the Sivak's chest in an instant. The dagger clattered to the floor, and the Sivak crumpled after it.

Palin, weak from the exertion and the wound on his arm, stumbled out of the room, closing the door behind him.

The corridor was empty. Palin stopped for a moment, steadying himself by leaning against the wall. He knew that a Sivak killed by a human assumed the appearance of his slayer—announcing the identity of the murderer to all those who found the body. The corpses inside the office would hold Palin's appearance for several days. There was no way around it, the effect being part of the enchantment Takhisis had breathed into them at their birth. The Dark Queen had wanted to know who killed her children.

Palin headed down the stairs quickly. His chest felt tight, his throat dry, and his wounded arm throbbed. The knight he had pushed down the steps was waiting for him at the foot of the stairs.

* * * * *

Rig moved down the corridor quiet and quick like a cat. A lone, guttering torch provided just enough light for him to see where he was going. The mariner's skin itched terribly from the blue paint, but he resisted the urge to scratch it off.

The air was hot and fetid and it carried the stench of sweat and urine. He turned a corner and saw a row of cell doors and another brute guard. This brute was massive, with tree trunk legs and thick, bulging arms. He was easily more than seven feet tall, and the sword at his side looked impossibly big and long.

The brute tilted his head and looked at Rig as the mariner's grip tightened on his dagger's pommel. He spoke a few words the mariner couldn't understand. The big brute's brow furrowed. The mariner shrugged and grinned, giving up on the charade and drawing out his dagger.

The brute charged forward in that instant, finally realizing Rig wasn't one of his kinsmen. The dagger flew from the mariner's fingers, and the blade sank into the big man's chest. Still the brute kept coming, and Rig pulled himself up against the corridor wall as the blue-skinned giant rushed past him.

Not even bothering to remove the dagger lodged in his chest, the brute turned and came back at Rig.

The two fought intensely, large blue blurs against the background of black sand walls. Rig eventually backed off a bit, deciding he was simply going to have to wear out the wounded brute. He dodged and ducked, thrust and withdrew, until the brute finally grew dizzy from the loss of blood and fell dead, face forward on the floor. Rig knelt and quickly found a ring of keys on the dead man.

Rig stepped toward the closest cell door, opened it, and shuddered as a nauseating stench wafted out. The cell had no sanitary considerations. Excrement lined one wall, and a half-dozen elves huddled in the rest of the space better suited for two or three. They were gaunt and expressionless, eyes staring unblinking from sunken sockets. Their clothes were filthy, stained with sweat and urine, and their skin was covered with grime. A couple of the elves who were pressed together on the sole cot in the room looked like corpses. Rig stared at them and finally noted the faint rising and falling of their chests.

He swallowed hard. "Let's get out of here." He motioned them out of the cell, but they held their position, continuing to stare blankly at him. "Look, I'm not here to haul you off and turn you into spawn." He rubbed at a spot on his arm until the blue paint came off and revealed dark skin beneath. Then he instantly realized that proved nothing—he had no idea what color the brutes were beneath their paint. "I'm here to rescue you. Palin Majere, Feril, and. . . ."

"Majere?" The faint male voice came from the direction of the cot. An elf with long, matted hair and a facial scar shakily stood up. "The sorcerer?"

"He's outside. We've got to hurry," Rig said. He motioned again, and this time the elves followed him, slowly shuffling out into the corridor. The mariner hurriedly unlatched the other doors.

One cell contained only women. Another contained more than twenty men who must have been fairly new arrivals because they appeared a little healthier and moved more quickly. One room contained a sole occupant—an elderly man madly clutching a small clay tablet to which he mumbled. Rig had to pick him up off the cot and carry him out into the corridor with the rest of the prisoners.

The mariner continued to free the captives, working rapidly and continually watching the hallway for fear that more brutes might come around the corner. "Leave us alone!" he heard from behind one cell door. He opened it and cringed when he saw a few women and more than a dozen girls and boys. The knights had kidnapped children, too. There were wooden bowls on the floor, filled with a pasty gruel that crawled with insects. It was the first sign the mariner had seen that the people were even being fed. The women stared at him defiantly and placed themselves in front of the youths.

"We'll not go willingly!" one spat at the mariner. She clenched her bony fist and waved it at him.

"It's all right," said the elf who had recognized the name Majere. "We're being freed."

The woman glared at the blue mariner skeptically, until the elf with matted hair reassured her and tugged her gently from the cell, the others following. Rig busied himself with freeing the rest of the prisoners.

Corpses were stacked like cordwood in the two cells farthest down the corridor. Rig guessed from the various states of decay that some had been dead less than a day, while others had been moldering here for weeks.

"Any more cells?" Rig asked the pathetic-looking throng.

The matted-haired man nodded back toward the way Rig had come. "I understand there are a few more cells upstairs. But they would be guarded, too."

The mariner drew his cutlass and edged past the group of prisoners.

* * * * *

Palin rushed down the last few steps and leapt at the knight. The air rushed from the man's lungs with a muffled "whoof," as the sorcerer knocked off his helmet, grabbed a fistful of dark brown hair, pulled the man's head back and flashed the dagger against his throat. He paused for an instant when he looked into the man's eyes. "Steel Brightblade?" the sorcerer whispered.

"The water!" the sorcerer heard someone outside yell.

The knight used the distraction to push Palin off him, but the young man's movements were clumsy and slow. Palin drove the dagger into the knight's chest, between a gap in the armor plates, and the man's mouth opened in a scream. The sorcerer thrust the blade in again, and the scream died as blood gurgled from the knight's mouth.

Palin, blood staining the front of his robes, struggled to his feet and out into the courtyard in time to see Rig leading out a throng of haggard-looking people. A brute trundled around the corner and pointed at the bloodied sorcerer.

"Trespassers!" the brute hollered.

"Our water's gone!" came another cry from somewhere in the inner courtyard.

"Look!" shouted one of the knights stationed at the top of the nearest tower. "The prisoners are escaping!" He drew a horn to his lips, and a shrill bleating sound filled the air.

"Palin!" Blister yelled. "Over here!" The kender was frantically waving her arms. At the edge of the stable, the sorcerer spied a trio of Knights of Takhisis, tied and gagged. Nearby, the Kagonesti was gesturing at four elephants. The beasts were charging toward a large group of knights and brutes who were racing toward them.

Almost in unison, three of the elephants raised their trunks and trumpeted, then their great feet pounded over the sand, following the Kagonesti's directions, and they charged at the onrushing knights. The fourth elephant thundered past them and headed around the corner of the fortress.

Palin shrugged off his bloodied robe. The tunic and leggings he was wearing beneath it were also stained. There'd been so much blood from the knights and the draconians that it had soaked through to his skin. He struggled for breath, and an incantation began to tumble from his cracked lips. Behind him he heard Rig shout to the prisoners. In front of him he heard the screams of the first knights to fall beneath the elephants' feet.

Chaos was erupting everywhere. The Kagonesti wrestled with a knight who had slipped past the elephants. The kender loaded her sling with elephant dung and pelted the knights. The largest elephant skewered a knight on one of its tusks and pitched the broken body to the side.

Rig motioned for the former prisoners to run, then left

them, dashing headlong into the fray. He slipped between two of the incensed elephants, his blade arcing down and drawing blood with practically every swing.

From somewhere in the inner courtyard, where the fourth elephant had gone, there were more screams and barked orders. "To the walls!" the sorcerer barely heard someone say. "Get the bows!"

Palin continued to mouth the words of his spell, and the energy in his hand surged outward, a catapulting magical force.

He stared at the castle of sand, at the black walls, the towers, and the ornate crenelated tops. Then he uttered the last syllable of his summoning spell, urging some of the castle's foundation to disappear.

At the same instant, a barrage of arrows filled the air. Arrows pelted the elephants, but only served to madden them. One found its mark, lodging in Palin's right shoulder. A second and a third struck his left thigh. The sorcerer groaned in pain, and dropped to his knees. Another arrow struck in the sand perilously close to him, and another. The pain was intense, but the sorcerer shoved it to the back of his mind. He couldn't let it overwhelm him, lest his concentration on spellcasting break. The magic was harder now, but not out of his reach. He bit down on his bottom lip and fixed his gaze on the castle's sandy base.

"Palin!" he heard Feril cry. She was running toward him. He heard her feet pounding across the sand, then felt the sand, the ground deep beneath him, vibrate. Then came the piercing pain of another arrow lodging in his upper arm. The sensations—the trumpeting of the elephants, the pain he felt, the warmth of his sunburnt skin, and the wet, sticky heat of the blood from his wounds—started to overlap one another.

"What's happening?" Palin heard a knight cry. "The Bastion! Run!" Other words were shouted, but the sorcerer could no longer make them out. He felt himself slipping toward a welcoming blackness.

Then he felt Feril tugging at him, helping him up. His legs were lead weights and didn't want to move, let alone support him, but she persisted. Was this what my brothers felt, what my cousin Steel felt? Palin wondered. Did they feel agony like this before they died?

Feril worked her way under his left arm, propped him up and started dragging him forward. The vibrations in the ground were increasing, and Palin tilted his head toward the stronghold. The walls were collapsing, and the towers were folding in upon themselves. Black sand exploded in all directions. Knights who were perched on the walls and towers pitched forward into the ditch, and those who survived the fall suffered further horror.

"The scorpions," Palin whispered.

A loud thud cut through the din and the ground shook. One of the elephants had fallen, slain by the knights. The other two elephants continued to trample the knights and the brutes creating a sea of limbs and blood.

Blister hurried to Palin and Feril, and then the trio saw Rig. He was covered in blood—his own and that of the knights he'd been fighting. The mariner was racing toward the path that led through the city gates and to the desert. The freed prisoners were already straggling down that path as his cries urged them to move faster. A few of the prisoners were being carried by their fellows, a couple of them were being dragged.

Feril and Blister guided Palin in that direction, too. The knights they passed were too busy to try to stop them. The knights were intent on staying alive, avoiding the elephants' feet and tusks, and staring wide-eyed at the thousands of scorpions pouring out of the ditch.

The scorpions swarmed over knights who had lost their footing, scrabbling over their plate armor and stinging their victims' hands, necks and faces. The knights screamed and writhed on the ground, trying to brush the creatures off. But for each one flung away, three more skittered up to take its place. Scorpions swarmed up the legs of the brutes, who tried frantically to brush them off. Distracted, the brutes couldn't defend themselves from the elephants' tusks or get out of the way of their massive feet. Many of the brutes were trampled as the elephants plodded past them on their way to join the Kagonesti.

"So much death," Palin whispered. His thoughts drifted back to the Chaos War where bodies of Knights of Takhisis, Knights of Solamnia, and dragons littered the floor of the Abyss.

"We'll be next," the kender said. "If we don't get moving."

Feril and Blister nudged the sorcerer forward. The two were practically carrying him. "We've got to stop, tend to your wounds," the Kagonesti was saying. "You'll bleed to death."

Palin shook his head. "Not that bad," he insisted. "Keep moving. Blister's right. We've got to get away from here—the scorpions." The elf protested, but they had reached the escaped prisoners who were poised on the lip of the depression and the murmurs of the many excited voices drew her attention.

Rig was talking to the gaunt elf with long, matted blond hair and ragged clothes who had urged the prisoners to trust the blue-skinned mariner. When Rig noticed Palin, Blister, and Feril, he rushed toward them.

"I've got him," Rig said. The Kagonesti and kender let Rig take over propping up the sorcerer.

"Palin Majere?" the prisoner said, meeting the sorcerer's clouding gaze. His voice was weak, but tinged with awe. "I've heard of you. I know your parents. You're the most powerful sorcerer on Krynn."

"I don't feel so powerful," Palin answered. "And you're . . ."

"Gilthanas." The man brushed a clump of hair behind a

dirty, but gracefully-pointed ear. "I was second to the throne of Qualinesti. You saved us. All of us." He swept his hand out to indicate the more than one hundred men, women and children. "We owe you more than our lives. We were destined to be . . ."

"Spawn," Rig finished.

"Not the elves," Gilthanas said. "It seems they don't want elves for their process. I was taken when I tried to keep the knights from capturing humans outside Palanthas. I was slated to be executed in front of the Blue for my insolence."

"Did you say Gilthanas?" asked Palin, blinking and looking around, as disoriented as if he'd just woken up. He turned to face the elf and almost lost his balance. "My father told me stories of the legendary Gilthanas. Where have you been? Your sister has long sought your return. We've got to get out of here before the dragon comes back."

The mariner nodded. "We've got a lot of sand to cover." Palin nodded and grew dizzy. Rig rushed forward and almost effortlessly picked up Palin. "Feril, do you think you can talk those elephants into accepting a few passengers?"

"I hope the dragon doesn't figure out who is responsible for all that carnage," Palin heard Gilthanas say. "Dragons are a vengeful lot."

"Skie will know," Palin whispered. The sorcerer pictured the dead Sivaks who now bore the face and form of their slayer. Then Palin gave into the pain and fatigue and slipped into peaceful unconsciousness.

Chapter 8

Magical Minds

"How are we gonna feed 'em?" Blister anxiously looked up at Rig, leaned against the rear mast, and yawned. She was not used to getting up at dawn, and she dabbed at the sleep in her eyes with the padded fingertips of her gloves.

No one had made her get up, especially after she had stayed awake half the night helping the freed prisoners on board— refugees, Rig was calling them. It was just too hard to sleep with all of these people milling about. There were too many chances that she might miss something, might miss out on some especially interesting conversation. "They're all so hungry. I can hear their stomachs growling from here. Wake up, Rig Mer-Krel! I'm down here! How are we ever gonna feed 'em?"

The mariner glanced down at her, and shrugged his broad shoulders. The kender made a soft huffing sound, crossed her arms petulantly, and returned to ogling the many people gathered on the forward section of *Flint's Anvil.*

Some were sleeping near the mainmast, others were too giddy with freedom to do anything other than stand at the railing, take in their watery surroundings, and chatter about the future. There were nearly as many below deck—the more malnourished and injured of the lot. Jasper had been tending to them. The ship was seriously overcrowded.

Blister had counted them seven times. It took her that many attempts to get the same number twice—one hundred and eighteen. Nearly all of them were human. Gilthanas was one of six elves.

"Where are we gonna get enough food?" the kender persisted.

"And you wanted to bring one of the elephants on board? Then you really would have had something to worry about." The mariner studied her. It was clear she wasn't going to drop the subject. "A couple of the men are in the galley fixing breakfast. Can't you smell it?" Rig took a deep breath, held it, and smiled at the scent of eggs and spiced pork lingering in the sea air. He was hungry too.

"What about after that?" the kender said, sniffing the air.

"We took on supplies before we left Palanthas—dried meat, plenty of grain for bread, and bins full of potatoes and carrots."

"All of which will last three days—if we're lucky. I already figured it out. The water should last six or seven—maybe." The kender pursed her small lips. "Saving all these people was wonderful, and I'm glad I got to help. But what are we gonna do with all of 'em?"

Rig shrugged again. The mariner knew the escaped prisoners couldn't be dropped off in Palanthas, the closest sizeable city. The Knights of Takhisis controlled the place—Khellendros's knights. Hiding them in the cargo hold while they took on more supplies in the city wouldn't work—the knights were inspecting practically every ship that pulled into the Palanthas docks.

"Gander, maybe," he said after a long silence. It was three and a half weeks away, perhaps a couple of days less if the winds were favorable. The kender was right, they'd have to take on food and water at some point, but any place before Gander was too close to the dragon as far as Rig was concerned. "Witdel, Portsmith, maybe Gwyntarr farther to the south," he added. "Maybe we'll drop a couple dozen off in each place to avoid too much attention. Those cities are all in Coastlund, and Skie doesn't make too much trouble there."

"So there wouldn't be as many knights around?"

"Right. Should be safer."

Blister shook her head. "I don't think any place is really safe anymore, but I definitely vote for Gwyntarr. It's the farthest from here. Besides, I've never been there, and I'd like to see it. Wonder how it got its name?"

The kender was determined to see as much of Krynn as possible during her lifetime. Itchy feet, she called it—the inability to stay in any one spot for too long. Her passion for traveling was the reason she had left Kendermore a few decades ago, and it had compelled her to join forces with Dhamon several long months ago. The prospect of travel made her continue to keep company with the mariner and Palin Majere. If she could fight a few dragons along the way, all the better.

"So what will they do?" she continued. "Provided that we can find enough food to keep 'em all alive?"

"I don't know. Start a new life in one of those towns. Stay out of trouble. Stay away from any Knights of Takhisis they might see."

The kender scowled and shook her head. "That's not what I mean. These people have no money, only the clothes on their backs—which aren't even very nice clothes. Look at that fella—he's got no shirt and his pants are ripped. And that one—the tunic has more holes than thread! How are they gonna start from nothing in a strange town? Who'd hire these beggars?"

Rig caught several of the former prisoners staring at him, smiling. It made him happy to think he had helped save them, had deadened some of the pain he was still experiencing over Shaon's loss.

"They might have to steal to get some money or food. And if they get caught they could end up dead or in prison." The kender was continuing to contemplate the freed prisoners' fate in a soft enough voice that they couldn't hear her, but loud enough that Rig couldn't ignore her. "And if they end up in prison, maybe more Knights of Takhisis will come along and kidnap them. Or maybe they'll starve. Maybe . . ."

The mariner looked down at the concerned kender and gave a hard tug on her braid. "Give it a rest, Blister," he said. "We'll give them a stake, some coins, help them start a new life."

"How? Palin isn't *that* rich. He's already paid for the repairs on the ship, bought us supplies. Paid for—"

"I'll take care of it."

"*You'll* take care of it?"

"Don't ask," he replied firmly. "I don't want to talk about it." He headed toward the wheel to relieve Groller. The money from the dragon's jewelry was going to be earmarked for supplies for the ship, and it would have lasted a good long while. There were pearls, rubies, emeralds—enough to buy a bigger ship and supplies for it if he wanted. Now Rig made the decision to divide most of it between the refugees, and he'd keep just enough to supply the *Anvil* for a couple of months.

Groller joined Jasper below decks. The dwarf was in the cargo hold, checking this bandage, feeling that bump, offering a reassuring word, and in general doing his best to make everyone feel better. Some of the refugees were helping the dwarf. The elf, Gilthanas, was passing around mugs of water. Several in the hold didn't need much tending. They were simply keeping their friends company or fighting off minor cases of seasickness.

Fury was busy sniffing everyone and lingering here and there to get his ears and belly scratched. The wolf eventually settled himself next to a young man who seemed to know just where to rub his neck.

The half-ogre waved to get the dwarf's attention. Groller pointed to his head with one hand, his stomach with another, and made a sad-looking face. Next, he brought his hands close together in front of his chest, then moved them about three feet apart.

"Sick." Jasper translated the first gesture. "Much." The dwarf grimaced, then his face brightened. "How much? How badly are they injured? Are they very sick?" The dwarf waved his arms around to indicate all of his patients, then he brought a thumb to his breastbone and waggled the fingers of that hand—the gesture for fine, all right, and a couple of other things. Groller got the gist of what the dwarf was trying to say.

"Allufem be all right," the half-ogre said. "Jaz-pear good healer. Jaz-pear suhmart. And tard."

The dwarf nodded. He hadn't slept since the refugees came onto the ship, and using his mystic magic to heal the worst wounds took a lot of energy. Initially he had spent most of his time ministering to Palin—and praying to the departed gods that the sorcerer would pull through. He motioned to Groller that he had to go check on Palin now.

* * * * *

Palin lay in his bunk, a damp cloth covering his eyes and forehead. His badly sunburned skin stood out against the white of the sheets. Feril sat near him, seemingly studying a spot on the floor. She looked up when Jasper and Groller entered, and drew a finger to her lips, signaling them to be quiet.

"He's finally sleeping," she whispered.

"No, I'm not." Palin tugged the cloth loose and opened his eyes. He tried to sit up, but quickly stopped himself. He winced and looked down at his chest, which was partially covered with a thick bandage. It effectively hid the claw marks from the spawn and the arrow wound in his shoulder.

"You're going to be hurting for the next few days," Jasper said. "You were badly injured. I did the best I could, but—"

"I owe you my life," Palin said.

"Well, you probably would've made it anyway. You're more stubborn than just about anyone I know." The dwarf stroked his short beard and shuffled over to examine Palin's bandages. He poked and prodded at the sorcerer's shoulder, ignoring Palin's painful expression. "Hmm. Still bleeding. Was worse than I thought. Must fix that."

Jasper had dug out two arrow heads the night before. It was a procedure that the sorcerer thought more painful than getting wounded in the first place. Then the dwarf had cast a couple of curative spells, which had gone a long way toward making certain that Palin would live.

The dwarf closed his eyes in concentration. He put his hand on Palin's shoulder and shut out the creaking of the ship's timbers and the sound of the waves beyond the porthole. He shut out everything until all he could hear was the beating of his own heart.

"Your heart gives you life," Goldmoon had lectured him. "But your heart also gives you strength and power." He remembered her words, heard her voice softly repeat them over and over in his mind. "The magic to heal is inside you," she had told him, "inside your heart." It had taken him a few years to discover that she was right.

A soft orange glow radiated from the dwarf's fingers, left his hand, and hovered above the wound for a moment. Palin's skin took on a warm sheen, and his chest rose and fell more quickly. Then the healing aura disappeared as quickly as it had come, Palin's breathing slowed, and the dwarf let out a deep breath, surveying his handiwork. He tossed aside the bandage. The spell had made the bleeding stop, and only a raw red patch of skin remained to remind the sorcerer of the arrow. "You'll scar," Jasper said.

"It's not where anyone would notice," the sorcerer said. "Thank you."

"And you'll be weak. You lost a lot of blood. Can't do anything about your sunburn. Yours either, Feril. Or Blister's. You all should've dressed better—going off into the desert like that. Your skin will be peeling for days. Can't do nothing about the boils on your feet either."

"Thank you," Palin said again.

"You're welcome."

Groller tilted his head to the side and laid it in his open hand, then he pointed to Palin.

Jasper nodded. "Yes, he needs rest. But first he needs to talk to one of the refugees, that old man with the tablet. The man keeps mentioning the Blue, Khellendros, and says he must speak to you. Frankly, the man babbles. I think he's a touch mad. But if you'll give him a few minutes, maybe he'll leave the rest of us alone."

Feril looked at Palin. "He tried to talk to you on the way from the stronghold."

"I don't recall much of the trip back," Palin admitted. With her help, the sorcerer sat up in his bunk and slowly swung his legs over the side. "All right, let's go see this gentleman."

"You're not going anywhere—Jasper's orders," the dwarf said. "We'll bring the old man to you."

Several minutes later, Gilthanas escorted the old man to Palin's quarters. The man was grizzled and bent, wearing tattered but clean clothes. He clutched a small clay tablet protectively.

"This is Raalumar Sageth," Gilthanas announced. The elf stepped back and let the old man shuffle closer to Palin.

"Call me Sageth," he said in a soft, cracking voice. "That's what my friends called me. But my friends are all dead now. Hamular, Genry, Alicia, all gone—old, dead, buried." His rheumy blue eyes carefully consulted the tablet he held, and he muttered to himself for several moments about age and wrinkles. "Southern Ergoth. You're going there, I heard the sailors say. Cold place." He cackled and wheezed. "Cold now in any event. Right place to go, wrong reason."

Palin cocked his head. Jasper sidled over and sat next to the sorcerer on the bunk. "Told you he babbles," he whispered to Palin. "Maybe this could have waited." Jasper turned to the old man and said, "What's wrong about our reason for going there?"

"Let's see, let's see." Sageth consulted his tablet and chortled. "Ah, here it is. Alicia could have told you quicker. Did I tell you she's dead?"

The dwarf and Palin nodded.

"Let's see. You mean to fight the White there. Right?"

Feril stepped up behind him, and noted that his tablet was filled with a myriad of symbols and scratchings she couldn't hope to fathom.

"Somebody needs to fight the dragon, any dragon," Jasper said. "If we don't stand up to the overlords soon, there'll be no spot on Krynn left free."

Sageth glanced at the tablet again. "I miss Alicia, poor Genry the most. Better use for your energies than fighting. Hamular could have told you that, too. The White has an ally now. You see, some of the overlords are joining forces, the White of Southern Ergoth with the Red near Kendermore."

"Malystryx," Palin said.

"Yes, the Red Marauder. It was inevitable." The old man wheezed and grabbed his side. "The Red seeks to establish a formidable power base. And something dreadful will happen if she is successful."

"So killing the White will help erode that power base," the dwarf said.

The old man closed his eyes. When next he spoke, his voice was clearer, as if he were putting all of his energy into talking. "Listen to me. Use your energies better. Forget about the White. Worry about magic first, the dragons second. The Blue, Khellendros, the so-called Storm Over Krynn, searches for the ancient magic—magic from the Age of Dreams."

Palin grew instantly interested. "What do you know of that magic?"

"Ancient, more powerful than all of the arcane items enchanted since." The old man opened his eyes, looked down at his tablet, then peered intently at Palin. "More magic pulses through those artifacts than does in the veins of the dragons. The Storm Over Krynn wants the magic, and because I know he wants it, the knights imprisoned me."

Feril walked over to face Sageth. "Imprisoned you? Why didn't they just kill you if they thought you were such a threat?"

"I'm no threat," the old man cackled. "My bones are old and brittle. Only what I know is a threat. But I think the knights would have killed me eventually—if you hadn't come along. I'd be seeing Alicia and Genry. Hamular, well, I don't know if I'd want to see him. See them soon enough anyway. I'm old."

"Just how do you know what Khellendros wants?" Feril persisted. "How did you learn the dragon seeks the ancient magic? Why should we trust you? Believe you? Why should we even bother listening to you?"

He sadly shook his head. "Ah, Alicia and Genry were more believable than me. They had a way with words and could make people understand. No one has listened to me yet, only the knights, and when they heard my dire warnings, they put me away in the desert."

He made a soft clucking sound and shook his head at Feril. "Dear elf, I was a scholar at the library in Palanthas. The contents of the building were stolen by a mysterious force more than thirty years ago, on the very day the Tower of High Sorcery collapsed. Alicia died in the attack; Genry and Hamular died years later of who knows what. The dragon wanted something there—in the library and in the tower, and I began to research just what that might be. I figured something important to a dragon, something that cost the lives of my friends, might also prove important to men."

Feril's expression softened. "So this ancient magic, what does the Blue intend to do with it?"

"He wants to keep the magic out of the hands of men because he believes destroying ancient artifacts would raise the level of magic permeating Krynn. And with that magic, men can maybe stand up to the dragons again."

"What?" Jasper blurted. "When the gods left after the Chaos War, they took magic with them. Most healers and sorcerers can cast only simple enchantments now. It would seem that truly powerful magic is beyond everyone."

"Powerful sorcerers can cast harder spells," Palin said.

The old man nodded and grinned. "There is so much power in the artifacts from the Age of Dreams that if several of those artifacts were destroyed at the same time, the energy released would permeate Krynn, would raise the level of magic to what it was before the gods left. The gods created those artifacts, after all."

"Goldmoon has such an artifact," Palin said.

"One will not be enough," the old man cautioned. "You will need at least three, four to be certain according to my research. And you will need to gather them soon. Time is crucial. With each passing day Khellendros moves closer to gaining the ancient magic."

"There are so few artifacts remaining from that age," Palin said.

"Precisely," Sageth continued. "That is why you must beat the dragon to them. There is little time, and I doubt the dragon knows exactly where to look. This is a race against time, and you must win it if Krynn is to—"

"If you've researched what the dragon wants, then you must have some idea where we can find the artifacts," Feril interrupted.

Again the old man consulted his tablet. "Some such remnants from the Age of Dreams are more powerful than others. These, I believe, are what the Storm Over Krynn will seek. According to my studies, and mind you some of this is cryptic, one can be found about the slender neck of an old woman who lives at the base of an ancient, glistening staircase."

"Goldmoon's medallion of faith," Palin whispered.

"Another is a ring, once worn by the sorcerer men called Dalamar. It sits about another's finger now, hidden and polished and in a building that calls no land home."

Palin's mind whirled. The building—the Tower of Wayreth? Did one of his associates possess Dalamar's ring?

"Another is a jeweled scepter that rests in an old fortress in the heart of a murky forest, a realm where elves once walked peacefully. The scepter is called the Fist of E'li, and it was once wielded by Silvanos himself. It lies within a realm that is overgrown, corrupted by the Green Peril."

"The Qualinesti forest, Beryllinthranox's realm," Palin

said. "I have scryed the dragon before, and I am familiar with the land; I know of the fortress."

"The fourth is a crown that lies far away beneath the waves. Elves once held sway in this land, too. Now they are prisoners, trinkets on a watery shelf."

"He's talking about Dimernesti, the sunken land of the sea elves," Feril said.

"The last I am aware of is a weapon, perhaps the most powerful weapon ever crafted. It was intended all along to fight dragons. Find it in a grave as white as the land that surrounds it, a resting place sealed with ice and legend."

"Huma's lance." Gilthanas had remained silent to this point. The elf stepped forward. "I know exactly where the tomb lies—in Southern Ergoth. I was to meet someone there years ago. I was . . . unable to make the journey. We should go after the lance first. It is the closest. I can lead you there." He directed the last statement at Palin. "Helping you is the least I can do. You saved my life and the lives of all the other prisoners."

The old man studied Palin and Gilthanas. "I had not thought there were any on Krynn who would believe me, let alone have the courage to attempt this. But perhaps I was wrong. Perhaps fate led me to be imprisoned so I could be rescued by you. If you can attain these artifacts, I will help you destroy them and return magic to the world."

The sorcerer made a move to rise from the bed, but the dwarf put a strong hand on his shoulder.

"You must get some rest first," Jasper said, waggling a stubby finger at Palin. Feril and Gilthanas helped the sorcerer lie down again. "Now, Feril, Gilthanas, Sageth, the three of us have some planning to do. Southern Ergoth, eh? I'll bet it's pretty cold there."

* * * * *

It was dark when Palin awoke. He was feeling much better, practically as good as new, he tried to tell himself. But he felt weak, felt older than his fifty-four years. He slowly dressed and took a few steps toward the porthole. Krynn's single moon hung low in the sky, sending a dazzling display of pale white light dancing across the choppy water. Palin realized he had slept the day away.

The *Anvil* creaked softly. Palin heard the faint snap of the sails. The ship was heading west. When it was beyond Palanthas's harbor, which would be in a few more days, it would round the tip of Tanith and start toward Southern Ergoth and Huma's Tomb.

"But will the old man's plan work?" Palin mused aloud. "I would like to be certain, to know that this isn't some goose chase, a waste of precious time. Perhaps my associates will know." He stared at the moon and pictured a tower sitting atop the water in its place. "The Tower of Wayreth," he whispered.

Palin was a master at transporting himself from place to place. Though magic was no longer easy, this spell—particularly when he traveled to and from the tower—came easier than all the others. Perhaps it was the tower's own residual magic that powered the enchantment. The ancient structure moved about at the behest of its occupants, calling no single place home.

" . . . *in a building that calls no land home,*" Palin recalled Sageth saying. "Has one of my fellow wizards been hiding something from me?"

Palin focused his thoughts, and the moon appeared to shimmer and turn as insubstantial as fog. In an instant an image of the Tower of Wayreth sat on the horizon in its place. The moon was not truly gone, nor was the tower truly there, but visualizing the building at the edge of his sight helped him to cast the spell. Dark, mysterious and illuminated only by the faint starlight from overhead, the tower beckoned.

The sorcerer steadied himself, closed his eyes, and felt the gently rolling deck of the ship turn to solid stone beneath his feet.

"Palin!"

"Usha?"

She was in his arms in a heartbeat, hugging him fiercely and causing his mending wounds to flare up with pain. But the sorcerer didn't mind. He returned her embrace and buried his face in her hair, inhaling her lilac perfume. After several long moments, she edged away from him, a slight frown on her unblemished face.

"Where have you been? Look at your face!" She ran her smooth fingers over the short beard he'd grown. He hadn't shaved since he'd left the *Anvil* to journey through the desert.

"I think it makes me look more distinguished."

"Liar," she tsk-tsked at him. "You're not a young man anymore, Palin Majere, but you've been running around Ansalon like one. And you're so sunburnt."

He smiled and stared wistfully at her, glad that his clothes covered his bandages so she wouldn't fuss over him. Usha Majere was only a few years younger than Palin, though she could pass for a woman nearly twenty years younger than that. Her silvery-white hair fell in soft curls about her shoulders, framing her face and her golden eyes.

Palin thought she still looked very much like the girl he had met more than thirty years ago. His love for her grew stronger with each passing day.

"What are you doing here?" he asked. He raised his hand, and cupped her chin. Her skin was soft and smooth and unblemished by the years. "It's not that I'm not glad to see you. I certainly am. But why aren't you in Solace?"

"I was worried about you," she said. "I hadn't heard from you in a while. And neither had they." She pointed to the cloaked men moving up behind her. "The Master brought me here, said he knew you'd be coming for a visit soon. I'm just happy he was right."

The Master of the Tower nodded to Majere. "You have news for us?" His voice barely rose above a whisper and was muffled by the folds of the hood of his black robe. The dark-cloaked man was the caretaker of the Tower of High Sorcery, hence his title. Despite all the time they'd spent together, Palin scarcely knew him. The Master kept his past a secret, dressed in somber robes that hid his features, and rarely talked about anything save magic and the dragons.

Near him stood the Shadow Sorcerer, an even greater enigma. Dressed in voluminous gray robes that effectively masked individual features, the sorcerer could have been a man or a woman. It was impossible to tell. The voice was too indistinct to provide a clue, and though the Shadow Sorcerer had spent much time over the years with Palin and the Master, there was never a revealing slip about his—or her—past.

Palin had given up trying to figure either sorcerer out. His Uncle Raistlin had been a bit eccentric; many sorcerers seemed to wrap themselves in secrets and puzzles. He knew only that they were able colleagues interested in combating the menace of the overlords. He trusted them and welcomed their counsel.

"We looked in on you," the Master began, gesturing toward a crystal ball on the shelf. "We saw you in the Blue's lair. You were most fortunate that he was not at home."

Palin smiled, and nodded his head. "It wasn't exactly the lair we were looking for, but the trip was valuable nonetheless. We learned how spawn are created." He continued to regale the sorcerers and Usha with the tale of his escapades in the Northern Wastes while the quartet climbed the stairs to the tower's topmost level.

* * * * *

A rectangular ebonwood table stretched nearly the length of the room. Maps detailing where dragons had claimed territory hung on all four walls. Palin sat at the head of the table and steepled his fingers. The climb had taken more effort than he had expected, and he didn't want his wife to realize that he was winded. Usha, who rarely joined the sorcerers' sessions, sat next to him, looking intently into his eyes.

"Khellendros is becoming an increasing threat," Palin said finally.

The Shadow Sorcerer brushed by the Majeres and stood in front of one of the room's windows. "All of the dragons are becoming an increasing threat, Majere. An army of blue spawn? If Khellendros has discovered the secret for making dragonspawn, the other dragons will learn it soon—if they don't know already. We'll be facing *armies* of spawn. But spawn are the least of our worries. Some dragons are gathering human slaves. Now you say Khellendros wants to gather ancient artifacts—magic from the Age of Dreams? If he seeks them, other dragons will, too."

"That ancient magic," the Master cut in. "It is more powerful than any could comprehend. Palin, I believe Sageth could be correct—destroying it might unleash enough energy to increase Krynn's magic."

"But something bothers you about the idea," Palin prompted. "I can tell by the tone of your voice."

"What troubles me is that the Shadow Sorcerer and I had not considered such a venue before. It took a half-mad old scholar from a prison cell to open our minds. Enhancing magic, if it could be done, sorcerers could command more powerful spells, and with them, the dragons could be challenged."

"That settles it, then," Palin said. "My companions and I will search for the artifacts. While we do so, I want you to research the matter. I want to be absolutely certain we'd be taking the right path by destroying the items once we found them."

The Master nodded. "Research takes time, and it doesn't always lead to the conclusion one expects."

"Time isn't something we have a lot of," Palin said. "But regardless of whether we decide to destroy the items, we need to find them before Khellendros." He inhaled deeply, looked into the recesses of the Master's shadowy hood, and then turned to glance at the Shadow Sorcerer. "I recently learned that a piece of the ancient magic sits within this tower. It is a ring."

"Dalamar's ring," the Master answered, his singularly soft voice even more difficult to hear than usual.

"*You* have it?"

The Master extended his right hand beyond the folds of his long sleeve. A thick band of braided gold encircled his middle finger. The entire piece gleamed with an eldritch light, and Palin felt the waves of its dark energy from several feet away.

The Shadow Sorcerer pushed himself back from the table. "And just what other secrets do you have?"

"Perhaps as many as you." The Master withdrew his hand back into his sleeve.

"How did you come into possession of such a ring?" asked the Shadow Sorcerer.

"Dalamar studied in the Tower of High Sorcery in Palanthas. It was one of the items he left behind, and I rescued it before the tower was destroyed many years ago."

"And Dalamar was a Wizard of the Black Robes, just as Raistlin was. And Raistlin would have known just where Dalamar left the precious ring."

"I have no qualms, Shadow Sorcerer, about surrendering this ring to Palin," the Master said. "It is a very powerful artifact. But first I would prefer to conduct the research he requires. I would prefer to know that my sacrifice of the ring will not be wasted. I'll review Raistlin's notes. Certainly they discuss the ancient magic. Raistlin knew how."

"Raistlin," the Shadow Sorcerer hissed. "Not even *he* could have hoped to stand against these dragons."

"You don't know that," the Master argued. "He was powerful. His books and tomes are filled with——"

"Words and suppositions about the arcane," the Shadow Sorcerer finished. "But do what you will. Maybe you will find something of use amid his musty ruminations."

The Master glanced at Palin. "Sageth spoke of needing four artifacts. When you've gained three, return to me. Then you can have Dalamar's ring—the fourth."

"Such a noble sacrifice," the Shadow Sorcerer whispered. "But then it's no greater sacrifice than any loving uncle would make."

Palin cleared his throat. "I'll return to the *Anvil*. We've people on board to find homes for. We'll be stopping in some of the coastal cities on our way to Southern Ergoth."

"Fine," the Shadow Sorcerer said. "You'll go sailing. The Master will delve into Raistlin's books; one of us studying the ancient magic is sufficient. I will busy myself with a more crucial task—looking in on the great Red to the west. I think she is far more of a threat than your Storm Over Krynn and more important than your artifact chase."

The Shadow Sorcerer returned to the window, looking out at the stars and at the surrounding orchard. "Tomorrow I will scry the Peak of Malys."

"I will leave in the morning," Palin said.

"So soon?" the Master asked.

"I didn't tell my friends I was coming here, and if they find me missing on the ship, they're liable to think I fell overboard."

"This time I'm going with you." Usha's voice was firm and invited no argument.

"So am I." The speaker stood in the doorway. His eyes

were golden, like his mother's, and his hair chestnut brown, just like his father's was many years ago. "It's past time I involved myself in all of this."

Palin smiled and nodded a greeting to his son. Yet the sorcerer was taken aback to see Ulin—he expected his son to be in Solace with his wife and children. "Very well, I welcome your help. I'll take us back to *Flint's Anvil* shortly after dawn—after we've thoroughly stocked up on food."

Chapter 9

Seeds of Atonement

"We found no survivors, Lord Khellendros." The Knight of Takhisis removed his helmet and knelt respectfully before the great Blue Dragon. His four fellows stood at attention behind him, their heads bowed.

Khellendros sat at the cave entrance to his northernmost lair and silently scrutinized his nervous pawns.

"The stronghold was in ruins, the brutes and knights all dead. Some had been trampled by elephants, others slain by weapons or poisoned by scorpions. All of the prisoners were gone." He looked up at the dragon. "It couldn't have happened more than a few days ago, judging by the condition of the bodies. We tried to track the ones responsible, but the wind had erased all signs of their footprints."

"The Sivaks?" Khellendros asked.

The knight shook his head. "Dead, too, my Lord."

The dragon snarled, the sound causing the desert floor to tremble beneath his massive body. The knight felt the tremors, but showed no fear. There was no point—Khellendros would either slay him and his fellows or not. Being frightened would not change the situation.

"The Sivaks," the knight added, "they provided the only clue. In their office we found two chained men—identical. They looked like Palin Majere, son of Caramon and—"

"I know who Palin Majere is," Khellendros said. His growl deepened, and his belly rumbled. Overhead, clouds started to gather, mirroring the dragon's dark mood. The wind picked up.

"We can assemble a unit and search for him," the knight continued. "We will contact our brothers and our spies along the coast. He is called the most formidable sorcerer on Krynn, so he is widely recognized. Sooner or later, someone will spot him, and alert us."

"*I* shall find Palin Majere, and *I* shall slay him." Khellendros raised his head and closed his huge yellow eyes. The clouds grew heavy with rain and lightning flashed. "The son of Caramon and Tika Majere—Kitiara's enemies—shall be mine alone to deal with. Do you understand?" The wind began to whistle, stirring the sand about the kneeling knight and finding its way into every crevice of his black mail armor.

"I understand, Lord Khellendros."

"I have a mission for you," the Storm began. "Take one of your dragon-prowed ships and sail to Southern Ergoth."

The knight looked quizzically at him. "The White Dragon is there. Southern Ergoth is his territory."

"And if you wish to live and serve me, you would be wise to avoid him," Khellendros continued. "There is a place called Foghaven Vale. Somewhere between a ridiculously large carving of a silver dragon and a ruined keep, there sits a simple building made of black glass. You must search for it somewhere amid all of the fog of the valley and all of the snow and ice Gellidus has created. Inside this black box is something I want. You shall retrieve it for me." The dragon went on to describe the item in great detail.

The knight nodded and rose. Fine sand stuck to the sweat on his face, but he didn't brush it off. He replaced his helmet and stepped back to form a line with his brethren.

"You shall need to take someone with you," Khellendros added. "Who you select is unimportant, just so he is moral and upright, of sterling character—a human idealist. What I want you to retrieve might burn your skin, perhaps be impossible for you to touch, but it should pose no threat to a pious man. There shall be other trinkets to gather, but first I must discover where those trinkets lie."

"We shall begin with this one, Lord Khellendros. We will not fail you," the knight spokesman stated.

Khellendros was pleased with himself. He was clever, indeed. Now he had both Fissure and the knights searching for the ancient artifacts. "See that you don't fail. Success shall help your order atone for your brothers' negligence at the stronghold."

* * * * *

"I've seen enough." Mirielle Abrena stepped back from a crystal bowl filled with water, on the surface of which were images of the knights and Khellendros. She nodded to the sorcerer who hovered nearby.

"Very good, Governor-General." He twirled a gnarled finger in the water, chasing away the picture.

Mirielle paced the length of the room, a richly appointed library filled with furniture made of dark wood. Her boot heels clicked harshly against the polished floor. She selected a high-backed chair and sat, steepling her fingers in front of her. "Tell me, Herel, if we were to acquire some of this ancient magic that Khellendros is looking for could you use it? To our benefit?"

The sorcerer pulled back his hood, revealing the craggy visage of a man in his late middle years. A scar, similar to the thorny vine embroidered on the front of his robe, ran down the left side of his face. "My dear Governor-General, I am most accomplished. Yes, I could use them, would thank our departed Takhisis for such an opportunity, and, most certainly, I could use them to advance our aims. But what will Khellendros do if he discovers his knights are trying to gain the items for themselves?"

Mirielle smiled slyly. "He won't catch on. The knights assigned to the Blue Dragon will do exactly as commanded. If they get to this magic first, so be it. But if my handpicked men discover some other examples of this ancient magic . . ." She let the possibility hang, and her eyes bore into the sorcerer's. "Khellendros is sending his knights to Huma's Tomb. We'll not bother with that quest, for it's a race we cannot win. You will endeavor to find out where more of this ancient magic lies, and we will direct our efforts there."

"But Governor-General, some of the old magic has been buried, hidden. Who knows where—"

"Not impossible for one so accomplished," she returned. "Not for someone who wants to please the governor-general of the Knights of Takhisis, and who will use any means necessary to serve her wishes."

The sorcerer visibly paled. "I will attend to the matter right away, Governor-General."

"See that you do," she replied evenly. "I believe time is—"

A sharp rap at the door cut off Mirielle's words. The sorcerer hurried to the door and placed his hand on the dark wood. "Lord Knight Breen awaits beyond, Governor-General."

"Show him in—and not a word of this to him, *to anyone*."

The sorcerer slipped out and hurried away as the big man entered. Gleaming black plate covered his large chest, and a black cloak, the shoulders of which were festooned with medals and bars, hung in thick folds behind him. His steely eyes fixed on Mirielle as he bowed slightly.

"Governor-General, our forces have taken four more ogre villages. We suffered considerable losses during our last advance. The village was large, and they were ready for us. Still, I believe Sanction will be ours before the year is out."

Mirielle nodded. "Anything else?"

"You asked for a report on our recruits, Governor-General. Youths from cities in Neraka and Teyr are flocking to the Order, and we are recruiting good numbers from Solamnia and Abanasinia. Our measures of persuasion are yielding a good harvest this year. Would that Takhisis were here to note our progress."

"We are stronger than ever before." Mirielle rose and glided toward Breen. "Select a dozen of your best men from the city and send them to me. I have an errand of considerable importance."

Lord Knight Breen cast her a brief, curious look, and opened his mouth to question this mission.

"Dismissed," Mirielle said.

Chapter 10

The Shadow Dragon

The dragon was huge, black and featureless, as if it were a silhouette cut from a piece of velvet and hung in the early evening sky. It hovered several yards above the twisted body of a green dragon, studying it. Then, like a child growing bored with a plaything, it banked away until it was but a tiny spot on the horizon. Then the spot vanished altogether from view.

"What do you make of it?" The voice was the Master's. He stared at the dead green dragon, at the blood that formed a spreading, dark pool about the body, and at the olive-colored scales that were scattered like fallen leaves over the ground.

The Shadow Sorcerer stirred the water in the large bowl in

front of him. Instantly the dragon's corpse and the scene that had played out on the water's surface disappeared. "In the Dragon Purge, the dragons killed each other and absorbed their essences, grew more powerful. This dragon is most likely doing the same."

"The dragon is black, but it is not a black dragon," the Master commented. "It did not breathe acid upon the young green. Its breath was like a suffocating shadow, a cloud of darkness we couldn't see through. I believe it to be a shadow dragon."

His colleague nodded. "They are rare on Krynn, but not unheard of. I first sighted it several weeks ago. I watched it kill a young red. I have noticed other dragon corpses—a white and two blacks, and I am wondering if this shadow dragon is responsible."

"Perhaps, though we will likely never know for certain," the Master replied. "It has no scales, no talons. It claims no land like the dragon overlords. I would deign to study it longer, as it has captured my curiosity, but I must continue my research on these ancient artifacts—and quickly. I agree with Palin that time is urgent. Perhaps I erred by taking even these few moments to spy on this creature."

"I would like to study this dragon as well, but I must devote my energies to Malystryx. The Red amasses a larger army of goblins each day. However, this shadow dragon seems not to threaten people, and so study of it can be postponed."

"But not indefinitely."

"No."

"Then let us agree that when our respective investigations are done, we will give this shadow dragon our attention." The Master moved away from the bowl and over to a bookshelf that covered an entire wall in the room in which they now stood, a chamber high in the Tower of Wayreth. The shelves stretched from floor to ceiling and were filled with thick tomes and yellowed scrolls. "These are Raistlin's notes and journals. I have been looking through copies of them, trying to gain information about magic from the Age of Dreams."

"Raistlin again," the Shadow Sorcerer whispered. From beneath the mage's hood, smoldering eyes took in the Master's every move. "You know your way through the sorcerer's writings very well."

The Master stopped before a section of black leather-bound books, turned his back on the Shadow Sorcerer and gazed up at the tomes. "I have read his words often." He reached up and tugged at a thick volume in the center of a high shelf. It resisted his first few attempts, but finally fell into his hands. "Yes, this is the book."

"You know certain passages by heart. I have heard you recite them."

"Some of his works greatly interest me." The Master held the book in front of him and ran his fingers over the cover, tracing the gold-inlaid letters. He opened it to the middle and studied a passage, his index finger out tracing the lines of text and his lips moving silently as he read the words.

"Yes, I am certain of it."

"Certain of what?" The Master closed the tome, and turned to face the Shadow Sorcerer.

"You are Raistlin."

The Master softly laughed. "I knew Raistlin Majere, knew him very well—perhaps better than even his own brother knew him. But I also knew a number of Krynn's greatest sorcerers. Justarius of the Red Robes, Dalamar, Par-Salian, Rieve, Gadar, Ladonna, and more. Raistlin was perhaps the greatest. You flatter me by your accusations."

"Do you deny it?"

"If I was Raistlin, what would I be doing in this tower with you and Palin Majere? Raistlin is gone. And for one thing, he always preferred solitude."

"There is solitude here. And Raistlin Majere would be interested enough in his nephew to—"

"Do I look like Raistlin? I am not so frail as he."

The Shadow Sorcerer took a step closer. "You cleverly mask your appearance."

"As you mask yours." The Master turned back to the shelf and replaced the tome. He selected the one next to it and tugged it down.

Beneath his metallic mask, the Shadow Sorcerer smiled. "I take my leave of you to study the Red Terror—as the kender are calling Malystryx. Alert me if you find something of significance in Raistlin's notes." The Shadow Sorcerer glided from the room, quietly adding, "*Your* notes, I think, my colleague. You did not deny my charge."

The Master opened the volume to the last section, searched for a well-remembered heading, and began reading.

Chapter 11

Trouble on the Docks

The blue dragon plummeted, taking Dhamon Grimwulf down in its deadly descent. Blood and scales fell, and Dhamon's sword tumbled quietly like a silver needle, small and insignificant. Dhamon looked like a discarded doll. The storm howled all about, hammering savagely against the plunging bodies and against Feril, who stared helplessly at the grim scene. The dragon and Dhamon struck the lake, sending a great shower of water up into the air. The two disappeared below the surface. There were ripples and bubbles at first, signs of life and hope. The Kagonesti's heart beat wildly in sync with the thunder. "Dhamon!" she cried. But then the bubbles disappeared, and the storm stopped, and she woke up sweating.

The same dream again—night after night. The only time she couldn't remember having the nightmare was when she was in the desert with Palin and Rig. There'd been so much to do and think about then that when sleep came, it had been from sheer exhaustion.

The Kagonesti lay in her bunk, listening to the waves lap against the hull, the gentle scraping sound the ship was making against the dock, and the gulls crying in the distance. She heard feet slapping against the deck above, someone in a hurry to go some place. She glanced out the porthole. The sky was rosy, but filled with low, gray clouds. It was nearly dawn. She heard more feet scurrying above.

They'd pulled into the Witdel port late last night. It was a deep harbor, so they could moor the *Anvil* at the docks. Rig had decided they would off-load the last of the refugees in the morning. But he hadn't said it would be this early.

Then she heard other sounds, her keen elven senses coming into play and focusing on the pounding of feet. On the docks, people were running. A scream pierced the air, and Feril bolted out of bed and grabbed her tunic and boots. She sniffed. Something was burning. It wasn't clouds she saw through the porthole. It was smoke.

* * * * *

A crash sounded behind Rig Mer-Krel as the rear mast toppled and rocked the ship. The sails were on fire, and as the mast struck the deck, flames streaked away in all directions.

The mariner dashed amidships, darting around the fires and drawing his cutlass high above his head. He brought the blade down hard, sinking it into the collarbone of an advancing Knight of Takhisis. Rig heard the mail split, the crunch of bone, and the gurgled cry of his opponent, who was already falling to the deck. The knight's sword clattered from his hand, and the mariner scrambled to pick it up.

Rig leapt forward to meet his next adversary and ducked just as a blade sliced through the air above his head. He thrust forward with his borrowed long sword, sinking it deep into the stomach of another knight. Rig twisted the blade as he tugged it free, and the knight pitched forward.

The mariner paused only a heartbeat to survey his grim handiwork, then he bounded over the body and met the rush of two more knights. Smoke billowed all around him as the fire spread across more sections of the deck. His eyes watered and he coughed to clear his lungs. Cutlass in one hand and long sword in the other, he waved the blades to keep the two knights at bay until he could find an opening. They crouched side by side, their swords in front of them, weaving to keep away from Rig.

Behind the pair, a black-robed man who was partially concealed by the smoke moved his fingers in front of his wrinkled face and mumbled unintelligible words. The mariner scowled and coughed again. The robed man wore the Knights of Takhisis emblem on his chest, but in place of the death lily was a crown dotted with thorns. "Stinking sorcerer," Rig whispered.

The mariner doubled over coughing, and the two knights moved in. Rig suddenly straightened up and impaled the knight on his right with the long sword. The man on his left dodged to the side, barely avoiding the mariner's cutlass. Rig yanked the long sword free and rushed toward the sorcerer.

"Barbarian," the sorcerer spat as daggers of dark red light flew from his long nails and struck the mariner in the chest. Red hot as coals, the magical shards melted into his skin, and the heat quickly spread to his stomach and shoulders, then raced down his arms. Rig's fingers twitched, and he had to concentrate to keep his hands locked about the pommels.

"Stinking sorcerer," the mariner repeated as his momentum carried him a few steps farther. He drove his cutlass into the belly of the black-robed man, who was in the midst of casting another spell. A look of surprise flashed across the man's face. Rig followed with the long sword, making contact with the man's leg. The sorcerer fell, and Rig tugged the cutlass loose, spun, and fell to a crouch when he spotted three more knights charging in his direction.

Several yards away, amidst the rolling dark gray clouds of smoke, Groller was grappling with the knight-officer. The half-ogre gripped the knight's upper arms and squeezed hard. The knight was yelling something, but the man's words could not distract the fierce half-ogre who slid his fingers up to the man's shoulders and toward his neck. At the same time, the knight leveled blow after blow against Groller's stomach. The man's lips continued to move, his face reddened and contorted, and bits of spittle flew from his mouth.

Pain exploded in the half-ogre's side as the knight-officer's mailed fist landed hard against a rib. Groller raised his leg and slammed his foot down on the knight's foot. Then the half-ogre pressed his attack by dropping to his knees and using his weight to pull the knight deeper into the growing smoke and heat. Coughs racked the knight-officer's body, and the half-ogre's meaty fingers found the man's neck again. The knight tried desperately to pry Groller's thick fingers loose. But the half-ogre held on, keeping the man from drawing any more of the hot, smoky air into his lungs. The knight-officer struggled feebly for a moment more, then fell limp. The half-ogre pushed himself up and rushed toward the rail, gasping for fresh air.

* * * * *

Feril nearly collided with Usha and Palin as they met at the top of the *Anvil's* steps and looked across to the deck of the Knights of Takhisis's moored schooner. Its hull was charcoal black. Smoke billowed from several places on the deck, and flames licked up the mainmast and the forward mast.

"Palin!" Feril cried.

"In the name of Paladine!" Palin breathed. The sorcerer wrapped his bed sheet tighter around him, took in the carnage, and began uttering the words to a spell.

Usha, dressed in a sleeping gown and robe, hurried to his side. "Ulin?" she whispered. "What in the gods' names is Ulin doing?"

Ulin Majere stood in the center of the knight's dragon-prowed ship, directing the fire. His hair was slick with sweat against the sides of his face, and his tunic and leggings were ashen and smeared with soot. He made a gesture, and a smoldering section of deck erupted into a bonfire, engulfing a quartet of knights. They thrashed about in the flames and rushed toward the rail, their tabards streaming fire as they plunged over the side. Their heavy mail quickly carried them below the surface.

A howl pierced the air as Fury leapt over the ship's railing and onto the burning schooner. Feril scrambled down the *Anvil's* plank and boarded the knights' schooner where she found her way blocked by Groller. His clothes were smudged and tattered, and blood ran from several cuts on his arms. He gestured toward her as if shooing away a fly. "Furl, go 'way! Ship burns. Farr everywhere!"

She vehemently shook her head. "Behind you!" Feril shouted. "I've got to help Rig."

The desperate look on the Kagonesti's face made his eyes follow the direction of her outstretched finger. A burly knight, his tabard on fire, was charging for the half-ogre, his sword high above his head. Groller spun to face him and tugged the belaying pin from his belt. As he crouched to meet the attack, a red-haired blur streaked past him.

Fury's front paws landed against the knight's chest, toppling him. The wolf's teeth closed on the man's wrist, forcing him to drop the sword. Groller took advantage of the situation and slammed his belaying pin against the side of the man's head.

On the deck of *Flint's Anvil*, Usha rested a gentle hand on her husband's shoulder. "Palin, can you . . . oh, you're doing something." Usha watched as her husband finished his spell and the energy he'd been summoning was channeled through him, whipping up both the air and the water around them.

The sorcerer stared at the mounting waves that had begun to toss both the *Anvil* and the dragon-prowed ship. He gestured with his hand, singling out a particular wave. Elsewhere the harbor was practically as smooth as glass. With a flick of his wrist and a few words, the sorcerer summoned the water from the wave and deposited it on the deck of the Knights of Takhisis's ship. A second wave from the harbor followed it, and a third, each called upon by the sorcerer. The water doused some of the flames and succeeded in washing several knights over the railing.

"Let me help," Gilthanas said. He, Sageth (still clutching his tablet), and the remaining refugees who had been asleep in the hold were now gathered behind the Majeres. Gilthanas tucked his blond locks behind his pointed ears and spread his fingers across the rail. He took several deep breaths, then closed his eyes and concentrated on the air blowing gently all around him. "Faster," he coaxed.

"Ohmygoodness!" Blister sputtered. The kender squeezed between the refugees, poking and prodding with her elbows until she was next to Usha. "I thought the cook was burning breakfast! Hey, what's Rig doing over there? And Groller? There's Feril! And . . . Ulin!" The kender pushed the rest of her questions aside as she thrust her gloved hand into one of the many pouches at her waist and found her sling. She pulled it free and immediately set her aching fingers to finding stones and marbles. Within moments, she was pelting the Knights of Takhisis who were fighting the mariner.

"Faster!" called the elf, his voice rising as the wind whipped about him. A gust caught another wave Palin was summoning and the water rose higher and crashed across the deck.

"Again!" the elf shouted, and another wave was augmented by his enchantment.

Her bare feet slipping on the wet deck, Feril dashed toward Rig. Not only did the mariner have three knights to contend with, but a fourth was headed his way. The Kagonesti barely managed to keep her balance as she darted toward the fourth knight, shoving her shoulder into his side and knocking him down.

When the next wave struck the ship, Rig reached back and grabbed the rail to keep from being knocked over as two of the three knights he'd been fighting were washed over the side. Rig dropped prone as the remaining knight rushed forward, madly swinging. The blade passed harmlessly over the mariner's head, and he rolled to the side to avoid another series of hurried thrusts. Rig retaliated by slashing upward with all of his remaining strength. The cutlass cleaved the knight's wrist, sending his hand and his sword flying to the deck. The knight screamed and grabbed at his stump, and the mariner kicked the wounded man, sending him to the deck.

Rig paused to take a deep breath and glance around the deck, catching Feril's gaze and smiling. Beyond her, an aging knight—a knight-officer by the look of his insignia—was rushing toward them. Rig sheathed his cutlass, and reached into the **V** neck of his tunic to retrieve two daggers. The knight saw Rig's intent and turned, running instead toward the far rail, the water washing across the deck threatening his balance.

"Honor is for fools," Rig muttered as he loosed the first dagger. It caught the man between the shoulder blades. He paused, and threw his second dagger at a knight who was closing on Ulin. The blade pierced the man's throat, and he fell dead at the young sorcerer's feet.

Feril stepped back and held on as one of Palin's waves, coaxed by a magical gust of wind, crashed over the starboard side and drenched her. There were few flames visible now, and most of the smoke had cleared. The Kagonesti took stock of the rest of her friends as the mariner slid beside her and put an arm around her shoulder, hugging her gently.

"A brisk morning exercise," he said. "Nothing like it to keep your sword arm in shape."

They spotted Fury and Groller, and Feril eased away from Rig and moved toward the pair. The wolf was trying futilely to shake the wetness from his coat. The half-ogre was driving his fist into the face of the last knight still standing. The knight refused to fall, until the half-ogre jammed his fist against the man's sternum. The blow cracked the bone and the man collapsed.

Rig looked across to *Flint's Anvil*, saw Palin, and grinned. "Interrupt your sleep?" Rig called, pointing at Palin's attire.

Palin felt the red of embarrassment rise to his face. "I'm going to get dressed," he told Usha. "Then we can talk about what happened here." The sorcerer headed below deck, just as Jasper Fireforge was climbing up.

The dwarf yawned. "What's all the noise? It's impossible to get any rest on a ship."

* * * * *

By the time Palin had dressed and returned to the deck, he found Jasper tending to the wounded. Rig was sitting against the *Anvil's* mainmast as Jasper applied a padded bandage that wrapped around the mariner's waist. Groller surveyed the dwarf's handiwork and then held still as Jasper poked and examined the half-ogre's ribs. "You should wear armor," Jasper grumbled, well aware the half-ogre couldn't hear him.

"Seems Rig started it," Blister announced to Palin.

"Started it?" the mariner blurted. "They started it. I just helped finish it."

Palin glared at the dark-skinned man. "What happened?"

"I was up early. Me and Groller were watching the knights. Seems their ship pulled in sometime after we did last night. Your son joined us, said he couldn't sleep. So we talked a bit. I wasn't that interested in the schooner until I saw a few knights leading all those people from town toward the dock. Nice and early in the morning, when the rest of the town was still sleeping."

"And?" Palin prompted.

"And I asked them what they were doing." Rig stopped to gently adjust his bandage. "They wouldn't say, but I figured they were capturing more people so the Blue could make spawn out of them."

"So you attacked the knights?"

"Not exactly." It was clear the mariner didn't like Palin's questioning. He rose, brushed by the sorcerer, and strode down the plank to the docks where Feril, Gilthanas, Usha, and Ulin were already talking to the former prisoners.

"Then *what* exactly?"

Rig didn't answer. Palin sighed, then followed the mariner onto the crowded dock.

"Rig didn't start the fight," Ulin said as his father approached. "I did."

"*You?*"

"Rig asked them to release the prisoners, and the knights threatened to add us to the lot instead. So I threatened to destroy their ship. They didn't believe I could. Fools."

Palin sighed.

"Remember the simple fire spell you taught me a few years ago? Well, I've been working on it, and I tested an improved version on their sails."

"Of course, the knights were none too happy about it," Rig added with a chuckle. "And when they started drawing their swords, I thought I'd oblige them." He patted the pommel of his cutlass. "I only worked up a sweat on a couple of them."

"Couldn't you have woke us before things got out of hand?" Feril asked. "I could've helped. Maybe all those knights wouldn't have had to die."

"Well, things got out of hand a little too quickly for us to call anyone," Ulin said. He grinned at his father.

"You were lucky," Palin told his son. "The fire could have spread to *Flint's Anvil*. One of you could have been killed if—"

"But it didn't," Ulin cut in. "And we weren't. And we managed to save a lot of people who were destined to become dragon food or spawn."

"Let's see to the last of our refugees and be on our way. We're in a hurry and we haven't any more time to waste on—"

"You're Palin Majere, the famous sorcerer!" A young man with an unruly shock of red hair stepped forward, nudging his way through the front rank of the freed prisoners.

"Yes I am, but—"

"You're one of the most powerful people on Krynn," the youth continued. Behind him, the former prisoners began murmuring excitedly, pointing at Palin. The sorcerer blushed.

"Palin Majere, he fought in the Chaos War," a thickset woman tittered. "He slew Chaos."

"That's not true," Palin cut in. "I only—"

"Your father's Caramon, one of the Heroes of the Lance," her companion said.

"And don't forget his mother, Tika!" the thickset woman added. "She was something in her day! Still is, I bet!"

"Palin studied at the side of Raistlin, the greatest sorcerer of Krynn!" another cut in. "They're related, Palin and Raistlin. Cousins or something."

"My uncle, actually."

"No, Palin's the greatest sorcerer, not Raistlin. My father said there'd be no magic at all if it wasn't for him. There'd be no Krynn if he hadn't fought in the Abyss."

"A real hero!" a young girl beamed. "Oh, please let me come with you!"

Palin took a step back toward the ship. Usha followed him, her twinkling eyes telling him she was amused by his embarrassment. "You definitely should get out of the Tower of Wayreth more often, husband. Look how you're appreciated."

"Appreciated?"

"I've got to tell all my friends I was rescued by Palin Majere!" The thickset woman tried to press closer to the sorcerer.

"Listen, I'm flattered, but we're in a hurry."

"But not too much of a hurry, I pray," the red-maned young man cut in. He had startling golden eyes, and a smattering of freckles crossed the bridge of his nose. "There are more knights around, in a clearing not far outside the city."

"Yes," a thin woman said, as she inched her way past the thickset woman and stepped forward to join the youth. "They've a camp a few miles out. That's where they held us for a while, I guess until the schooner came into port. They told us they were going to take us north, to some stronghold."

"And they said they were waiting for more prisoners that would be arriving any minute," the youth added. "What if those prisoners are there now? Do you think you could help them? Like you helped us?"

Palin let out a deep breath. He wanted desperately to search for the artifacts from the Age of Dreams. It was a "race," Sageth had said, and Palin agreed. Yet he couldn't say no to these people. "How far?"

A cheer went up from the crowd on the dock.

"Not more than a few miles," the thin woman said. "I can take you there. I know the way."

"Great!" Rig had been silent up to this point. He wrapped his fingers around the pommel of his cutlass. "A few knights will present no challenge. We'll have your friends free within the hour. I can handle it myself."

"You've got a death wish, Rig Mer-Krel. Don't deny it," said Feril. "I watched you on the deck of the schooner—you took on three knights at once, and more were coming. I should've realized it when you wanted to tackle Khellendros's strong-hold in the desert. There were only four of us, but you didn't care. That's how Shaon's death has affected you." She took a deep breath and continued her tirade. "You don't like living without her, so you're doing your best to join her!"

Rig stared slack-jawed at the elf. "That's not true. I—"

"Isn't it? You were never this reckless before. Daring, yes, but not so blasted foolhardy." She spun around and glared at Palin. "These other prisoners"—she tilted her head toward the thin woman and the red-haired youth—"I'm going to help them."

"I'll join you," Rig cut in.

"No!" Feril practically spat out the word. "You'll stay here and help the rest of our refugees. Then you'll figure the best course to take us to Southern Ergoth and get us more sup-plies. Palin, Gilthanas, you can come with me," she contin-ued, "Ulin, you too. I think we can manage a handful of knights. We've got magic on our side, not just swords. Maybe we won't have to kill them all."

She turned, and threaded her way through the crowd on the dock, hesitating only long enough to make sure the red-haired youth and the woman were following her.

Ulin was quick on her heels. Palin paused to kiss Usha and whisper something to her.

Gilthanas approached the mariner. "I don't solely rely on magic," the elf said. "If you've got a blade I could borrow?"

The mariner unsheathed his cutlass. "Here, I have plenty of others."

"Are you men coming?" Feril was halfway down the dock with Ulin and their two guides. "Rig, be sure to get a map of the eastern coast of Southern Ergoth while we're gone."

"Yes, Captain Feril," Rig whispered when he was certain the Kagonesti and her entourage were out of earshot. He smiled as he watched her cut through the crowd and head into the city. "I'll follow your orders, ma'am."

Rig returned to the deck of *Flint's Anvil* and drew his lips into a straight line when he saw Jasper, Blister, and Sageth staring at him. His dark skin hid his embarrassment. "Well, what are you people ogling me for? We've got work to do. Jasper, you'll have to . . ." The mariner's words were lost on the dwarf, who turned and headed below deck. "Blister?"

The kender shrugged. "Sorry Rig, I've got to help Jasper with whatever he's doing," she said as she bounded away.

"I've got nothing better to do at the moment," Usha offered, as she walked up the plank. "I'll take charge of getting the rest of our refugees settled in town—after I'm more properly dressed." Her eyes twinkled. "Get on that map right away, and begin to plot a course. Palin and the others won't be gone that long."

"Yes, Captain Usha," the mariner softly muttered as he ambled away. "I never minded an occasional order from Shaon."

On a ship filled with people, Rig felt suddenly alone.

Chapter 12

The Kender's Discovery

Blister heard voices in Jasper's cabin. The dwarf and a woman talking. Goldmoon? There was something familiar about the woman's voice. But it wasn't Usha, who was up on deck seeing off the rest of the refugees—except for Sageth, who had agreed to stay with them. And it definitely wasn't Feril, who'd left the ship several minutes ago. It wasn't any of the crew because with Shaon gone there were no other female sailors.

The dwarf's door was open a crack, or rather not latched, and to the kender it was an invitation to confirm her suspicions. She nudged it wide and slipped inside.

"Goldmoon," she said, pleased that her guess was correct.

"How did you get here?"

Jasper turned, sighed, and rolled his eyes but Blister didn't see his exasperated expression. She was too busy staring at the woman in the center of the small room. The kender shuffled forward, past the dwarf, and gazed up at the beautiful human face.

Goldmoon floated several inches above the floor. She wore a pale rose cloak draped over her slender shoulders, and her tunic and leggings were the color of sand. The hem of the cloak swirled outward around her sandaled feet, reminding the kender of the glow that spread from the sun setting on ocean waves. Her long blonde hair fluttered about her neck and shoulders as if there were a strong breeze teasing it, but the air was completely still inside the cabin. The kender tentatively reached a gloved hand forward and her fingers passed right through Goldmoon's knee.

"Oh, you're not here, not really. Just a magical picture," Blister said.

The first time the kender had seen Goldmoon, the healer looked well into middle-age, with several streaks of gray hair. That had been hundreds of miles from here and several months ago at the Citadel of Light on the island of Schallsea. Goldmoon looked a little younger today, and a touch more lively. She had fewer wrinkles, but her eyes were sadder.

"Remember me?" The kender smiled cheerily and waved a gloved hand.

"Blister," Goldmoon said warmly. "Of course I remember you. It is good to see you again."

The kender beamed, deepening the wrinkles about her eyes. Jasper grumbled something behind her, then coughed, as if clearing his throat.

"I was looking in on Jasper," Goldmoon explained.

The kender pursed her lips. "Well, the door was open a little bit." The kender kept her eyes on Goldmoon.

"It wasn't open," said Jasper.

"Well, it wasn't locked. I must have accidentally bumped it open when I was walking by. You know how the ship rocks all the time, even in port, and makes you lose your balance. And since I accidentally opened it, I figured I might as well come inside—just in case Jasper needed to talk to me about something."

Goldmoon cast an amused glance at the dwarf, who was scowling. "Jasper has been telling me about the fight with the Knights of Takhisis this morning."

"Did he tell you what a hero I was in the desert? That I helped rescue prisoners? There were elephants and everything."

She nodded.

"Did he tell you about the old magic we need?"

"I was just getting to that," Jasper said.

"Palin wants us to get magic from the Age of Sleep."

"The Age of Dreams," the dwarf corrected.

"That's what I meant to say," Blister continued. "Well, Sageth, one of the people I heroically helped rescue from the desert, told us where some of the powerful old stuff can be found. He was kind of cryptic about it, but Palin figured it out. Anyway, we're going to Southern Ergoth where it's really cold and snowy. We're not going now, but as soon as the others get back from rescuing more people, that's when we'll go, Feril and Palin and Ulin and Gilthanas." She paused. "You might not know Ulin and Gilthanas. Feril used to live there—in Southern Ergoth. But she left because of the White and all the snow and cold. It was a good thing she left, because we wouldn't have met her otherwise. And—"

"Huma's lance," the dwarf said simply.

"I was getting to that," the kender huffed. "That's what we have to find in Southern Ergoth. And then we're going to the Qualinesti forest to look for something there."

"Provided we're still alive," Jasper muttered under his breath.

"But that's only two, and we need three or four according to what Sageth said. Old magical artifacts, and one of them is around your neck," the kender concluded.

Jasper smiled weakly at her lack of tact. "Your medallion of faith," he said. "It's from the Age of Dreams. And Palin and Sageth think that by destroying the old artifacts—"

"Enough magic will be released to bring powerful magic back to Krynn," Blister added.

"And then we'll have an easier time stopping the overlords." The dwarf was determined to have the last word.

Goldmoon raised an insubstantial hand and ran her fingers across the disk's surface. It was silver, and hung from a thin silver chain that sparkled like a string of miniature stars. The kender looked at it closely. Engraved on the disk's surface was a design—the outline of two closed eyes joined, or perhaps two eggs touching at their narrowest ends. It was the symbol of Mishakal, the Healing Hand, the departed goddess whom some called the Light Bringer and whom Goldmoon still worshiped.

"You might need to use it," Jasper said.

"Yes, but yours is the greater purpose." Goldmoon's voice was soft, but intense. "I believe the gods are merely away, watching us from some distant place where Chaos does not see them. I believe they are giving men and women the opportunity to fail or succeed on their own, to find the strength in themselves to overcome whatever obstacles are placed before them."

The kender listened with rapt attention. "But the dragon overlords—"

"Are one of those obstacles. There are smaller obstacles, too." Goldmoon's radiant blue eyes bore into the kender's. "Things each of us must overcome."

Blister's glance fell to her gloved hands. "Some things just can't be overcome."

"Take off your gloves, Blister."

Goldmoon's voice compelled the kender to tug off her soft tan gloves, revealing her crippled hands. Her fingers were bent and scarred, covered with blisters and sores, and she turned her back to Jasper so he couldn't see them.

"I don't like the way they look," the kender explained. "So I keep them covered. And it hurts when I move them."

"The pain isn't in your hands, Blister. The pain is in your heart and spirit. That is also an obstacle to be overcome. Look at me and move your fingers. Think about me, Blister, not your hands."

The kender gritted her teeth and complied, flexing first the fingers of her left hand, then her right. She stared at Goldmoon's eyes and moved her fingers again, making fists, releasing them, then clenching them tighter. At first she felt a familiar dull ache, but when she prepared herself for the throbbing sensation that would follow, it didn't come. The ache faded. She balled her fists again. There was no pain now. She looked at Goldmoon, astonished.

The healer seemed different, younger, more full of life. There were no wrinkles, no gray hairs. Her shoulders were straight, her eyes impossibly clear.

"I don't understand," the kender said, as she continued to move her hands. She couldn't find anything else to say, unaccustomed to being at a loss for words.

"You were punishing yourself for a past deed—the thieving expedition in which you fell victim to a magical trap. Your hands were scarred, will forever be scarred, but the physical pain fled you years ago. Have more faith in yourself, Blister. Your faith colors what you feel."

Faith also colors what you see, the kender said to herself as she continued to stare at the now-vibrant Goldmoon. Before, the kender saw her as middle-aged, and that must have meant her faith was waning. Now she saw the healer differently, signaling a regeneration in the kender's faith and convictions. Blister's eyes grew wide.

"We'll locate Huma's lance, and whatever it is we're supposed to find in the forest. And some ring—Dalamar's. I just know we can do it."

Goldmoon smiled softly. "And when you visit with me at Schallsea, Blister, I will give you my medallion. Until we meet there . . ." Her image faltered. The magical breeze picked up, and blew Goldmoon away.

"Wow," the kender said, "I gotta tell Usha and Rig. Jasper, you'll have to tell Groller. I haven't figured out those hand signals yet, but I can now." Blister spun on the balls of her feet, sidestepped Jasper, and hurried from his cabin.

Her gloves lay on the floor, forgotten and no longer needed.

* * * * *

Goldmoon walked down the twisting staircase in the Citadel of Light, pausing at a window that overlooked the bright blue waters of the bay.

"I must teach my pupils," she said aloud to herself. "They're an attentive bunch and show promise, but I myself am not feeling so attentive today." The healer twirled a strand of silver-blonde hair around her finger. "What's that you say? I'm always attentive? No, dear Riverwind. Today my mind is on Palin and his friends. I truly believe that the fate of Krynn is on their shoulders, and I'm not so certain their shoulders can bear such weight. Why do I have doubts?" Goldmoon's eyes fixed on the waves washing gently against the shore.

"I told you my meditations led me to believe Dhamon Grimwulf was the one, the man who could lead them to some measure of victory. My meditations reveal nothing of Palin's chances now that Dhamon is gone." She cocked her head to the side, listening intently. "I worry too much? I never worried so much when you were by my side. But Krynn's future was never so grim when you were alive, dear Riverwind. And the dragons were never so large."

Chapter 13

Beginnings

Dhamon Grimwulf toyed with the aging Solamnic
Knight by rushing in and retreating, slashing high at the
Solamnic's chest then jabbing at his legs. Dhamon was
wearing the older man down. In the process he was ferreting
out the Solamnic Knight's weaknesses and learning to pre-
dict his swings.

After several minutes, Dhamon realized that the Solamnic favored his right leg; his left foot edged slightly forward
before he swung, his shoulders dropped before he thrust,
and the man always glanced toward the spot where he
intended his sword to strike. It was a mere practice session
to the young Knight of Takhisis, who'd come upon the

Solamnic on the trail between Kyre and Solanthus. And it was achingly easy.

Dhamon feinted to the right and swept his long sword in a broad arc to the left. The Solamnic barely dropped his shield in time to parry the blow. The young knight could have swung faster, darted in and employed wide strokes to lure the Solamnic into using his shield to cover his chest so that his belly was exposed. It would have been more honorable to finish him quickly, the young knight thought, and he did believe in honor. One deep thrust into his heart or lungs would do it, only one sharp, brief moment of pain. He usually made quick work of his enemies.

But the Solamnic Knight was alone, and Dhamon was bored; those two factors changed matters. Drawing out the fight was a way to get some exercise, he rationalized, and he wasn't being entirely unchivalrous. There was a fairness to this duel.

Dhamon's opponent was armed and armored. He hadn't ambushed the Solamnic—though he saw him coming down the trail and easily could have lain in wait. He didn't kick or throw dirt into the air to temporarily blind the older knight, as some other fighters did to gain the upper hand. And he used only one weapon against his foe in order to match the Solamnic's solitary blade. There was an equality to this duel.

The Solamnic's moves were polished but slow and becoming increasingly more labored and predictable. Dhamon effortlessly parried each stroke. He watched the beads of sweat run down the older man's face, smiled as his opponent's chest heaved with the exertion.

The young knight almost backed away at one point, for as the duel wore on he felt an uncommon pang of guilt. The aging knight was terribly outmatched—an old, tired mouse fighting a very hungry young cat. But Solamnic Knights were enemies of Knights of Takhisis, and therefore the Solamnic was Dhamon's enemy.

"Fight me!" the older man bellowed. Sweat clung to his upper lip, dripped from his chin. "Stop playing with me and fight! Or did your commander not teach you well enough? Hmm? Perhaps you're not playing at all? Perhaps this is the best you can do!"

The taunt powered Dhamon's next thrust. The young knight's long sword, issued to him by his commander for bravery in battle, was a fine blade, keenly balanced, with an ornate black pommel set with a perfect ruby. Now the blade bit into the older man's side as a punishment for the verbal jab. The Solamnic retaliated, not even bothering to glance at the wound, and drove his own blade toward Dhamon's abdomen. The young knight effortlessly stepped aside and laughed.

"They taught me to fight, old man! And they taught me very well. But did your commander teach you how to die?" Dhamon rushed the Solamnic then, swinging high to his left and then down at the older knight's chest. The Solamnic raised his shield, as Dhamon had expected, but he brought the shield down quickly, knocking away not only the first blow, but the second, killing stroke aimed at his stomach.

The older man was moving swiftly now, stepping toward Dhamon and using his shield to parry a succession of the younger knight's frenzied blows. The Solamnic's sword thrusts were no longer sluggish. He moved like lightning, flashing in and cutting, then flashing higher.

Too late Dhamon realized it was the older man who had been toying with him, studying his weaknesses. The young Knight of Takhisis now put all of his effort into avoiding the Solamnic's dancing blade. Sweat ran down Dhamon's face, and for the first time in his life he felt his confidence melt away. He began to truly worry.

He'll tire. He has to tire, Dhamon told himself as the contest wore on. He's three times my age, and he can't keep this up. Watch for an opening. Watch. "No!" Dhamon cried as he felt the Solamnic's blade slide between his ribs, felt the warm stickiness of his blood flow out. The young Knight of Takhisis dropped to his knees as the older man pulled free his sword. Then Dhamon felt the ground rush up to meet him as his knees and thighs refused to support his weight. His face slammed against the ground, and the wind rushed from his lungs. He tasted blood in his mouth. He was dying. The Solamnic rolled him over, stood above him. There was compassion, not hate, in the older man's rheumy eyes.

"Finish me!" Dhamon spat at him. Finish this, he prayed to Takhisis, the Dark Queen, his absent beloved goddess. Grant me a quick death. Don't let me linger in front of my enemy.

But a quick death didn't come, and the Solamnic bent closer, hoisted Dhamon over his shoulder and snatched up the young man's blade. The Knight of Takhisis felt cold, so terribly cold. It was a summer day, and he'd been sweating from the fight. But now his limbs felt like lead weights, and he was freezing, the warmth rushing from his body as the blood continued to pour from his wound. Darkness enveloped him, and he continued to pray for the release of death.

* * * * *

Dhamon felt so very cold—and to his amazement, alive. His eyes shot open, and he gasped for air. A pair of enormous emerald eyes stared back, practically filling his vision.

"You wake, at last. I was worried that you might sleep forever, that I might have to bury you or feed your corpse to the fishes." The words came from the owner of the eyes—a massive creature, with an almost equine face covered with coin-sized bronze scales and jagged ridges along the jowls. It hovered mere inches from him. The emerald eyes, wide set and rimmed by tiny, seemingly identical scales, blinked several times and seemed to soften and become a shade paler.

Dhamon noted at once that the head was attached to a long, serpentine neck. The belly of the creature, which Dhamon could easily see from his prone position, was covered with horizontal bronze plates that shimmered in the meager light. Its long tail twitched lazily back and forth, and was crowned by a spiky ridge that ran to its very tip. A similar ridge ran down the center of the dragon's back.

The bronze dragon pulled its wings to its sides and eased a few yards away to give Dhamon room to sit up. He tried to take in his surroundings—an immense cave with smooth gray walls and a flat, almost slippery floor. Faint light filtered down from a patch of luminous lichen overhead. At his side was a dragon's scale, inverted so it resembled a large, scalloped bowl. It was filled with water. Dhamon ran his tongue around the edges of his lips. They weren't cracked, and he didn't feel overly thirsty. The dragon must have been forcing him to drink somehow. But his head pounded and his stomach ached. He felt dreadfully hungry.

The coldness was leaving him, though not entirely. He was naked, and the air that only faintly stirred around him—the dragon's breathing—was undeniably chilly and stale. For an instant he felt self-conscious and looked around to find something to cover himself with. He guessed he must have been resting here for quite some time. His muscles were stiff, and it felt as if he'd lost quite a bit of weight. The hunger continued to gnaw at him.

"Who are you?" Dhamon asked. His voice cracked, and his tongue felt a little swollen. He cupped his palm and dipped it in the water. It was cool and felt good in his throat.

"You may call me Shimmer," the bronze dragon replied. "My true name is too complex for your tongue."

"You saved me." It was a statement. Dhamon was certain the dragon must have rescued him from the lake.

"I watched you battle the blue." The dragon studied Dhamon's expression. "I was a fish in the water, for such is my ability to manipulate my shape. I did not intervene then. It was not my fight, and you were both strangers to me. But when it was finished, and when you fell into my domain, I watched as you struggled to the surface for air. I felt your blood seep into my water, and I pulled you under and brought you here. I cared not if the dragon died, desired it in fact, for blues are creatures of corruption. But you seemed brave and worthy of life."

"This cave is under the lake?"

"A safe lair," Shimmer continued. "Safe from the eyes of the overlords and from Krynn's inhabitants who seem to fear all dragons now."

Dhamon's fingers explored his chest and his legs, where he'd been sliced by Gale's sharp scales. There were no scars, and only a few tender spots. His palms were healed, too. He reached his hands up to his face, where a short, uneven beard grew. His fingers combed through his hair, which was a little longer than he remembered and much more tangled. He glanced again at the dragon.

"I peeled your clothes from you, healed you," Shimmer explained. "I have such talents. But there were serious injuries beneath your flesh, and those took a long while to mend."

"How long have I been . . ."

"You have slept for a month or more, as humans count the passing of time. I was able to feed you some, but I suspect you are hungry. Yes?"

Dhamon nodded.

"I will return with something for you to eat." Shimmer slipped into the darkest shadows of the cave, and Dhamon heard a splash. He pulled himself to his feet, using the cave wall for support.

"A month," he whispered. "Feril must think I'm dead." He

felt a little lightheaded as he forced himself to walk. His legs protested, but he pushed himself to explore the cave. The floor sloped downward to his right and the passage narrowed. Too narrow for the dragon, he thought, but not a dragon that can turn itself into a fish—or likely other creatures. Blackness engulfed him for a moment, but he followed the passage, until it widened and brightened. Luminous lichen covered the ceiling of a chamber that was filled with piles of steel pieces, gems, jewelry, weapons and shields, urns, golden candlesticks, and more. So my savior dragon is covetous, Dhamon thought. But then all dragons were said to crave wealth.

He slowly returned to the scale and drank his fill, then sat and leaned back against the wall to wait for the dragon. He did not have to wait long. Shimmer glided into the cave, moving quickly and quietly despite her bulk. She opened her mouth and three large fish spilled out, flopping onto the cave floor. Dhamon quickly grabbed one and struck its head against the stone wall to stun it. He sliced open its belly on the edge of the scale, careful to not let its entrails spill into his drinking water. Gently prying the fish apart, he tugged at its flesh and began to eat.

"Feeling better?" the dragon asked when Dhamon had finished all three fish.

"Yes, thank you."

"I would know of you, then. What you call yourself, what you are about. Then I will decide just what to do with you."

Dhamon's brow furrowed. He hadn't considered the possibility that the dragon might not let him go. Bronze dragons sided with the forces of light, and in decades past they had aided Krynn's humans and demihumans. But times were different. Naked and without a weapon, he could do little to stand up to Shimmer. He was at her mercy. Dhamon took a deep breath and stared into the dragon's emerald eyes.

He told her briefly of his youth, of how he had been recruited into the Knights of Takhisis, lured by thoughts of pomp and battle and his admiration of the knights in his town. He had distinguished himself in battle after battle, and finally was paired with a blue dragon, Gale.

Dhamon was apart from Gale when he met the old Solamnic Knight—Sir Geoffrey Quick—in the woods. The Solamnic had carried the grievously-wounded Dhamon to his home, and during the next few months gradually nursed the young man back to health. During that time, the Solamnic's words eventually swayed Dhamon away from the Knighthood of Takhisis, made him realize that the Order had little to do with chivalry and honor anymore, and had grown into an organization of armored bullies striving for power and the accomplishment of dark goals.

The day Dhamon left the Solamnic, he buried his black mail armor and the sword with the ruby in its pommel, and set about trying to cleanse his spirit.

"I am not proud of what I was," Dhamon concluded. "But I am not that man anymore. I owed the Solamnic for saving my life, and now I owe you as well. But do not think to keep me here."

The bronze scrutinized Dhamon's tanned face. "No. I do not think you would reveal my lair. You are free to go."

Dhamon grew silent. A month had passed—at least. Rig, Feril, and the others would no longer be in Palanthas. Once they had contemplated going after the White in Southern Ergoth—perhaps he might find them there. Or perhaps they were on their way back to Schallsea. He wanted desperately to see Feril again, to explain about his past. He'd need clothes first, and a weapon, as well as a way to get to Schallsea island.

"Join us, Shimmer," Dhamon said simply. "We stand against the overlords and we could use your help. If good dragons were to join forces and fight against the evil dragons, then we . . ."

Shimmer emphatically shook her head. "Most of my brethren are in hiding. There are more evil dragons than good now, and the evil ones are ruthless. It is impossible to save all the people from the overlords. If we tried, if we fought *for* you, we would be dying *with* you, not saving you. We will pick our own battles, in our own time." The dragon glanced toward the darkest part of the cave. "You are free to go. I will take you above the lake. I've invested too much effort in you to see you drown. You can go wherever you wish."

Dhamon paused. "A weapon," the former knight said. "You've several in your cave. Could you spare one?"

Shimmer's eyes narrowed. "The glaive. You can have it. Take it from my treasure chamber. But take nothing else."

Dhamon hurried through the passage. He had no intention of taking any of Shimmer's wealth. He had no intention of risking certain death for a bit of treasure—even though a couple of coins would buy him something to wear. The glaive leaned against the farthest wall. Dhamon picked his way over a mound of coins and gems. The weapon's curved edge glinted in the light from the lichen. It had a long haft, nearly five feet in length and was intricately carved with the images of birds of prey in flight. The blade secured to the top resembled a large axe head, and it was crowned with a spear point. The glaive was light and well-balanced, its metal a silvery-blue.

He returned to Shimmer and ventured to ask another boon. "It would take me a long time to walk anywhere. Would you take me to the healer Goldmoon on Schallsea? The island?"

He heard a gentle rumble, the dragon laughing. "You ask much; that is near Sable's realm."

"Yes."

"No. Name another destination."

Dhamon thought for a moment, then named another

possibility. The dragon nodded. Her emerald green eyes bore into his, filled his vision. The cave seemed to melt around him, the grays and browns of the rock melding with the green, swirling about him like wind-whipped leaves. Then the stone floor vanished beneath his feet.

Chapter 14

A Dangerous Reunion

Gilthanas tugged the cord free from the neck of his bright indigo tunic and tied back his hair, tucking the loose strands out of the way behind his prominent elven ears. Then, without slowing his stride, he straightened the tunic and brushed at a couple of loose threads. It was one of the garments Rig had bought for him not quite a week ago in Gander, where most of the Northern Waste refugees had been sent on their way—thankfully easing the severe overcrowding on the ship.

The mariner had purchased colorful clothes for everyone, and gave each passenger a purse of steel coins. Gilthanas remembered that Feril was pleasantly surprised by Rig's generosity, but that generous act wasn't enough to save the dark-skinned man from the Kagonesti's tongue-lashing several minutes ago.

Gilthanas varied his stride a bit, working to break in his new leather boots. Feril walked to his right—they had fallen behind the Majeres so they could talk a little. He had decided that the Kagonesti was a formidable person, and he was glad he was on her good side. She was someone he'd like to continue to be friends with. He ran his fingers over the pommel of his borrowed cutlass and caught Feril staring at him. She swallowed hard and looked away.

"Don't like my ears?" he teased. "I don't have the slightest problem with yours—though it's almost impossible to see them under all of those curls."

She shook her head. He was referring to the fact that she was a Kagonesti, and he was a Qualinesti—quite a bit taller and paler, almost aristocratic, in comparison with the wild elves. Historically, the disparate races of elves did not see eye to eye, though that was starting to change under the tyranny of the dragon overlords. Qualinesti, Kagonesti, and Silvanesti were banding together in some lands. One such colony was on the southern shore of Southern Ergoth.

"Your ears," she laughed softly. "No, it's not that at all." She paused. "Dhamon had blond hair, and he used to tie it back like that, too."

Gilthanas gave her a sympathetic look. "I heard a lot about him from the others on the ship. A former Knight of Takhisis, but a good man from what I understand. I take it you were close."

"We were trying to be. Fate just wouldn't give us a chance." Feril took a deep breath, turning her tanned face toward the sky. "Wouldn't have worked out anyway. He was human."

"Something wrong with being human?" Gilthanas asked just loud enough so that Palin and his son, walking a few paces ahead, could hear. Both Majeres glanced over their shoulders, and Gilthanas grinned mischievously at Feril. Ulin scowled, shook his head.

The Kagonesti blushed, offering Palin and his son a weak smile. "There's nothing wrong with humans. I like humans—truly." Softer, once the Majeres had turned around to continue following their guides, she added, "But they're not like us. Their life spans are so short, burning out like stubby candles. They look at things differently. They like cities; I prefer the wilderness. They're better off with their own kind. Things wouldn't have worked out between Dhamon and me. And there's no point in thinking about it now—he's dead."

"Decades ago I thought like you," Gilthanas said. "I was younger, definitely more foolish, and I almost cost my sister Laurana her happiness. I doubt she would have ever forgiven me of my ignorance."

"Laurana fell in love with a human?"

"Yes, a half-elven man named Tanthalas."

"Tanis Half-Elven" Feril said excitedly. "I've heard of him. He was a hero with Caramon and Raistlin, and he died before the Chaos War. I don't know much more, though."

"His mother died giving birth to him, and my family took him in. He was a playmate, a confidant. But he was different, tainted I used to think, not as good as the Qualinesti, and certainly not good enough for my sister. She was infatuated with him from the beginning. One day when they were playing together, she made him promise that they would marry when they were older. He thought it was a jest and I heard him promise, felt the blood pounding in my ears. I realized it was no game to my dear sister; she wasn't kidding. I drew Tanis aside, intent on keeping my family's pure elven heritage alive. I threatened him, I guess. I most certainly threw our friendship out the window by calling him a half-breed unworthy of my sister."

Tanis left and my sister was heartbroken. I was very pleased with myself, so happy that I'd saved her—until he came back a few years later. Laurana pursued him again, with more of a passion than ever. But Tanis was wise enough to heed my words. He kept his distance, and I kept my eyes on him."

"So, they never got together?" Feril asked quietly.

"During the War of the Lance, fate took all of us to Icewall, then up to Southern Ergoth, your home. The three races living there—your people, mine, and the Silvanesti—were at odds. Though they lived side by side, they weren't civil to each other. And it opened my eyes. You see, I fell in love with a Kagonesti. Being with her made me realize that elves are elves, and the names and happenstances of birth are irrelevant. It's what's inside a person that counts. The shell isn't what matters."

"Where is she now? What happened to her?"

"I pledged my love to her, fell so deeply that she became my entire world, and all thoughts of Laurana and Tanis were pushed aside. But then," Gilthanas said, pausing to stroke his chin, "she showed me her true nature. She wasn't a Kagonesti after all, and I turned away."

"Her true nature?"

"I felt betrayed. She wasn't who she claimed, *what* she claimed. She hadn't been honest with me. I thought I knew her, but I didn't know her at all. I felt that she'd tricked me, made a mockery of my feelings. I was no longer willing to trust her or to accept her. I refused to acknowledge my feelings for her. Then, I disappeared. Disappeared? Ha!"

"That's when you were imprisoned?"

"Yes, by the Silvanesti. Spending years alone in that cell made me think about my life, my very haughty life. My own people gave me over to the Silvanesti. First, I focused on Tanis being not good enough for my sister. Thank the gods, the two were finally married. Then, I fixated on Verminaard. He killed my people, and I vowed vengeance, no matter what. Next, I was obsessed with Silvara. I loved her deeply, then rejected her just as passionately. I later realized I should have given her a chance, our love a chance. When I finally escaped from the prison, I began to travel all of Ansalon in search of her. Ultimately, I was betrayed again by elves and wound up in the prison where you and I met."

"Maybe you could still find her."

"Maybe," Gilthanas said, so softly that Feril had to strain to hear him. "How petty I was. And how entirely unworthy of her. Race has nothing to do with love, Feril."

The Kagonesti studied his face for a few moments, and considered asking him more about Silvara. Gilthanas stared straight ahead. Feril looked down. "Dhamon and I never had enough time together," she said quietly.

Gilthanas remained silent for a while. The thin woman and the red-haired youth led the small entourage through Witdel. The city was for the most part impoverished. At one time it had been prosperous, but it had gone through hard times, starting with the Chaos War. Most of the buildings were made of wood, and they were weathered from neglect and the ravages of the sea—paint was peeling, doors hung a little off-center. Business signs were crude, some with paint chipping so badly that they couldn't be read.

However, a few establishments seemed to be faring better. A small boardinghouse two blocks from the docks was in better shape than most. Flowers bloomed in baskets hanging from the porch, and the trim around the windows looked newly painted. Nearby, a store that catered to fishermen and hunters was in the process of being renovated and expanded.

The thin woman glanced at her reflection in the window of a cobbler's shop, frowning at her disheveled appearance. She didn't walk very fast, exhausted from her ordeal as a prisoner of the Knights of Takhisis, but her stride was a determined one. "You can't free them all, can you?" she asked Palin. "I mean, the Knights of Takhisis are probably taking prisoners in other cities, too. And you can't save all of them."

Palin didn't answer, didn't think she really expected one.

"Even saving one person is important," Gilthanas interjected. "Nobody should be a slave to the knights."

The Qualinesti knew what it was like to be held captive. Gilthanas had been a prisoner for more than ten years at the hands of the Silvanesti. Second in line for the throne, his confinement had been a matter of political expedience. It was a short time in the life of an elf, but hardly a pleasant experience. And then he'd fallen afoul of a band of Knights of Takhisis and was again taken captive. He was grateful to Palin, Rig, Blister, and Feril for being rescued.

On both occasions of his imprisonment, Gilthanas had thought about a lot of things—and one female in particular. She was not of his race, and Gilthanas had therefore denied his feelings for her. However, confinement provided a lot of time for thinking, and during those long hours and long years the elf had come to the conclusion that love transcended race.

Decades ago, he had been supposed to meet his love near the Tomb of Huma on Southern Ergoth, and he felt certain that breaking that appointment had been the greatest mistake of his life.

At the edge of town, Palin asked their guides to stop. "Down this road?"

The thin woman nodded. "A couple of miles. Their camp is in a clearing that the road cuts through. It didn't take us long to walk from there to the docks—even though it was dark. Just follow us."

"I think we can find their camp from this point," Palin said.

The woman started to protest, then gave in when the red-haired youth tugged on her arm. "We'll wait for you here," she said.

Feril glided past Palin and knelt at the edge of the small dirt road that lead southeast from the city. "The knights travel up and down this road." She pointed to broken twigs and crushed fern leaves, running her fingers along the outlines of several bootprints.

"How do you know a Knight of Takhisis made that print?" Ulin asked.

"All of these prints are deep and relatively uniform, like they could've been made by people in armor—soldiers— except for these prints, which were probably made by the prisoners they took to the docks." Feril glanced at Palin. "I'm going to scout ahead."

The Kagonesti moved a few dozen yards beyond the sorcerers. She was in her element, focusing her acute senses on the plants and the ground, looking for traces of the knights. She dropped to her hands and knees when she heard voices ahead, quietly crawling forward until she came upon a campsite in a clearing. Hiding behind a large bush, she parted its leaves and watched a knight dragging an elk into the clearing, a single arrow protruding from the creature's chest. He tugged the elk near a fire that another knight was building and began to skin and gut it.

Behind the pair, two more knights guarded a group of people who were tied together with lengths of rope, bound at their wrists and ankles. Feril could see ten knights altogether, and she counted forty-three prisoners. She watched for several more minutes, then hurried back to the sorcerers and relayed the information.

Ulin shook his head. "I don't like the odds."

"Rig would say we have them outnumbered," Feril added.

"It's not that I don't think we can take them," the younger Majere quickly returned, "I just think the odds are high that some of the prisoners could get hurt in the process. Still, I've an idea."

* * * * *

A lone Knight of Takhisis staggered into the camp, the front of his tabard coated with blood from a gaping chest wound, his face streaked with dirt. He was weaponless and shieldless, and his helmet hung from his hand. At once the other knights were alert, all of them jumping to their feet. As one, they drew their swords and looked past the wounded man. The knight who'd been skinning the elk stepped toward his injured brother, ready to steady him. But the knight stepped back, refusing the aid. He flung his arm toward the road that led back to Witdel.

"Hurry!" he panted, "the ship." He dropped to his knees and held his chest. "It's been attacked, the prisoners freed. You must hurry. The attackers are coming here. They've weapons and—" He gasped for air and pitched forward, his face inches from the fire, his helmet rolling away.

The knight-officer motioned for his men to form ranks. "We'll meet them on the trail!" he snapped. "Move!" He gestured for two of his men to stay with the prisoners, then led the way back toward Witdel at a hurried march.

"Is he dead?" one of the remaining knights asked after the rest of his brethren had thundered away. He cast a curious and sympathetic glance at the fallen knight. "Know who he is?"

"Never seen him before. Must have come from the ship in Witdel," the other replied. He took one step closer to the knight, glancing over his shoulder at the prisoners. "He breathes—but barely, and with all that blood he's as good as dead. We'll be burying him before dawn."

"Maybe we can do something for him."

"You heard the officer," the second knight said, "he told us to watch the prisoners."

The wounded knight raised his head slightly, staring at the flames only a few inches away. He could feel the warmth on his skin. The smell of the partially gutted elk nearby was practically overpowering. The fire writhed as he gazed at it, becoming more animated. Its tendrils swayed, not teased by the wind, but by the fallen knight's mind. His mental commands urged it to dance higher and to consume the wood as if it were a ravenous beast.

"Hey! What's going on?" one of the knights hollered.

All traces of the blood and wound had vanished. The knight stood, shedding his black armor. He was a tall man with shoulder-length brown hair, and was clad in a simple tunic. The man slowly rose to his feet and reached for the staff at his side that had been magically disguised as the knight's helmet.

"Sorcery!" the other shouted. "Stay with the prisoners. We've been tricked!" He drew his blade and charged Ulin, who was stepping back from the fire.

Ulin gestured toward the knight, sending a spark to the man's tabard. The knight paused only a moment to swat at the flame, and in that time, Ulin had scrambled back farther and willed the campfire to erupt into a great ball of fire that quickly overpowered the two knights.

The prisoners gasped, recoiling as much as their bonds allowed. The flames licked dangerously close to them, but Ulin called the fire back, mentally urged it to fold in upon itself until all that remained were glowing embers.

"It's all right," he told them. "Everything's going to be all right. My friends and I will take you to the city." He stepped toward them and noted that most were leery. He tried another tact to relax them a little. "My father's Palin Majere. He's nearby, dealing with the other knights." Those words seemed to do the trick, and he began untying the prisoners.

* * * * *

Feril lay on her stomach among the ferns off to the side of the road. The Kagonesti breathed deep, taking the heady scent of the loam into her lungs. Her fingers stretched forward, touching the leaves—so delicate, yet strong. She closed her eyes and vividly pictured the ferns.

"Join with me," she softly called, her words sounding like the wind blowing gently across the fronds. "Feel with me." The Kagonesti fluttered her fingers and moved her head from side to side. The ferns followed her movement, and she felt the energy that flowed in their stems, surged from their roots. She felt the nourishing sun on her back. She seemed to drink in the energy. "Join with me," she repeated.

A sound intruded on her private world—it was Gilthanas. "The knights are coming," he said. She heard the shush of leaves being brushed aside. Palin was kneeling down beside her. Feril heard other sounds then, frantic and hurried ones—leather boots running over the earth. She redirected all her attention to the fern.

"Join with me," she breathed. And suddenly, her vision pulled back and she saw the bush near the fern, the veil-like leaves of the willow birch that stood a few feet away. She saw the tall grasses, the moss, the wild roses that grew in profusion.

The sound of bootsteps came closer, and the plants began to move, swaying in time with the Kagonesti's fluttering fingers. The vines from the oak overhead, the willow birch veil, the ferns, and more, all swaying, stretching, grasping. The oak groaned and dipped a branch, whipping like a noose around the neck of the lead knight. The willow birch's veil enveloped two more, holding them as tightly as though it were a spiderweb trapping helpless insects.

Feril clenched her fists and the tall grasses lashed out at the Knights of Takhisis's ankles, tripping those not held fast by the trees. The roses lashed their thorny stems around the knights' calves, and the fern leaves encircled the wrists of the knights who fell to the forest floor.

The Kagonesti felt pain intrude on her private world, the sensation of the knights fighting against the plants, trying to rip the grass from its earthy bosom. She felt what the plants felt.

But Palin was moving through the ferns now, casting an enchantment of his own. Feril kept her senses focused on the plants and was only dimly aware of the sparks of fire that flew from the sorcerer's fingertips. Then she felt a warmth on her back and limbs, the perception of blood. Gilthanas was swinging Rig's sword, the knights' blood splattering the plants. The Kagonesti directed the willow birch to wrap more of its tender lengths around the knights to bind their arms.

The plants responded, moving faster now, drawing strength from Feril. The wild roses recoiled, dragging a knight into their thorny embrace. As he fought against the plant and struggled to rip off the stems, Gilthanas darted in and slew him quickly. Another knight was nearly free, squirming out of his mail shirt to elude the oak. But Palin stopped him with more sparks that struck his chest, penetrated, and made him go limp.

"Move with me," Feril was talking louder now, easing herself off the ground as she continued to direct the plants. The forest all around her was more alive than ever, moving and grasping, branches and stems lashing out like cobras, vines working like lassos. She pointed to a small patch of wild raspberries growing by the road, and in response, the coiling, reed-thin stems entwined around calves and ankles, pulling the remaining knights down. There, the moss waited, releasing an intoxicating, dizzying scent. *Join with us,* the moss urged the knights, relaxing them, lulling them into a restful state, which made them easy to dispatch.

Palin and Gilthanas had been forced to slay half of the men. Feril sluggishly detached her senses from the plants and staggered onto the trail. She took several deep breaths and steadied herself. The enchantment had enervated her. Four of the knights were tied with vines against the largest trees. Gilthanas was removing their boots, slicing the footwear in half with his cutlass and tossing it into the underbrush. Palin was gathering the men's swords.

"They'll be barefoot and weaponless," Palin informed her. "So if they work themselves free, they'll pose little threat. You all right?"

She nodded and smiled. "Fine. Just tired. Let's see how your son fared."

* * * * *

Ulin had freed nearly all of the prisoners by the time Feril, Palin, and Gilthanas entered the clearing. Gilthanas was carrying the knights' weapons, and he quickly distributed them to some of the former captives. Ulin snatched up his staff and nodded to Palin, who was inspecting the charred remains of two knights.

"Let's move out," Gilthanas urged, pointing toward the trail that would lead back to Witdel. "We should be on our way in case there's more of them."

"Something's wrong," Feril said. The Kagonesti turned about, scanning the trees that ringed the campsite, sniffing and listening intently. "There's—"

"More knights? Reinforcements?" came a sultry voice. A stocky woman clad in a black robe stepped into the clearing. At her side were Knights of Takhisis, their weapons drawn. More knights ringed the campsite, nearly two dozen of them. Four had bows drawn and pointed at the prisoners. The stocky sorceress gestured at Gilthanas and Ulin, who flourished weapons. "Make a move to fight, and the men will loose their arrows."

"Put down your weapons," another knight said. This one was clearly in charge, the insignia of a subcommander visible on his shoulder.

Her eyes narrowed as she spotted Palin, and the sorceress nodded to get her commander's attention. "Subcommander

Gistere," the robed woman said. "We have a very important person in our midst—Palin Majere."

Gistere's face remained impassive, but his gaze locked onto Palin's. "Put the swords down. And you, put down the staff." The last order was directed at Ulin. "Keep your hands where I can see them." The officer scrutinized them. "Your weapons!" he barked.

Ulin dropped his staff, and the prisoners behind him reluctantly dropped the weapons they'd been given. Palin slowly raised his hands out to his sides, watching the knights. He knew there were more behind him, and his mind whirled with the spells he might cast. He couldn't catch all of them in an enchantment—not without also injuring the prisoners and his companions.

Feril's lips curled back as she dropped her arms to her sides. "How did you know we were here?" she asked, her tone venomous. "And how did you sneak up on us?"

The Knight of the Thorn took a step toward her. "There are enchantments that can make a talon move as quietly as a dying breeze, my dear wild elf," she hissed. "It's a spell that can stifle the clink of armor. We were to meet the men guarding these prisoners. Fortunately I sensed something was wrong. Tell me, did you slay them all?"

"Enough!" Subcommander Gistere spat at the sorceress. "We haven't the time for this. You—I said to drop your weapon." He was pointing at Gilthanas, who stood with his legs slightly spread, Rig's cutlass unsheathed and at his side. "My men will fire on the prisoners—do you understand? I'll order them to slay the unarmed women and men. Their blood will be on your spirit. I'll give you no more warnings."

"Don't do it!" a new voice intruded.

Feril's eyes grew wide as a man stepped into the clearing. He was naked except for a Knights of Takhisis tabard that was draped over him, no doubt taken from one of the knights they'd captured on the road. And he had moved so quietly because he had no boots or armor. He looked like a wildman, a mass of tangled hair and a beard.

Dhamon? Feril mouthed. Her heart beat faster.

"Dhamon?" Palin asked in disbelief.

"Another fool to join you," Subcommander Gistere sneered. "And a fool who will die very quickly if he doesn't put down the weapon." The subcommander motioned to one of his archers, who trained an arrow on Dhamon's chest.

Gilthanas looked uncertainly between Dhamon Grimwulf and the Knight of Takhisis. Dhamon kept a firm grip on the glaive and protectively stepped between Feril and the knights. A second archer drew a bead on the wildman. "Dhamon," she breathed as he passed by.

"The Knights of Takhisis used to be noble," Dhamon said. "Years past they wouldn't have threatened unarmed people, used weapons of distance on foes who hadn't the same advantage. Only fair fights." He looked directly at Gistere and raised an eyebrow when he spotted the red scale on his lily emblem. "But that was before they chose to bow to the overlords, to serve dragons instead of men. You should order them all slain," he said, waving his free hand at the prisoners for emphasis. "Killing them outright would be a far better fate than what's likely in store for them."

Gistere's eyes narrowed, and he raised his hands to signal the archers to fire. Then instantly his eyes grew wide and he held his gesture. He felt the presence of the Red Dragon in his head, felt the scale imbedded in his chest tingle.

This one intrigues me, Malys hissed. *I could use someone with the tenacity to stand up to so many of your men. I want him—alive and whole. Slay the others as a lesson.*

The subcommander swallowed hard and motioned to the archers, pointing out different targets—Palin Majere, Gilthanas, Ulin, Feril, and the burliest of the prisoners. In that instant, Dhamon rushed forward. Gilthanas joined his mad charge, even as the sorcerer had begun an enchantment.

Feril, stunned by Dhamon's arrival, quickly came to her senses. There'd be time for an explanation later—if they lived. She reached inside her pouch and tugged free a sea shell. Ulin was behind her also, mumbling the words of a spell.

Palin had settled on an incantation just as Dhamon arrived. The astonishing return of the former knight threw him, and he had to concentrate to keep from tripping over the words to the enchantment. As he recited the arcane syllables, an arrow streaked by him, piercing the throat of one of the prisoners. Another streaked by, and he heard Ulin groan behind him.

"Son?" Palin whispered as the spell finished and tiny fragments of gold and silver, of ruby, emerald, and jacinth filled the air. The dying light of the sun touched the objects, and as the pieces spun about, they reflected a kaleidoscope of blinding color. Some of the knights threw their arms up to shield their eyes. But too late, Palin's spell had blinded them—and practically all of the prisoners as well.

The sorcerer glanced behind him. Ulin was on the ground near the dying campfire, an arrow protruding from his back. "Ulin!"

Gilthanas darted toward his intended target, the Knight of the Thorn, but his path was quickly blocked by a knight wielding a two-handed blade. The elf barely stepped aside as the sword arced down, whistling through the still air.

Dhamon was near the Qualinesti, swinging the glaive in wide, sweeping motions. He was unaccustomed to the weapon, used to fighting with swords. At first this weapon seemed unwieldy, then it seemed amazing.

The glaive glowed faintly blue as it struck the raised long sword of a charging knight and cut the blade cleanly in half. The glaive continued its arc, slicing through the black mail of the knight as if the armor were thin cloth. It easily parted the man's flesh beneath, blood spurting out to cover Dhamon's chest and face. The Knight of Takhisis was dead before he struck the ground.

Dhamon spun about, blinking to clear his eyes, and found himself facing a pair of advancing knights. Holding firmly to the lower part of the glaive's haft, he swung the weapon at waist height. Again it sliced through weapons and armor and two more men fell.

Subcommander Gistere saw his archers aim at Dhamon, and yelled to them to redirect their arrows. "At Palin Majere!" he shouted. "This one's mine."

Dhamon cut down three more knights as Gistere took a step forward, then halted in a defensive stance, with his long sword in one hand and a buckler shield in the other.

Dhamon whirled, dropping two more knights. Though he was practically covered in blood, none of it was his own. He eyed the subcommander. "Call your men off!" Dhamon cried. "There doesn't have to be any more killing."

Gistere shook his head and raised his long sword. Perhaps if he could wound the man just enough to make him drop that cursed weapon. . . . He glanced at his four archers, and noted with relief that they all still lived. Two were peppering the prisoners and the third had struck the younger sorcerer in the back and the Qualinesti in the shoulder. The fourth was sighting the Kagonesti. "His shoulder, his legs!"—the subcommander shouted to the fourth archer, pointing to Dhamon—"nothing else!"

The archer complied and sank two arrows into Dhamon's right thigh, just enough to hobble him. The subcommander stepped forward and adjusted the hold on his sword so he could swing with the flat of his blade. *Alive,* Malystryx hissed a warning inside his head. *And I want his weapon.*

Meanwhile, the Knight of the Thorn crouched behind a fellow knight, protecting herself from Gilthanas. The sorceress pointed a long-nailed finger at the Qualinesti, who had been slowed by an arrow lodged deep in his shoulder. The sorceress smiled at the elf's pain and uttered a string of words indecipherable to those around her.

But Gilthanas knew what the woman was saying. A spell-caster himself, though he often relied more on a sword, the elf gritted his teeth, thrust forward with the cutlass, and waited for the inevitable. A streak of orange-red light extended from the Knight of the Thorn's finger to the elf's chest. Prepared for it, Gilthanas was better able to take the electrifying pain. He thrust forward again, this time slipping past the mailed knight's defenses. Rig's cutlass carved deep into the man's belly, and he fell to the ground.

The magical beam continued to pulse from her finger as Gilthanas tugged free the sword with a considerable amount of effort. The elf glared at the black-robed woman and dropped to his knees, the pain starting to overcome him and paralyze his limbs. Gilthanas tried to lift the blade, and cursed when another jolt rushed through him. His fingers trembled uncontrollably, and the cutlass slipped from his hand.

"Die, Qualinesti," the Knight of the Thorn commanded. It was all Gilthanas could do to keep from crying out. He fell forward on his hands, his entire body quivering. "Die, elf!"

"No!" Feril shouted. The Kagonesti had completed her own enchantment and hurled the sea shell at the Knight of the Thorn. The shell stopped in midair above the woman's head, and a heartbeat later the air surrounding her shimmered blue-green. Beads of water stood out against her black robes and spread like a sheen of sweat across her face.

The sorceress gasped and drew her hands to her chest, ending the spell that had tormented Gilthanas. More sea-scented water collected on her skin and garments. The Knight of the Thorn whimpered and fell, foam flecking about her wide nostrils and mouth. Even Gilthanas was impressed by the unusual magic. Feril had turned the air to sea water in the atmosphere immediately surrounding the sorceress and had drowned her.

The Qualinesti struggled to his feet and wrenched free the

arrow that was stuck in his shoulder. "My thanks," he nodded to Feril, as he snatched up the cutlass and looked about. His shoulder throbbed and his arm was growing numb, but he shoved the pain to the back of his mind. Feril was occupied with directing the trees and vines in the area to join the struggle. They were snaking forward to bind the men.

When a knight rushed up to check on the fallen sorceress, Gilthanas hurried forward to meet him. Their blades clashed, and both drew back to raise their swords again. The Qualinesti dropped to the ground, rolled forward under the knight's next swing, and drove Rig's cutlass into the man's stomach.

Gilthanas heard startled cries from somewhere behind him. Feril's plants had entangled several of the knights, and they were panicked by what was happening. The elf charged at another knight. Out of the corner of his eye, he saw Dhamon slice through two more, then pause to tug the arrows out of his leg. The ground was red with blood, and the wild-looking fighter had to be careful not to stumble over so many fallen bodies.

Palin Majere glanced over his shoulder and breathed a sigh of relief. His son still lived. Ulin had pushed himself into a sitting position. Palin returned his attention to the scintillating lights that still filled the air of half of the clearing. Focusing, he increased the potency of the spell. The gem shards and bits of gold and silver glowed brighter—like sparks from a fire— and spun toward the knights, burning the faces and hands of those who were not entwined by the foliage.

Ulin added to the threat. The younger sorcerer was directing all of his waning energy at the embers in the campfire. The pieces of wood, hot as coals, rose under his command and streaked toward the men. His fingers pointed out targets, and the coals unerringly obeyed. Ulin could barely maintain consciousness. He knew he was losing a considerable amount of blood.

Feril crouched as two arrows cut through the air only a few inches above her head. She reached into the pouch at her side, dropped to all fours, then rolled as another barrage of arrows shot by. She sprang to her feet and stumbled toward Dhamon in time to see him carve through another knight and take a step closer to the subcommander.

"We can end this!" Dhamon called. "You've six men left. Six—and you! With one word you can end this. Let them live."

"Surrender?" Gistere asked. He raised his buckler and again felt the presence of Malystryx's mind. The dragon hissed that giving up was not an option. She did not want her knights caught and questioned within another dragon's realm—better that they die if necessary—even Gistere. The subcommander waved to four of his surviving knights, ordering them to charge. "I want them alive!" Gistere bellowed.

One knight continued sparring with Gilthanas as the other dashed toward Palin. Feril glanced around, concerned about Dhamon, but more worried about Palin, who was weaponless and too spent to cast another spell. She rushed toward the sorcerer.

In that instant, a howl cut through the clearing. Fury raced down the road and into the campsite, a mass of flying red fur that slammed into the knight attacking Palin. Palin grabbed up his son's staff, and the wolf fell to tearing out the throat of the fallen knight.

A few feet away, Dhamon drew his lips into a snarl and gripped the glaive tighter, swinging it in a tight arc to keep four knights at bay. One tried to leap past the weapon, but Dhamon kicked forward, his foot landing hard against the knight's mailed abdomen. The glowing blue edge of the glaive sang through the air as he raised the weapon and brought it down on the man's shoulder, slicing halfway into the knight's chest. The glaive came effortlessly free, and Dhamon swung at a second knight who had dared to inch closer. The edge cut through the man's sword and continued its deadly path, quickly dispatching him.

Dhamon faced only two knights now, and both gave him an increasingly respectful distance. They circled him, looking for an opening. They were constantly stymied as he continued to pace them and use his glaive to keep them at bay.

When the knight fighting Gilthanas risked a glance toward the others, the Qualinesti swept in, striking the knight's gloved hand with his cutlass. The long sword flew free, and the knight was forced to retreat a step. Gilthanas motioned with his head, nodding toward the trail that continued on the opposite side of the clearing. "I'd get out of here if I were you," he whispered.

The knight glanced at his subcommander.

"I won't offer again," the Qualinesti said.

The knight backed up another few steps, keeping a wary eye on Gilthanas. Then he spun on his heels and dashed away. Gilthanas saw Palin kneeling by his son. The Kagonesti was speaking to the Majeres, hovering over them, but her words were too soft for Gilthanas to hear.

The elf turned his attention to Dhamon. He had cleaved through another knight, and the remaining one had dropped his sword and was begging for mercy. The subcommander snarled "coward" at his man as he brushed by, extended his weapon, and offered a mock salute to Dhamon. "Barbarian, I will take you alive. Although you may lose a few limbs in the process."

"I'll not be bested by the likes of you," Dhamon returned, as he stepped forward to meet the man.

Gistere was nimble, despite his heavy mail, and he effortlessly dodged Dhamon's first several swings. He darted in close, inside the blade of the glaive, and thrust at Dhamon's already wounded leg. Gistere's sword managed to graze the leg, and swinging again and again he forced Dhamon to retreat.

"You're good," Dhamon observed, as he took a defensive stance, "but I have the better weapon."

"But I am the better weaponmaster," Gistere sneered. The subcommander sprang forward, leaping over the path of the glaive as Dhamon swung it too low. Gistere landed next to the man and raised his sword high, bringing it down, pommel first, on Dhamon's shoulder.

Dhamon fell to his knees. The blow was almost impossibly strong and was followed by another of equal force. The air rushed from Dhamon's lungs and he scuttled away, gripping his weapon. "No!" he shouted to Gilthanas, who was coming forward to help him. "This fight's mine."

Gistere smiled, stepping closer. The strength in his arms and legs were a gift from Malystryx. He hadn't yet worked up a sweat, though his opponent had. His body was soaked with sweat—wherever it wasn't soaked with blood. "It will be a short fight, I think," he said as he stroked down with his blade.

But Dhamon leapt to his feet at the last moment, spun his weapon, and brought the glaive's edge up. It cut through the subcommander's sword and continued toward the man's mailed chest. The glaive's keen edge parted the black links as if they were cloth, then struck the red breastplate beneath. It sank no deeper, but bounced off.

Gistere pushed off against the ground, vaulted over Dhamon and rushed toward the body of one of his men. There the subcommander snatched up a fallen sword, and turned just in time to see a flash of silver descend toward him.

Dhamon had spun as fast as the knight, wielding his weapon in the widest arc he could swing. Now the edge of the blade cut into Gistere's stomach, just below the red breastplate.

The subcommander's fingers released their grip on his sword and flew to his wound. Blood flowed over his hand, as he dropped to his knees. *You have failed me, Subcommander Rurak Gistere,* Malys hissed inside his head.

"Not yet!" he shouted. Then he felt a rush of dizziness, and his legs began to tremble. Gistere fell to his back, felt his throat filling with blood.

Dhamon was at the subcommander's side. He knelt, trying to listen to something the man was trying to say.

"My mail," Gistere breathed, "please, off." He coughed and blood ran over his lower lip. Dhamon pulled the man to a sitting position and tugged the shredded chain shirt free. Gleaming on his muscular chest was a red scale.

Gilthanas had come over, curious at what was transpiring. "What is this?" the elf asked, pointing at the scale.

Feril joined them, and her breath caught at the sight of Dhamon. He looked like an animal, practically naked, his hair a snarled mass. Singlehandedly he had slaughtered more than half of the knights. Fury, his muzzle dripping with blood, padded to her side and sniffed at Dhamon.

As the subcommander's lips moved, Dhamon bent closer, putting his ear next to the dying man's mouth. Gistere's fingers found the edges of the scale, dug in, and with the last bit of strength he could summon, he dug it loose.

Gistere screamed as he tore it free. His fingers burned like his chest had stung when Malystryx placed it on him. Dhamon cradled the man and stared at his chest, at the bloody indentation that remained, and at the scale he clutched.

"You can't hope to win," the subcommander gasped. He felt Malystryx's mind drift from his, and he suddenly felt very cold. He shivered and gazed into Dhamon's eyes. "You don't know what you're up against." A smile formed on his lips, and he slapped the scale against Dhamon's bare thigh. "Take it off, and die like me."

The scale instantly adhered to Dhamon's flesh, wrapping around his leg like a second skin and searing the former knight as if he'd been branded. Dhamon moaned as a jolt of heat shot from the scale and through his entire body, making his throat tight and dry. He fell back, releasing the knight and clawing at the dirt. The pain continued to race through him, waves of agony that surged in time with his heart. He writhed on the ground.

"What did you do?" Feril screamed at the subcommander. But her cries fell on deaf ears; the man was dead. She dropped to Dhamon's side and tried to help him, but she couldn't stop his contortions.

Fury paced around Dhamon, growling softly and keeping his distance. Palin nudged the wolf aside as he stepped closer, still supporting Ulin. "Dark sorcery to be sure," the elder Majere stated.

"We've got to take it off!" Feril shouted, grabbing at the scale.

"No!" Gilthanas warned, pulling the Kagonesti away. "The knight said Dhamon would die if he removed it. He might have been telling the truth. We don't know what kind of enchantment was involved."

"It's killing him! We've got to do something!"

"Wait," Palin told her, "watch." He readjusted his hold on his son, who was drifting in and out of consciousness.

Feril and the three men watched as Dhamon's contortions gradually subsided. He lay on his back, taking great gulps of air into his lungs. After several moments, his eyes met Feril's, and the Kagonesti helped him to stand.

"I'm all right," he said. In truth, he felt better than he had a few moments before, stronger somehow, though his leg tingled oddly.

"I don't understand," she said. "What did he do? The scale? And how did you get here? How did you get here—"

"Alive?" The tingling sensation had left him, and he could no longer feel the heat of the scale, though one glance confirmed that it was still there. "Feril, I—" She was in his arms instantly, tugging at his beard to bring his face down to hers.

"My survival is a very long story," he said between her kisses. "There'll be time for it later." He held her tighter, desperately, and their kisses deepened. "As for this scale, we must cut it out," he said when he finally came up for air.

"Ahem," Gilthanas politely coughed after a moment.

Dhamon and Feril slowly separated. His fingers drifted down to entwine with the Kagonesti's, and his eyes reluctantly left hers to take in Palin, Ulin, and Gilthanas. Curiously, the wolf continued to keep his distance, growling.

"It's obviously a dragon's scale," Palin said, pointing to Dhamon's leg. "I want to study it as soon as we get back to the ship. We're not going to take a chance on losing you a second time by cutting it out here."

Gilthanas retrieved the glaive and pressed the haft into Dhamon's free hand. "Quite an amazing weapon," the Qualinesti said.

"It's part of the long story." Dhamon looked at the elf for a long moment and then turned to Feril.

"Oh, this is Gilthanas," she said. "We found him in the desert." She kissed Dhamon again. "But all that can wait for later, too."

"Then let's be on our way," the Qualinesti said. "There might be more knights close by, and even with your remarkable weapon, we're not in fighting shape anymore."

Dhamon nodded. "Wherever *on our way* is," he said. "I . . . uh . . . have no idea where we are."

"However you managed to end up here, it is good to see you," Palin said. The sorcerer looked the former knight up and down and then nodded toward Ulin. "Dhamon, this is my son."

"Let me carry him," Dhamon said, passing the glaive to the sorcerer, and effortlessly scooping up Ulin. "Oh, he's not as heavy as he looks."

The group turned and headed back to Witdel, Feril leading the way with Dhamon at her side. Behind the entourage, the freed captives chattered animatedly about their rescue.

"Good thing Feril has nothing against humans," Gilthanas said, winking at Palin. "Otherwise she and Dhamon would never work out."

Chapter 15

Dividing to Conquer

They reached Witdel shortly before noon. Jasper barely
had time to register surprise at Dhamon's return before Ulin
was thrust at him. The dwarf quickly fell to tending the
younger Majere, while Usha and Palin hovered around trying
to help.

Rig acted pleased to see the former knight, but his expression didn't match his words, and his eyes wouldn't hold
Dhamon's gaze. Groller was another matter however. The
half-ogre warmly clapped him on the back, pointed curiously
at the scale, and then found some of the mariner's old clothes
for Dhamon to wear.

Blister chattered nonstop—about Khellendros's cave, the

prisoners, and anything else that popped into her head.

Dhamon thrust the kender's animated banter to the back of his head and watched Feril. The Kagonesti directed him to sit on a barrel, and she stood behind him as she set about cutting the tangles from his hair and shaving his uneven beard. Dhamon could have easily handled the tasks himself with the proper tools, but he enjoyed being fussed over. In the end, he looked far better than he had in a long while. His hair was short now—falling in one neat length that just brushed the back of his neck and the bottoms of his ears. Feril smiled apologetically and said there were just too many knots to do anything else with it.

"It'll grow back," he told her. "If I let it." Dhamon reached out to her, drawing her close, then scowling when Blister raised her voice so they could hear her better.

"Your hair looks good. Since it's all one length, it's more swingy," Blister said as she surveyed Feril's handiwork. "Well, it definitely looks better than it looked a few minutes ago. How come you're not dead?" It was a question she'd wanted to ask since she spotted him and the others heading toward the ship, but she'd restrained herself for what she considered a polite, but inordinately long time.

Dhamon offered a brief version of his rescue by Shimmer the bronze dragon. "The dragon gave me the glaive and agreed to send me someplace—a place not held by an overlord. I thought about you," he said, as he brushed a curl away from Feril's face. "And somehow the dragon transported me nearby."

"But not your clothes," the kender cut in. "Nice weapon, from what I hear, though. The spell probably only worked on flesh and metal."

"A part of me died when I thought you had died," Feril said. She cupped Dhamon's face and ran her fingers along his lips.

"I wonder if Palin knows the spell that got you here?" the

kender continued. "Say, Dhamon, how long were you with the Knights of Takhisis?"

Dhamon sighed and stared down at the kender. "Six years, nearly seven. I was young when they recruited me." He hoped the kender wouldn't press the matter, as he had no desire to talk anymore about it, and hoped she'd get distracted with another topic.

"What rank did you hold?"

"I was promoted to knight-officer before I left."

"And just why did you—"

"We'll be pushing off within the hour," Gilthanas announced as he stepped between Blister and Dhamon. "Feril's probably told you that we're in a hurry—a race to gain some ancient magic. You've got just enough time to run into town and buy yourself a few clothes." The elf extended a handful of steel pieces, which Rig had hesitantly surrendered a few minutes earlier. "I know Feril's not especially enamored of cities, but I bet she could help."

The Kagonesti happily tugged Dhamon toward the docks, and away from Blister's suggestions about colors, styles, and fabrics.

"Within the hour!" Gilthanas called after them. The Qualinesti turned his attention to the kender, who wanted to hear his version of the fight with the knights outside Witdel.

* * * * *

Later that night, when *Flint's Anvil* was again heading toward Southern Ergoth, Palin and Usha called a meeting. Sageth paced near them, consulting his tablet and speculating as to whether the ship or the dragon would reach the artifacts first.

"Ulin, Gilthanas, and Groller will be traveling to the Tomb of Huma to find the lance," Palin began.

"And he with the purest heart should carry it," Sageth

interrupted. "It will scald the soul and body of an evil man— burn the flesh, singe the bone, destroy the—"

"We're all good people here," Ulin said.

Palin nodded. "And we all understand the importance of what we're undertaking. While they search, the ship will continue to Ankatavaka near the Qualinesti lands. From there, Feril, Jasper, and I will . . ."

Blister waved her hand to get the sorcerer's attention. "Since Feril's from Southern Ergoth, why isn't she going to the tomb?"

The Kagonesti, who was clutching Dhamon's hand, leaned close to the kender. "My decision, Blister. It *is* my home. And because of that, I would be distracted, thinking about the land and the dragon, the wolves I left behind. Nothing must interfere with getting the lance. Beside that, I don't know where the tomb is. Gilthanas does."

Blister thought about it for a moment. "Good idea," she said finally.

Palin cleared his throat to get everyone's attention again. "In the Qualinesti forest, we will search for the scepter—the Fist of E'li. I know those lands well, and Feril knows forests. Hopefully we can find the tower that Sageth has spoken of, even though the land has been altered."

"An old tower," Sageth clucked, "older than me and standing straighter."

"Rig, Dhamon, Blister and Sageth will go to Schallsea to meet with Goldmoon and ask for her medallion." He looked at Dhamon. "Perhaps Goldmoon can do something about the scale."

The former knight turned to Feril. "I don't ever want to leave you again."

"This won't take long," she finished. "Then we'll have the rest of our lives together."

Rig rolled his eyes at the pair. "Anyway, that's only three artifacts," he said to Palin. "Where do we get the fourth?"

"Yes, must have four," Sageth said.

"I know where to find Dalamar's ring," Palin replied. "Obtaining it will not be difficult."

"Good, the land of the sea elves is too far away," the mariner said.

"I will reunite us all in the end," the sorcerer concluded. And may we be successful, he thought, before all the free lands of Krynn go away forever.

* * * * *

Palin slipped away from the others briefly that night, journeying hundreds of miles to the Tower of Wayreth.

The Shadow Sorcerer greeted him, telling him of the Peak of Malys—a lofty ridge ringed by volcanoes. Several glowed orange, and lines of vermillion ran down their sides, ribbons of steaming lava that in the scrying bowl looked like bright strands of thread sewn against dark fabric.

The Master of the Tower interrupted their discussion. "I have found nothing in your Uncle Raistlin's notes about dragon scales embedded in humans, nothing to even hint at how or why it might be done. Perhaps it has never been done before." He closed a thick tome and replaced it on the shelf. "In any event, I do not like the sound of it. Such a graft is evil magic to be certain and should be removed immediately."

"The knight said that would kill Dhamon."

"The scale itself might kill him, might be killing him now," the Master said. There was an edge to his soft voice. "You have a healer with you. Perhaps the dwarf can save your Dhamon Grimwulf after the scale is extracted."

"Do you want to take that chance?" The Shadow Sorcerer asked. "I would trust the knight's words, Majere. The scale was on him, and you said when he pried it off he died quickly. You are wise to wait and have Goldmoon attend to the matter. She is a much more accomplished healer than your dwarf."

Palin glanced at both of his robed associates. Their features obscured by their hoods, it was impossible to read their expressions or guess what they were thinking. "The scale seems to be doing him no harm at the moment. Perhaps there is time to wait until Goldmoon can look at it."

The Shadow Sorcerer bowed slightly to Palin. "She is the one who selected him as her champion. Let her deal with him."

Chapter 16

Across the Ice

Bundled in furs they'd purchased in the last port, they looked like bears walking on their hind legs. Groller was distinguishable because of his size, but from more than a few feet away it would have been impossible to tell Ulin and Gilthanas apart. Fury plodded through the snow several paces behind them, his whiskers and jaws sheathed in ice crystals, and his nose quivering, taking in the scents of the frigid place.

The Qualinesti's teeth chattered. "From the deserts of the Northern Wastes to the windswept barrens of Southern Ergoth in less than two months," he said aloud, knowing Ulin couldn't hear him through his muffled hood and over the whipping wind. "And it's noon here, the hottest part of the day. How will I endure the coldest?" He knew that the former homeland of the Kagonesti would be icy because the White had altered the climate, but he hadn't fathomed that the cold would be so intense. The cold seeped through the seams in his fur garments and stung his skin and eyes. His feet were likewise chilled—despite the leather and fur boots he wore.

The wind keened like a clan of maddened ghosts. The sound unnerved Gilthanas and Ulin. The Qualinesti looked over his shoulder and caught a glimpse of *Flint's Anvil*—the carrack's sails specks of white against a bay dotted with miniature icebergs. Then he turned back toward the frigid heart of Southern Ergoth and continued walking. Despite the snow cover he knew he could still find his way to the tomb.

In most places the snow was packed so hard that a glistening sheet of ice had formed over the top, a thick crust that was relatively easy to walk over—even though the heavy furs they wore were cumbersome and made the going slow. In other places the snow was loose and fluffy, and Gilthanas, who was in the lead, found himself floundering up to his waist, like a man caught in quicksand. Groller helped him up each time, careful not to get caught himself. Then Gilthanas would probe ahead with the dragonlance Rig had reluctantly loaned him, hoping to find the safest places to walk. Midway through the afternoon the sky became completely overcast, making everything look even bleaker and more foreboding.

"One month," the Qualinesti whispered. "It will take us one month to reach the tomb and find the lance." He glanced at Ulin. "Maybe just a little longer. Have you been away from your wife this long before?"

Ulin shook his head.

"I'm sure it's hard."

"I love her, and the children," Ulin said. "But love isn't enough. Something's missing in my life."

"And you expect to find it in a snowdrift?"

"I need to make a difference in this world, whether with my magic or my wits."

"There's too much of your great-uncle and your father in you."

The younger Majere would contact Palin if they, *when they*, Gilthanas corrected himself, attained their goal. Then his father would magically whisk them all out of here. Bringing someone home was a lot easier than sending them someplace he wasn't sure of. "You could end up in the middle of a glacier," Gilthanas remembered Palin saying.

Fury seemed to handle the climate much better. He strayed from the trio only occasionally, and that was when he smelled something particularly interesting. Ears laid back against the sides of his head, the wolf would creep forward, sniffing and stalking. Gilthanas, Ulin, and Groller slowed their pace to a crawl at those times, glancing about furtively.

Ulin had the feeling they were being watched, or followed, and he was certain that was why Fury seemed so wary. They could find no signs of tracks, but twice the younger Majere swore he saw a man-shaped thing standing on the drifts behind them. But by the time he got Groller and Gilthanas to look, the creature had vanished. There were no tracks to be found, and Fury could pick up no trace of a presence.

Nightfall found them sitting against a curving bank of snow that resembled a frozen wave. It provided shelter against the still-blowing wind. Ulin was still nagged by the memory of the shape he was certain he had seen, and worried that their position wasn't defensible enough. But they were too tired to search for a better spot, so they quickly settled in.

The cloud cover thinned and the stars poked through, reflecting off the snow and making the landscape breathtakingly beautiful. Gilthanas admired the view, all the while silently cursing the cold and keeping his eye trained on the horizon. Perhaps Ulin had spotted an ogre, Gilthanas speculated, or maybe a Kagonesti bundled in furs—a lone wild elf who hadn't left when the dragon took over and who didn't want to approach strangers.

Protected by the bank and shielded from the whistling wind, they could hear each other for the first time since they had set foot in Southern Ergoth. Ulin shook his head, saying that what he had seen was not like any creature he had ever looked upon before, and it certainly wasn't an elf bundled up. The manlike shape was large and bloated, but too far away to describe in any more detail.

Gilthanas leaned back against the hard-packed snow, closing his eyes. He had suggested leading this small expedition to Huma's Tomb, and his words had been persuasive enough to put him in charge. His own lanky elven legs were having trouble with the rigors of the trip. He set the lance against the drift behind him. "I hope we won't need this," he told Ulin. "Rig's been itching to use it against a dragon. Even though it was forged to slay them, I doubt it would do much against an overlord."

Ulin nodded and closed his eyes. He had decided to come to Southern Ergoth of his own accord. Though he admired his father greatly, the opportunity to be out from under Palin Majere's formidable shadow while doing something important on his own appealed to him. "I'm a grown man who'll always live in my father's shadow," he said to himself, "but not here."

The Qualinesti drew the furs tighter around himself and scooted closer to Ulin to gain some semblance of warmth. He tried to picture sand and sparkling waters, and tall oak trees in the spring—anything to keep his mind off this cold. But nothing worked.

* * * * *

One week later, they saw two of the manlike creatures, and this time they carried spears or staves. "And not friendly," the elf observed.

That day they also spotted boot tracks that led in the direction of the tomb. There were nine distinct sets of tracks, and none of them were large enough to be ogres or the bloated creatures that were stalking them.

"I don't like it," Gilthanas told Ulin that night. This time they'd found shelter in a small clearing in a grove of pine trees. "For a place as desolate as this, there shouldn't be any signs of company."

"But someone is here," Ulin said, "ahead of us and going in practically the same direction—a straight line to the Tomb of Huma. And those things behind us," he added as he munched on a strip of dried beef from his rations, "wonder what they are? I guessed they were hostile when I saw their spears, but so far they have stayed away. Perhaps it is they who are afraid of us."

Groller, oblivious to their words, stood and sniffed the wind. The half-ogre glanced nervously about, smelling something out of place—something that he couldn't identify. Yet the scent seemed familiar. Fish? The sea? He cocked his head to the side and headed away from his companions.

Fury growled, the hair standing in a frost-covered ridge along his back. The wolf crept forward, slinking between a pair of smaller pines. Groller threw off his hood so he could see better.

Suddenly, the wolf howled and jumped back from a deep drift. Groller saw a spear jab into the wolf's side. Reaching into the folds of his fur cloak, the half-ogre tugged free his belaying pin and churned forward, the snow spraying Ulin and Gilthanas who were behind him.

Erupting from a drift ahead of him, between a pair of tall

pines, were four creatures. They were man-shaped, but the moonlight filtering down through the branches softly illuminated their grotesque features so that the men could finally see them clearly.

They were taller than the half-ogre, each at least eight feet in height, blue-gray, with shoulders a yard or more wide. They were exceedingly muscular, despite the thick folds of blubber that hung about their waists. Appearing to be a cross between men and walruses, they had thick torsos from which sprouted humanlike arms that ended in stubby, webbed claws. Their walruslike heads were set on short, thick necks. Twin tusks nearly two feet long curved down from mouths filled with blunt teeth. Their eyes were small, shiny black and set atop rows of bristles that grew down to their upper lips. And the skins they wore were crude and poorly cured.

They jabbered something, deep and guttural. Groller only saw their mouths move, clouds of vapor steaming from them as the heat of their breath met the chill air. The half-ogre slammed his belaying pin against the chest of the nearest one, but so thick was the creature's hide, that the blow was virtually ineffectual, bouncing off.

"Get Groller away from the trees!" Ulin called to Gilthanas. The younger Majere crouched in the snow, mouthing the words to an enchantment he'd been discussing with his father, and keeping his eyes on the boughs of the pines. "If this worked against the Knights of Takhisis's ship, it'll work against pine trees!"

The half-ogre spotted the other three closing in on him, and he backed up a few steps until he was against the trunk of one of the thicker pines. The creature directly in front lunged forward with the spear, and Groller didn't sidestep the attack. Instead, his hands shot forward, dropping the belaying pin and closing about the haft. The half-ogre's muscles tensed, and he just barely managed to keep the spear tip from its target. Then he tugged upward, wrenching the spear away from the walrus-man. The other three closed, and Groller used the spear to parry their weapons, alternately defending himself with it, then striking out.

Fury howled behind him, then sprinted across the snow, launching himself against the weaponless creature in front of the half-ogre. The frenzied wolf began tearing at the walrus-man's folds of blubber. The creature flailed about, trying desperately to dislodge the animal. The wolf, though wounded, nimbly dodged the creature's tusks as it darted in closer. Blood soaked the snow, looking rosy beneath the pale moon.

"I can't get Groller's attention!" Gilthanas cried as he scooped up the dragonlance and started toward the half-ogre.

"Stay back!" Ulin called. "Can you shield him?" Ulin's hands were glowing faintly red and he was angling his fingers, thumbs touching and pointing toward the tree that Groller stood beneath.

The Qualinesti closed his eyes and shrugged the fur cloak off his shoulders. He felt the wind whip about his body, felt it as if it were a living thing, a lover caressing his skin. He beckoned to the wind, urged it closer, tugging the energy from each gust. The energy pulsed through him, not warming him, but giving him magical strength.

He tugged more, and his lips began to tremble from the cold. Gilthanas felt ice forming under his nose, though he continued to coax the energy. His fingers and toes grew numb. He felt himself shivering uncontrollably, but finally the wind was his to control, and he cupped his hand in front of his face, mimicking a shield.

"Finish, Ulin!" the Qualinesti shouted as he tried to hold his concentration. "I can't keep this up forever!"

As Gilthanas's words died, Ulin released his spell. Instantly the large pine Groller stood against turned into giant kindling. Its trunk and limbs were suddenly coated with brilliant red-orange tendrils of fire. Flaming needles fell from the branches and coated the creatures. None touched Groller, however, as the wind formed a dome around the surprised half-ogre, effectively insulating him from the magic.

The creatures, unaccustomed to the heat, writhed on the ground as more needles and bits of branches fell on them and caught their fur cloaks on fire. The air was filled with the scent of burning wood and flesh, and the stench from the dying creatures was overpowering. Groller watched in fascination and horror, glancing toward Fury. The wolf was just beyond the circle of destruction and continued to tear at the remaining walrus-man, whose struggles were becoming increasingly feeble.

"We've got to get out of here!" Gilthanas shouted above the wind as he picked up his cloak and wrapped it around himself. He hefted the lance over his shoulder. "That fire can be seen for miles!"

"The White," Ulin breathed, realizing he might have made a terrible mistake.

"Frost might notice it," Gilthanas replied, as he started from the clearing. "And if he sees us—unless I'm very, very lucky with this lance—we're dead."

All that was left of the large pine was a black silhouette that creaked in the wind. The fire had left almost as quickly as it had come, and Groller carefully edged away from the tree. Fury, his muzzle red with blood, followed. The trio stared at the wolf. The wound from the spear had healed in the passing of a few minutes.

"No time to wonder about that now!" Gilthanas shouted, pointing at the wolf. "Let's move!"

Groller and Fury took the lead, cutting toward the edge of a canyon. It stretched like a deep scar across the land, the moonlight hitting the edges of it and filtering down to the snow-covered floor far below.

They descended the terrain for hours, and dawn found them at the bottom of the canyon. They rested there, sleeping in shifts to keep watch for more of the creatures and ice bears.

They'd found tracks of the latter just before they started down the ridge, and at the bottom they had found nine additional sets of boot tracks.

Then they spent days wending their way through the canyon, which had the advantage of offering considerable protection from the wind. They could hear each other without shouting, and Gilthanas passed the time asking Ulin questions about his magical training. They diligently tried to follow the boot tracks, jumped at every unusual sound, and contemplated what was so extraordinary about Fury that had made him heal so easily.

A three-day blizzard slowed their progress to a crawl, completely covered the boot tracks they'd been following, and had them wondering if they would die before reaching their destination. But finally the blizzard broke, and the sun made a rare appearance.

"Three weeks. At least I think it's been that long," Ulin said as they neared the end of the canyon.

"Closer to four," Gilthanas returned.

"It seems like we've been here forever." The mouth of the canyon widened, opening onto a vast plain of ice. "You said a month right?"

"My best guess," the elf replied. "Decades ago, when this was all scrub, it would've taken me two or three weeks to traverse this ground. So I guessed a month given all the snow."

"I think you were being optimistic," Ulin said. "I wonder if my father has found the scepter yet. He'll probably be safe and sound with Goldmoon at the Citadel of Light long before we ever locate the tomb."

"And warm," Gilthanas added.

"I can't remember what warm is like."

"Don't worry. It's not much farther. A few more days from my recollection," the elf replied. "It's just past the plains." He shook his hands. His fingers were numb beneath his gloves, and he could barely feel his frozen toes. He and Ulin had taken turns complaining about the cold for the first week or so of the journey. Now the Qualinesti kept all the complaints to himself. He glanced down at the ground, and sucked in his breath. Just ahead, there were traces of crimson in the snow. Frozen, it was impossible to tell how fresh the blood was.

"Ize bear!" Groller hollered. The half-ogre spun and hurled the spear he'd appropriated from one of the walrus creatures. A large ice bear, easily a dozen feet tall, was poised to strike a little more than a dozen feet from them. Nothing but white fur against all that snow and ice, it had been difficult to see. Only its black eyes and nose had given the half-ogre an inkling. The spear sank into the bear's stomach, but the bear didn't move, and it didn't growl. It remained frozen and unblinking, with the spear protruding from it.

The wolf's hair stood in a ridge along his arched back. Fury hunkered low in the snow, his nostrils quivering and his tail straight out.

Groller stood puzzled as Ulin shuffled toward him. The younger Majere wished he would have paid more attention when the half-ogre was teaching the Kagonesti and the dwarf some of the hand signals he employed for words. Ulin tugged on the half-ogre's furry sleeve, then balled his gloved hands and vigorously shook them in front of his chest. It was the gesture for cold, frozen. Ulin pointed to the bear and repeated the gesture, trying to explain to Groller that somehow the bear had died frozen in that position. But the half-ogre shook his head.

"Dno," he said to Ulin. "Ooo-lin wrong 'bout bear." Groller sniffed the air and plodded toward the bear, pulling loose his spear and gazing beyond the unfortunate creature. Ulin and Gilthanas followed him, but Fury held his position, refusing to go any closer and growling all the louder.

"In the name of Paladine," Ulin whispered.

Groller brushed away some of the snow along the wall behind the frozen bear, revealing a thin sheet of ice that cracked quickly after the half-ogre pounded on it several times. Also revealed was the entrance to a massive cave. Inside were more frozen bears and dozens of seals. A whale, looking like it somehow had beached itself upon the cave floor far from the sea, was also there.

"Here, over here."

At first Ulin thought it was the wind whispering, but the sound repeated itself, with a little more volume this time. Glancing deeper into the massive chamber, Ulin spied nine figures—eight of them wearing the mailed armor of the Knights of Takhisis beneath their furry cloaks. The ninth, a young woman, was clad in the silver-plated armor of a Solamnic Knight of the Crown. Frost covered her exposed face and hands, but her eyes blinked.

"Here!" one of the Knights of Takhisis called.

Ulin and Groller rushed forward. Gilthanas stood at the cave entrance, swallowing hard. "Gellidus's larder," he whispered. "Ulin," the elf said a little louder, "If we're going to try to free anyone alive, we've got to do it quickly. We can't afford to stay here. Who knows when the dragon will get hungry and come back here looking for something to snack on?"

Ulin and Groller chipped frantically away at the ice. Only two of the eight Knights of Takhisis lived—and the young Solamnic, though just barely. The other Knights of Takhisis had been smothered by ice that covered their entire forms. Practically all of the other creatures in the larder were covered with ice, too, and in some cases the coating was an inch or more thick.

"The White," the first Knight of Takhisis to be freed said. He wobbled, unable to stand on his frozen legs. "He came upon us in the valley. I thought he meant to kill us all there."

"But he wanted to save you for later," Ulin surmised. The younger Majere helped the Solamnic Knight, while Gilthanas and Groller each supported one of the Knights of Takhisis as they hurried from the cave.

It wasn't until they were well away from the valley that they stopped and interrogated the knights.

"Fiona Quinti," the Solamnic introduced herself. She took off her helmet and a shock of curly red hair cascaded out. "I'm new to the order at Castle Eastwatch on the westward side of Southern Ergoth."

"You were headed to Huma's Tomb," Gilthanas said in a hushed voice. "What did you want there? And what were you doing in the company of Knights of Takhisis?"

"I was with four others, hunting for deer, when the Dark Queen's men came upon us. They slew my companions, kept me alive." She cast a sullen look at the Knights of Takhisis.

The younger of the two knights glowered at her. "We needed at least one alive," he hissed. "To carry the lance."

"For Khellendros," the older knight added. "We couldn't have safely touched it. She posed the least threat, was the easiest to handle."

"Are you going to kill us now?" the younger asked.

"I'd like to," Gilthanas replied. "But I suspect Ulin and Groller might object. They seem a little more kind-hearted than me." The elf looked at the ground, remembering his time spent as a prisoner of the Dark Knights. His brow furrowed, and he looked to the knights standing before him. He let his gaze drift from the knights to the sky above. He was still more than a little worried about the White Dragon.

"And if you had managed to get Huma's lance?" Ulin pressed.

"We were to deliver it to the dragon," the older knight quickly answered.

"And then?"

"We would have received other orders, been sent elsewhere."

"Are there more knights searching for other magic?"

The older knight shook his head. "I don't know. I was only privy to our unit's orders. I will not speculate on what the Storm Over Krynn desires."

Ulin turned his attention to the young woman and noticed that she had dark green eyes. She seemed so incredibly young. "There are other Solamnics at Eastwatch?"

"Yes, nearly two dozen of us," she answered. "We protect the elves and humans there. I'm certain my brethren are looking for me. My senior knight won't rest until she knows what has happened to me and the others."

"When we're finished here, we'll find a way to get you back home."

"My thanks, stranger," she replied.

Ulin introduced himself, Groller, and Gilthanas. Fury was quick to make friends with Fiona, settling next to her while they rested, then walking at her side when they resumed their trek toward the tomb.

Indeed, by the end of the following day even the Knights of Takhisis had agreed to join the quest, vowing to leave their Order. To return to the Blue empty-handed would be to invite death, and to return to their commander would invite nearly the same thing.

Ulin believed, however, that the knights accompanied them solely for the chance of finding the lance and salvaging their mission. He kept a prudent eye on them, and noted that Fiona was doing the same.

* * * * *

The heroes quietly passed by the stone ruins of a small keep as they entered Foghaven Vale. They slowed their pace as they descended a treacherous, snowy slope, and then the thick mist that hung over Foghaven Plain enveloped them.

"Stick together, and keep heading north," Gilthanas directed. "The tomb is somewhere straight ahead."

Ulin turned to cast a wary glance at the group of Knights of Takhisis. It was going to be hard to keep an eye on them in all of this fog. "How long is this going to take?" he asked, rushing over a few small snowdrifts in order to catch up with Gilthanas.

"About an hour," answered the elf, quickening his pace.

Meanwhile, Groller, who along with Fiona and Fury brought up the rear, seemed particularly troubled about having another of his senses hampered. He took slow, heavy steps, his feet often breaking through the snowdrifts to the ground below. "See," he asked Fiona repeatedly, "see?"

Fury darted in and out of the fog nervously, disappearing for a few moments, and then reappearing at Groller's side. The half-ogre, unable to hear the wolf approach, jumped a little each time Fury materialized out of the mist.

The group slowly made its way across the plain, pausing when it came to a bridge. Made of marble, the wide arch rose over bubbling water that gave off steam and coated the bridge with a sheen of ice.

"The fog is created when the hot springs on the right side of the valley and the cool lake on the left side run together," explained Gilthanas. "We're going to cross over their meeting point now. Of course, thanks to the White the fog is even thicker because both bodies of water now mingle with cold glacial air."

One by one, the adventurers crawled across the slippery span on all fours. They had all gathered together on the other side of the bridge when the fog slightly parted to the north.

"Look! Right up there!" cried Ulin. "It's the White!"
A great dragon emerged from the swirling mist, its massive, rock-solid body wrapped in undulating gray and white vapors.

The group quickly disbanded, some rushing forward to attack, others retreating to the bridge.

"Hold it! Hold it!" called Gilthanas, waving his hands and laughing. "That's only a statue! That's Dragon Mountain! It's not moving, see?" The giant carved visage disappeared behind a veil of fog.

Ulin relaxed his defensive stance and then sighed. "Anything else you forgot to warn us about?"

The group fell back into line, and Gilthanas trudged ahead, still chuckling to himself. He stopped suddenly, then straightened. "Now that you mention it . . ."

Directly ahead of them a dark figure rose out of the fog. It stood in their path—solid, glistening black and unmoving.

"This is a guardian," said the elf, gesturing to the dark form, "we are very near the tomb."

Groller pushed his way through the assembled adventurers and moved forward to regard the nine-foot-tall, obsidian statue closely. He turned to look back at Ulin, beckoning the young mage forward. The half-ogre repeatedly pointed to his own eyes and then to the guardian.

"It's a nice likeness of your father," said Gilthanas.

Ulin joined Groller in front of the statue. "Father? Why?"

"We see Palin Majere because we have only good intentions in coming here. Because we bring no evil to this place, we see this guardian as a friend, a loved one, and we can pass by it easily."

"*This* guardian?"

"There are more; carved pillars ring the entire tomb. But enough of likenesses, let's get to the real thing."

The group formed a line and began to move past, giving the large statue a wide berth. But it wasn't wide enough.

The Knights of Takhisis were overcome with fear, and could not pass by the pillar. They scrambled backward, colliding with Fiona and Fury.

The red wolf snapped at their heels, urging them forward. Fiona struggled to get them to cover their eyes but their hands inexorably slid away from their faces. They could not look away, could not stop staring in terrified fascination at the guardian. They could not move. It was as if they had become statues themselves.

In frustration, Groller finally tromped back to where they

stood. One at a time, he scooped them up and carried them past the pillar, their bodies rigid, their heads turning to continue staring at the statue as they moved by.

None of them noticed the figure flying overhead, the dragon whose immense form briefly darkened the snow beneath its sparkling white wings. The dragon craned its neck so it could better see the tiny figures below, then it started to circle.

The group assembled in front of the tomb. The small rectangular building sat upon an octagonal base against which snow had drifted. A great deal of the obsidian structure was covered in snow and ice, but sections of its smooth black exterior were visible where small avalanches had slid down its sides.

"There are stairs under here somewhere," said Gilthanas, gingerly climbing up the snow covered base of the building and toward its shiny, ice-encrusted brass doors. He reached the top of the platform, and a crack spread down the center of the icy doors. They swung open silently.

Gilthanas glanced back to smile at the band of adventurers, and then entered the tomb. Ulin stood transfixed, as did Groller, Fiona, and the Knights of Takhisis behind them. Fury sensed the warmth spilling outward and brushed by them, padding inside. Beyond the threshold he shook himself, snow flying onto the marble floor, and instantly melting into dozens of puddles. The wolf looked over his shoulder, and as if motioning for them to follow him, went deeper inside.

Inside, the walls of the tomb bore torches that burned but produced no smoke, their flickering, yellow glow playing along the black, shiny interior. The room was empty except for benches that lined the walls, an obsidian dais upon which rested an empty sarcophagus, and an altar at the far end of the tomb.

"Those were Huma's," said Gilthanas, gesturing to a sword and shield at the foot of the coffin. He was silent and still for a moment, then he quickly walked over to the stone altar. The others quietly joined him.

"The Order of the Sword . . . Crown . . . and Rose," said Fiona, pointing at the carvings in the altar's surface.

She quickly pulled her hand back, for fear of coming too close to touching the altar.

Gilthanas crouched on the floor. "Down here," he said.

Centered below the altar was a large, iron plate. Its surface was flush with the floor, so it could only be lifted by pulling up the iron ring in its center. Gilthanas tugged the plate free, and slid it to the side.

"After you," the elf said to Ulin.

The young mage warily looked down into the black hole. "Something else you forgot to mention?"

Gilthanas laughed, and pointed to the opening. "This is our route to Dragon Mountain. In order to get inside, we have to ride in this windpipe, which leads us underground and then, up into the interior of the mountain."

The elf gained Groller's attention, pointed at the half-ogre, and then pointed down the hole. Groller blinked slowly, then repeated the gestures, directing them back at Gilthanas. "Yes, me, too," said the elf, nodding.

"I'll be first," said Fiona, striding forward. She sat down on the smooth floor, slid herself over to the hole, and situated herself so she was perched on its edge, her lean legs dangling into the dark expanse. "I can feel the air moving, like a warm wind pulling me down."

Fury settled by her side, then jumped to his feet as she began to lower herself down into the hole. "There are hand-holds down here," came an echoing voice from inside the shaft. "I'll just climb—"

Her voice disappeared in a sudden gust of wind that made them all rush forward to the edge of the opening. "She's probably almost inside Dragon Mountain," said Gilthanas. "It's that fast."

Fury yapped, his long muzzle directed down the hole. His claws slid against the obsidian floor as he readied himself to jump, then hesitated and backed up a few inches. Groller moved behind the wolf, and stroked Fury's magnificent red coat of fur. The wolf suddenly sprang forward, silently disappearing into the darkness of the shaft.

One by one the remaining adventurers lowered themselves into the windpipe and were instantly whirled away on great columns and gusts of air to the interior of Dragon Mountain. They emerged in a brightly illuminated chamber, climbed a great curving staircase and discovered the Hall of Lances in the upper gallery.

Many of the lances were ornate, with handles of silver and gold that practically glowed. Some looked so very similar to Rig's lance that the elf suspected they were made by the same craftsman. Others were made of intricately carved wood while still others were plain—merely functional weapons that stood out among the others because they were so proudly unadorned. Not a speck of dust was on any of them.

"Which one was Huma's?" Ulin asked.

"I think that could take us a while to find out," Gilthanas answered. "Unless our friends here have some clue we're unaware of." The Qualinesti looked at the Knights of Takhisis. Neither offered a suggestion. "Fine. Then let's everyone relax. We've reached our destination, and I for one would like to be out of the cold for a while. And I'd like to catch some sleep." He walked several feet down the corridor, yawned for emphasis, and dropped his fur cloak on the floor. "Ah, here's a good spot." He quickly settled on it. "I don't intend to inspect any of these lances until I've inspected the inside of my eyelids for a few hours."

Fiona stood at the entrance of the hall, her eyes searching the rows of weapons fading into the distance. Ulin followed her glance, and swallowed hard. He put his furs on the floor, and arranged them into a makeshift bed. Finding Huma's among all of these was just about impossible, he thought. But he would do his best in trying. He took a deep breath, and relished the novelty of the warm air spreading over his face and hands. "Warm," Ulin said to himself. "I do remember what warm feels like."

Chapter 17

A Curious Malevolence

Curling wisps of steam drifted upward from the Red Dragon's cavernous nostrils, mingling with the heat from the volcanoes that ringed her plateau. Heat rose from the craters and from the rivulets of lava that ran down their sides. The air was oppressively hot, the way the dragon liked it, and tinged with the agreeable scent of sulfur. And the rocky ground she rested upon was seared and lifeless, the way she preferred it.

The Red Marauder, as those humans in her realm called her, spread her wings and stretched her neck, working out an uncomfortable kink while admiring her surroundings. She pointed her massive head down and opened her maw. Fire rushed out in a great gout of blinding red, the flames crackling. The flames raced to touch the farthest edges of her plateau, moving like a crashing wave of boiling crimson to flow over every crevice and rock.

The flames licked about Malys's claws and rose higher, and still the dragon continued to dispense fire. The blaze grew and flowed about her belly now, lapping against her scarlet scales, soothing her with its smothering, comforting heat. The great red dragon paused only to draw a breath of air before she again unleashed her brilliant flames.

This blessed heat, Malystryx purred to herself. It helped to placate her temper and ease the loss of one of her pawns. The Red had been watching through Rurak Gistere's eyes, and she had witnessed the destruction of the subcommander's unit. Malys was only mildly upset at losing Gistere, who had shown slightly more promise than the other Knights of Takhisis she had toyed with.

But more than Gistere, she had wanted the man who singlehandedly cut down half the knights in the woods in Khellendros's realm. She thought the man would make an even more suitable pawn. And when she had him, she would also have his magnificent weapon to study. Through her link with Subcommander Gistere, she had sensed the magic in the blade and wondered how a mortal came into the possession of such a deliciously deadly thing.

The Red knew that one of her consorts, Khellendros, was searching for ancient magic from the Age of Dreams—though the Blue was unaware she knew. Such magic was powerful, and Malys intended to snatch her share, to fuel her own dark schemes. The glaive the man had wielded was obviously a relic, one capable of parting armor as if it were cloth and easily slicing through the skin and bone underneath. Malystryx would have it—and she would get the man to bring it to her.

"It will be mine," she hissed.

Though Gistere had failed her in life, he had succeeded—at least partially—with his death. He'd grafted her scale onto the man and established a tenuous link with her that the new pawn seemed to know nothing about.

Malys looked through the man's eyes now, seeing polished wood beams several feet above him, a swinging wrought iron candle holder, and the top of a bookcase against a far wall. The man was laying on a bunk below the deck of a ship, his bed swaying with the motion of the waves. She had tried to peer through his eyes many times before, but without success. The link was far from perfect; still, with repeated efforts and great patience, she was certain she could make it work. Propped against the wall, at the edge of the man's vision, was the glaive, its sharp edge beckoning to her in the afternoon light that spilled in through the porthole.

"That weapon will be mine."

The man closed his eyes, and Malystryx saw darkness. She turned her attention inward, looking into the man's mind in an attempt to fathom his spirit. *What are you about?* she entreated. Resting, his mind was not so active, his defenses down. She slipped beyond them.

* * * * *

Dhamon Grimwulf tossed fitfully in his bunk, just as *Flint's Anvil* tossed on the frigid seas. In his dreams he wore his Knights of Takhisis mail and stood on a battlefield, fallen enemies all around him. He walked from the field, his feet passing directly through the bodies and floating over the pools of drying blood as if he were as insubstantial as a wraith. The blood couldn't touch him. Death couldn't reach him.

The Dhamon-wraith walked toward an old cabin, well tended and nestled against the side of the hill. He glided to the door, which somehow swung open for him, and he spotted a familiar figure inside, a tall, aging Solamnic Knight bent over a bed on which rested a young Knight of Takhisis. Dhamon realized he was staring at himself.

The man Dhamon knew as Sir Geoffrey Quick placed cool cloths on the young knight's head. He painstakingly gathered a mixture of herbs to make a poultice that he spread on strips of linen and applied to the deep wound in the young knight's abdomen. Rags dark with blood lay on the floor, staining the polished wood. The thin, quiet Solamnic paid them no heed.

The young Knight of Takhisis wanted to die, prayed not to be healed at the hands of his enemy, concentrated on the pain and beseeched it to take him beyond the man's control. But the Solamnic was stubborn and refused to give up. The wraith floated closer and watched the older man intently as he changed the bandage. Quick's long fingers worked deftly. Strands of his dark hair fell forward into his face, and he tucked them behind his ears. His large brown eyes scanned the bandage repeatedly and then he nodded, apparently satisfied with his work.

Sir Geoffrey Quick filled young Dhamon's mind with rousing tales of the Solamnic Order, of courage and sacrifice, and of noble deeds so unlike those committed by his Takhisis brethren. Most of all, he spoke of simple kindness.

Lies, Malys hissed. *The man speaks falsehoods. His words are deceptive.*

The Dhamon-wraith shook his insubstantial head, and the dragon's voice dropped to an unintelligible growl. At the same time, the younger man on the bed tried to ignore the Solamnic's words, and fought to recite the Blood Oath in his head over and over in order to block out the older knight's voice. But eventually he listened. And eventually he realized Quick spoke the truth.

Malys felt her link weakening.

The Dhamon-wraith watched his younger self leave the cottage and bury the black armor of his former Order beneath an old oak. The sword given to him by his previous commander was laid there, too. But his past could not be completely buried, his spirit still bore the scars of dozens of battles and he felt the lingering ties of friendship to his blue dragon partner.

The Solamnic gave him another weapon—the first sword the older knight had used in battle—to replace Dhamon's discarded sword. That precious sword, it was all Dhamon had with which to remember the Solamnic—Geoffrey Quick—who was later killed by Knights of Takhisis.

Dhamon hadn't been there that day, else he would have given his life defending the man. But he had heard of the man's fate, and despite his best attempts, he had not been able to discover who killed him.

The years melted, and now Dhamon stood on a peak south of Palanthas. The wraith watched an older version of himself fall into the lake, the precious sword slipping from his fingers even as he slid from Gale's blood-slick back. He watched himself struggle in the water, sensed himself being dragged under the surface by a massive bronze claw. Feril stopped searching for him along the shore, gave him up for dead, and he imagined her turning to the mariner for comfort.

Then suddenly the water in the lake disappeared, replaced by fire. Dhamon panicked at first, thrashing as he sank down into the flames, gasping for air, again trying to wake up.

Malys concentrated, and the link grew stronger.

Breathe, a voice hissed to him. *Breathe in the fire.* And suddenly he realized that the flames weren't burning him; he was no longer drowning. The fire was in fact soothing. Its fiery tendrils wrapped around his arms and legs, teasing his face and nuzzling his chest. The scale on Dhamon's leg pulsed, and sent waves of calm through his body. The scale quietly throbbed in rhythm with his heartbeat.

The Dhamon-wraith heard faint words. *The Peak. Come to me.*

"No." The wraith spoke. "Feril. I must stay with Feril."

The words closed the link between Dhamon and the Red. Malystryx snarled as again she saw the streams of lava winding their way down from the peaks of her precious volcanoes. The man's spirit was strong—stronger than Gistere's had been, stronger than her other pawns scattered throughout Ansalon.

She could try to impose her will again, she knew, but she didn't want to push him too much—not yet.

"No longer does someone from the Tower of Wayreth scry upon us, my queen." The speaker interrupted Malys's thoughts. A growl started in her throat, but she quickly suppressed it and looked admiringly at the creature that emerged from between two volcanoes. It walked through the lava and across the heated plateau without flinching.

"You have done well, spawn," Malys hissed.

The Red appreciatively eyed her firstborn. It stood little more than five feet tall, with rippling muscles covered by tiny red scales that glittered in the bright rays of the late afternoon sun. When the creature moved, its legs looked like twin columns of writhing flames. Its hands and feet bore impossibly sharp ruby-colored talons. And its tail, viciously barbed, undulated slowly about its ankles like a hypnotically swaying snake.

The creature's face was nearly human, but covered with a thick red hide dotted here and there with crimson scales. Its eyes were orange, the shade of glowing coals, and a rough ridge ran above them, lengthening into a spiky growth that started at the top of its shiny pate and continued to the base of its tail. The spawn's wings swept outward from its back, batlike and as dark as dried blood. They flapped slightly as the creature walked, giving it a buoyancy so that it almost floated toward Malys. The creature did not want its claws to mar its queen's throne room.

"You have something else for me to do, my queen?"

"The kender," Malystryx replied. "My informants in the

villages say they have found a hiding place within my realm. Find it."

"Yes, my queen." The spawn bowed deeply, paying proper homage to its creator and master, then it flapped its wings harder and rose from the plateau, disappearing in the steam that continued to curl upward from Malystryx's nostrils.

Chapter 18

Dreams

Ulin stretched out on his makeshift bed of furs in the Hall of Lances. It felt good to be out of the cumbersome clothing, and even better to be inside of a building. He was exhausted, but he was having trouble falling asleep.

"Who would've thought there'd be more than one?" he mused aloud as he stared up at the rows of lances—some obvious works of beauty, others simple and crude weapons. "How are we ever going to figure out which was Huma's? The oldest? The most ornate?"

He listened to the wind howling fiercely outside of the mountain. Inside it whistled through the hallway, flowing around the lances, muted, but eerily persistent.

In the space of a few heartbeats his companions had fallen asleep. Gilthanas, several feet away from him, slept with his arm protectively draped across Rig's dragonlance. Groller snored softly next to Fury. The red-haired wolf's legs jerked and his tail twitched, as if he were running in a dream. The two Knights of Takhisis also dozed. As a precaution, their legs and ankles had been bound together with belts.

Fiona Quinti, the young Knight of Solamnia, sat cross-legged, her back rigid against the wall, her eyes wide.

"Can't sleep?" Ulin whispered.

"I'm uneasy," she softly replied.

"We're safe in here," said a voice equally soft, but masculine and unfamiliar.

Ulin tossed off his furs, leaping to his feet and glancing around to see where the unexpected words came from. Around him, his companions still slept. He crept to Fiona's side and extended a hand to help her up.

"Show yourself!" Ulin exclaimed loud enough to rouse Gilthanas, the Knights of Takhisis, and Fury. Groller alone, oblivious to the commotion, continued to sleep.

"As you wish." The speaker stepped out of a narrow alcove flanked by silver lances. He was thin and small, seemed no older than twelve or thirteen, and he was dressed in a simple white tunic that hung to his knees. His legs were bare, as were his arms and feet.

Fury padded toward him, growling softly.

"What is a child doing here?" Gilthanas asked. The elf was alarmed, more so because of the wolf's unease, and he gripped Rig's lance tightly.

"Be careful. He's more than he seems, or else he is not alone," Ulin cautioned. "No child would be living here."

"I am not a child, though I favor this form. I have spent more years upon this earth than you. Would this make you more comfortable?" The youth shimmered, and in the blink of an eye he grew taller. His skin paled to the hue of parchment, hanging on him in wrinkles. Age spots were spattered across his bald head, and his narrow shoulders sagged forward. "Or perhaps this?" He grew taller still, squarely broad-shouldered now and darkly tanned. A thick mane of blond hair cascaded to his shoulders. The muscles in his arms bunched, and veins stood out on them like cords.

"Who . . . what are you?" Gilthanas pressed. "Explain yourself."

"I am the keeper of this place," the being answered as he resumed the form of the youthful innocent and glided closer to the sorcerers and the knights. He reached out a slender hand, stroking the wolf. Surprisingly, Fury stopped growling and wagged his tail. "It is you who have some explaining to do—else I'll turn you out into the cold."

The strange youth questioned them extensively about their quest and their desire to obtain Huma's lance. Yet he would answer none of their questions about himself, and only a few about the tomb and the land surrounding it. "Gellidus, or Frost as most men call him, knows I am here," was all he would say. "But the White cannot enter this sacred place, and so I am safe from him."

"You are a sorcerer or a faerie," Gilthanas stated.

"You may believe what you wish."

"Whatever you are, you'll not keep us from Huma's lance," the elf ventured.

"I'll not stop you," the youth returned. "Provided you can find it."

The Solamnic Knight cleared her throat. "Their purpose is just," she said, indicating Ulin and Gilthanas. "If you are just, you would help them, tell them which lance is the one they seek."

A faint smile crept across the young man's unblemished face. "I would help if I could. For unlike your two companions there," he gestured toward the Knights of Takhisis, "I sense great goodness in all of you. But I truthfully have no idea which lance Huma wielded."

* * * * *

Groller stirred, but didn't wake. The half-ogre was dreaming. In his dream he could hear, plainly, just as he had years ago before a green dragon destroyed his home, his family, and his life. He could hear the cries of the dying. The wailing of the wounded.

Why had he and a small handful of others been spared? he continued to ask himself. Why had he been left alive to hear the screams and to pray to the departed gods for the horrifying noises to stop?

All of the noises did stop that day for the half-ogre, and he had heard no sounds since. He had buried his wife and children and left the village, never to return.

Groller never knew whether a malicious god listening from afar had heard his plea for silence and made him deaf, or whether the atrocities he witnessed that day were responsible for his handicap. The cause didn't matter, only the unending, empty silence.

But he did hear things in his dreams. At first he thought it was the wind whistling, a sound he'd almost forgotten. The whistling grew deeper, then formed words. *Huma,* a distinct, musical voice said. *Lance.* The half-ogre saw the image of a man, statuesque and thick-chested. His armor gleamed, looking golden in the light of the torches.

These lances were used in the Chaos War, a disembodied voice said. The words didn't come from the image of the man in golden armor. Nor did they come from the dozens of wraithlike figures that suddenly materialized. The wraiths wore the armor of Knights of Takhisis and Knights of Solamnia. A few wore no armor at all, just simple tunics, and they carried translucent shields. Each seemed to be linked to a particular lance.

Wielded by Knights of Solamnia, these lances were, and by brave men who claimed allegiance to no knighthood but who fought for the glory of Ansalon, the voice continued. *Fought alongside the gods in the war against Chaos.*

How . . . how did the lances get here? Groller heard himself asking. He could hear himself speaking, and was able to correct his pronunciation. The words were plain and rich, not broken and nasal.

I called them, the voice replied. *Such weapons of honor deserve a final resting place, too.*

The images of the knights wavered, then disappeared.

Are you Huma? His spirit? Who are you?

I am what you seek.

Huma's lance? A weapon speaks to me?

I yearn to be wielded again—by one who reminds me of my former master. Come. I wait for you.

Groller listened intently, following the sound of the disembodied voice. In his dream, he was alone in the hall. Ulin, Gilthanas, Fury, the young Knight of Solamnia and the two Knights of Takhisis were gone.

The half-ogre eyed the lances surrounding him. Some of them whispered to him, recounting tales of the last battles they were used in, describing Chaos and the dragons, proclaiming the number of lives they claimed, mourning the loss of the men and women who once carried them. The hall stretched into the distance, and the torches burned brighter, their light casting long shadows on the floor. As he walked the hall, the floor sloped steeply downward. There were more lances along this hall—lances as far as his keen eyes could see. They were all whispering to him, but there was one talking louder than the rest, and he continued to pursue that voice.

After what seemed like hours the hallway leveled out and a circular room hove into view. It was lit by more torches that burned but did not smoke. The walls were made of glistening white marble. The floor was black with specks of white, looking as if a piece of the night sky had been cut away and installed here. In the center was a long rectangular block of green stone decorated with the image of a golden lance. A single piece of jade decorated the lance's handle.

Wield me again, the voice beckoned.

* * * * *

"If you don't know which lance was Huma's, and you're the keeper of this place, how will we ever find it?" Ulin asked.

The youth shrugged his shoulders. "You're a sorcerer, as is your companion here. Perhaps you've the means to—"

"Wait a minute," Ulin interrupted. "How could you know that?"

The youth smiled.

"My magic is limited," Ulin continued.

"I am not a sorcerer," the keeper said. "But I have the means to enhance your magic, great-nephew of Raistlin Majere. I have been looking for an opportunity to work with one with such skills as yourself."

"How? You won't even explain yourself or—"

Ulin was interrupted by the sound of footsteps on the staircase.

"For a very long time no one has come here," the youth sighed. "Tonight, it seems there is a convention."

Climbing the last step was a striking woman, with white-blonde hair that flowed out from a silver helmet, and startling blue eyes that sparkled in the torchlight. She was dressed in the shining plate armor of the Knights of Solamnia. Behind her came a half-dozen men, also Solamnic Knights.

"Lady Plata!" Fiona called. "See, Ulin, I told you someone would come looking for me!" The young Solamnic was quick to join her comrades and they formed a tight circle. The hall was instantly abuzz with their reports to each other, Fiona gesturing toward Ulin and pointing to the Knights of Takhisis.

Gilthanas stared at the group of Solamnics for a moment.

He placed his hand over his heart, and slowly walked up behind one of them. "Silvara?" he whispered.

Ulin cleared his throat loudly so as to gain everyone's attention. "What do you mean 'enhance' my magic?" he asked the youth.

"There is a bit of magic in my veins."

"You state the obvious."

"You can draw on that magic. I can show you how."

"We can find the lance that way?" Ulin dragged his fingers through his hair, then glanced over his shoulder at the Solamnics.

"We can try."

Gilthanas still stood behind the Solamnic. "By all the gods! Silvara?" The Qualinesti reached out to touch the knight's armored shoulder, and the woman quickly turned around.

"My name is Lady Arlena Plata now. I'm with the East-watch Solamnic Knights," she said, not making eye contact with Gilthanas. "My life is tied to the Order. I am happy and satisfied, and there is purpose to my life. Silvara is a name I used in the past. What we once had . . . is also in the past." Despite the coldness of her words, she allowed him to draw her away from the other knights.

"Forgive me, Silvara . . . Arlena," Gilthanas choked out. His voice was strained, and a sob caught in his throat. "I was confused decades ago. I should have met you here. I was so very wrong and foolish. I should have—"

"We came in search of Fiona," Lady Plata continued. "I was . . . worried about her. I didn't know . . . what had happened to her," she said, her voice breaking. She looked down at the floor and swallowed hard. "We determined that the Dark Queen's knights would bring her here. We'll take them along with us. Justice will be served."

"Silvara," Gilthanas was insistent, "I never thought I'd see you again. Somehow we've been given a second chance."

"Have we?" she asked, looking up. She made eye contact

with him for the first time. "It was you who decided there was no chance for us. I waited for you. I waited here for months, nearly a year."

"I didn't understand my own feelings."

"I loved you."

"I still love you," Gilthanas replied, his voice cracking, "more than life. Please, Silvara . . . you have to feel something for me. I've learned that love transcends everything—race, flesh. Although you now look human, I still *knew* it was you. We are connected."

For an instant the knight's face softened. She appeared to hesitate. "I don't know," she said.

"Please."

"Gilthanas," Ulin cut in. "I'm sorry to interrupt. But if we're not going to get any sleep tonight—except for Groller who is blissfully unaware of all this racket—we might as well look for the lance. The keeper thinks he can help."

Groller was about to get a rude awakening, however. Fury nudged the half-ogre with his wet nose. Groller was twitching, his big hands opening and closing, his brow furrowed. The wolf barked, licked Groller's face, and eventually resorted to pawing the half-ogre until his eyes fluttered open.

Groller groggily got to his feet. He looked back and forth between Ulin and Gilthanas, and his face registered surprise at the addition of the small band of Knights of Solamnia.

The sorcerer drew his lips into a thin line and brought his hand to his face, cupping it just above his eyes, as if he were shading them from the light so he could look for something. Then he pointed to the weapons and raised his index finger to signal the number one. He repeated the gestures for emphasis.

"Uma'z lanz," Groller said. "Ino where. Foddow me." The half-ogre walked down the hallway. Ulin, Gilthanas, and the keeper exchanged puzzled looks as they fell in step behind the half-ogre. The Knights of Solamnia were quick to join the procession. Fury walked at the half-ogre's side.

Groller took them to a niche made of green marble that housed a gold breastplate. He opened a panel that revealed a small room.

The keeper was visibly surprised. "Few know of this," he said.

Groller stepped inside, talking about specters of men and his brief vision of Huma in gold plate. "Uma's lanz zaid come. Wands to be uze."

He led them into the round chamber he'd seen in his dream and reverently circled the coffin-shaped block of green marble. He ran his hand across its surface, over the gold lance design. His index finger paused on the oval piece of jade. "Uma waz great man." Groller pressed on the stone and a part of the circular wall behind him slid away. The lance beyond hovered in the air, suspended by magic cast long before the Chaos War. It was an elegant weapon, a lance with a satin steel tip. The handle was polished brass with gold and silver relief—the images of dragons circling and fighting.

The keeper's mouth fell open. "Here, and I never knew it," he said, a hint of awe in his voice.

The half-ogre stepped forward, and reverently plucked the lance from its resting place. Then he returned to the coffin and again depressed the stone. The wall slid back.

Groller, oblivious to their words, led the way from the chamber back to the hall of lances. "And-vel now?" he asked Ulin.

The sorcerer shook his head. He held his hands out to his side, palms facing each other, and then slowly drew them together. It was the gesture for near . . . soon. Then he laid his head on his shoulder, closing his eyes. "Magic is difficult when I'm this exhausted," he said, hoping Groller would understand his message. "I won't be able to contact my father until I've slept a little."

"Ulin tard," the half-ogre said. "Rest. Go morrow?"

Ulin nodded, settling on his bed of furs. "It must be late," he said to the Solamnic knight. He was uncertain whether to call her Arlena or Silvara, so he avoided using any name. "You might as well stay with us and get some rest, too."

"We'll leave in the morning." She turned to the keeper. "Sunrise, do you mind if we pass the night here?"

So the keeper has a name, Ulin thought to himself as he drew one of the furs over him.

"You are always welcome here, my friend," the youth returned. "Ulin, we will talk later." He pivoted on his bare feet and disappeared into one of the alcoves.

"You know the keeper?" Gilthanas asked the knight.

"I know him very well."

"Is it possible we can learn to know each other again? Or is it truly too late? Has my past foolishness doomed us?"

She pursed her lips. "I don't know," she finally answered.

"Is there someone else in your life? Something between you and . . . Sunrise?"

Ulin didn't hear the woman's answer. Sleep claimed him.

* * * * *

The sorcerer suspected it was morning, judging by how rested he felt. He rose from his furs, began to descend the stairs, and immediately spotted Gilthanas and the Solamnic woman engrossed in a discussion. The men were just rising, and they were urging the Knights of Takhisis to their feet. Groller and Fury stood in the area where the windpipe had deposited them. The half-ogre was clutching Huma's lance.

Ulin cleared his head to concentrate on *Flint's Anvil* and his father. He pictured the elder Majere's face, reached out, and felt—nothing.

"Your magic will not work in here." The keeper had joined them. "The walls are so enchanted as to permit no mortal-cast spell to function within its confines. It keeps this place safe."

Ulin started putting on his furs. "Then we'll go back to the tomb and go outside."

"I would first like to talk with you about magic," the youth persisted.

"Well, some other visit, perhaps," Ulin returned. "We're in a hurry. There's a race for this ancient magic, and we need to take the lance to my father as quickly as possible."

The youth sighed. "I can help you, Ulin Majere, teach you things about magic you've never dreamed."

"And-vel now?" Groller asked Ulin, moving toward the open hole in the floor of Dragon Mountain.

The sorcerer nodded. "Coming, Gilthanas?" Ulin turned and asked.

The elf shook his head. "To the tomb? Yes. But to the *Anvil*? No, actually. I'm staying," he said. "I'll return with . . ." he paused. "Arlena. To Castle Eastwatch. We're going to see if we can patch things up a bit."

The room grew silent. "Well, then, let's get going," said Ulin, ushering everyone toward the shaft.

They each made it through the return trip in the windpipe safely and gathered by the tomb's doors, which again swung open without the slightest touch. Immediately snow began to blow inside the small room.

Ulin gestured, and the half-ogre plodded out through the snow, the wolf behind him, following in the trench he was creating.

"I'll tell the others of your decision. I doubt my father will be pleased. Rig's lance?" Ulin held out his hands, and Gilthanas handed it over.

"Tell Rig thanks for the loan," the elf said. "And tell him I was glad I didn't have to use it."

Ulin headed out into the frigid landscape. Behind him, the Solamnic Knights gathered their weapons and prisoners, and followed after. The keeper sadly shook his head, and joined the procession.

The magic came easier with his fatigue gone, and when the sorcerer again concentrated on the visage of Palin Majere, an image of his father's face appeared almost instantly in his mind. "We're ready, father," Ulin stated simply.

"Dragon!" one of the Solamnics cried, shattering Ulin's enchantment. "Frost!"

The sorcerer's gaze shot skyward as a great shadow passed over the snow.

"Gellidus," the keeper announced. "Everyone, back into the tomb!"

The dragon swooped closer. Stark white against the pale blue morning sky, he was at once terrifying and exquisite, his scales glimmering against the snow that swirled around him. The dragon streaked toward the ground, opening his maw and blasting forth an icy breath.

"No time to get inside!" Ulin shouted to the others. He held out the lance. It was unwieldy, and he wondered how Sturm Brightblade could have ever handled it with ease.

The keeper rushed past the Solamnics, who were drawing their weapons and spreading out. Barefoot, and seemingly mindless of the cold, he waved his spindly arms, trying to draw Frost's attention. "Here, creature of evil!" he called in a deepening voice.

Ulin stared at the strange youth, who had begun to change his form again. His skin sparkled, then turned golden and rough. Scales began to cover his body, and his hair melted away leaving a spiky ridge that ran across the top of his head and down his back. His face cracked and popped and extended into a snout; his arms and legs rippled and thickened and grew longer. Gold talons replaced his fingers, and small wings sprouted from his back. Gleaming gold barbels dripped from his lower jaws, and darker gold horns, like those of a ram, curled backward from atop his equine-shaped pate.

The gold dragon stretched more than a hundred feet from nose to serpentine tail. He opened his mouth, revealing an astounding number of iridescent teeth.

"Fight me, Gellidus!" the gold dragon bellowed. "I'm what you want—not these people!"

"Sunrise!" the Solamnic called. "You can't fight him alone!" She was racing through the snow toward him, her plate mail shimmering, her form shining.

The White plummeted toward the gold, opening its maw and expelling a cone-shaped blast of ice particles. The ice struck with the power of a hail storm, pushing Sunrise back into a snowdrift and practically burying him. But the young dragon was up in a flash, opening his own mouth and sending forth a deafening roar. The sheer force of the noise repelled Groller, who had been advancing with Huma's lance, and even Ulin and Gilthanas felt the sound waves and struggled to keep their footing.

The White Dragon's eyes grew wide in anger, as he pulled his wings into his sides and dropped to the ground. Landing, he sent a great deluge of snow in all directions, and the vibrations from his impact knocked Groller over backward.

The half-ogre struggled to his feet, grasped the lance more tightly, and slogged forward. Then his mouth fell open as he noticed Silvara, several paces ahead of him, launch into an extraordinary transformation.

The elf's armor flowed outward across her limbs until her skin was sparkling silver. Her hair also became silver, grew down her back and changed into a jagged, imposing ridge edged in pale blue. A tail grew and her arms elongated and spread to her sides. Wings sprouted from her underside. Her neck snaked forward and her head enlarged, the tips of her ears shooting up to become twin horns the color of burnished platinum. Silvara's mouth pushed outward until it was filled with sharp teeth, and her eyes became great oval pools of gleaming sapphire.

She was a most impressive silver dragon, more than double the size of Sunrise. She had immense wings that swept away from her sides. Her muscular legs pushed off from the ground and Silvara leapt into the air.

The sorcerer was in the midst of casting a spell. The magical lance tingled in his hands. He was drawing some of its power into himself, using it to channel his enchantment. Even as Ulin finished the last arcane phrase and pointed his finger at Frost's head, the White opened its maw, and the sorcerer felt an icy blast of wind and saw ice crystals speeding toward him. At the same time, a ball of fire raced from his fingertips toward the dragon. The ball of flame struck the ice missiles. Steam filled the air outside Huma's Tomb, and then the fireball struck its intended target and erupted inside the dragon's mouth.

The White Wyrm howled as the heat exploded inside him, and Groller darted in, angling Huma's lance upward.

Wield me! the lance cried inside Groller's head. *For such was I forged!*

So massive was the great dragon that the half-ogre could only hope to reach the tip of Frost's belly. The lance struck the white plates and easily passed through them into the soft flesh beneath. Cold dragon's blood rained down on the half-ogre. He withdrew the lance and stabbed upward again, eliciting another chill shower of red. A third time he tried, but the White was no longer within his reach. Gellidus was winging upward, away from the annoying little man who'd hurt him so terribly.

The silver dragon darted after Frost, lashing out with her claws. But the overlord was faster and larger, easily eluding her, and slamming his tail against her side as he dodged. He sent her catapulting through the sky.

"Silvara, no!" Gilthanas cried.

"We can't help her!" a Solamnic cried. "Our weapons are useless against Frost!"

The White Dragon searched the ground below for the spreading pool of his blood, the half-breed mortal, and the ancient lance. Malys had assured him that men could not stand up to dragons any longer, promised him that they posed no significant threat and could not challenge the overlords. But Malys was not here, facing gold and silver dragons who had allied themselves with a little man who wielded a weapon of power.

The dragons had hurt him, but the man had drawn blood. Gellidus had not felt such pain since the Dragon Purge, when he battled the good dragons who once lived in Southern Ergoth. He sensed the magical energy in the lance, felt the pain in his belly where it had pricked him, and he roared in anger. His ice-blue eyes glared at the small form of the half-ogre, and his mind reached out to the wind. *Colder, quicker, harder,* he urged it. The snow came in a driving, icy sheet now, nearly obliterating the sky. The White beat his wings faster, aiding the frigid wind and knocking the little man to his knees.

The hateful half-breed was now an easy target, Gellidus decided, as he opened his maw and breathed. But a streak of silver cut in front of him. Silvara had returned and took the brunt of his frosty attack. The extreme cold wracked her massive form, but she mastered the pain and managed to keep herself aloft. She flew past him, then banked around and dove toward him, claws outstretched.

"Sorcerer!" Sunrise hissed. "To me! We can work together." The gold dragon pulled himself from the deep bank as Ulin slogged through the snow toward him. With considerable effort the sorcerer climbed onto the dragon's back, sitting at the base of his neck and clasping Rig's lance.

"I've never used this before!" Ulin shouted over the wind. "And I'm crazy to be doing this," he added so softly the gold couldn't hear him. "Riding a dragon."

"The lance is for warriors, not wizards," Sunrise said as he pushed off from the ground. "But you'll not need it, Ulin Majere." His small wings beat furiously, propelling him toward the overlord as he opened his mouth and let loose another roar. Ulin flung his hands about, trying to find purchase, and he watched in horror as Rig's dragonlance fell from his grasp. His gloved fingers grabbed onto a scale, and he felt the sharp edge cut through the material and his skin beneath. He winced and tried to hold on.

Below, Gilthanas rushed for the falling lance. Fury raced at his side, nipping at the White Dragon's shadow along the ground.

Frost steeled himself against the sonic pain, and plunged toward the younger dragon, a malevolent grin splayed across his massive visage.

"Draw from me!" Sunrise called to Ulin. "Feel the magic in me. Use it! Hurry!"

The sorcerer began an incantation. The words tumbled from his lips, then were interrupted as Frost struck, and Gellidus's claws dug into Sunrise's side. Blood and gold scales fell to the snow and were lost in the blinding blizzard.

"Hurry!" Sunrise hissed, as he banked away from the white monster and closed again.

Ulin forced the words, feeling an energy grow beneath his fingers. The energy flowed into him, invigorating him. As the last word of the enchantment fell from his tongue, the wind gusted wildly outward and curled about the White's wings, folding them at odd angles. The overlord was tossed off balance. That was all the distraction Sunrise needed. The young gold closed, raking his claws against the White's belly. Then he bit down on the white overlord's neck. More blood spattered the ground, coloring the snow crimson.

Frost screamed, the mournful wail sounding like the howling wind. He unleashed another blast of his icy breath that struck Ulin. A wave of numbness spread from his heart to his limbs. He couldn't feel his legs or his fingers, couldn't feel the dragon's scale he'd been clinging to. Instead he felt himself falling, the wind rushing around his body as he toppled from the gold dragon's back.

Ulin plummeted, flailing and screaming as he fell nearly one hundred feet to the ground.

Above, the White Dragon pushed his front legs against the younger dragon, propelling the gold away.

At that instant, Silvara slammed into Frost's back, throwing Frost off balance and knocking him toward the ground, where Gilthanas and Groller waited with their lances.

Gilthanas hoisted his lance and stared up, squinting his eyes so he could see through the blowing snow. "Silvara!" he shouted.

Gellidus spun about in midair and unleashed his icy breath once more. It struck the charging silver dragon in the snout, icicles finding their way into her nostrils and mouth, and temporarily choking her.

"I give you this battle, Silvara!" Gellidus cried. "But only because you caught me off guard. I will return—rested and ready. Enjoy your sweet, brief victory. You'll not have another."

"You will not win!" Sunrise called, streaking toward the White. "We will find more of our kind, band together and fight you!"

"Foolish youth!" Frost threw back his head and laughed. He rose higher into the sky and beat his wings faster, stirring the wind into a frenzy. "It matters not how many of your kind you find!" he called above the noise. "You will lose in the end. Takhisis is returning!" He banked away, his laughter trailing after him and echoing off the nearby mountains. "Malystryx is bringing back the Dark Queen. And she will rule Krynn!"

The wind howled and the mountains shook, threatening to cause an avalanche.

"Takhisis!" Ulin breathed, as he clawed his way out of the snow. He was alive, miraculously, and sensation was already returning to his tortured limbs.

The gold dragon landed near him.

"I must hurry back to the ship, and tell my father," Ulin said. He stumbled toward Sunrise. "Takhisis. I heard the White say the Dark Queen will return."

"Back inside!" Silvara shouted. As she lowered to the ground, her form shifted again, and within a heartbeat she had resumed the appearance of the female Solamnic. "Hurry!"

Sunrise glided toward the tomb, his form shimmering and changing as he went. In a moment, he too was back in the form of the young man with shiny blond hair and bright green eyes.

Ulin took one last look into the sky, then motioned to Groller and Gilthanas, who were quick to enter the tomb. The Knights of Solamnia, herding their prisoners, followed. The rest of the group rushed inside the tomb, the brass doors swinging shut behind them.

"To reveal ourselves is to risk destruction by the overlords," Silvara said, gasping for breath. "And now that Gellidus knows I am in his land as well, he will try to take action. Maybe he didn't consider Sunrise much of a threat. But two dragons . . ." She turned and looked at Sunrise. "Fortunately, he cannot enter here, nor can he damage the powerful exterior of Huma's Tomb."

"Though he can choose to bury it with snow," Sunrise explained. "He does that often enough."

Silvara nodded. "There is something about the magic that was used to construct this place that keeps evil at bay. The tomb is stronger than even the White."

"But the Knights of Takhisis?" Gilthanas pointed to their bound prisoners. "They came in here, and they are evil."

"You *brought* them in here. They didn't enter of their own volition. Too, their evil is not so great as the White's. There must be a spark of good within their hearts."

Ulin tried to collect his thoughts; this news about Takhisis returning was amazing.

"Goldmoon believes the gods are merely away, watching mortals," he said. "She believes they will someday return. But Takhisis . . ." He sagged against the smooth wall, sliding to the floor. "If the Dark Queen comes back, all is lost."

"She *will* come back. It has been prophesied," said one of the Dark Knights, standing up a bit taller.

Sunrise shot a glare at the prisoner. "Palin Majere must be told of Frost's words," Sunrise said. "He can warn others, including the other sorcerers he knows. But it is not Ulin who must do the telling." The dragon-youth's eyes sparkled.

Ulin returned the dragon's gaze, remembering how he had called upon Sunrise's magical aura to power his spell. "Gilthanas, I'm staying here, too."

Chapter 19

Beryl's Forest

The dragon skimmed just above the lush canopy. Black as night, it stood out in the pale morning sky. The shadow dragon craned its featureless neck this way and that so it could better see through gaps in the branches. Not spotting what it was looking for, it reached out with its magical mind, searching for the lesser dragons in Beryl's forest. The Green Peril, the great overlord who claimed the Qualinesti lands, had minion green dragons living in her realm.

It growled softly, a noise sounding like the wind blowing through a crack in a window, and clenched and unclenched its jet-black claws. It had planned to slay a green dragon this day, though by now it would settle for a black. And so it had confined its search to the rich forest and swampland where those types of dragons were more likely to be found.

"Perhaps to the northeast," the shadow dragon growled, sounding like a gusting wind now. "A small black in Onysablet's swamp. Or to the . . ." The words hung in the air. Something had caught its attention. It opened its black eyes wide and peered at two humans, an elf, and a dwarf who were working their way through the dense undergrowth.

"Palin Majere," the shadow dragon observed. "And his wife, Usha." It followed them, hovering so close to the canopy that its claws touched the topmost branches, listening to the sorcerer and his friends' unnecessary banter and guessing at their purpose. "The elf. She has magic about her, too. Fascinating. And foolish. They have no clue they are being watched."

The dragon had the patience to watch and wait—until it picked up the scent of a more interesting quarry only a few miles away. Its midnight nostrils quivered, and its eyes narrowed. "A black," it breathed. It sniffed again. "A young one. Another time, Palin Majere."

The shadow dragon banked to the north and let its magical mind lead it to its prey.

* * * * *

There was too much green as far as the dwarf was concerned. So much green he could barely see the sky or the ground. Of course, there was considerable variety in the shades—light green, dark green, drab green that matched Usha's tunic and leggings, emerald green, olive green, green so dark it looked nearly black, and green so pale it looked practically white.

If the dwarf looked closely at the ground, between the swatches of thick grass and spreading ivy, he could also see dark brown—the mud left behind from the torrential rain that had washed over them just before dawn. They'd been put ashore a few days ago—when the sky was a brilliant blue and there were no hints of clouds. That quickly changed, however, and it had been raining every day since. The dampness made the green colors seem more vivid.

But if Jasper stared at the trees, he could see the lighter browns and grays of the trunks between the large patches of lime green moss and the thick veil of vines. There were bits of blue and purple here and there too, and splotches of red—flowers. But they were essentially beneath his notice next to all of the green. All that green made him sneeze and made his eyes water. "Gilthanas thought I'd slow them down in Southern Ergoth," he chuckled as he wiped his runny nose on his sleeve. "Oh, nuts." He felt his foot step on something soft, and at first he figured it was a patch of moss. But a quick glance revealed that in his effort to avoid a mud puddle, he'd just stepped into a moss-covered, rotting log. "Nuts. Nuts. Nuts." He struggled to yank his foot free.

"Jasper, what's wrong?" Usha asked.

"It's not the green," he muttered in answer. "It's this place. I should've gone with Gilthanas. How are he and Ulin gonna be able to talk to Groller anyway? Should've argued with them."

"Jasper?" It was Feril's voice. The Kagonesti and Palin had been walking a few yards ahead, discussing Dhamon and the problem of the scale on his leg. They had noticed the sudden silence—the absence of the dwarf's thrashing through the brush behind them.

"There was mud surrounding the log," Jasper said. "I was just trying to keep my boots clean."

Usha and the Kagonesti softly laughed. "There's no way Jasper will truly appreciate these surroundings," Feril told Palin's wife.

"I'm having a little trouble appreciating them myself,"

Usha softly returned, as she backed away from the struggling dwarf. "Maybe I *shouldn't* have insisted on coming along. I'm just tired of hearing about all of Palin's exploits secondhand. I like to be part of them myself every now and then."

Palin fell to freeing the dwarf. The rotting log was filled with mud, moss and insects. When the dwarf's foot finally came loose, he hopped about on the other and looked for a relatively dry spot of ground. He found one at the base of a massive oak. The dwarf tugged off the offending boot, and water and mud spilled out. A cloud of gnats instantly formed around him.

Palin was patient enough to wait, gazing at his wife while he did so. He hadn't protested too loudly when she said she had wanted to come along. He knew it might be dangerous, but Usha was right—no place on Krynn was truly safe anymore. He offered her a slight smile. Her eyes twinkled merrily. He thought she looked beautiful with all of the greenery around her.

"Didn't mean to slow things," the dwarf apologized. Until now he hadn't slowed them down much, despite his short legs. He tugged his dagger free and ran the blade around the inside of the boot to get out as much of the mud as possible. Next he loosened his sash and used it to dry out the inside. Afterward Jasper stuffed the muddy sash in his pocket.

Usha offered him a kind word here and there, while Palin swatted at a foglike swarm of mosquitoes that had augmented the gnats. The Kagonesti stepped a few feet away, and listened to the peaceful woods.

"I could live in this place oh so easily," she said.

"Bet Dhamon wouldn't like it," Jasper cut in. "Too many bugs." Satisfied with his cleaning effort, he thrust his foot inside the boot and grimaced. "Still a little wet," he mumbled. "Well, it could've been worse. Could've stuck both feet in."

Palin helped the dwarf to his feet. "Feril, decades ago this was a temperate forest, vastly different from this . . . jungle. I visited here then."

"Beryl has changed it," Feril said, frowning and glancing upward.

The largest trees stretched well more than a hundred feet into the air with trunks wider than a house, forming a dense canopy through which only the brightest light filtered down. Dozens of heady scents assailed her—rotting wood; the wet, rich earth; a profusion of wildflowers, most of them hidden behind giant fern leaves; the thick moss that spread across the ground and over stones and up the trunks of the trees. There were the scents of animals, too. The Kagonesti recognized fox, bear, raccoon, squirrel. There were other odors, musky ones she couldn't quite identify, and these intrigued her.

The elf thrust to the back of her mind the fact that the forest was a corruption of nature, an abomination, and an affront to the absent gods who once helped fashion this world. It was such a wondrous abomination. The Kagonesti needed to explore it for just a brief while. She'd been on *Flint's Anvil* for so long that it was almost as if she'd forgotten how exciting a forest was.

"I wish we had the time to explore Beryl's forest," she said, adding to herself that she wished Dhamon were here to explore it with her. "I'd like to discover what animals are responsible for some of these smells."

"To talk to this place," she mused aloud. The rustling leaves seemed to be talking to her. *Join us*, she imagined them saying. Perhaps if she and her companions were successful in obtaining the four artifacts, she would come back here and do just that—with Dhamon in tow. The Kagonesti hoped if the Green was eventually vanquished, the forest would not revert quickly to its original form. "This is so beautiful."

"Yes, it is," Usha agreed.

"And green," Jasper added.

Feril took the lead as she headed deeper into the tropical woods. Her eyes lit on a trillium, a three-leaved dark red flower that grew amid a patch of velvet ferns. The plant should have been ankle-high, the bloom about the size of her thumb, but this one reached nearly to her waist. She moved toward it and ran her fingers over its fist-sized, cone-shaped blossom. Its fragrance was intoxicating. She breathed in deeply.

"Nuts!" She heard wood snap behind her, and turned.

"Sorry," the dwarf offered as he tugged his foot loose from between two protruding roots. "Don't mean to insult your beautiful forest, Feril. It's hard to get around in here. Everything's so big."

"You wanted to come along," Palin reminded him.

"Only because Gilthanas didn't want me to go to Southern Ergoth. And only because I wasn't about to get left behind on the ship again. Look what I missed by not going into the desert with you—elephants and everything."

"You could have sailed to Schallsea with Dhamon and Rig," Usha reminded him.

Jasper caught up to the Kagonesti. "If you ask me, *you* should've stayed on the ship. Dhamon didn't look too happy to see you go."

Feril frowned. "I wasn't too happy about it either. But we'll have time together later. Besides, Goldmoon needs to do something about that scale."

The dwarf smiled. "If anyone can do something about it, it's Goldmoon. Let's pick up the pace; there's not much day-light left."

Feril smiled down at him. "There's lots of light left. Just not much of it is reaching down here."

"Night'll be real dark, then."

"Like a cave," Palin mused.

The dwarf sighed.

Monkeys chattered and leaped from branch to branch. Birds were in abundance, some screeching shrilly, others singing melodiously. There were plenty of parrots—tropical birds that normally wouldn't be found here. Lured by the warmth and dense vegetation, they were thriving. Throwing her head back and peering between the branches, Feril could see the orange and yellow feathers of the largest macaws. She pointed them out to Jasper, who seemed only politely interested. Usha, however, was enchanted by them and walked with her head tilted up. She watched them glide from branch to branch, while she held onto Palin's arm.

They had traveled for more than an hour when the noise abruptly stopped. Feril was the first to notice the unnatural silence. She stopped and concentrated on her other senses—her elven eyes peering into the foliage, her nostrils quivering, trying to pick up new scents—perhaps a large carnivore, something that might have scared the birds.

"Palin, look over here. There's some kind of net on the ground!" Jasper called.

"Don't touch it!" Feril called, as she darted forward. Palin and Usha were fast behind her. The Kagonesti reached the dwarf then felt herself yanked off her feet and rising into the air along with Palin, Usha, and Jasper. The net shot high into the trees, biting into their skin. Thorny branches scraped them, tearing their clothes and striping them with welts.

When it came to a stop, the net dangled more than twenty feet above the forest floor, swaying and causing the branches that held it to groan in protest.

"I didn't touch it!" Jasper shouted. He looked down and then slammed his mouth shut, fighting the sensation of his stomach rising into his throat.

Feril also looked down at the ground, then at her companions. Usha was holding tight to the net, her knuckles white. Palin was trying to move his legs. The sorcerer had a dagger he'd been carrying since the Northern Wastes. Jasper had one too, and a hammer strapped to his belt. Between the two of them, maybe they could cut their way free, swing the net toward a tree first, snare a branch and climb down. Something moved below, skulking from bush to bush, before finally stepping out into the clearing. Feril tugged on Palin's sleeve, and pointed to the solitary Qualinesti gazing up at them.

The elf wore a long green dress that nearly matched the shade of the velvet ferns. Her hair was short, the color of honey, and her bright blue eyes peered up at them with curiosity. "Spies of the dragon," she pronounced after looking them over. "You are dead."

More than a dozen elves rushed out of the foliage to join her, several of them with bows trained up at the net, arrows nocked. She raised her hand, signaling them.

"Wait!" Palin shouted. He pressed his face through a gap in the net. "We're no spies! We work *against* the dragons— not for them. I'm Palin Majere and—"

"Majere?" The word rolled off her tongue. "One of the few survivors from the battle with Chaos?"

"Yes, I fought in the Abyss!" Palin returned. "I'm still fighting!"

"*If* we let you live, you'll still fight." The woman stood directly beneath the net now. "Apparently the most famous sorcerer on Krynn is tangled up in our net," she said, looking over at the other elves. She turned to look back up at Palin. "Apparently you must think us complete fools!"

"No, he really is Palin Majere," said Feril.

The woman glared up at her. "Kagonesti," she said loudly. "Fled from Southern Ergoth. Perhaps you spy for the White?"

"We will not harm you," Palin said calmly.

"Oh, I know that. After all, you and your sorcerer friends

from the Tower did save our race from the Green Peril. And you still help some Qualinesti escape to safety, when you're not hanging around in nets, that is." The elven woman burst into laughter, her companions joining her.

"You? Stand up to the Green Peril?" one of the archers asked Feril. Those beside him chuckled, their soft laughter sounding like leaves rustling in the breeze.

"We oppose Beryl, too—and the White in Southern Ergoth," Feril added. She turned her head and whispered to Palin, "The resistance is made up of scattered groups of Qualinesti linked by a network throughout the forest. I've heard they monitor the dragon and strike with military precision against her minions."

"We're trying to stand up to all the overlords," Usha called.

"And just how do you expect to fight the great dragons?" The woman's tone was heavy with skepticism. "Four against the dragons."

"There's more of us," Jasper finally spoke.

The elven woman whispered an order to one of the archers. He lowered his bow and slipped into the dense undergrowth.

"Not here!" the dwarf called. "In Southern Ergoth and Schallsea. Oh, what's the use? You're not listening."

"What measure of trust do you offer us?" she returned. "What proof is there of what you claim? Speak quickly, or my men will loose their arrows."

"This trust," Palin answered. The sorcerer took a deep breath and told her the truth about their search for the artifacts and their hope to restore magic to Krynn. "We were heading to the old stronghold, the old tower," he concluded. "One such artifact, a wooden scepter known as the Fist of E'li, is said to rest there."

"A tale, and a good one," the elven woman said. "And if it is true, you are on a fool's errand. Only death awaits you in that place. It is a crumbling tower that even our greatest warriors avoid. What matter if we kill you, or if you die there?"

She again nodded to the archers, who raised their bows.

"No!" Usha cried. "Why won't you believe us?"

"We believe in ourselves."

"You are right to be wary of strangers, and I will ask for no special treatment," said Palin.

"Keep me here with you. I am Palin's wife. I was in the Abyss. I watched the dragons die, too. Let me be the guarantee that he told you the truth. Let him go to the stronghold and try to find what he's looking for."

The Qualinesti leaned her head to the side. "Whoever you are, you are brave." She pursed her thin lips, running a slender finger across her chin. "But is your offer sufficient?" She closed her eyes and her brow furrowed, as if she was considering the matter.

"Don't do this," Palin urgently whispered to his wife. "My magic . . ."

"You'd rather us all die by their arrows?" Usha said softly. "Are your spells quicker than those archers?"

"We accept your offer," the elf finally answered, taking note of Palin's admirable concern. "Sorcerer—it is a long walk to the stronghold—for those who move awkwardly through the woods. Three weeks we will give you for your fool's errand. If you have not returned to this clearing at the end of that time with proof that all you seek to take from this land is the scepter, we will know that you failed, or that you lied to us and are indeed spies. Your woman's life will be forfeit. And, if you still live, we will track you down and finish this job."

The elf motioned to the archers. They lowered their bows and backed into the foliage. Within a heartbeat, she had disappeared amidst the leaves, too.

The net jerked violently, then plummeted like a rock.

With no room to maneuver in their hemp cocoon, the quartet couldn't brace for the landing. The ground rushed up to meet them, and they hit with bone-jarring impact. Feril crumpled on her shoulder, her arm pinned beneath her, and Usha on top of her. Palin landed partly on his stomach and partly on Jasper.

The sorcerer unsheathed his dagger, and began cutting at the net. Several moments later, they were free. They gingerly moved their limbs to make sure nothing was broken.

Palin held his wife close. "I should stay, not you."

"I'll be all right. Don't worry. You're the only one who's been to the tower before."

"That was years ago, when I was helping Gilthas try to find Beryl's lair. The place has changed so much. If only I could visualize it enough to summon us there . . ."

"Really, I'll be all right. Just don't dawdle."

He stared into her golden eyes, as he'd stared into them years ago before he had ventured into the Abyss during the Chaos War.

"There's no sign of them," Jasper said. He looked about on the ground, seeing no footprints and noting that the trampled grass was already beginning to spring back up.

"They're here, watching us," Feril said.

Palin cupped Usha's chin with his trembling hand, kissed her, and took a last lingering look into her eyes. "We'll be back in time," he promised.

"Then let's move," the dwarf said. He looked about, an uneasy expression on his wide face. He couldn't see the Qualinesti, but he knew Feril was right. A prickling feeling on the back of his neck told him they were being watched. His tunic was muddy and grass-stained, his face striped with red where the net had pressed against it. And his companions looked equally disheveled.

Palin pointed to the east. "This way."

A week later they found the stronghold—barely. They had passed by the area twice, and only Palin's insistence that it was somewhere nearby kept them from moving on and looking elsewhere.

The tower was wedged into a crevice in a moss-draped, rocky hillside. It was as if the forest and the land were trying to swallow the structure, not wanting a work of man to mar this place's primitive beauty. What little bits of stone were visible were tinted green with moss and looked as if they were part of the hill. Thick patches of well-established ferns grew all around it, and a riot of vines stretched from the base of the tower to its crenelated top more than fifty feet above the forest loam. More vines grew from the top of the hill to the bottom, practically blanketing the structure.

Spider monkeys cavorted up and down the vines, and dozens of the orange and yellow parrots had made nests within niches. Several thick vines had pulled away from the top of the tower, as if something too large, like an ape or gorilla, had tried to use them for climbing. A shadowy recess covered by a draping of ivy strands marked the doorway at the base.

Feril and Palin stared at the structure, while Jasper struggled through the bushes that barred easy access. "You two coming?" The dwarf pulled at a stubborn, broad leafed plant, not noticing the Kagonesti hesitate.

The wooden door, warped from moisture and age, stood slightly ajar.

"Someone's been here," Feril whispered.

"Maybe the elven resistance," Palin speculated. "Maybe the woman lied about her men avoiding this place."

"Or maybe the dragon's been here," Jasper wondered aloud.

Palin took a deep breath, parted the leafy curtain, and

tugged on the rusted latch.

The old door swung open with a gentle groan, revealing shadows and blackness. A pair of glowing yellow eyes peered out from the darkness beyond.

Chapter 20

Toward Schallsea

"Thinking about her, aren't you?" Blister stood at the ship's railing, looked up at Dhamon, and repeated the question more loudly. She gave him a pouty face when she received no reply. "Well, I'd certainly be thinking about her if I were you. She's beautiful and smart, can talk to all sorts of animals. She has tattoos, and she obviously is in love with you. I'd be thinking a lot about her, especially after the past few days."

He finally nodded. "Yes, I am thinking about her." He was staring at the coast of Abanasinia, at a city called Zaradene that they were swiftly approaching. Rig planned to stop there for the better part of the day to have the mizzen sail replaced and to pick up some fresh water and fruit before heading on to the Silver Stair on Schallsea.

The mariner slowly steered the ship toward one of the deep-water docks. It was a sizeable town that obviously relied heavily on sea trade. The docks were nearly full of ships—two- and three-masted schooners primarily, and several caravels. It took big ships to brave the treacherous waters between Southern Ergoth and Abanasinia. A couple of massive merchant galleys were anchored out in the harbor, their longboats in the process of transporting some of the crews ashore.

The smaller docks were filled with local fishing vessels that ran the gamut from large boats in good repair, newly painted and with several hands on board, to scows with warped wood that seemed to barely stay afloat.

The shore was busy this late afternoon. Fishermen sold their wares to all manner of customers, from men and women picking out a fish or two that would be their evening's main course, to inn owners buying barrels full of them. Young women in multicolored dresses danced, entertaining the sailors for a few coins. And the street was thick with urchins looking for handouts from sympathetic travelers and keeping an eye out for bulging purses that could be easily snatched.

This would be a fair place to live, Dhamon thought to himself. Perhaps he and Feril could find a measure of happiness in a cozy stone cottage in a town like this, he mused—after they made their stand against the dragons. And if they lived through such foolhardiness.

Spaced evenly along the city's shore and along its southeastern boundary were numerous towers, atop which stood men with spyglasses pressed to their eyes. Some scanned across the water to Southern Ergoth, Frost's realm. Others looked to the far south where Beryl held sway. So far the White had stayed put on his icy domain, and Beryl's forest hadn't grown any farther north in the past decade, hinting that the Green was content to lord over the Qualinesti home-land.

Rig said he'd heard from sailors in the last port that seers here were constantly asked to consult their bones and tea leaves in an effort to learn what the dragons were doing, and that occasionally patrols were sent to Ankatavaka and the forest beyond to learn what the Green was up to. The patrols never went too deep into the forest—at least not the ones that were lucky enough to come back.

Zaradene's waterfront businesses looked like they were thriving. Most were one- and two-level stone buildings with gaily painted trim and placards advertising the specials of the day. A few were made of wood with thatched roofs, and these appeared to be of newer construction. One sizeable wood building, painted light brown with ivory and pale blue trim, had a large glass window. It caught Dhamon's eye. He squinted to make out a few dresses on display.

"I bet you're thinking they'd look pretty on Feril," Blister said, following Dhamon's gaze. "But I don't think she likes long skirts. I could help you pick something out for her. She seems to favor green. Maybe she'd wear a dress if it was green and—"

"I don't have enough steel left," he replied. He'd spent most of the coins the mariner gave him on clothes and boots for himself.

"Well, I've a few coins, and an old friend's collection of silver spoons," she offered. "We could guess at her size and . . ."

He shook his head.

"So you're not going into town with me and Rig?"

"Not this time."

"That's 'cause you're worried about her, I bet." Blister fussed with her braid. She had on a pair of pale blue gloves this morning that matched her shirt and the trim on her dark blue leggings. She was wearing the gloves because she was going into town and didn't want strangers staring at her scarred hands. The kender hadn't been wearing any on the ship, and had explained to everyone at least three times that a vision of Goldmoon made her realize she could move her fingers without pain. "I guess I'd worry too if I was in love with—"

"No reason to worry. Feril can take care of herself." The voice was Rig Mer-Krel's. He'd turned the wheel over to one of his mates and had moved silently up behind the pair. He laughed and patted the top of Blister's head. His eyes narrowed when he looked at Dhamon. "Feril will probably end up taking care of Palin and Usha—and Jasper, too."

The kender smiled. "You never worry about anything, Rig."

"That's not true," he said. The ship eased up to the dock, and he frowned when the hull scraped softly against a piling. "I worry about the *Anvil*. And I worry about the dragonlance. Dhamon said I could keep it for now, and I went and loaned it to that elf. Gilthanas better bring it back to me—without a scratch on it."

* * * * *

While Blister and Rig busied themselves in port, Dhamon turned his attention to Sageth. Sitting by the capstan and earnestly consulting his tablet, the old man clucked to himself.

"I've decided," he said when he finally acknowledged Dhamon's presence.

"Decided what?" Dhamon knelt next to him and tried to make some sense of the scratchings on the clay.

The old man rubbed his bald head and seemed lost in thought for a moment. Then he drummed a finger in the center of the tablet. "See, it's very clear," he said. "The ancient magic. The best time to destroy the items would be at night—with the one moon in full view, low on the horizon. And in a barren place. The earth could well shake as the deed is done. Don't want people to get hurt. Or buildings."

Dhamon followed the man's finger across the scratches. He could read well enough, but not whatever language was on the clay. "Why at night? Why does it make a difference?"

"It might not," the old man tsk-tsked. "But then again it might. Don't you understand? It's probably not the night, it's probably the moon. It was left by the gods—in place of the three we used to have, Lunitari, Nuitari, and Solinari. So there is a bit of god magic in the single moon, as there is still a bit of god magic in Krynn. But until the ancient artifacts are destroyed and their magic released, well . . . perhaps even the three moons will return. Oh, to bring such magic back to Ansalon." Sageth pursed his lips, staring into Dhamon's eyes. "I know you don't understand all this magic prattle. Most warriors don't. But your elf lady does. She knows magic. She knows it's important."

"I know it's important," Dhamon replied testily. "With more magic, the sorcerers would have a better chance against the overlords." He rubbed his leg, feeling the hardness of the scale beneath his pants and shivering involuntarily.

"So it's all up to your friends," Sageth continued. "I certainly hope they're successful, and can gain the pieces before the dragons can. Now, this medallion we seek, on Schallsea?"

"Goldmoon's."

"Yes. Well, it won't be enough. Must have four, I think. Four should do it. See my notes here? Three might do it, might. But four to be certain. We must be certain because there might not be time for a second attempt."

"My friends will be successful," Dhamon said. "Or they will die trying."

Chapter 21

General Urek

The yellow eyes blinked, then separated from the darkness, edging toward the faint light spilling in through the doorway and revealing the tower's occupant. An Aurak, one of the rarest and most powerful of the draconians, stood before Palin. The creature was gold, though in the scant light he looked more ochre. He was wingless and had a pronounced, lizardlike snout filled with an abundance of pointed teeth. His taloned hands flexed slowly, and the claws of his feet clicked harshly against the stone floor. Tiny scales covered every inch of him, including his stubby tail, which undulated slowly. Palin guessed the Aurak must be nearly eight feet tall, remarkably large and powerful for a draconian.

The creature's muscles were thick, its chest broad.

The Aurak extended a scaly arm and crooked a long talon at the sorcerer, as if beckoning him.

"I'm not going in there," Jasper announced, peeking from behind Palin's leg. The dwarf glanced over his shoulder at the Kagonesti as he contemplated a route of escape.

"Draconians are creatures of evil," Feril said in a hushed voice. "I think we should—"

"Enter, of course, since we've been invited." The sorcerer glided inside, leaving the door open so Jasper and Feril could follow. "What we're looking for is somewhere in here. And we have to get it, or Usha is lost."

The dwarf offered a silent prayer to Reorx, a god favored by dwarves who was long-since absent from Krynn. Then he followed after Palin. Feril was the last to step beyond the doorway.

Inside, where the heady scents of the plants and the earth were subdued, another smell assaulted the trio. The odor of death and the coppery scent of blood hung heavy in the air, even overpowering the musty dampness of the stone and rotting wood. The dwarf's hair stood up along the back of his neck, and his stubby fingers drifted to the haft of the warhammer hooked in his belt. Feril's fingers rested on her bag, and the Kagonesti mentally went over the items inside— clay, arrowheads, stones, things she could focus her magic on to use against the scaly creature.

The door boomed shut behind them, and torches were instantly lit. Fat-soaked, they sputtered, but provided enough light so that the trio could inspect their surroundings. They stood in a large room that occupied the entire first floor of the tower. At one time there had been wooden walls to divide the space, but they had long since rotted away, their remnants in moldy shards on the floor. A curving stone staircase wound up the wall and disappeared into darkness overhead. There were broad scorch marks on the stone floor and along the walls, as if several magical bursts of fire had been released—or a few draconians had exploded there.

Suddenly more than a dozen draconians surrounded the trio, stepping away from the wall and revealing themselves as Kapaks, cunning creatures who were typically employed as assassins. Copper-hued muscles bulged and rippled, shimmering like polished coins in the torchlight. Their wings flapped slowly, and their green eyes were riveted on Palin.

The sorcerer took a step toward the Aurak and opened his mouth to speak, but the draconian, who sparkled darkly in the torchlight, held up a clawed hand to silence him.

"You are not allies of the Green Dragon, elssse the elves would have ssslain you." The Aurak had a deep, resonant voice, and sounded like a giant, hissing snake. "But you are not friends of the elves either, elssse they would not have captured you, and they would not be keeping one of your allies for insurance."

"These people are not our friends!" one of the Kapaks shouted. His scratchy voice echoed eerily off the damp walls. The Kapak clenched and released his fists. "Humans and elves are not our friends. We should eat them."

Jasper bristled at being overlooked, but decided to stay silent. He glanced around the spacious room. Three against thirteen, he thought. With Palin's and Feril's magic, that shouldn't be too unfair. Killing these foul things would be the only way to get the Fist of E'li, and would probably benefit Ansalon. Thirteen fewer draconians would be a good start.

He felt a pang of guilt at having such bloodthirsty thoughts. Goldmoon had taught him to love peace. His grip loosened around the hammer haft, then he heard footfalls from above. The dwarf glanced at the Kagonesti. She had heard them also. Her gaze drifted to the stairs, and Jasper looked up, then swallowed hard.

Scaly legs descended from the darkness. Copper-hued, they were Kapaks. Another dozen of them. The dwarf sucked in his lower lip. The Kapaks were followed by a trio of immense Baaz—draconians made from the eggs of bronze dragons. Their snouts were shorter, and their skin was smoother, looking more like bronze leather than scales. But patches of scales glimmered in the torchlight here and there, around their broad shoulders and at the tips of their tails. Their legs were thick and powerful, corded muscles standing out.

"This is getting worse," the dwarf whispered. He heard more footfalls above, hinting that there were at least several more draconians somewhere. "Great idea coming here. *Abandoned* tower," Jasper said. "Abandoned, my Uncle Flint's beard. Why--"

"Sssilence!" the Aurak snapped. The draconian turned toward the staircase, watching a lone draconian come into the room. This draconian was slower than the others, taking shaky steps and holding a clawed hand against the wall for support. His gold scales gleamed as if each one were carefully polished. His breastplate of silver was equally shiny and was bound by strips of leather. It had obviously not been made for him, so it did not fit him well. The breastplate bore an etched rose, a symbol of the Knights of Solamnia. A dark red skirt hung below the armor, and a worn and threadbare cloak hung from the creature's shoulders. A formidable-looking axe hung from a belt about the Aurak's waist.

As the creature reached the bottom of the steps, all the draconians bowed to him. He was smaller than the others. The leathery flesh about his jowls sagged, and his muscles were ill-defined. But there was an aura of power surrounding him, and it was clear he had the respect of all of the draconians in the room.

"General Urek," the Kapak at the base of the stairs announced. He waved a coppery arm toward the trio, "Our prisoners."

"Prisoners!" Jasper sputtered.

The draconians closest to the dwarf raised their claws and stepped forward. Jasper took his hand away from his hammer, held his outstretched fingers to his side. The Kapaks paused. Feril's fingers slipped into her pouch, and she tugged free an arrowhead, which she quickly hid in her palm. She glanced at the general. If need be, she'd call on her magic and send it his way. She would not be taken prisoner by these hideous creatures, even if defying them meant her death.

"Prisoners?" General Urek said. His voice was soft, yet intense. "I would not consider holding Palin Majere prisoner."

The sorcerer was visibly surprised that the old Aurak knew who he was. Palin nodded to the Aurak, showing a semblance of respect. Feril seemed to relax just a bit, but Jasper grew even more nervous. A few more draconians filed into the room.

"And perhaps I will not hold his associates captive either," the old draconian continued, "if I hear in good faith that he intends to keep our presence secret."

"You would trussst the word of a human?" the other Aurak asked. He strode toward the general, towering above the older draconian. "Trussst a sssorcerer?"

"This human, I would trust," General Urek returned. "Besides, there has been enough killing this day." The general waved a thin arm, and several of the Kapaks stepped away from the far wall. Cloaked by the shadows, in a section of the room where the torchlight barely reached, was a mound of bodies. More than two dozen reasonably fresh corpses. Their blood had congealed about them on the stone floor, looking black as oil. Their weapons were piled near them.

"Knights of Takhisis," Palin said. If the draconians killed that many of them, they could well overpower he, Feril, and Jasper. The sorcerer knew he had the strength to cast a spell or two that would bring down the tower and most of the draconians in it. But that would make recovering the scepter impossible, which would mean Usha would die. And they themselves might not escape the disaster.

"The knights came upon us only a few hours ago," the general explained. "We could make no peace with them. They were agents of Governor-General Mirielle Abrena."

Jasper risked a question. "How would you know that?"

"A few . . . talked . . . before they died," the old Aurak answered. "We could not risk their returning to their vile master—the woman who holds some of our brothers as slaves in Neraka."

"She ssserves the Red, the overlord, Malysssstryx," the large Aurak added.

"So you're hiding," Feril said. "You don't want the dragons to know where you are."

General Urek nodded. "We are a dying race," he said, his voice growing softer. "There are few females among our kind, and none here. They are rarer than Auraks. A few of us die when the dragons create spawn but most feel it is our chance to reproduce. We have only a few opportunities to procreate, and many draconians welcome the spawning process. I am not one of them."

"Did you say 'dragons'?" Palin asked. "You mean dragons other than Khellendros."

"The Red knows how to fashion spawn, too. And she is teaching her allies as well. Though the Green is not one of her cohorts, we suspect she has learned the secret, too."

The sorcerer let out a deep breath. Multiple dragon armies could be being birthed while they stood here talking. Perhaps the Shadow Sorcerer was right, the Red was much more of a threat than Khellendros.

"So we hide from Beryl and the other overlords, and we watch. Perhaps one day we will learn how to procreate on our own using this spawn process. Perhaps we will not die out."

"My friends and I are working against the dragons," Palin said. "We're here looking for a scepter—the Fist of E'li."

"What *they* were looking for," the general said, again indicating the fallen knights.

Palin stared into the old Aurak's rheumy eyes. "We need the scepter. It's powerful, and no doubt you could benefit by keeping it for yourselves. But we intend to use it to raise the level of magic Krynn already has, and in turn to defeat the overlords, if possible. If you would give it to us, we could—"

"We did not know it was powerful until the knights came," he said. "We thought it merely a curious treasure, a bauble to hold and admire."

"With it . . ."

"We no longer have it, Palin Majere," the general said. He shook his scaly head. "While we battled these knights, more of their forces climbed the tower and entered our treasure room, absconding with the Fist of E'li. When darkness falls, we will pursue them. They cannot move through the woods as fast as we can, and we have Sivaks among our ranks. We intend to leave no witnesses among them to lead others back to our stronghold."

Palin knew that Sivak draconians were created by Takhisis from the stolen eggs of silver dragons. They could fly; unhampered by the thick ground cover they would have little trouble closing the distance to the knights. Mirielle's Knights of Takhisis would undoubtedly take the shortest route out of the forest, heading toward the coast or directly north into Abanasinia. The Sivaks would capitalize on this knowledge.

"You have a few hours of light left, Palin Majere." General Urek walked toward the sorcerer, the claws of his feet making dull clicking sounds against the stone. "If you gain the scepter before us, it is yours and we will not challenge you for it. But if we regain it first, we will keep it. Perhaps we could find a way to harness its magic against the Green."

Palin heard the door open behind him.

"I would hurry," General Urek said.

* * * * *

"No wonder the elves stay away from that place," Jasper said once they were safely away from the draconians' tower. The dwarf was sweating profusely, his stubby legs propelling him as fast as possible. But it wasn't the heat or the exertion making him sweat. It was fear. The dwarf had felt the sensation before—long months ago on the deck of the ship as it made its way from New Ports to Palanthas. They'd nearly all been pitched into the icy water near Southern Ergoth and swallowed by the White who swam far below them. And he'd felt fear when the blue dragon called Gale had appeared above the ship and killed Shaon. He was almost getting used to fear.

When they were about a half mile from the hidden tower, Feril urged Palin and Jasper to stop. She dropped to her knees and dug her fingers into the damp ground. "We can only guess which way the knights are heading," she said. "But the earth can tell us for certain."

"We have to hurry," Palin said.

The dwarf studied him. The sorcerer was sweating, too, and had a troubled expression on his face. "So I'm not so alone," he whispered to himself.

"If we don't find the scepter and return to the elves, I'll lose Usha," Palin said.

Feril gently swayed back and forth on her knees, keeping time with the movement of the branches blown by the breeze. She started singing, a tune that sounded like water softly splashing. "Mother earth," she whispered, ending her song, "give me your secrets. Tell me where the men walk. The ones in black, with hard shells like beetles." She hummed again, and felt her mind slipping from her own fleshy husk, flowing down her arms and into her fingers, then into the loam. It was rich earth, full of moisture and life and strength.

Magic usually drained the Kagonesti, but not this enchantment. She felt energized by it, and she suspected it was because the dragon had ensorceled the land. Her senses slipped around the bits of rock lodged in the dirt, around rotting pieces of wood. Dead plants added to the life that sprung from the soil, added to the energy and the power of this great forest that pulsed into her. As she probed deeper, there were tiny skulls—squirrels and rabbits that had died and were joined forever with this place. She felt the fervor of their spirits in the soil.

It was then that the earth spoke to her, revealing its birth at the hands of the gods and how time had nurtured it. Centuries passed in the elf's mind while only moments passed around her swaying body. The Kagonesti listened to the stories of how the dragon had added to the forest's power, enabling the giant plants to grow, the ferns and bushes to cover every inch and to send their leaves rocketing toward the sun. The earth reveled in the dragon's presence, considering it the source of much of its nourishment. The earth also liked the elves, who had protected it in the years before the dragon came, and did not object to the presence of the draconians.

Feril sensed that the earth was puzzled, torn between the two sides, and well aware that the dragon had slain elves and other creatures. But the essence of the dragon's victims joined with the soil and the forest, and added to its unique energy. Death was life in the Qualinesti woods.

"The men with shells," Feril whispered.

Like beetles, the earth answered.

"Yes," the Kagonesti replied, gaining a mental picture.

And the men the color of the sky and of the jays and of the sweet, juicy berries that ripen in the spring.

Feril was bewildered, but she continued. "These men, they serve another who serves a dragon—one who cares nothing for your beautiful forest. Her realm is barren and hot, lifeless."

Hot lifelessness, the rich soil replied. *I know where these beetles scamper.*

The rocks and bits of wood, tiny skulls, and sprouting acorns flashed by Feril's senses. The Kagonesti's mind sped ahead, arcing to the north and following the pull of the earth. All of a sudden she felt a great weight upon her back, though there was nothing there save the soft leather tunic she wore. But the weight she felt seemed oppressive, and she directed her senses upward, recognizing mailed, thick-soled boots that trod heavily on the ground and trampled the ferns.

"There are only four of them," she whispered to Palin. "Two knights and two blue-painted brutes. I think they're lost. They're not going in a straight line. The path they're making looks like a snake." She knew it was easy to get lost in a forest this dense. "We should catch them by sundown."

"About the time the draconians come out of their tower," Jasper said.

Feril let her senses stay with the earth for a few more moments, relishing the sensation and the perceptions, before almost reluctantly drawing her attention back to her companions. She hesitantly rose and started to brush the dirt from her fingertips, then stopped herself. "This way."

The Kagonesti flitted through the underbrush, as Palin and Jasper struggled to keep up. Neither asked her to slow her pace, however, as they knew how important it was to reach the scepter while it was still light.

They were weary by the time the shadows were thick and by the time they caught up with her, thrashing ahead of them. The meager sunlight was tinged orange, and hinted that soon the forest would be plunged into darkness and the draconians would begin their hunting. They crouched behind an immense, velvety fern and parted the leaves. The two knights were in the lead, using their long swords like machetes to hack at the plants and clear a path. Feril cringed at their careless brutality.

The shortest brute, a stout man of perhaps six feet, carried a leather sack over his shoulder. A wickedly spiked club was clenched in his left hand. The other brute was a foot taller, and was busy scanning the greens all around, alert for trouble. An uneasy expression shrouded his chiseled face. His wide nostrils quivered, and Feril knew he had already smelled them.

She touched the fern leaf in front of her and addressed the plant. "Join me," she whispered. Her senses easily slipped into the leaves, the stems, then flowed into the roots. The enchanted forest made her nature spells come practically effortlessly, and her mind quickly touched the other plants around the knights and brutes. She felt Palin crouch near her.

The tall brute stopped and whirled toward the fern where the trio was hiding. Jasper stood, his hammer hefted in his right hand. Judging the distance between himself and the man, he hurled the weapon. It spun over and over, until it struck the man, thumping hard against his abdomen and knocking him backward.

Palin had begun his own enchantment. One of the first spells he'd taught his son, it was a clever use of heat, and it would produce no actual flame to threaten the forest. As the last words to his enchantment ended, the knights dropped their swords and cried out, tearing at fastenings on their armor. Their metal had grown hot, and was progressively becoming hotter, their skin sizzling.

Meanwhile the tall brute had struggled to his feet. His companion dropped his leather sack and hefted the spiked club to his shoulders. He spied the dwarf, charged toward him, and quickly fell face first into the velvet fern. Vines had slithered across the ground and wrapped themselves about his ankles. More vines were encircling his wrists and neck, flowing like water over his body and holding him tightly in place, nearly smothering him beneath their leaves.

Other plants were grabbing at the tall brute. He fought against them as Jasper darted forward, picked up his hammer, and waved it threateningly. The brute broke free and glared at the short bearded man.

Palin and Feril stepped toward the knights, picking up their swords and kicking away pieces of the discarded armor. The heat did not affect Palin, and he watched as the moss and the vines spread to obscure most of the discarded mail and helmets. His eyes widened when he spotted a lord knight's insignia on one of the breastplates.

The knights were down to the padding they wore beneath the mail. They wisely made no move to attack Palin, but they couldn't help but glower at him.

"Don't make us kill you," the sorcerer said. He studied the men's faces. "Lord Knight Breen," he recognized the older man, Mirielle's heir-apparent, "we've more than enough blood already on our hands. If I were you, I'd leave this forest quickly."

Palin saw that the lord knight looked relieved, believing that his life and the lives of his men had been spared. The Knights of Takhisis didn't know the draconians would likely find them, and that the draconians had no intention of letting them escape. "No witnesses," Palin remembered the old Aurak saying.

"It's in here!" Jasper said. The dwarf glanced in the leather sack, then returned his gaze to the tall brute and flourished his hammer for emphasis. Softly, he said to Palin, "The knights will follow us, you realize. If a lord knight's involved, they'll not give the Fist of E'li up. Probably wait until we're sleeping, or . . ."

Palin motioned to the dwarf and Feril, and backed away from the men, following the path the knights had carved back toward the draconian's tower. "If you're right," Palin told the dwarf, "and they follow us, the Aurak's assassins will find them that much quicker."

When they'd put some distance between themselves and the knights, they darted behind a fragrant bush and waited. "Of course I was right," the dwarf smugly whispered. "See?" A moment later the brutes thundered by. The knights followed, weapons outstretched.

Palin was disappointed to see the dwarf proven right. After all, Steel was a Dark Knight, but he had acted honorably—escorting Palin's dead brothers home, praying over their graves, facing execution without excuse when Palin had escaped.

Feril motioned Jasper and Palin north, leading them toward the clearing where they'd left Usha. She talked to the plants as she went, coaxing them to cover up their trail. They pressed on even when the blackness settled around them, and she continued to use her keen elven senses to guide them.

More than a week later, and only one day shy of the Qualinesti's deadline, they found Usha in the company of a half-dozen elven archers.

Jasper pulled the scepter from the sack and held it up for them to see. It looked like a small mace made of polished wood. Its haft was trimmed with alternating bands of silver and gold, and its bulb-shaped top was encrusted with diamonds, garnets, and emeralds.

"So you were successful," the tallest elf observed, his eyes mesmerized by the glittering gems. "We are glad. We are only sorry that we were not able to help you as you have helped the Qualinesti, Palin Majere."

Usha ran to embrace Palin. "You're all right!"

"Your wife convinced us of the error of our ways. You spoke the truth, but we would not hear it. We hope you will hear our apology."

"She can be very persuasive," said Palin, smiling down at her. "No harm has been done. We have the scepter, and I have my wife back."

The tall elf nodded, and the band of elves quickly and silently melted into the foliage.

Usha kissed Palin deeply, then pulled back, wrinkled her nose, and looked closely at her husband.

·Like Jasper and Feril, the sorcerer was exhausted and filthy, and smelled strongly of sweat. Usha, however, looked as fresh as if she'd just gotten up from a long nap.

"Ankatavaka isn't far," Palin said, grimacing when he noticed some of the grime of the forest had rubbed off on Usha. "New clothes, a bath, and when we're rested, I'll transport us to Goldmoon's Citadel."

"Ulin?"

"He hasn't contacted me," the sorcerer replied. "I'm hoping he does so by the time we reach Ankatavaka."

Usha inhaled sharply. "I must believe he's all right."

"Of course he is," Jasper offered as they walked toward the coast. "He's a Majere, isn't he? And Majeres are made of very stern stuff. He'll be back with us in no time. Now, about those clothes . . ." He opened the leather sack, so Usha could look inside.

The brutes, who had climbed the tower wall, had stolen more than the Fist of E'li from the draconians' treasure room. Also inside were handfuls of rubies and sapphires, and strings of pearls.

"New clothes, some dwarven ale, a side of beef for Fury, maybe a nice necklace for Goldmoon since we're going to need her medallion, and . . ."

Palin and Usha walked hand in hand, she softly telling him of her few weeks with the elves.

Feril shut out the dwarf's musings and the Majeres' conversation and concentrated on the beautiful sounds of Beryl's forest. I will come back here, she told herself. With Dhamon Grimwulf.

Chapter 22

Red Hands

Dhamon had kept to himself during most of the journey. He ate sparingly, having little appetite, and he slept only briefly, feeling little need for rest and preferring to stay awake and forestall any further dreams. The few hours of sleep he grabbed here and there were filled with images of a red dragon made entirely of flame. Sometimes the dragon was ringed by erupting volcanoes and surrounded by red-scaled spawn that breathed streams of fire. Sometimes there were legions of goblins, hobgoblins, and Knights of Takhisis behind her—all of them made of fire, crackling and hissing malevolently.

The dreams became less and less frequent as *Flint's Anvil* neared Schallsea Island, then one day they vanished all together. When the Silver Stair came into view beneath the full, pale moon that illuminated it—the Citadel of Light where Goldmoon made her home—Dhamon felt relaxed. The ship dropped anchor in the bay, and Dhamon, Blister, and the mariner took the longboat ashore. After two guards admitted them, they passed by a large number of Goldmoon's students before making their way to her chamber.

The former knight had decided to show Goldmoon the glaive and tell her about the bronze dragon Shimmer. Perhaps she would have a clue to the weapon's origin and how the dragon came by it. But first she needed to look at the scale imbedded in his thigh. Though it had caused him no pain since it was first put there, he feared it might be the true source of his nightmares.

* * * * *

The stars winked down on the Peak of Malys, and a single pale moon that hung low on the horizon. The Red raised her head to the heavens and roared. Flames leapt into the sky, a burst of searing heat that helped to vent her great anger. She roared again, the sound so intense this time that it made her mountain tremble. In response, the volcanoes that ringed the plateau belched sulphurous gouts of black smoke.

A rumble started in Malys's belly, and the volcanoes thundered in chorus and began to erupt anew. Thick streams of lava raced down their sides and pooled at the Red's taloned feet. Their smoke continued to rise to mingle with her flames and to blot out the stars and the moon.

Her link with Dhamon Grimwulf had been tenuous, but as he neared the cursed Isle of Schallsea, it seemed to disappear entirely. The Red knew of the healer, one of the most powerful Heroes of the Lance, and she knew it was the woman—deity-touched—who was interfering with her influence.

"I will have the man and the weapon," she hissed. "I will

not be cheated of so great a prize." There were other exceptional magical items to be had, Malys had learned—a lance wielded by a man named Huma, a crown that rested beneath the waves with the Dimernesti, a ring languishing on a mysterious man's hand. Still, the Red sensed that none of those things could surpass the glaive.

Her fire continued to fill the sky, the lava surged about her claws, and Malystryx the Red closed her eyes and summoned all of her arcane strength.

* * * * *

Usha Majere stood on the outskirts of Ankatavaka and stared into Groller's eyes. The half-ogre reached out a big hand, trying to provide some comfort. His other hand firmly grasped Huma's lance. He offered her a smile, but didn't offer her any words of explanation or understanding. Words weren't needed—there were plenty of them on the parchment Palin was reading for the second time.

The red-haired wolf sat at Groller's feet, and Fiona Quinti, the young Knight of Solamnia from Castle Eastwatch, stood nearby, clutching Rig's dragonlance.

Ulin and Gilthanas hadn't appeared when Palin magically summoned them from Southern Ergoth. Neither had Ulin offered a clue as to what he was planning when he had contacted his father more than an hour ago and asked for the summoning enchantment.

Palin's spell brought only Groller, Fury, and Fiona—and the parchment on which Ulin sought to rationalize his and Gilthanas's absences.

"I came to help explain their decision," Fiona began. "I was given leave to join you for a time. I realize I cannot replace Ulin and Gilthanas, but my sword is yours."

"Do you know anything of this gold dragon? Sunrise?" Usha asked.

Fiona shook her head, glancing at Palin.

The sorcerer was visibly rattled by the words on the parchment. His eyes watered as they met Usha's. "Ulin is a grown man, with a wife and children. But to think he would abandon them—for who knows how long—to study magic with a dragon. He and Sunrise have also gone to the Dragon Isles to tell the good dragons about Takhisis's imminent return. He feels it a mission of great import."

His shoulders slumped. He couldn't control his son's life. He didn't want to and wouldn't dream of trying. "But the twins are so young. He has a family. How can he do this— what I did too often to you?"

Usha released Groller's hand and moved toward her husband. "He can do this *because* he is your son and because he is tied to magic. Magic was always at the heart of the reason why you left me."

"I always came back."

"Ulin will, too."

But will he? Usha wondered. She knew her son better than Palin did. And she knew that magic was Ulin's passion, perhaps even more so than it had been his father's.

Palin crumpled the parchment in his fist. Usha wrapped her arms around her husband. "We will travel to the Tower of Wayreth," he said softly into her ear. "This matter of Takhisis . . ."

"And if it is real?" Usha asked.

"We'll gain Dalamar's ring, and rejoin the others at the Silver Stair. The overlords are threat enough, but if the Dark Queen aids them, the danger is tenfold." He felt a lump rise in his throat and thought briefly of the Chaos War and all the death and destruction it had brought. Takhisis and the overlords could wage a battle that Krynn probably wouldn't survive—at least not the world's races of humans and demihumans.

"You'll send the others to Goldmoon's?" Usha interrupted his musings.

Palin nodded. "Yes, now. I suspect Goldmoon is waiting for them—as the Master and the Shadow Sorcerer wait for me."

* * * * *

"They're coming," Goldmoon said to the air. She stood at the window, looking up at the stars. "Yes, Dhamon is with them. I was so glad to learn he lived. I sensed he was the one, dear Riverwind. I'm still certain of it. What's that? Oh, yes, the mariner is with him, the one Palin trusts. And Blister as well. There is hope yet for Ansalon."

Her fingers fluttered over the surface of the medallion she wore. "Of course I will give this up," she said, her eyes fixed ahead. "Yes, it does mean a lot to me, husband. But they think it will return the gods' magic to Krynn. Do you remember when we worked so hard to bring back clerical magic to the world? We were so young then, and the task seemed impossible. But we succeeded, and it seems like it was only yesterday. You were here and—"

"I think she's got company." The kender's voice drifted up from the curving stairwell. "I hope we're not interrupting anything important. Wonder who'd be visiting her this late at night?"

Blister was in the lead because she was tired of getting left behind. Her short legs carried her up the twisting staircase that seemed to wind itself through every vacant room and alcove of the crystalline dome. She was sticking to the middle of the stairwell so Rig and Dhamon couldn't squeeze around her and with their longer legs leave her behind. Eventually they reached an oval chamber at the top, where Goldmoon seemed to be conversing with someone. Rig and Dhamon emerged from the stairwell behind the kender.

"Guess she doesn't have company," Blister decided, as she took in the immaculate room. "Must have been hearing things." The room's polished, curved white walls and its marble floor reflected the starlight and made it seem as if a dozen lanterns were burning. "Guess I was imagining her talking to somebody." Gauzy curtains hung here and there, more for decoration than function. The pale birch furniture, though sparse for the size of the room, appeared newly made and delicate.

As Goldmoon stepped away from the window and faced Blister, the healer's lips edged upward in a smile.

Though she was over eighty, she didn't look quite that old, nor as old as Dhamon remembered seeing her long months ago when he had first answered her summons. Her blonde hair streaked with silver rested in stray curls about her shoulders. Her blue eyes were pale, but not dull and cloudy as he recalled. Jasper once told Dhamon that his faith colored what he saw whenever he visited the famed healer. The moonlight revealed the lines on her face, and Dhamon could see that the flesh on her arms and along her jaw sagged.

Blister saw a different image, however, one full of life and promise, with sparkling clear eyes and no trace of lines or stooped shoulders. "Your faith indeed colors what you see," the kender whispered.

Goldmoon glided toward the trio, carrying herself with a quiet grace. There was a stately demeanor about her, a feeling of quiet power. "It does truly gladden my heart to see you, Dhamon Grimwulf." She took Dhamon's hand, and nodded to the mariner, offering him a smile. Then she winked at Blister.

Rig was awed to be in her presence, but kept silent. One of the Heroes of the Lance. She was the stuff of numerous tavern tales he'd heard throughout the many nations he'd visited. He suddenly wished Shaon was here to share this moment with him.

"It's good to see you, too. I'm sorry to be so abrupt, but my leg," Dhamon began, "there's a red dragon scale on it, in it actually, and—"

"In a minute," Blister interrupted. She trotted up to Gold-moon, turned her face up to stare into the healer's brilliant eyes. "Your medallion. You said when I came to the Silver Stair that you'd give it to me. Well, to us really. Palin and Feril and Jasper are looking for a scepter, and Ulin and Gilthanas are with Groller and Fury looking for Huma's lance. I hope they've found everything by now, or else some of them will be very, very cold. There's a ring, and Palin said he'd take care of that. But—"

"My medallion," Goldmoon said, releasing Dhamon's hand and again running her fingers along the medallion's shiny edges.

The kender's fingers moved almost nimbly now, and they reached up to grab the precious medallion, with its string-of-stars silver chain. But Blister's mouth couldn't help but fall open. Goldmoon placed the medallion in the kender's hands, but an exact duplicate of the medallion remained around the healer's neck.

Even the healer was surprised. "By my faith in Mishakal! The medallion can duplicate itself," Goldmoon whispered.

"Wow," was all Blister could manage. The kender stared at the two medallions and scratched her head. "They certainly look the same. Hey, I wonder why you couldn't just have made four of them, so Groller wouldn't have had to go to Southern Ergoth, and Palin and Feril to the forest."

"I don't think it works that way."

"Oh, I suppose you're right." Blister beamed at the healer, her scarred fingers closing tight about the medallion. "I'll take real good care of this for Palin. Maybe I could wear it until he needs it. Do you think I could?"

Goldmoon nodded, and Blister instantly put the chain around her neck, careful not to let it get caught in her braid. The kender had a dozen or so more questions, but decided now wasn't the best time. She turned to Dhamon. "What are you waiting for? Why haven't you told her about that scale on your leg?"

* * * * *

They appeared at the base of the Citadel of Light. Jasper grabbed his stomach, and fought the wave of dizziness that swept over him as Palin's spell ended. Feril marveled at the sensation, then was quick to inhale the sweet sea air.

"If we had more time, we could have sailed here," the dwarf told Fiona. "This magical moving about is all so disorienting. Interesting, but definitely disorienting." He slumped on the bottom step with a deep sigh. "Give me a moment to feel myself again, then I'll introduce you to Goldmoon."

"The Mistress of the Citadel? I would be honored." The young Knight of Solamnia grinned down at him. "And this Rig you mentioned, he's inside?"

"With Dhamon," Feril said.

"Rig's here," the dwarf replied, pointing at the shore where a longboat was tied to a spiky hunk of granite. He gestured out into the bay, where *Flint's Anvil* sat. "That's his ship. I bought it—with a piece of jasper my Uncle Flint gave me. It's a long story. I'm sure Blister will tell you about it some time. And that's his first mate sitting on the shore, Groller Dagmar."

"I'd like to return this to him," she said, hefting the lance over her right shoulder. She patted the long sword that hung from her left hip. "This isn't so unwieldy, or heavy, but Rig must be pretty strong if he uses the lance."

"Hasn't used it yet," Jasper said as he pushed himself to his feet and started up the steps. Feril slipped by him, taking the steps two at a time. She was anxious to be with Dhamon again.

"Ah, love," the dwarf mused. "If they're with Goldmoon,

they'll be on the top floor. Better get started, it's a consider-able climb. You coming, Groller?"

The half-ogre, who was sitting on the shore with Sageth, didn't budge. The dwarf cocked his head, and held up his index fingers and crooked them toward his chest. "Coming?" Then he pointed at the door.

Groller shook his head, scratching Fury's neck. "D'no," he answered. "Like it here. I'll sday here a while wid old man." The half ogre stared at the water and the reflection of the stars that danced on the waves. "Weel wade fer you, Jaz-pear."

"Suit yourself," the dwarf said.

"Save myself the climb," the old man said. He ran his fin-gers over his beloved clay tablet, which he could barely read in the moonlight. "My legs don't like stairs. Besides, the moon's low, a perfect night for this. We'll want to destroy the artifacts on solid ground. Somewhere over there might do." He pointed his spindly arm to the north side of the island, where a plain stretched. "No buildings around, no people. Maybe Groller could help me pick out a spot."

Jasper balled his right fist and set it down on his open palm, then he brought the left hand up, as if he were giving his fist a helping boost. The dwarf pointed to Sageth and repeated the gesture.

Groller took a last look at the bobbing ship, then assisted Sageth to his feet. "I'll help you," he said.

"We're going to be a while," the dwarf called over his shoul-der. "Goldmoon and I have a lot of catching up to do. But we'll find you out there when we're done chatting."

* * * * *

Dhamon wore loose fitting trousers that he tucked into the tops of his boots. Holding his glaive with his left hand, he pulled the trouser leg up with his right, showing the scale.

Goldmoon knelt in front of him and stared at it, her red-tinged face reflecting back at her. A shiver raced down her spine, and she frowned. "By my faith in Mishakal," she said in a hushed voice. "Magic so dark. It feels . . ." She tentatively touched the scale and then shuddered, as if she'd pricked herself on a needle. Then she listened in horror to Dhamon's explanation of how the dying Knight of Takhisis had forced it on him. "This is an incredibly powerful enchantment," she said, looking up at him. "Dragon magic."

"He said I'd die if I pulled it off," Dhamon said.

"Do you think you can fix it?" Blister moved closer, concern showing on her cherubic face. The mariner, equally curious, looked over the kender's head. He had heard Feril and Dhamon discussing the scale, but until now hadn't seen it.

"I'm not sure," Goldmoon said, staring into Dhamon's eyes. "I'd like to try. I don't think you should keep carrying this . . . thing . . . around with you. It could be risky to remove it, but with your permission?"

"Please." The former Knight of Takhisis looked into her eyes, then felt a presence at the back of his mind, one he'd not felt for several days. The face of the Red Dragon loomed before him, gauzily superimposing herself over the image of the healer's face.

The scale throbbed, stronger than it ever had before, and he felt his will slipping away and his body growing warmer. He clenched his fist around the glaive handle and clenched his jaws together so tightly that they ached.

"Dhamon, is something wrong?" He heard the mariner ask. It sounded like Rig was far away, the dark man's voice muffled.

"No!" Dhamon moaned, as he fought to push aside the dream. For an instant the Red's visage flickered like flames, but then the dragon's head came more sharply into focus, the scales glittering, and her dark eyes, like molten pools of magma, boring into his, burning through him, and filling his vision.

You are mine, Dhamon Grimwulf, Malys hissed as she stretched out on her plateau and purred.

The dragon's voice sounded so close and distinct, as though it were coming from Goldmoon. Dhamon shook his head, trying to clear his senses. Was he asleep? he wondered. Dreaming again?

My pawn, the red dragon hissed. *Mine to—*

"No one's pawn," Dhamon said.

My pawn, the dragon reiterated, louder this time, her voice echoing inside his head. *My pawn to control. The glaive you hold, use it!*

"Dhamon?" Rig stepped forward and pulled Goldmoon and the kender back. He heard footsteps echoing in the stairwell. "I hope that's Palin," he said to the pair, feeling suddenly very uneasy.

Dhamon's eyes glazed red and he let the trouser leg fall back over the scale. He felt his hands grip the glaive, felt the dragon power his limbs. He was a marionette, and Malys was pulling his strings. Flames licked about the Red's mouth and formed a wreath around her massive head.

The glaive—use it now!

He stepped forward, feeling a strength in his muscles that wasn't there before, feeling a fresh force guide his arms and legs.

"What are you doing?" Rig shouted, as Dhamon charged forward. The mariner tried to grab the former knight. But Dhamon was already past him, lunging toward Goldmoon who was backing away.

"Stop!" Blister screamed. "Dhamon! Leave her alone!"

"My faith will protect me," Goldmoon breathed as she backed toward the window. "Mishakal will save me."

Dhamon raised the glaive and rushed toward her.

Feril reached the room just as Rig sped toward Dhamon, barreling into him and sending him sprawling on the marble floor, the glaive clattering away. She was obviously startled and unsure of what was going on. Then she caught sight of Blister loading her sling. Who was the kender aiming at, Rig or Dhamon? Feril wondered. And what had started the ruckus? Below came the footfalls of the dwarf and the Solamnic Knight. What was happening?

"Are you mad?" Rig bellowed. Dhamon had regained the glaive, only to have Rig kick it away.

Dhamon shook his head, trying once again from the small faraway place in his mind to take control of himself. "Mad?" he heard himself say. It was his voice, but not his words. "I'm far from mad. I've finally come to my senses!"

The former Knight of Takhisis leaped up and slammed both fists into the mariner's stomach. The blow was strong, enhanced by his link with the Red, and it caused the mariner to double over and drop to his knees.

A volley of rocks shot toward Dhamon, expertly hurled from Blister's sling. But the former knight's reactions were heightened, and he dodged them, stepping toward the glaive.

"Dhamon!" Feril rushed toward him. "What's happening?"

His fingers closed about the haft, and he felt a burning sensation on his palms. The weapon was scalding him.

A weapon of good, Malys hissed to him. *And your acts, dear pawn, are far from good now.*

Dhamon concentrated, trying to force his fingers to release their grip on the haft, praying that Rig would get up, that Feril would stop him.

No, you don't, Malys communicated. *Your skin will heal, and you'll hold onto this weapon. I'll make you master the pain. You, and the glaive, are mine. Use it! Slay the elf!*

"No!" Dhamon screamed as his arms swept in an arc, angling the glaive at the charging Kagonesti. A look of horror crossed Feril's face as she dropped to her stomach to avoid the blow. And from the small place in his mind, he watched in terror as he brought the butt-end of the haft down on the back of her head.

Feril crumpled.

"Guards! Guards!" Blister screaméd, looking towards the stairway. "Dhamon, please stop!"

But Dhamon didn't stop. He was moving toward Rig, who was rising and drawing his cutlass.

"Never cared much for you," the mariner said between clenched teeth. "Put up with you because of Feril and Palin. *Former* Knight of Takhisis? You had us all fooled." He danced to his right as Dhamon swept the glaive toward him. The blade passed through the mariner's voluminous sleeve and sliced his arm. Pain jolted the mariner's shoulder and spread to his chest. He fought to keep hold of his cutlass. "Better not have killed her," he said as he dodged a second blow and risked a glance at Feril.

Dhamon was forced to sidestep this time, as Rig jabbed forward with his cutlass. As the mariner retreated, he balanced his blade in his right hand, and thrust his left into the V neck of his shirt. He retrieved two daggers, hefted them, then threw them as Dhamon closed.

The first blade flew over Dhamon's shoulder, clattering impotently on the floor near Goldmoon, who seemed to be in the midst of a prayer or spell. The second lodged in the former knight's left shoulder. Dhamon felt the pain, still felt the intense burning sensation in his hands from the glaive, but Malys allowed him no further hesitation. She forced his body forward, and he swung the weapon again.

This time the glaive grazed the mariner's stomach, drawing a glistening line of blood. The mariner's left hand flew to the wound, and he backed up several steps.

"By Reorx's beard! What's going on here!" Jasper cried.

"It's Dhamon! Go get some guards!" Blister squealed, as she let loose with another volley of stones. Her aim was true, and they pelted Dhamon's chest. "We've got to stop him!"

More pain. Dhamon wanted to double over from the pain, crawl away and heal and get Malys out of his head. He wanted Feril to be all right. And he didn't want to hurt anyone else.

The former knight turned toward Goldmoon. "The healer!" Malys hissed with Dhamon's voice.

With her back against the window, Goldmoon stood and stared defiantly. "Fight this," she said in a voice barely above a whisper. "Whatever's taken hold of you. I've looked into your spirit. You're strong and good. You can fight this!"

Not strong enough, Malys communicated to Dhamon. *I want her dead.*

Stiffly Dhamon took a step toward her, and another. Behind him he heard Rig moving again. With incredibly sensitive hearing, he followed the mariner's soft footfalls over the marble. Without warning, the former knight drove the butt-end of the glaive backward—straight into the already wounded stomach of the dark man.

The sensitive ears heard the mariner groan, the cutlass clatter to the floor, and the big man drop. Dhamon now heard the pounding of the dwarf's feet, and of another's—someone he couldn't place. He heard the *shush* of more rocks being hurled at him, felt them rake the side of his face.

His body ached terribly, he shouldn't even be standing. But Malys gave him superhuman strength. *The healer! Slay her!*

"Dhamon! That's Goldmoon! Are you out of your mind?" Jasper was running now, sliding across the marble and interposing himself between Dhamon and Goldmoon.

Blister was running too. It was no great feat for him to thrust out his leg, connect the heel of his boot with her face, and send her flying backward. At the same moment, his arms were moving up and forward, swinging the burning, magical glaive.

Then the blade was arcing down, reflecting the light of the stars that shone through the window, dancing toward the dwarf's chest.

Jasper raised his hammer, trying to ward off the blow, but it was useless. Jasper hadn't been in the clearing to see Dhamon's weapon slice through the swords of the Knights of Takhisis and their armor like cloth.

The dwarf saw the weapon arc down, saw his hammer rise up to defend himself and Goldmoon, saw the glaive slice through the thick metal and continue on its deadly path. Jasper felt the blade pierce his chest, then felt excruciating pain, and his own blood splattered everywhere. The dwarf sobbed involuntarily and clutched his chest, warm and wet. Then he suddenly felt very cold, and all he saw was darkness.

"My faith will protect me," Goldmoon, her eyes closed, whispered as Dhamon took a step closer.

Malys was moving her pawn's legs very slowly now, savoring this moment. From behind him, Dhamon heard the sharp hiss of a sword being drawn, heard the frantic breathing of a woman. Who?

Dhamon turned his head. Malys wanted to see who was there. A woman, young and uncertain, clad in the hated armor of the Solamnic Knights. She crouched and waved the blade in front of her.

Kill her, Malys ordered.

Dhamon stared at the armor, at the crown and kingfisher etched into the breastplate. Sir Geoffrey Quick had saved him years ago, turned him from a life of evil. Could this Solamnic save him now, run him through before he killed again?

You can't fight me! Malys hissed inside his head. *You are mine!*

The woman edged to her right, started circling. She glanced down at the dwarf, noted Rig and Feril and Blister, all still.

"You'll not kill Goldmoon!" Fiona Quinti spat. "Whoever you are, you're done with killing!" She had maneuvered herself in front of Goldmoon, and now she raised her blade, bringing it down in one smooth motion toward Dhamon's chest.

But the former Knight of Takhisis was quicker. He parried with the glaive, slicing the woman's long sword in two. Then he swept forward with his leg, catching her ankles and knocking her to the floor.

In two more steps he was upon Goldmoon, raising the glaive and bringing it down one last time.

No! Dhamon cried from the small place in his mind as he watched the blade cleave deeply into her shoulder. *By all the gods!* He watched the healer fall, a blossom of red forming on her white tunic and spreading over the floor. *No!*

On her plateau high in what had once been called the Goodlund Peninsula, Malystryx roared in pleasure. Her mountain trembled, her volcanoes erupted, and the small army of red spawn who stood about her struggled to retain their balance.

"You are mine, Dhamon Grimwulf!" Malys cried in her sibilant inhuman voice. "Come to me, my pawn. And bring your enchanted weapon."

I am damned, Dhamon thought. As his feet rushed across the blood-covered floor, and his hands continued to burn, he caught a last glimpse of his fallen comrades. How many of them had he killed? How many were only injured? Feril? His feet were flying down the curving staircase, through the lower levels of the Citadel of Light, then across the shore and toward the longboat.

From somewhere behind him his keen senses picked up more footfalls, a large man. The mariner. Rig still lived.

He jumped in the boat and pushed off from the shore, laying the glaive in the bottom of the boat. Dhamon was thankful to set aside the burning thing. The skin of his hands was cracked and red, but the Red forced them to close around the oars and to head out to the ship.

On the shore, he spotted the mariner. Rig was screaming something, vile words that he knew he deserved. The mariner charged into the water, fists raised and shouting. But the dark man couldn't catch Dhamon, and eventually Rig retreated, returned to the Citadel and disappeared inside.

Dhamon was near the *Flint's Anvil* now, could see the few deckhands at the rail. They were calling out questions, but the dragon ignored them, wouldn't let Dhamon reply. She directed Dhamon to again grab the hurtful weapon, to aim it at the ship, at the waterline. Blow after blow landed against the prow, shattering the hull and eliciting cries from the startled deckhands. Again and again the glaive cleaved through the wood as if it were cloth. Water poured in, the ship listed. Only when the dragon was certain the ship was doomed and when a rain of arrows from an archer on deck started to fall upon the former knight, did she have Dhamon row away.

Come to me, she hissed. *Come to the Peak of Malys. You are a most worthy pawn.*

* * * * *

In the highest room in the Citadel of Light, Feril regained consciousness and crawled toward Blister. The kender lay unmoving, breathing awkwardly. Her lips were cracked and bleeding, her nose broken from Dhamon's kick. Feril shakily got to her feet.

Fiona was unconscious, but at first glance seemed otherwise unhurt. Goldmoon was dead. And Jasper. . . .

Feril knelt by the dwarf. There was so much blood. The cut through his chest was deep. It had parted a couple of his rib bones and punctured a lung beneath. But somehow he lived, for the moment at least.

"I know of healing magic, but I can't do it alone," the Kagonesti said softly. "Help me, Jasper." She clutched his stubby fingers and brought them to his chest. She laid his hands across the wound, as he had laid them across Palin's wound long weeks ago. She fought back the tears that filled her eyes. "Please help me, my friend."

* * * * *

A few miles beyond the Citadel of Light, Groller and the old man examined a wide patch of ground. Fury sniffed about the perimeter, only occasionally raising his furry head and staring at Sageth. They were oblivious to what had transpired in Goldmoon's room.

"Good you can't hear me," the old man tittered to Groller. He glanced at the tablet and spoke to it. "This spot will do nicely. It shouldn't be long now."

Chapter 23

Loose Ends

The blue dragon banked over the Northern Wastes. The moon was so large and bright and low against the white sand that it cast the dragon's shadow ahead of him. The silhouette passed over the ruined Bastion of Darkness, glided over a decimated barbarian village and a small oasis. The dragon smelled the fresh, sweet water below and idly considered stopping to quench his considerable thirst and to feast on the camels and riders he could also smell sleeping beneath the palms. But he decided such a luxury would have to wait.

The dragon continued on toward a rocky rise, where a massive cave was partially hidden by the ridge's shadow. Tucking his wings in close to his scaly body, he disappeared inside the cave, leaving behind the comforting warmth and accepting the cooler confines of the underground lair.

"Khellendros," the blue dragon began. He lowered his sapphire head, showing proper homage.

"Gale," Khellendros replied. "What has delayed you?"

The younger blue dragon related the tale of his battle with Dhamon Grimwulf, and how the human—his former partner—had wounded him seriously, blinded him. He had to rely on his other senses now, and on his rage, which was unstoppable. The dragon knew Dhamon Grimwulf lived, and he swore the man would die for leaving him in a world of darkness.

Behind Khellendros, a talon of Knights of Takhisis rested. They had managed to retrieve a set of crystalline keys, magic from the Age of Dreams. They listened intently as the younger dragon retold the story of plunging into the cold lake, sinking to its bottom and laying still for so long. He had expected to die, felt his blood and energy leave him, felt sadness and anger that his once-partner, whom he had considered a brother, delivered the killing blow. The dragon wanted to die in a glorious battle. He had been on duty in Northern Ergoth during the fighting in the Abyss, and had lived through the Chaos War. This death seemed such a waste.

It was perhaps those thoughts, he told Khellendros, that kept him alive. Gale stayed at the bottom of the lake for hours, the air stored in his great lungs keeping him from drowning. He had sensed two humans and an elf standing on the shore of the lake, and he hadn't wanted to crawl out while they were there and he was weak and at their mercy. So he waited until he was sure they were gone, then slowly made his way into the hills around Palanthas.

Gale spent months there, nursing his wounds and recovering his strength, sleeping for several weeks at a time and learning how to exist by his heightened senses of hearing and smell. Even now traces of the battle lingered. His eyes were fixed and pale. A scar stretched nearly two feet along the side of his neck. The cut had been deep, and the wound festered. No scales grew along the wound, and never would again. There were other scars, one near the base of his neck, another on his side where Dhamon had buried his sword up to its hilt and used it as a mountain climber would, lodging a piton in rock to haul himself up the creature's back.

Khellendros was relieved his lieutenant had survived the ordeal. The dragon was as loyal as any dragon could be, though Khellendros would never completely trust him—or anyone. The Storm Over Krynn had not killed him during the Dragon Purge, and had in fact kept other dragons from killing him, too.

"My purpose now is to serve you, and slay Dhamon Grimwulf," Gale growled, the deep sounds reverberating off the cavern walls. Sand trickled down through the cracks in the rocks.

"His death shall come in time," the Storm answered. "For now, I would have you watch my desert. I have something to attend to."

Chapter 24

Age of Dreams

The spot Sageth had selected, a few miles north of the Citadel of Light, had once been the courtyard of a castle. The afternoon sunlight revealed bits of high crenelated walls that girded what was decades ago an octagonal white stone tower. The little ruins that remained hinted that the castle must have been impressive in its time.

Jasper choked back a sob, and inspected the wide bandage that was wrapped around his chest. Somehow, with Feril's help, he had managed to heal himself—though he would never be quite the same. Walking was now a chore. His lung was punctured, and his chest ached.

"I should've saved her . . . like she saved me." His frame

shuddered as he thought about the healer, whose body was wrapped in a shroud in a small dome in the Citadel of Light. She would be buried as soon as Palin and Usha arrived.

Rig stood near the dwarf, looking out to sea. "We're stranded," he said. "Dhamon sank the ship." He was responsible for Shaon dying, he added to himself. He was responsible for all the bad things that had happened since they joined forces with him. "I intend to kill him."

"You don't mean that," Feril said.

"I think he does mean that," Jasper said. "And if I'm feeling up to it, I'll help him."

The Kagonesti walked toward the pair. "I want to know what happened, what came over him. I believe it was that dragon scale. Something possessed him."

"Maybe it was nothing," the mariner replied. His dark eyes flashed at her. "Maybe he was just biding his time, playing us all for fools and waiting for the best time to strike. Maybe he even orchestrated the blue dragon's attack on the *Anvil*, purposefully caused Shaon's death. If that blue dragon's alive somewhere, you'll know for certain that Dhamon was in cahoots with it, that this was all part of some grand stinking scheme of his. If Palin doesn't come soon, I'm leaving. I'll find passage in the port of Schallsea. It might take a while, but I'll hunt him down. That glaive can't cleave weapons Dhamon doesn't see coming." For emphasis, he rubbed the pommel of a dagger that stuck out of his boot.

The Kagonesti was silent, listening to Rig's tirade and watching Groller and Sageth pace off the clearing. Fiona Quinti stood apart from everyone else, and looked around cautiously, occasionally meeting the Kagonesti's gaze.

Feril felt a tear edge over her left cheek.

"Lady elf," Sageth called, as he checked his tablet and hobbled toward her. "We can't wait much longer for Palin Majere. Should have destroyed the artifacts last night—despite the havoc in the Citadel. The moon was low, perfect.

We must do it tonight. We'll not have a better time for at least a month."

"We don't have enough artifacts," she answered.

"But we do." His rheumy eyes sparkled. "We've Huma's lance, and the Fist of E'li you retrieved from the forest." He nodded toward the leather sack at the dwarf's feet. "Then there's Goldmoon's two medallions."

"Two?" the Kagonesti asked.

"That's right." Blister came forward. "The one she gave me, and the one that's still around her neck. I can go get it if you want."

"No," Jasper answered. "Let me." It was an effort to stand, an effort to take a few steps. And he knew it would be a great chore to walk the few miles to the Citadel and climb the steps again. But he wasn't going to have anyone else remove Goldmoon's medallion. "I'll be back here by nightfall."

The half-ogre spotted Blister fingering the medallion around her neck and guessed what they were talking about. He retrieved Huma's lance, and padded toward them, Fury at his heels.

"So, you see, we have four after all," Sageth concluded. "Tonight, when the last bit of sunlight fades, we shall change the course of Ansalon's future."

* * * * *

Palin had spent several days meditating alone at the Tower of Wayreth, while the Master concluded his research on the ancient artifacts. The Shadow Sorcerer was helping him, temporarily putting aside his studies of the overlords. In that time, Palin and Usha had tried to discern how the dragons could bring back Takhisis. His colleagues were skeptical. If the dark goddess could return, would the other gods follow?

Usha urged Palin to focus on the matter at hand, one even more pressing than speculating on the return of Takhisis.

"Dhamon and the others," she began. "they're waiting for us—and the ring you said you could get."

Palin climbed the tower steps. The Master was in the room where all of Par-Salian's journals were stored. He was hunched over a thick volume written by the former head of the Conclave of Wizards. The book was bound in dark green lizard hide. Palin cleared his throat to get the man's attention.

"It could work," the Master said. The wind was blowing strongly outside the room's lone window, and Palin had to strain to hear his colleague's unusually soft voice. "Magic from the Age of Dreams was created by the gods, as is all magic. Destroying the items should release an incredible amount of energy."

"Enough to permeate Krynn?"

"I do not know if it will be enough to heighten the level of magic," the Master continued, "but according to Par-Salian's journals on the Age of Dreams, the artifacts are so saturated with arcane power that they should be able to at least increase the general level of magic in a good-sized area."

"The Shadow Sorcerer claims you are Raistlin."

The Master pushed himself away from the table and faced Palin. "So you believe the Shadow Sorcerer's assumption? Just because I am so familiar with your uncle's works? And just because there is something familiar about my presence?"

"You do seem familiar."

Beneath his hood, he smiled, but offered no reply.

"If you're not Raistlin, then just who are you?"

"It took you all these years to ask me," the Master said.

"I respected your privacy, the secrecy you seemed to enjoy."

"And now you don't respect it?"

"Now I need to know. If you are Raistlin, you're far more powerful than I am. You could help us."

"I'm not your Uncle Raistlin," the Master began. "But I knew him well. And Dalamar. And many, many others. There is some of Raistlin in me—just as there is a bit of every mage who ever took a Test of High Sorcery. All who take the Test become a part of me. I think, however, that Raistlin was the most formidable of those who studied within my walls."

"Within *your* walls?"

"I am the Tower of Wayreth."

"Preposterous! You're a man, not a building." Palin's voice rose and he felt anger color his cheeks. "Palanthas's Tower of High Sorcery was destroyed more than thirty years ago. There's nothing left of the building."

"But the magic that pervaded its stones remained. I am a living manifestation of the tower. I am *all* of the towers. I am the essence of all of the old magic of High Sorcery"

The Master raised his hands to his hood and drew back the heavy cloth. For an instant the face Palin saw beneath was his Uncle Raistlin's, the familiar silvery-white hair spilling over the man's shoulders. Then the visage changed, becoming Par-Salian of the White Robes. Next, Gilthanas's face appeared, then the visages of Dalamar, Ladonna of the Black Robes, Fistandantilus, and Justarius of the Red Robes. There were others, some Palin only guessed at from descriptions he'd heard. He had no clue as to who others were.

"All of these people came to the tower, studied there, left an impression on me. Their power helped create the essence you see before you." The Master pulled the hood back over his head. "I am the Master of the Tower and also what is left of the tower."

"The Shadow Sorcerer . . ."

"Thinks I'm Raistlin. And I've no intention of telling the Shadow Sorcerer otherwise."

Palin pulled out a chair and sat heavily on it. "I thought you were a man."

"I am—in a sense. I am your colleague. And I've come to think of you as a friend."

Palin nodded. "You *are* my friend."

"Now let us move on to more important matters," the

Master urged. "This Age of Dreams magic. It has been hard for me to come to terms with destroying such magnificent artifacts, but Sageth is to be heeded in the matter of gaining the ancient magic. I believe it is the answer, our best hope at defeating the overlords. The more of it you can find, the better. The more divinely crafted power we have to work with, the greater our chance of success."

"There's something more. What?"

"Let me show you." He went over to a large bureau and opened one of the drawers, retrieving a crystal ball on a hammered bronze pedestal. He gingerly carried it to the table and held his hands a hair's breadth above its shimmering surface. "This is what I saw this morning when I finished my research and tried to find Sageth. No man with any sorcerous ability matches his description. The crystal could not locate him. But it did reveal this."

A tiny image appeared in the center of the ball. It was small at first, looking like a raven. But it grew larger until it filled the crystal.

"Khellendros!" Palin exclaimed.

"He is the power behind Sageth. The man is his puppet, I suspect. Look closer, there's more."

The Blue Dragon faded, and the Red filled the crystal. "Malystryx the Red, the one our associate the Shadow Sorcerer concerns himself with. She too is involved in all of this somehow. And a woman." A face imposed itself over Malys's, a young human woman with curly black hair and soft brown eyes. "Kitiara uth Matar," the Master said. "She died several years before your birth, and yet somehow her spirit has a hand in all of this."

He drew his hands away from the crystal, and the images faded. "Don't let your friends relinquish the ancient magic. They'll be putting it in the hands of an overlord. I'll give you Dalamar's ring—when we know for certain how to use the artifacts—and when no dragon is involved."

"I've got to stop them." Palin pushed back from the table and hurried from the room, the spell that would transport him to Goldmoon's dome already racing through his mind. He bumped into the Shadow Sorcerer as he flew down the stairs. The mysterious sorcerer nodded a farewell.

"Did you enjoy your chat with your Uncle Raistlin?" the sorcerer asked.

But Palin Majere couldn't answer. He was already growing transparent, the stone beneath his feet becoming the shore outside the Citadel of Light.

* * * * *

Thick gray clouds filled the sky shortly before sunset. Jasper struggled toward his friends, gathered about the clearing. He hoped that the storm would hold off until after dark, when the stars came out and they could perform whatever ceremony they had in mind to destroy the artifacts. Then the magic could increase on Krynn, the sorcerers could band together and would have a hope of standing up to the overlords, and then at last he could properly mourn Goldmoon.

As the sun edged toward the horizon, thin flickers of lightning began to dance between the clouds, and the thunder that followed was soft, like a distant drum beating.

Sageth selected a spot where there were no stones, and where the ground was flat. They waited there as the sun dipped lower, the last of its orange-red rays all but obscured by the still-darkening sky.

"The magic," he said, as he consulted his tablet. "It's time."

Blister wondered how an old man could read when it was this dark out. She made a mental note to ask him about it when the ceremony was over. The kender didn't want to distract him now.

"The lance first." Sageth looked up at the sky, pointing with his finger through a gap in the clouds where a faint star could be seen. "Put the lance here."

Jasper translated Sageth's words, and Groller took a last look at Huma's prize, then carefully set it on the ground where Sageth indicated.

"Now the Fist of E'li. See that it touches the lance." Jasper wheezed as he walked forward, still exhausted from his trip to the Citadel. "And the medallions. Make sure the chains touch both weapons." Blister came forward and took the medallion off from around her neck. She did as she was instructed, then backed away, not wanting to take her eyes off Goldmoon's gift. Jasper pulled the other one from his pocket and laid it next to the first.

"No!"

All of a sudden Palin was among them, running toward them, the white of his tunic illuminated by flashes of lightning. "Don't give him the medallion! Don't give him anything! It's a trick!"

Rig reacted first. He leaped forward, and grabbed the wooden haft of the scepter. In that same instant, the ground beneath the mariner seemed to melt; the grass dissolved and the dirt turned to quicksand. Rig felt himself sinking into the sucking, wet earth. He gasped and tried to free himself, but only sank deeper, faster. He was completely covered now, his chest tightening and then feeling as if it would explode with thirst for air. Shaon, he thought. Perhaps we'll be reunited sooner than I expected. Then he felt big hands fishing about and latching onto his legs. Groller's hands. They pulled Rig to the surface, and the mariner coughed up a mouthful of sand and slime.

The half-ogre pulled his friend away from the area. The mariner could see that Palin, Jasper, Feril, Fiona, and Fury—all of them were also running away. The patch of quicksand was growing, racing outward to engulf them.

Fiona charged forward, her long sword reflecting the lightning as she skirted the growing pool of quicksand.

Palin held something in his hands and recited arcane words. Feril was doing the same, but their words weren't coming fast enough—the sand was going to overtake them. It swelled like a tide around their ankles, sloshed up to their knees.

On the other side of the sandy pond, Sageth threw back his head and laughed. The stone tablet melted from his arms, forming a foot-high man who joined in the malevolent laughter.

"You did well," Fissure replied. "I am quite proud of you." The diminutive gray man looked up at his accomplice and blinked his large black eyes. He smiled, showing a row of tiny pointed teeth. "The Storm Over Krynn will be most happy. And when this is all over, he will suitably honor both of us."

The gray man motioned to the sand, and it belched forth Huma's lance and Goldmoon's medallions. The objects fell at his tiny feet. Then he gestured at the sand again, and it grew hard, turning to stone, trapping Palin and his friends.

Lightning arced to the ground, striking near Rig, and making the ground tremble. The thunder boomed deafeningly, and the rain began. It was a hard, pummeling rain. It was a warm rain, too, uncomfortably so, and it came at them sideways now, driven by a fierce wind.

Palin continued the words to his spell, a complex enchantment that he couldn't afford to cast improperly. Feril's spell finished first, and a chunk of the solidified quicksand shot up and struck the gray man in the side of his head. He reeled from the blow, but quickly regained his balance. A master of the element of earth, he could not be truly hurt by it, nor could it much slow him down.

He dropped the medallion over his short neck, picked up the handle of the dragonlance, and dragged the weapon behind him. Sageth turned and followed the diminutive man.

Lightning flashed again, illuminating the pair's retreating forms—and highlighting another approaching one. A dragon was slowly dropping toward them through the clouds. His sapphire scales slick with rain, his eyes glowing yellow, the dragon snarled. Lightning danced along his teeth and talons and raced to meet the earth.

"Khellendros!" Feril cried.

Sageth and the huldrefolk continued to walk in a northerly direction. "It looks like everything is progressing smoothly," the old man said. "How long before I receive my reward for my part in all of this?"

"Now, I think," Fissure replied. He faced the elderly man and stretched out his long thin fingers. He touched the man's side, and within a heartbeat the huldrefolk had drained away the scant remainder of the man's years. Sageth turned to stone and then crumbled to dust that was swiftly washed away by the rain.

Fissure grinned and continued north, occasionally glancing back to see if the Storm Over Krynn was finished playing with the foolish people.

"Majere!" The word exploded like a clap of thunder from the dragon's mouth. "I've let you live long enough!" Khellendros beat his wings, spurring on the rain and hovering in one position, angling his head toward his captured, squirming foes.

His eyes fixed on the struggling sorcerer, and he thought of Kitiara. "Whelp of Kitiara's enemies!" he bellowed. He wished his once-cherished partner were here to see this victory, to savor this success. She would know of it, he vowed. When he again found her spirit, and brought her back to Krynn, he would regale her with tales of the day he had destroyed Palin Majere and stolen the magic that made it possible for her to return. He would let one or two of the others live so that they would continue to hamper Malys.

Fiona, meanwhile, had barely managed to avoid being trapped in the stone. She stood defiantly, waving her sword and daring the dragon to come closer. The young Knight of

Solamnia knew to face a dragon of this size would mean certain death, but not to stand up against it would mock everything she believed in. "Skie!" she cried, using the name humans had given the dragon. "Fight me! I'm not some helpless target!"

Behind her, Rig held the scepter over his shoulder. "This is supposed to be such a very powerful artifact," he said to himself. "Let's see if that's so." He drove the Fist of E'li against the stone that held him, clenching the haft in his sweating hands. The macelike head connected with a sound like breaking glass that split the air and parted the stone, sending spider-web cracks racing in all directions away from his feet. "Magic indeed!" The mariner quickly broke free and raised the scepter near Feril's feet. "You next," he told her.

Above, Khellendros opened his jaws and unleashed a bolt of lightning, thick and bright. The dragon overlord sped toward the ground, landing mere feet away from Feril and Rig. The Kagonesti was in the midst of another spell, but Rig struggled to keep his footing and drove the scepter at the stone in front of her. Seconds later, she was climbing out.

Jasper gave up struggling against the magically hardened earth. His breaths were shallow, and he felt incredibly dizzy. "If it is Reorx's wish, I will join you, Goldmoon," he said.

Several feet away, Palin clenched his teeth and fought to keep his concentration. His own spell was almost complete. It might save us, he thought. It *has* to save us or we are dead, and everything will be lost.

Somehow Fury had freed himself, and now the wolf was at Palin's side, growling at the dragon. The energy the sorcerer had been gathering from the air and ground about him came faster now—and stronger. He felt the arcane force race outward into his limbs as the last word of the spell fell from his lips. Fury howled, and the sorcerer sagged, spent from his effort.

As the Blue swooped overhead, Fiona swung at it, grazing

its underside. Unfortunately, her blade was unable to penetrate the hard scales.

"Don't ignore me, dragon!" she cried. "Fight me!"

"Do you fear death, Majere?" Khellendros hissed. "Do you fear me?" He opened his mouth to breathe lightning again, but suddenly a stream of quicksilver struck his side, pushing him away, ruining his aim.

"Jasper" the mariner cried, seeing that the dragon had been distracted, "I'm coming!" He raised his scepter and brought it down. The dwarf gasped, prodding his side. Then he gratefully accepted the mariner's help getting out of the hole in which he had been stuck.

Khellendros turned to the south, where a silver dragon was banking toward him, skimming just below the clouds. The dragon looked gray under the cloud cover. A rider was on her back, and behind her trailed a gold dragon, younger, with a rider also.

The Storm Over Krynn roared his defiance. Neither of them was large enough to defeat him. Even if the approaching dragons worked together, they would not win. But he knew they might hurt him, and he had no time to waste on licking his wounds. He would not let these dragons keep him from the artifacts, from Kitiara.

As the gold and silver beat their wings in an effort to close the distance, he gazed pitilessly at the sorcerer and his friends. Perhaps he would kill them all. His thick blue lips pulled back, and he unleashed a barrage of lightning bolts. The forks of yellow-white light rebounded off the figures below—the female kender, the short-bearded dwarf, the wolf, and the defiant Kagonesti. They also struck Rig Mer-Krel, the dark-skinned man with even darker eyes, and Palin Majere, the sorcerer.

Khellendros's lightning rained down again and again—and all the while his massive blue body withstood the blasts of quicksilver emanating from the silver dragon and the gouts of fire from the gold. He ignored the tremendous pain, thrust it to the back of his consciousness, and directed one last barrage.

The lightning and thunder rocked the earth. Chunks of hardened quicksand flew into the air, then fell down again on the broken form of Palin Majere, covering the sorcerer and his friends in an impromptu mass grave provided by the Storm Over Krynn.

Then, with the gold and silver nearly on him, he beat his wings to carry himself higher, beyond their attack. He'd won, garnered magic from the Age of Dreams, blessed artifacts that he could use to return Kitiara to his side. And he had destroyed his enemies in the process.

The gold and silver would try to pursue him, but they were smaller, and their wings could not take them as far and as fast as Khellendros's. They would not be able to catch him. The Storm Over Krynn ached from absorbing the impact of their dragon breath, but his heart soared with pride.

Higher he flew, until he buried himself in the thickest cloud overhead. Lightning skittered down his sides and helped to ease his agony. The fierce wind washed over his massive head, and the rain refreshed him.

Then he climbed higher still, heading north, swooping below the clouds only once, and that was to snag Fissure in a great claw—and the lance in the other.

"The Storm Over Krynn shall triumph!" the Blue bellowed to the heavens. "With this magic I will bring Kitiara home!" His triumphant cries turned to shrieks of agony as the lance burned his evil flesh. Still, the dragon flew higher.

The clouds thinned and the rain lessened. The gold and the silver gave up their chase and returned to the scene of the carnage.

"Father! We answered your call too late!" Ulin gasped as he slid from Sunrise's back and stared at the rubble strewn over the shattered bodies. Tears welled up in his eyes, and spilled down his cheeks. He felt faint with grief and tried to stifle a sob—which quickly turned into a cry of surprise.

A portion of the clearing shimmered. As the dragons and Gilthanas and Ulin watched, shapes formed, transparent at first, but then growing brighter, appearing solid. There were eight figures—Palin, Rig, Fiona, Groller, Fury, Feril, Blister, and Jasper.

The elder Majere dropped to his knees. The spell he had cast to cloak their presence and make false images of themselves had sapped the last of his energy. He was exhausted, and his sides heaved mightily as he tried to suck air into his lungs. He had not cast that type of illusion since the gods of magic had withdrawn from the world.

Gilthanas, Silvara, Ulin, and Sunrise had provided a much needed distraction and had made it easier to fool the Blue. Now the dragons kept their necks craned toward the thinning clouds, wanting to make sure Khellendros would not be returning.

"We still have a chance," Rig said, as he shouldered the Fist of E'li and helped Palin to his feet. At least he had one artifact, and Palin knew where Dalamar's ring rested. There was Age of Dreams magic with the Dimernesti beneath the sea. And there was Dhamon's glaive, which the mariner intended to claim after he slew the treacherous ex-knight.

"Goldmoon is dead. We're wounded. What chance do we have?" Jasper asked.

"A chance," Rig said quietly. "And it's a chance we have to take." He stared at the scepter in his hands. "If we give up now, all of Krynn loses."

* * * * *

It was a place of swirling gray mists—insubstantial, yet solid enough to stand upon. Goldmoon stood there, the tendrils swirling about her legs, and wrapping tight as if to hold her there, to keep her from falling or floating away.

She was dressed in leather breeches and a fringed leather tunic that hung to her thighs. The clothes looked new and fit her perfectly. Her long, gold and silver hair was braided, as she had worn it in her younger years, with beads and feathers stuck here and there as adornments.

Though there was no sun or moon, there was a hazy light, provided by the gray mists. Her hair shone in the light, and her eyes sparkled as her lips crept upward into a smile.

Goldmoon looked as she did then, on that first day they met, her eyes wide open and fixed on the man's handsome form.

Riverwind stood before her, with tanned skin, jet black hair, and eyes that were piercing and filled with a quiet mirth. He was just as she had remembered him being at their first meeting that seemed like yesterday, though it was long ago. He reached out a hand and touched her smooth face.

"Husband," she said simply.

"I have been waiting for you," Riverwind replied.

~

**If you enjoyed reading *The Day of the Tempest*,
be sure to read these other books in the
DRAGONLANCE® Saga:**

~

The first novel in Jean Rabe's FIFTH AGE™ trilogy is *The Dawning of a New Age*. Inhabitants of Krynn, reeling from the departure of the gods, are besieged by powerful dragon overlords that have the run of the land. Magic has waned, and Goldmoon—one of the last original companions—searches desperately for new heroes to fight the overlords. One troubled man, a sorcerer by the name of Majere, answers her call.

~

Readers will find that events made familiar to them through other DRAGONLANCE novels seem very different when told from the perspective of the dragons themselves. The great wyrms take center stage in *The Dragons*, a sweeping novel that follows generations of both metallic and chromatic serpents as they battle over Krynn with a fury that threatens to annihilate nations and whole races—even dragonkind.

~

The sixth novel in the Warriors series, *Lord Soth* details the exploits of the famous Knight of the Rose whose jealous passions and neglect of duty lead him to lose all that is dear to him—his love, his life, his very spirit. This is the tale of Lord Soth's descent into darkness and evil, one that has remained untold . . . until now.